LUCY'S CHILD

•

SLUGS

SHAUN HUTSON OMNIBUS

LUCY'S CHILD
•
SLUGS

LITTLE, BROWN AND COMPANY

A *Little, Brown* Book

This first edition published in Great Britain in 1999 by
Little, Brown and Company.

A CIP catalogue for this book is available from the
British Library.

ISBN 0 316 85368 2

Printed and bound in Great Britain.

Little, Brown and Company (UK)
Brettenham House
Lancaster Place
London WC2E 7EN

LUCY'S CHILD

MUCH OF WHAT FOLLOWS IS TRUE

PART ONE

'Welcome to where time stands still,
No one leaves and no one will . . .'

                                                    – Metallica

'There are maladies we must not seek to cure
because they protect us from others that are
more serious.'

                                                    – Proust

One

There was an audible thump as the insect hit the windscreen of the Astra.

Beth Parker had no idea what kind of insect it was. The only immediately apparent fact was that it had been large. The second fact was that it was now coated across most of the glass.

Beth sprayed the windscreen with water and flicked on the wipers in an effort to clean off the worst of the mess, smiling to herself as she thought of the old gag about the last thing that goes through a fly's mind when it hits a windscreen is its arsehole.

The windscreen was spotted with the debris of numerous similar encounters, the kind of hazard drivers came to expect in such warm weather. Beth was delighted that the day had turned out fine, and hoped it signalled the beginning of a decent spell. She smiled contentedly as her thoughts were confirmed by the weatherman on the radio.

She pushed a cassette into the machine, tiring of the mindless burble of the DJ, and soon the car was filled with the steady thud of music. Beth turned up the volume, singing along whole-heartedly as 'Another One Bites the Dust' came thundering from the speakers.

Quite appropriate, she thought, as another fly smacked into the windscreen.

The drive home usually took her less than twenty minutes but she noticed road works up ahead and a queue of traffic forming at some temporary lights. Beth pulled up alongside a white transit van and opened her window. Exhaust fumes rolled in like noxious fog. Oblivious, Beth drummed gently on the steering wheel as she waited for the lights to change. The car in front of her had a sticker on the back window that proclaimed CHILD ON BOARD. As if failure to display the sign might somehow provoke other drivers to slam into the vehicle. She grinned at her own musings and glanced to her left.

A man was staring down at her from the transit, a smirk on his face. He was in his early twenties, the sunlight glinting on the silver earring dangling from his lobe. He was making no attempt to hide his interest in Beth's legs, visible because of the shortness of her skirt. She tried to ignore his prying gaze, concentrating on brushing her long brown hair away from her face. She reached into the glove compartment of the Astra and put on a pair of sunglasses, as if the dark shields would somehow protect her from this man's intrusive inspection.

Her blouse was undone slightly and she wondered if this smirking half-wit could see more than he should from his elevated position, but she decided that he was more concerned with her legs.

Beth's mood changed somewhat and a slight smile spread across her lips.

And why *shouldn't* he be interested in her legs?

She glanced down at them herself.

She had good legs. She'd always thought so and to hell with false modesty. Let him look if he wanted to. Beth made an exaggeratedly slow attempt to wipe away some fluff from the hem of her skirt, rubbing her thigh in the process. She heard a muted murmur of approval from the transit.

It was all she could do now to prevent herself laughing aloud.

What next?

Was this acceptable behaviour for a twenty-six-year-old married woman? What *would* her mother have said? Beth

4

finally *did* laugh aloud, noticing that the lights were changing. She looked up at the man in the transit, smiled, then waved and drove off.

Behind her, the transit stalled and in her rear-view mirror she caught sight of the two men in it gesturing angrily at each other.

Free of the choking exhaust fumes, Beth wound down her window fully, allowing the breeze to gust into the car. It whipped her long hair about her face, the strands flowing like so many pendants in the bluster. It was pleasantly cool in the Astra.

There was still a fair amount of traffic on the road although she'd missed the worst of the rush-hour. Even small towns like this one had their own version of the rush-hour. About fifty miles north of London, Oakley was a combination of the traditional and the obscenely new. It was on the outskirts of what was euphemistically called a New Town. A term used by planners to denote a cramped and over-populated confusion of yellow-bricked monstrosities, each almost identical to the next. Oakley was being swallowed up by one of these New Towns six miles to the east. Every day on her way to and from work, Beth seemed to notice new building sites springing up. Construction seemed geared to cover every single acre of land. But, for now, there were still fields and trees. There was even a farm close to where she lived.

She swung the Astra into the narrow road that led towards the house, noticing some people working in their gardens, enticed out by the warm weather. The smell of newly cut grass filled the air, and plastic garden furniture had appeared in many gardens on the estate.

A turn to the right and she was nearly home. A couple of kids were kicking a football about in the garden of the house opposite.

Beth swung the car into the short driveway of the house but decided not to put it in the garage.

She saw the figure as she swung into the drive.

5

Sitting by the front door. It looked as though someone had dumped a bag of washing there.

As Beth switched off the engine, the figure turned to face her.

Beth swallowed hard, felt the colour drain from her face.

'Oh Jesus,' she murmured under her breath.

Two

For long moments Beth sat holding the wheel, as if reluctant to step out from the Astra.

She glanced up at the figure standing by her front door and noticed that the newcomer was making no move one way or the other, either. At last Beth closed the car window, fastened the sun-roof, then swung herself out of the car. She reached for her jacket and laid it across one arm, heading up the short path towards the door.

And the person waiting there.

The newcomer was in her late teens, possibly her early twenties. Even Beth couldn't remember immediately. She had always looked older than her years, the cigarette stuck between her lips contributing to the illusion.

The girl was roughly the same height as Beth, not dissimilar in build. Both were slim, both had fine high cheekbones. The newcomer had long hair, too, but it was a deeper, richer shade of brown than Beth's, almost auburn.

The figure was dressed in a pair of jeans that looked as though they'd been sprayed on. The voluminous folds of a T-shirt effectively hid most of her upper body but the strap of a bra or body suit was visible where the baggy garment had slipped to reveal one bare shoulder.

On her feet she wore a pair of Reeboks, her jeans tucked

into a pair of white socks that looked as if they could do with washing. Beth noticed that the jeans were worn about the knees, one threadbare. The T-shirt she wore was faded from constant washing and a hole was visible beneath one armpit.

Across the front, emblazoned in cracked white letters, were the words: FUCK DANCING, LET'S FUCK.

As Beth drew closer, the newcomer took the butt of her cigarette and dropped it, crushing it beneath her foot. She kicked it aside, past the small duffel bag which lay nearby. The bag was stuffed to overflowing, the draw-strings barely meeting around such a bulging load. Propped against it was a Sainsbury's carrier, also full and tightly packed. A walkman was lying on top of the duffel bag.

Beth shook her head, almost imperceptibly.

'You're the last person I expected to see,' she said, flatly.

'That's a nice greeting for your own sister.'

They fixed stares for a moment then Beth fumbled in her handbag for her keys, inserting one in the lock.

'You'd better come in,' she said, stepping into the welcoming coolness of the house.

Lucy Morton followed, bringing the duffel bag and the Sainsbury's carrier. She dropped them at the foot of the stairs and pushed shut the door behind her.

'How long have you been here?' Beth wanted to know, hanging up her jacket.

'About two hours,' Lucy told her, looking around at the immaculately decorated hallway.

'You've been sitting on the doorstep for two hours?'

'What else was I supposed to do? I didn't know where you worked. I had no way of getting in touch with you.' She walked past a vase of flowers and flicked at a carnation with her index finger, knocking a couple of petals free. 'Some old bloke asked me what I was doing sitting on your doorstep.'

'What did you say?' Beth enquired.

'I told him to mind his own fucking business.'

'As charming as always,' Beth said, humourlessly, pushing open the kitchen door and walking through.

Lucy followed.

The kitchen was large and airy, well lit by two big windows that offered a view on to a grassy back garden framed on two sides by conifers and at the bottom by a high wooden fence.

Beth crossed to the sink and filled the kettle while Lucy sat down on the wooden bench by the kitchen table. She loosened the laces of her Reeboks then reached for another cigarette, watching Beth, running appraising eyes over the neatly tailored skirt – part of a suit that was completed by the jacket Beth had hung in the hall – the immaculately pressed blouse, and the suede high heels.

'Very smart,' Lucy said, smiling.

'It helps when you have to work for a living,' Beth said, acidly. 'Not that *you'd* know about that.'

'You know, Beth, you haven't changed, either,' Lucy said, taking a long drag on her cigarette. 'You're still a bitch.'

The kettle boiled and Beth made two mugs of tea. She carried them back to the table and sat down opposite her sister.

A heavy silence descended, finally broken by Beth.

'OK, Lucy,' she said quietly, her eyes narrowing. 'Now tell me what the hell you want.'

Three

Beth Parker regarded her sister balefully over the rim of her mug, waiting for her to speak.

She watched as Lucy sipped at the warm liquid,

studying every line and contour of her face. Her sister looked thinner than the last time she'd seen her, but how long ago had that been? Two years? Three? Maybe longer.

Lucy put down her mug and traced an index finger around its rim.

'I'm waiting,' Beth said.

'Yeah, I know,' Lucy told her.

'Why are you here, Lucy?'

'The truth?'

'It'd be nice.'

'I'm in trouble, Beth.'

'So what else is new?'

'Ha bloody ha. Look, I need somewhere to crash for a few days, right?'

Beth didn't answer, merely held her sister's gaze.

'You want to stay here?' she said, quietly. 'You've got a bloody nerve, Lucy. I don't see or hear from you from one year to the next and then you just turn up out of the blue expecting me to put you up.' Beth shook her head and smiled.

'I don't want this any more than you do,' Lucy told her. 'But I've got nowhere else to go.'

'So I'm the last resort, is that it?'

'Beth, I need your help,' Lucy said, quietly.

Beth sighed.

'What happened?' she demanded.

'I was living in London, here and there. It was OK. I'd met a few guys. I even lived with one of them for three months.' She raised her eyebrows. 'But it didn't work out. I ended up in a squat in Bermondsey. There were four of us there.'

'So what went wrong?'

'The fucking police raided it. They said we were using drugs, they reckoned one of the guys was dealing. Bastards.'

'And was he?'

'How do I know, we all kept ourselves to ourselves.'

9

'Oh, come on, Lucy,' Beth said, indignantly. 'You were living under the same roof. If one of your friends had been a drug pusher I think you'd have known about it.'

'It happens all the time, Beth. So what? You don't know what it's like. You're so wrapped up in your nice cosy little middle-class life here, with your nice cosy little middle-class job and your nice cosy little middle-class husband, you haven't got a fucking clue what's happening in the *real* world.'

'In *your* world, you mean,' Beth snapped.

They regarded one another silently for a moment.

'So what happened?' Beth asked, finally.

'I got out,' Lucy told her. 'I thought it'd be better to get right away from London.'

'And there was no one there you could have stayed with? What about some of these blokes you'd met?'

'They weren't love affairs, you know.'

'Just quick fucks, eh?' Beth said, flatly.

'There's no law against it, Beth. If a bloke sleeps around no one bats an eyelid. His balls start aching and he goes off and does something about it.'

'Where did *you* start aching?' Beth said, scornfully. 'How many were there?'

'I didn't keep a fucking scorecard. Six or seven.' She shrugged.

Lucy blew out a long stream of smoke and looked down at her hands, fingers spread on the kitchen table. There was dirt beneath most of the nails.

'So, what do you want me to do?' she said. 'Beg you to let me stay here?'

'Don't be so bloody ridiculous,' Beth said, wearily. She ran a hand through her hair and looked at her sister appraisingly. 'These drugs that the police came for, were you involved?'

Lucy shook her head.

'Do you want to check?' she said, extending her arms to show that there were no marks or bruises in the crooks.

'I might be a lot of things but I'm not a junkie,' she said. 'Don't start preaching to me, Beth. The last thing I need now is a lecture from big sister.' She emphasised the last two words with a tone bordering on contempt.

'So, how did you get here?' Beth wanted to know.

'I hitched from London, I didn't have the money for the train and before you start lecturing me about how dangerous it is to hitch-hike, I can take care of myself.'

'Tough nut. You always liked to think you were.'

'So what's your answer?'

Beth shrugged. 'What do *you* think? You know I'm not going to throw you out on the streets again. Though by the sound of it you wouldn't be out of place there.' She sucked in a deep breath. 'You can stay but I'm telling you, Lucy, it won't be for long. Just until you get yourself sorted out.'

Lucy smiled thinly.

'I'll have to check with Simon, anyway,' Beth added.

'You have to square it with hubby, do you?' Lucy said, sarcastically.

Beth glared at her for a moment.

Lucy took another cigarette from her packet and jammed it between her lips, flicking at the Zippo.

'I'm going to warn him,' said Beth. 'After all, it's his house too. He's got a right to know that you're going to be stuck here for a while. First thing tomorrow you go out and look for a job, I don't care if you have to clean toilets. You're not lounging around here all day.'

Lucy smiled and nodded.

'I appreciate it, Beth,' she said, still flicking at the lighter, which finally sparked into life.

Beth watched as she lifted the flame to the end of the cigarette, her gaze drawn to the flickering plume of fire as surely as a moth to a lightbulb.

She closed her eyes.

Conflagration

The windows exploded outwards, glass spraying in all directions like crystal shrapnel.

Those nearby ducked or raised their hands as the blast showered them with debris.

Flames were leaping madly from both of the upstairs windows now, smoke belching into the night air in a spiralling pall which carried thousands of tiny cinders with it.

Two powerful jets of water were directed at the fire, one at the downstairs windows, which had already been destroyed by the ravages of the flames. The other jet was being played over the upper storey, across the stonework made hot from the temperatures inside and the blazing holes where the windows had once been. The air itself seemed to be on fire.

Uniformed men were running back and forth, shouts were heard, competing with the roaring flames for supremacy. A ladder was propped against the wall but there was no one on it. The fire had taken too strong a hold from the beginning, the men who'd arrived to fight it had known that there would be no survivors from this particular ruin.

The house was detached, fortunately for them. It had been relatively easy to prevent the spread to those buildings nearby. The men had been thankful too for the stillness of the night. Any strong wind might have sent pieces of flaming debris flying in all directions. They could do without the problem of secondary fires as well.

There were two fire engines parked in the road, their blue lights turning silently. They had been joined by two police cars and an ambulance.

From the houses nearby, those roused at such an ungodly hour *by the commotion, either watched from the safety of their own homes or ventured out. Some to speak to the emergency services, others for a better view.*

The emergency services had seen it before. At other fires, at road accidents, at any scene of suffering or death. They had seen it and they all agreed. The public were morbid bastards.

The ambulance had its back doors open and, as he made his way from the house to the parked vehicle, PC Vince Durban could see the occupant of it seated there, wrapped in a blanket.

Seventeen years old, someone had told him.

Christ, she was still a kid.

Mind you, to Durban anyone under fifty was a kid.

He watched her sitting there, numbly, sipping at a warm drink one of the neighbours had made. Sitting and staring at the flames that were busily engulfing the place she had called home.

He shook his head.

As he drew nearer he could see her more clearly.

Pretty little thing.

Her hair was plastered across her face and there were smudges beneath both her eyes, but otherwise she seemed relatively calm.

Shock, he guessed. It didn't always hit them at the time.

Seventeen years old. Jesus. It wasn't fair.

There was a WPC with her too, standing beside the open ambulance doors, occasionally reaching out to brush some strands of hair from the girl's face. She seemed unconcerned by the attention, her eyes fixed on the burning house before her, the fire reflected in her wide, watery orbs.

Durban looked at the WPC as if for reassurance that it was safe to speak to the girl. The uniformed woman nodded gently and pulled the blanket more tightly around the girl.

'They didn't get out, did they?' she asked, quietly, her eyes never leaving the hungry flames.

Durban shook his head.

'Are both my parents dead?' the girl wanted to know.

'I'm afraid they are. I'm sorry,' the policeman said quietly, resting one large hand on her shoulder. 'You were lucky to get out.'

13

She smiled, her eyes still fixed on the blazing house.
'Yes, I was,' said Lucy Morton, softly.

Four

'This bedroom is bigger than my whole flat,' said Lucy, looking around approvingly. She turned and glanced at her reflection in the tinted-glass mirrors that formed the doors of the wardrobe, running a hand through her hair, then she pulled the sliding doors back and looked inside.

Beth crossed to the window and opened it, pushing it open to allow some of the warm air in.

Lucy joined her at the window and looked out.

At the bottom of the garden there were more houses, only their upper floors visible. She could quite clearly see someone moving about in the window opposite.

Beth opened a door to their left.

'There's a toilet and shower in here,' she said, indicating the small vestibule.

Lucy popped her head in and nodded approvingly.

'It's a big house,' she said. 'How the hell do you afford it? I mean, you're not much more than a secretary, are you?'

Beth regarded her sister coldly for a moment wondering if the question had been clumsily put or whether it was just another of Lucy's jibes.

'It was a repossession,' Beth told her. 'The guy who lived here was a builder and he designed it, but his firm went bust and he got behind with his mortgage. We got it cheap. Anything else you'd like to know about our finances?'

Lucy shook her head and tossed her duffel bag on to the large double bed.

14

A number of framed photos were dotted around the room, some on the bedside cabinets, others on the windowsill. Lucy crossed to the first of them and peered at it. It was a wedding photo: Beth resplendent in her white gown, beside her, in a dark suit, her husband.

'Is Simon still looking after loonies, then?' Lucy wanted to know.

'He's still a psychiatrist if that's what you mean,' Beth said, walking out on to the landing. She returned a moment later with some towels which she placed on the end of the bed.

'I remember one of his friends at the wedding, an usher I think he was,' Lucy said, still gazing at the photo.

'I'm surprised you can remember anything, the amount of booze you got through,' Beth said.

'I remember *this* bloke.' She grinned. 'While everyone was slapping you and Simon on the back at the reception, him and I nipped around the back of the hotel. Just for twenty minutes.' She chuckled at the recollection. 'He kept saying, "What if they notice we're gone?" He seemed to forget about that once I got his trousers undone.'

There was a moment's silence then Lucy spoke again.

'How long have you been married now? Two years?' she enquired.

'Three, it was the year after Mum and Dad died,' Beth told her, lowering her voice slightly as if in deference. 'That was what I missed more than anything, having Dad give his speech at the reception. I missed them both more on that day than at any other time since it happened.'

There was a photo of their parents on the bedside table and Lucy glanced cursorily at it.

'I just wish they'd been there,' Beth continued.

'To see their little girl get married,' Lucy said, scornfully.

'You were their *little* girl, Lucy.'

'You wouldn't have thought so. It was always Beth this, Beth that.'

'And that really pissed you off, didn't it?'

'They made our lives a fucking competition, Beth. Whatever you did I had to match it. If you got six A levels, I had to get seven. If you went to college, I had to go to university. They were always comparing us.'

'And you always came off second best. That's what you didn't like, wasn't it?'

'I didn't give a fuck,' Lucy snapped.

'Yes you did and you still do.'

'Well, at least they're not around to make judgements any more.'

'You hard cow,' Beth hissed.

Lucy saw more pictures on the windowsill. Pocket-size snaps in tiny gilt frames.

Children.

A smiling, red-haired boy about two.

A blonde girl grinning happily at the camera.

'Who are the kids?' Lucy asked.

'They belong to friends of ours,' said Beth.

'I'd have thought you and Simon would have had a kid by now. You were always very maternal, Beth.'

Beth swallowed hard.

'So, when does the family start?' Lucy persisted.

'There won't be one,' Beth told her. 'I can't have kids.'

'Perhaps you're doing it wrong,' Lucy chuckled.

'You'd know, wouldn't you? You're the expert when it comes to that. You should be, you've had enough practice.'

Beth regarded her angrily.

'Remember?'

The word hung in the air as if suspended on the warm breeze.

'Who was it who paid for your abortion, Lucy?' she continued, angrily. 'Who saved up two hundred quid so you could have the bloody thing done?'

'So, I'll pay you back one day,' Lucy said, dismissively.

'The money's got nothing to do with it,' Beth snapped.

16

'I did everything for you. Christ, I even covered for you with Mum and Dad. What do you think they'd have said if they'd known? You were fourteen, Lucy.'

'I didn't *ask* you to help me,' she said, quietly.

'You ungrateful little bitch,' Beth rasped. 'I didn't want your fucking thanks then and I don't want it now. I helped because I *wanted* to.'

'How much of that help was to stop Mum and Dad finding out? You didn't really care whether I had the kid or not, did you? You just didn't want *them* upset.'

They glared at each other for a moment, then Beth jabbed an impatient finger towards Lucy's bag.

'You'd better put your stuff away,' she said, heading for the door. 'When you've finished you can give me a hand in the kitchen. I'm going to get changed.'

Lucy heard Beth's footfalls moving across the landing, then she heard the bedroom door slam.

She sat down on the edge of the bed and turned to face the photo of her dead parents. She looked at each face in turn.

'It's *still* a fucking competition,' she murmured.

Five

As Beth made her way back across the landing she heard the sound of running water. The steady sputtering of the shower from the guest room.

She pushed the door open slightly and saw that Lucy had, indeed, unpacked her things. Most of them were strewn over the bed. It was a pathetic little collection. A couple of T-shirts, two pairs of jeans, some leggings, a few pairs of knickers. There was a toothbrush, even the

17

remains of a battered tube of Colgate. A dirty make-up bag bulged with lipstick and eyebrow pencils but precious little else. She saw a walkman and half a dozen tapes, one of which was cracked and broken, the thin brown tape dangling from it like a glistening streamer.

The Sainsbury's carrier had not disgorged much more. A pair of grubby black high heels which looked as though they hadn't tasted polish for years. A couple of packets of cigarettes. A pair of ankle boots with the laces missing, and two pairs of white socks balled up.

Beth exhaled wearily.

So this was the sum total of her sister's possessions, was it? She looked down at the duffel bag, preparing to move it from where it had been dropped in the middle of the floor.

As she did, she heard the door of the shower room open.

'What are you doing?' Lucy said, emerging with a towel wrapped around her, water dripping from her long hair, which was plastered around her face like auburn snakes.

'I wondered if you needed a hand,' Beth said. 'It doesn't look like you do.'

Lucy snatched up the duffel bag and placed it beside the bed.

'Are these the only clothes you've got?' Beth asked.

'I packed what I could get in the bag,' Lucy told her.

'You can borrow some of my stuff if you like, we're about the same size, aren't we?'

Lucy nodded slowly. 'Thanks,' she said, smiling.

'Some of this stuff looks like it needs a wash, I'll show you how the machine works when you come down.'

Lucy began drying her hair, sitting down on the edge of the bed.

Beth hesitated a moment longer then headed for the door. She paused as she reached it, turning to look at her sister.

'Lucy,' she said quietly, 'I'm glad you're all right.'

Then she was gone, her footsteps echoing away down

the steps as if she were anxious to escape before her sister could reply.

The younger sister ran both hands through her wet hair then patted her body dry, glancing at her reflection briefly in the mirrors opposite.

She dressed hurriedly, pulling on a pair of jeans, not bothering with knickers beneath. She eased into a T-shirt then stepped into her Reeboks.

It took her just a moment or two to place some of her clothes in the drawers of the bedside cabinets, the rest of the stuff she bundled up, ready to carry downstairs.

Before she did she looked at the photo of her parents on the bedside cabinet. She gazed at the two smiling faces looking back at her, then she reached for the picture and gently laid it face down on the top of the cabinet.

Below the drawer there was a cupboard and she found that the duffel bag fitted inside. She pushed it in and closed the door, checking that it was secure.

She didn't want Beth seeing inside.

Six

The office was huge. Not just large or spacious. It was enormous. Simon Parker had always thought so. The walls were painted a dull beige colour and they seemed to stretch up endlessly towards a ceiling that hung fully thirty feet above him. Two lights with very broad shades dangled from the ceiling on dirty-looking wires, which looked as though they hadn't been cleaned for years.

The size of the office was accentuated by the fact that the walls were completely unadorned by pictures or photos or anything to break up the vast, turgid expanse of beige. Only the odd crack in the paint from years of neglect served to deviate from the characterless vista. Perched somewhat incongruously atop one of the banks of filing cabinets opposite his desk was a vase which Parker could never remember seeing filled with flowers. But, otherwise, the ornamentation in the room was as spartan as its decoration.

His own desk was large too, an unwieldy oak monolith which looked to have been hewn from one enormous piece of wood rather than assembled from several smaller pieces.

Other than an anglepoise lamp, several pads, a blotter and some plastic trays, the desk, too, was unadorned apart from one single photo.

A five by eight colour picture of Beth Parker beamed back at him as he looked across the desk. The picture had been taken a year ago. She'd booked a session with a professional photographer in Oakley and, along with his other Christmas presents, she'd framed then wrapped several pictures of herself for Parker. He studied the image for a moment, taking in the details before him as he did every day. Her long dark hair cascading over her bare shoulders, exposed by the black strapless dress she had worn for the shoot. She was seated with her legs curled beneath her, smiling softly at the camera. At him.

He locked the picture away when there were patients in his office.

Parker got to his feet and stretched, wincing as he heard his knees crack.

Rheumatism at twenty-nine? Surely not.

He smiled to himself and walked across to the massive window, which offered a panoramic view of the grounds of Brackley Heath Psychiatric Hospital.

The building was in several acres of its own grounds, separated from the outside world by a high perimeter wall. Beyond were fields and some farmland.

The closest house was almost two miles away.

Like most of the mental homes in the country, the building was Victorian. A great, grey monstrosity constructed in the shape of a capital H. Forced to operate on a minuscule budget and with staffing levels way below those recommended for an institution so large, Parker couldn't help but feel apprehension about the future of the place and more particularly about those who lived or worked within its walls.

There were currently three hundred patients in residence, at least three quarters of them formal.

Parker smiled wryly. No one used words like 'committed' any more.

Not even for those on the Secure Ward.

There were three of them at the moment.

The following day they would be joined by another.

Parker glanced at his watch and decided enough was enough for one day. He'd stayed later than usual to complete some paperwork on a patient they'd admitted two days earlier.

The man had been a nurse, dismissed from a nearby hospital, caught in the act of removing a catheter from an intensive care patient and drinking the contents of the bag.

Parker yawned and fumbled in his jacket pocket for his car keys.

He'd reached the door when his phone rang.

'Shit,' he murmured, wondering whether or not to answer it. He glanced across and saw the button marked 'Internal' flashing. Parker hesitated a moment longer then turned and picked up the receiver.

He recognised the voice immediately.

'Simon, I was hoping I might catch you,' said Dr Marcus Flynn.

'I was just about to leave,' Parker told him.

'This won't take long.'

Parker sighed.

'I'll be there in a couple of minutes,' he said, wearily.

Seven

As he pushed open the door of Flynn's office, Simon Parker glanced down at his watch. He hoped the old man wouldn't be too long.

Flynn was sitting behind his desk and he looked up briefly as the younger man entered, motioning for him to be seated. Parker did as instructed and settled himself in one of the high-backed leather chairs facing the desk.

Behind Flynn, through the window framing the desk, the sun was sinking lower in the sky. The clouds were now tinged orange with the fading colour, the heavens beginning to take on a purple tinge with the onset of dusk. Parker studied his older colleague, watching as he scribbled something on a sheet of paper, seemingly oblivious to the younger man's presence.

The old man. Most of the staff referred to Flynn that way, even though at fifty-six he could hardly be called old. His cheeks were ruddy, giving him the appearance of a man who either has just finished running a very long race or is a long-term drinker. As far as Parker knew, the latter did not apply. He'd never seen Flynn with a drink during the four years he'd been at the hospital. What he did in his spare time, of course, was a different matter but Parker neither knew nor cared how his colleague spent his hours away from work. The older man's hair was snow white, combed back from his forehead so severely it looked as though it had been tacked on to his skull at the base.

Flynn had been senior consultant at Brackley Heath for almost seventeen years, before that he'd spent time at a number of other psychiatric hospitals around the country

22

including Rampton and Broadmoor. Brackley Heath was a promotion but it was also his swan-song. Flynn and everyone else knew it but the older man seemed happy enough to see out his time quietly.

Unable to restrain himself any longer, Parker coughed somewhat theatrically and smiled when the older man looked up.

'Sorry to keep you waiting,' Flynn said.

Are you?

Flynn put down his pen and clasped his fingers together on his desk top.

'I don't know if you're aware,' he began, 'but we are expecting a new arrival tomorrow for the Secure Ward.'

'I'd heard.'

'Are you familiar with the details of her case?' Flynn asked, handing a manilla file to the younger man.

Parker took it and flipped it open, scanning the information within.

'Karen Gregson, twenty-six years old,' he murmured, reading aloud. He glanced at the typewritten sheets.

'She lives nearby. I believe the case was widely reported in the local papers,' Flynn said, watching as Parker read.

'She killed both her children,' the younger man said, flatly.

'Apparently, she was so fascinated by the fontanelle of her baby, she pushed two fingers through its skull. The child was three months old.'

'She killed the older child too. Cut out both their eyes according to this,' he tapped the report.

'And fed them to a neighbour's dog,' Flynn added.

'The police psychiatrist reported paranoid delusions, hallucinations and extreme mood swings.'

'Any theories?' Flynn wanted to know.

'The youngest child was three months, the eldest nearly eighteen months.' Parker shrugged. 'It looks like some kind of post-natal trauma.'

'My thoughts too,' Flynn echoed.

Then why did you need me for a second opinion?

'I want *you* to deal with her when she arrives,' said Flynn.

'Why me? There are five consultants here. Why should I be selected for this particular honour?'

Flynn caught the scorn in Parker's tone but ignored it.

'I thought you were better equipped to deal with a patient like this.'

'I'm no better qualified than anyone else at Brackley Heath.'

'But dealing with a case like this will help you progress, won't it?'

Parker didn't care for the patronising tone that had slipped into Flynn's speech. 'Meaning?' he said, irritably.

'Promotion. You can't deny that's what you're looking for. Possibly even *this* job. *My* job.'

Parker exhaled wearily. 'I seem to remember we've had this conversation before,' he said. 'I don't *want* your job, Doctor Flynn. I've got enough on my plate coping with the patients here, we all have. There aren't enough of us to adequately cope with the numbers here at Brackley Heath, *you* know that. My ward rounds take up all my time, I don't want to be here until eight or nine every night like you are. I'm not interested in the administrative side of what you do. I'm only interested in dealing with people. Not figures. I'm a psychiatrist not an accountant.'

'So you're telling me you'd refuse promotion if it was offered to you?' Flynn persisted.

Parker held his gaze for long moments.

'That's not relevant now,' he said, quietly.

'You're young and you're ambitious, Simon. I envy your youth and I applaud your ambition.'

'As long as it doesn't threaten you?' Parker said, defiantly.

Flynn picked up his pen and began writing once more.

'Take the file home,' he said, tersely. 'Familiarise yourself with all aspects of the case. I want a full report after you've seen Karen Gregson tomorrow.'

Parker got to his feet and looked down at Flynn for a moment, then he turned and headed for the door.

'Good evening, Simon,' said Flynn, stuffily, without looking up. 'We'll speak tomorrow.'

'Yes,' said Parker and slipped out.

He stood on the other side of the door, the knot of muscles at the side of his jaw throbbing angrily.

Parker looked down at the file which bore Karen Gregson's name, then he tucked it under his arm and headed for the main exit.

Eight

'So, what am I supposed to do?' Lucy Morton said, picking up the paper that lay beside her. 'Take any old job I can find?'

'I told you, Simon and I aren't supporting you, you can pay your way while you're here,' Beth reminded her. 'Go down to the Job Centre in the morning, I'll drop you off on my way to work.'

'Aren't there any jobs at your place I could do?'

Beth smiled and shook her head.

'No way,' she said, dismissively. 'It's bad enough having to share a house with you for a few days, let alone work with you too.'

Lucy chuckled.

'You mean to say my big sister can't have a word in the boss's ear?' she said. 'His own personal private secretary.'

Beth caught the familiar edge to Lucy's voice but chose to ignore it.

'Haven't you *ever* worked?' she wanted to know.

Lucy shrugged.

25

'I worked in a Burger King in London for a few days,' she said. 'And a pub where I used to go needed a barmaid for a couple of weeks so I filled in for the usual girl while she was away.'

'What a full and varied career you've had, Lucy,' Beth chided.

'So what does everyone else around here do to make ends meet? What about your snotty neighbours?'

'Everybody seems to keep themselves to themselves most of the time.'

'I thought the middle classes were always in and out of each others' houses having dinner parties or cocktail parties.'

'Not around here, Lucy,' said Beth, fixing her sister in an unblinking gaze.

Lucy got to her feet and walked across to the front window, peering out at the houses across the street.

'Mum and Dad would have been proud of you,' she said, quietly.

'Meaning?'

'Nice house, good job, nice husband, posh neighbours.' She turned and looked at Beth with something approaching anger in her eyes. 'You've got it all, haven't you, Beth?'

'I wouldn't say that but what we have got we've worked hard for. What's the matter, Lucy? Jealous?'

'I couldn't live like this.'

'What's wrong, too clean for you?'

'I mean, surrounded by all this bullshit, tied to a house and a bloke.'

'Perhaps you hate it because you really want it.'

'Don't start the psychology on me, Beth. I thought Simon was the fucking shrink, not you.'

'Why shouldn't you want it? You've wanted what I've had all your life. Every time I got something you wanted it too. Boyfriends, money, attention. If I had it, you wanted it.'

'But I ended up with nothing.'

'From jealousy and anger to self-pity, I really am getting the full range of your emotions tonight, aren't I?'

'Fuck you, Beth.'

'No, fuck *you*, Lucy,' Beth hissed. 'I told you you could stay, I can just as easily tell you to pack your bag again.'

An uneasy silence followed, finally broken by Lucy.

'Yeah, you're right,' she said, a dry smile spreading across her face. 'You're the boss.' She turned her back on Beth and continued gazing out of the window. 'So, what *do* the neighbours do to earn a crust? I bet at least one of them is an accountant.'

'Are you really interested?' Beth said, challengingly.

'I'm curious.'

'One guy works for a newspaper, he's a photographer. They've got a couple of kids. The couple on the left-hand side are retired; on the right, Bill works for the Post Office.'

'No one *works* for the Post Office,' Lucy chuckled.

'His wife, Suzie, she runs her own press agency. She works with local firms mostly,' Beth continued. 'They've got a son of about four.'

'What about the house at the back? I can practically see into one of the bedrooms from my room.'

'That's Val and Ted. He works for one of the satellite TV companies. They've got a son called Mark who's at college.'

'How old is he?'

'Seventeen.'

'Is that his bedroom looking on to mine?'

'Yes.'

'So, when do I get to meet them all?'

'You're staying here because you've got nowhere else to go, Lucy. What do you expect me to do, throw a bloody party to welcome you to the neighbourhood?'

'I can't ignore them if they speak to me in the street.'

'I'm not asking you to. No doubt word will get around who you are.'

'You don't stand around gossiping over the fence, do you?' Lucy said, smiling.

Beth shook her head, wearily.

'So they've all got kids,' said Lucy. 'Except you and Simon. You must feel like the odd ones out.'

Beth swallowed hard.

That's right. And that's the way it was going to stay.

'I told you,' she said, quietly. 'I can't have children.'

'Oh, yeah,' Lucy murmured. 'I forgot.'

Beth glared at her but her sister merely continued gazing out of the front window.

She was the first one to see the car pull into the driveway.

Nine

Simon parked his car behind Beth's Astra, swung himself out from behind the wheel and slammed the door. He sucked in a weary breath and locked the red Peugeot, picking up his attaché case.

As he headed up the short path towards the front door he saw a shape at the window, hidden by the diaphanous folds of the net curtains. He could just make out the dark silhouette of hair. And he remembered.

Shit. It was Lucy.

She watched him as he approached the front door.

He'd forgotten about her. Beth had called him earlier and he'd said yes, unsure of what he was agreeing to.

As he reached the door she stepped away from the window.

Lucy.

Parker let himself in, the hallway offering a welcoming coolness from the humid evening.

Beth emerged from the sitting room and smiled at him.

He put down his case and embraced her.

'Hello, you,' he said, kissing her gently on the lips. 'What sort of day have you had?'

'Not bad, what about you?' Beth asked, sliding away from him towards the kitchen.

'Don't ask,' said Parker, sliding off his jacket. 'Where's Lucy?' he asked, following Beth into the kitchen.

Beth nodded in the direction of the sitting room.

'We've already eaten, I saved you something,' she told him, dishing up food from a saucepan on top of the cooker.

Parker crossed to the fridge and took out a can of beer, rolling it between his hands before pulling off the ring tab. Not bothering with a glass, he drank it straight down.

'That bad, eh?' Beth said, grinning.

Parker nodded.

'Hello, Simon.'

He turned as he heard his name spoken and saw Lucy standing in the kitchen doorway.

She smiled briefly at him.

'Hi, Lucy, how are you?' Parker asked, taking in the details of her face and body. The long red hair, the high cheekbones and pointed chin. The slender legs encased in tight denim. He looked again at her face, surprised at how different she looked to the last time he'd seen her. Older, obviously, but there was something else in those green eyes. An intensity in her gaze he'd forgotten.

'Long time no see,' she said, smiling.

Beth looked across at her sister who noticed the glance.

'I'm going to leave you two in peace for a while,' Lucy said. 'I'm going upstairs to listen to my tapes. If that's OK.'

'You don't need my permission, Lucy,' Beth said.

'See you later,' said the younger woman and she disappeared. They heard her footfalls on the stairs.

29

The humidity of the evening had given way to an unexpected coolness with the onset of night, and as Parker sat at the kitchen table, he could hear the branches of the small willow in the back garden being rustled by a breeze.

Only one of the spotlights in the room was on, throwing the other half into deep shadow.

'So, how long is she staying for?' Parker asked, sipping from his third can of beer.

'I told her it was only short term,' Beth informed him. 'I don't want her here any more than you do, Simon.'

'I wasn't complaining, I was just curious. And a little surprised.'

Beth raised her eyebrows quizzically.

'Well, there's no love lost between the two of you,' he continued. 'From some of the things you've told me about her, stuff that's happened in the past, I'm surprised you didn't tell her to fuck off when she asked to stay here.' He smiled.

'She's family, Simon. No matter what's happened between us in the past, I couldn't see her on the streets,' Beth explained. 'I know you think that's stupid . . .' She allowed the sentence to trail off.

Parker reached out and touched her hand, squeezing it.

'She's *your* sister,' he said, quietly.

'You don't have to remind me.'

There was a weariness to Beth's tone Parker wasn't slow to pick up.

'What's wrong, Beth?' he wanted to know.

'It's Lucy,' she said, unhesitatingly. 'She's my sister, I'm supposed to feel close to her, and yet when I saw her standing there today when I got home, I just thought, "Why did you have to turn up?" I know that's wrong but I can't help it. I don't trust her, Simon. I honestly thought that when she went to live in London after Mum and Dad died it'd be the last I'd ever see of her and I was glad about that, and if that sounds terrible, I'm sorry.'

'You still hold her responsible for their deaths, don't you?'

'She didn't have a scratch when she came out of that house, Simon. She even had time to call the fire brigade. If she had time to do *that* why didn't she have time to get Mum and Dad out of there? She left them to burn in that bloody house.'

'Beth, you can't ever know that.'

'I know *her*,' Beth snapped, angrily.

She stood up and crossed to the fridge, reaching in to take out a half-full bottle of wine. He watched as she retrieved a glass from the nearby cupboard and poured herself some of the white liquid.

'Cheers,' said Parker, raising his can in salute.

Beth managed a smile and sipped at her own drink.

'You look tired,' she told him.

'I'm OK, just pissed off,' he informed her. 'It's Flynn again. I swear to God that old bastard is getting paranoid. He's convinced I'm after his job.'

'Are you?'

'I wouldn't have his job for double the salary. I told him that.' Parker stroked his chin thoughtfully, the tone of his voice softening slightly. 'There's a new patient coming in tomorrow on the Secure Ward. He wants me to take on her case.'

'Is it a problem?'

'No. But I've got enough to do with my ward rounds. We all have. Flynn has fewer patients than any of us, he could have taken her. But he wants my perspective on the case,' Parker said, disdainfully.

'What did she do?' Beth wanted to know.

Parker swallowed hard. 'She murdered her two children.'

'How?' Beth asked.

Parker told her.

31

'Why?' she said softly when he'd finished.

'That's what I'm supposed to find out.'

'It's always children, isn't it? There's always something to do with children.'

He reached out and took her hand once again.

'Beth—' he began, as if to silence her.

'People who don't want kids, who don't care about them, why do they have them?' Beth asked, imploringly. 'It's not fair. We want them so much and yet we can't have them. *I* can't have them.'

'Beth stop it. It's not your fault.'

'But it *is* my fault, isn't it? I'm the one who can't conceive. I'm the one who can't bring a child into the world. And don't tell me it doesn't hurt you too, Simon, because I know it does.'

He got up and walked around the table, sitting down beside her, pulling her close to him. He could hear her crying softly and he held her close, finally putting one finger beneath her chin and raising her head. He wiped the tears from her cheeks.

'I love you, Beth,' he said, softly.

They embraced, clinging to one another almost frenziedly as if each was afraid the other might slip away.

'How could she kill her own children?' Beth whispered.

Parker shook his head and kissed her forehead, still holding her tightly to him, hearing her murmur quietly.

'How could *anyone* do that to a child?'

Termination

The stainless steel felt cold against her skin and she shivered, as much in fearful anticipation as at the chill of the metal.

A waking nightmare?

A vision?

She lay almost immobile as her feet were lifted into the stirrups, her skin prickling, her heart thudding faster against her ribs.

There was a huge circular light above the operating table and she found herself looking up into it, ignoring the afterburn it left on her retina. Every time she closed her eyes she could see that cold white glow.

The white tiled walls only added to the feeling of cold. Everything in the room seemed designed to draw heat from her. The cool steel, the icy gleam of the tiles, and the unblinking stare of that huge white light. She looked up at it to avoid seeing too much more of what was dotted around the room.

She had heard a small trolley being pushed alongside the table, had glanced briefly towards it and seen a row of gleaming instruments waiting there. She had hardly noticed the jab of the needle into the back of her hand and the introduction of the thin tube that would carry the anaesthetic. She tried to clear her mind, to push aside thoughts of where she was and what was about to be done to her. She heard mutterings from round about, heard the odd word from doctors or nurses who wandered around clad in their blue or green overalls looking like alien beings.

And all the time that white light bore down on her like some huge, godlike eye. Ever watchful. All seeing.

The smell was strong too. Nauseating sometimes it was so intense. The antiseptic odour seemed to fill her nostrils and head until she felt her skull would explode.

One of them had told her it would all be over in less than two minutes.

It was a simple operation.

The entire process, from the ward into the theatre and back again would take less than an hour.

So simple.

Two minutes. Two hours. It would make no difference to her.

She opened her eyes once more and looked across at the row of instruments that lay there. The range of speculums, which looked to her like duck bills on long handles, varying in size from the length and width of a man's fingernail up to what resembled a shoe-horn. There were small clamps there too and an instrument that looked like a metal loop on the end of a long thin handle. It was called a curette but she didn't realise. She didn't really care.

Instead she closed her eyes once again and tried to blot out the goings-on around her.

She felt a hand on her belly, pressing around her navel then moving lower.

When a mumbled question was asked she answered it with little more than a grunt, her eyes now screwed up so tightly white stars danced behind the lids.

She felt more hands on her ankle as the stirrup was re-adjusted. Then someone spoke softly into her left ear, told her to count to ten and she began counting, feeling the glorious oblivion of unconsciousness creeping over her. It was as if someone had injected liquid night into her veins.

She opened her eyes one last time before she drifted into sleep.

That cold white eye still stared down at her.

The nurse found the other girl immediately. The older one.

She guessed that she must be about twenty. A pretty girl with long dark hair who looked as pale as a ghost.

There was a strong resemblance between the two girls, the nurse thought, apart from the fact that the one in the operating room had deep red hair and was much younger.

Fourteen it had said on the form she'd read.

34

Fourteen.

The older girl saw the nurse approaching and moved agitatedly towards her.

'Is she OK?' she asked, worriedly.

'She's fine,' the nurse told her. 'We'll be taking her back to the ward in ten or fifteen minutes.'

'I'll wait. She'll want to see me when she wakes up.'

Beth smiled thinly at the nurse and watched as she turned and walked away back up the corridor.

She was glad Lucy would be all right.

The abortion had taken less time than she'd thought.

Ten

The papers fell to the floor as Parker woke with a start, looking around in bewilderment, shaking his head in an effort to rouse himself.

'Shit,' he murmured, leaning forward to pick up the scattered sheets before him, pushing them back into the thin manilla file which had been balanced on his lap.

'That interesting, eh?' said Beth, stretched out on the sofa next to him. She prodded him in the side with one bare foot, her eyes still fixed on the television screen.

Parker rubbed his eyes and yawned, dropping the file on to the small coffee table beside him.

'It's Flynn,' he muttered, blinking myopically. 'Wants me to read some case notes on Karen Gregson, the new patient. It's not even standard procedure, for Christ's sake. I'm sitting in during her physical tomorrow. *That* isn't standard either.' He exhaled deeply. 'The trouble with Flynn is, he thinks he's a fucking extra from *Silence of the Lambs* sometimes. You'd think he was senior

35

consultant at Broadmoor, not some pissy hospital no one's ever heard of.'

Beth looked at her husband for a moment, studying his creased brow and angry expression, then she smiled.

'Perhaps I should go to bed and let you rant on your own,' she said, chuckling.

'Was I ranting?' Parker said, smiling.

He grabbed her foot and ran his finger along the sole, tickling her. She tried to shake loose but he held her and she giggled as he stroked again, finally letting her go.

'Time for bed, I think,' said Beth, grinning.

She got up and crossed to the TV set, switching it off.

'What happened to Lucy?' Parker asked, getting to his feet. 'She didn't come down again, did she?'

Beth's smile faded slightly.

'I'll check on her on the way to bed,' she said, heading out of the sitting room first.

Parker heard her footfalls on the stairs as he ambled around the room turning off lights, taking a final look around before closing the door and following Beth up the stairs. As he reached the landing he saw her standing outside Lucy's room, heard her tap on the door gently as he passed.

Beth waited a moment, thought about walking straight in then tapped again.

'You can come in, I'm not asleep,' Lucy called from inside.

Beth stepped inside and found that the room was in darkness. The only light was coming through the window, the first silvery beams of moonlight jabbing across the blackness.

Lucy was sitting up on the bed, naked but for a long T-shirt which reached to just below her buttocks. The headphones of her walkman were still around her neck.

'Are you all right?' Beth asked. 'When you didn't come down we thought . . .' She let the sentence trail off.

36

'I thought I'd leave you and Simon in peace,' Lucy told her.

'Thanks. Look, we're going to bed now, if you want anything in the night you know where it is.' She hesitated in the doorway. 'I'll wake you when I get up in the morning, run you into town.'

Lucy nodded in the darkness, her expression hidden by the deep shadows.

Beth took a step back.

'Goodnight,' she said, flatly.

Lucy echoed the word and watched as the bedroom door was closed. She heard Beth padding across the landing to her own bedroom.

For what seemed like an eternity, Lucy sat motionless on the bed, the silence of the darkened house closing around her like an ebony fist. Finally she got to her feet and crossed to the bedroom window, pushing it open a few inches, allowing a chill breeze to whip inside. She leaned on the sill, gazing out at the other houses round about. Most were in darkness, in others lights burned. Through a gap between two houses at the bottom of the garden she could see the sodium glare of a street lamp.

As she watched a light came on in the house directly at the foot of the garden.

She saw the silhouette of someone moving past drawn curtains.

It was the outline of a man.

Lucy watched until the light went off then she closed her window and turned back into the room.

She crossed to the bedside cabinet and pulled open the door, retrieving the duffel bag which she dropped on to the bed, then she padded across to the bedroom door and opened it a few inches, peering out on to the dark landing.

There was no movement.

She could hear no sound from Beth and Simon's room across the other side of the landing.

Lucy pushed the door shut once more and hurried back

to the bed, pulling open the duffel bag, reaching inside.

Her hand closed over the first thing she sought and she lifted it into view.

The contents of the plastic bag seemed fluorescent in the dull glow of the moonlight. She held it flat on her palm, smiling as she prodded the bag of cocaine.

After a moment she replaced it and retrieved the other object, studying it with similar care and fascination.

It was fully nine inches long. Double edged and razor sharp.

The hunting knife glinted wickedly.

Lucy smiled and ran the tip of one thumb over a cutting edge.

The slightest touch was sufficient to open a small cut on the pad.

She watched as blood welled up from the slit then licked the coppery fluid away.

She was still smiling when she slid the knife back inside its sheath and into the duffel bag.

Eleven

'She doesn't look like a murderer, does she?'

Damian Wilks ran a hand through his hair and watched as the young woman with the blonde hair and milk white complexion climbed from the back of the police car.

Beside him, his companion watched in silence.

Frank Jennings used a thumbnail to remove a small piece of bacon from between two of his front teeth and kept his gaze firmly on the new arrival.

She was pretty. Slim, fragile almost. He guessed no more than five three, dressed in a pair of jeans, trainers and a white T-shirt. She had a dark blue jacket draped around her shoulders.

Very nice.

'I said . . .' Wilks began.

'I heard what you said,' snapped Jennings, still struggling to pick the pieces of his breakfast free of his teeth. 'What did you expect her to look like?'

'I don't know really. Just different.'

'That's one thing you should never do in this job,' Jennings said. 'Judge by appearances. They're all different, every one of them in here. They're either mad, sad or bad. That's what one of the older nurses said to me the first day I started here.'

'Very profound,' said Wilks, smiling.

Jennings offered him a cautionary stare.

'That was his advice to me,' the older man said. 'I'll give *you* some now. How long have you been here? A week? Best advice I can offer is keep your mouth shut and always watch your back, you can't trust any of the bastards in here. That goes for the staff too.'

'How long have you been a nurse here?' Wilks wanted to know.

'Twenty-two years,' Jennings told him. 'Not many last that long. How old are *you*?'

'Twenty-three,' said Wilks, defensively.

'Fucking hell, you'll be gone before you're twenty-five.'

Wilks was about to say something when Jennings took a couple of steps forward towards the policeman and his ward.

Karen Gregson looked up at the older man then swiftly lowered her gaze, staring down at the gravel driveway which ran along the front of Brackley Heath. Her feet crunched the stones as she shifted slowly from one foot to the other.

The young policeman who was escorting her handed a small hold-all to Jennings.

'Her clothes are in there,' he said.

Jennings nodded and took it from him, beckoning Wilks forward to join him, passing the hold-all to the younger man.

'Sign this, please,' the policeman said, pushing a clipboard towards the older male nurse, watching as he scribbled his signature on the bottom.

'Goodbye,' said Karen Gregson as the policeman turned to walk away.

He gazed at her, startled by the unexpected utterance.

She smiled wanly then looked down at the ground once more.

'Come on, Karen,' said Jennings and took her arm gently, guiding her towards the main entrance of the hospital. Wilks walked behind them, carrying the hold-all. As they reached the double doors Jennings pushed one and held it, beckoning Karen through. She hesitated until the older nurse placed one hand on her bottom and pushed gently.

Wilks grinned but the smile faded as Jennings shot him an angry glance.

He returned his attention to Karen, his gaze roving up and down her body.

Very, very nice.

He wasn't sure of her age but he guessed she was about twenty-four. About half his age.

As they approached another set of doors Jennings stepped in front of her, one arm brushing against her left breast as he ushered her through.

He could feel the warmth through her T-shirt, the firmness of that concealed fleshy globe.

She didn't even look at him, merely walked through.

Wilks followed.

The trio turned right at the end of the corridor and Jennings knocked hard on a large door there. He looked first at Wilks then at Karen who kept her gaze lowered.

Jennings looked at her breasts, the outline of her bra visible through the material.

40

'You'll be fine, Karen,' he said, quietly.

Yes. You'll be just fucking great.

A voice from inside beckoned them in.

Twelve

Miserable day, Lucy Morton thought.

Miserable fucking day.

A steady drizzle was falling from the banks of grey cloud that clogged the sky, the moisture forming into rivulets on the thick glass windows of the Job Centre, trailing down.

Beneath the canopy covering the main entrance of the building two young men, a little older than Lucy herself, stood smoking, peering in at her every now and then. She saw their interest and smiled to herself as she turned her back on them and began another circuit of the large boards dotted around the inside of the place, each bearing cards promising jobs.

Lucy scanned them disinterestedly.

A school cleaner. Barmaid. Shop assistant.

There were plenty of vacancies there. Small wonder considering the pittance most of them offered by way of remuneration.

Fuck it.

She'd have to find something, she had no doubt that Beth would carry through her threat to throw her out if she didn't find work.

As Lucy turned to consider the cards on the board behind her one final time, again she noticed the two men looking at her. This time she held their gaze, chuckling to herself when first one then the other looked hurriedly away.

41

She glanced across at the row of desks on the other side of the room. Job Centre employees were seated behind most of them. One was on the phone, another was chatting to a middle-aged man.

There was a woman in her late twenties pushing a buggy around, up and down the aisles. The child in it was asleep, its head lolling on one side. Lucy watched the child for a moment then turned her attention back to the noticeboards.

Petrol station attendant. Another cleaning job. Trainee cook.

She made a mental note of two of the job reference numbers then ambled over towards one of the empty desks and sat down.

The woman with the buggy trundled past, the baby still fast asleep.

Lucy looked round at the middle-aged man, catching a few words of his conversation.

The words executive and large salary seemed somewhat incongruous in these surroundings.

'Can I help you?'

Lucy turned to see that someone had returned to the desk at which she was seated. The woman smiled efficiently at her, running swift appraising eyes over her.

'There are a couple of jobs I'd like some information about,' Lucy said, wearily.

'I need the reference numbers, please,' said the woman, reaching for a pen.

'Yeah, I know, I've done this shit before,' Lucy muttered. She repeated the numbers and waited while the woman flicked through the roladex before her.

'Have you worked behind a bar before?' the woman wanted to know.

'Once or twice. I can add up and that's about the only qualification you need.'

'A friendly attitude helps too,' said the woman, acidly, pulling a form towards her. 'I'll need some details from you. Your name.'

'Lucy Morton. I'm twenty.' She gave her birthdate. 'No qualifications, I was expelled when I was fifteen before you ask.'

'What previous job experience have you had other than bar work?' the woman wanted to know, her gaze once again straying to Lucy's face. 'It's a bit limited.'

'I'm applying to be a barmaid, not a brain surgeon,' Lucy said, tersely.

'You won't be the only one for the job, Miss Morton. Jobs aren't easy to come by, you know.'

'Tell me about it. Have you got any jobs going in here? It looks like a piece of piss.'

The woman glared at her, pulling the phone on her desk towards her.

'I'll ring the employers and make appointments for you,' she said, irritably.

Lucy nodded and reached into her handbag for a cigarette, watching as the woman dialled. She was about to light up when the woman tapped her desk and motioned towards the NO SMOKING sign displayed on the wall.

Lucy smiled and made an exaggerated gesture of removing the cigarette and dropping it back into the pack. She barely heard the woman as she chatted on the phone. Lucy glanced again at the woman with the buggy. The child was waking up now, blinking and looking around at these unfamiliar surroundings. Lucy seemed transfixed by the baby, her gaze glued to it.

She heard the woman on the other side of the desk speaking but the words didn't seem to register.

'Miss Morton.'

The child was beginning to cry, its face turning red as it started to wail unhappily.

'Miss Morton,' the woman persisted.

Lucy looked round.

'I've arranged interviews for you at ten and at three tomorrow,' the woman told her. She gave her the locations, the names of the people to ask for.

Lucy nodded and got to her feet.

'Thanks,' she said, disinterestedly, and headed for the door.

The woman with the baby had lifted it into her arms and was attempting to silence it. Other eyes turned to look at her.

Lucy walked out, glad that the drizzle had stopped.

As she walked away one of the men standing by the door whistled loudly at her.

Lucy turned round to face him and saw him smiling inanely.

'All right, gorgeous?' he said, grinning.

'Fuck off, dickhead,' Lucy snapped and walked on.

'What's your fucking problem?' the other man called, irritably.

Lucy smiled to herself and walked on, glancing up at the sky. The clouds were parting, revealing blue behind them.

Perhaps it wasn't going to be such a miserable day after all. She looked at her watch.

10.25 a.m.

It was still early.

She had plenty of time.

Thirteen

Beth sat with the tip of her pen resting against her notepad, glancing occasionally at the tall figure of David Manning who had his back to her, his attention caught by something in the car park below.

She waited a moment longer then coughed theatrically.

Manning turned and smiled at her.

'Sorry, Beth,' he said. 'I was miles away. Where did we get to?'

She read back what she'd already scribbled down.

'That'll do,' Manning told her. 'Just finish it off with yours etc., etc. You've been doing it for long enough.'

Beth nodded.

Two years to be exact, she thought. Manning had joined the company about three months after her, walking straight in to replace her old boss who'd been given a substantial golden handshake amidst rumours of fraud. Rather than risk their good name in a well-publicised court case, Jaguar had preferred the option of paying the man off.

Manning couldn't have been more different to his predecessor. He was in his early forties but looked younger, due in no small measure to the amount of sport he played. His eyes, particularly, seemed to blaze with an almost intimidatory ferocity irrespective of his moods. Beth had yet to see the angry side of her boss, she knew him only as a thoughtful and efficient man who respected her abilities in her role as his personal secretary. His skin was lightly tanned and she had noticed a lighter band on the third finger of his left hand. Perhaps the indication that a ring had once been worn there. No longer was that the case. From what little she knew of him she understood he was divorced. His marriage another casualty of his rapid rise to one of the top positions within the company.

'Did you get the messages I left on your desk earlier?' she asked, getting to her feet, smoothing creases from her skirt.

Manning nodded, allowing his gaze to focus on her legs.

As she looked up he glanced at his watch.

'It's almost lunch-time,' Manning said. 'Can I buy you a drink, Beth?'

She smiled wanly.

'I'd better get this typed up,' she said quietly, waving

45

the pad before her.

'It can wait until later, can't it?'

'A boss advising his secretary to take it easy,' she chuckled. 'I've never heard *that* before.'

Manning smiled even more broadly.

'So, what about that drink, then?' he persisted.

'Maybe some other time,' she told him and headed for the door.

'I'll hold you to that,' he said.

I bet you will.

She closed the office door and wandered across to her desk, looking down to find a slim black wallet of photos lying there.

Beth picked it up and flipped it open, reaching inside to pull out the prints.

Manning emerged from his office and breezed past her.

'See you later,' he said and was gone.

Beth returned her attention to the pictures.

They were of a child, no more than six months old.

A little girl.

Beth held the pictures between the tips of her fingers, as if anxious not to touch the surface. She handled them as if they were contaminated, her gaze fixed on the face of the child.

There was one of the baby with its mother, shortly after the birth she guessed. The mother was smiling happily into the camera.

Another of the father, holding the child aloft like some kind of trophy.

Beth swallowed hard and pulled out the next print in the pile.

The mother breast-feeding.

Something *she* would never be able to do.

As she held the picture she noticed that her hand was trembling slightly.

'It's my sister's baby.'

The voice startled her and she looked up quickly.

'Beautiful, isn't she?' said Caroline Seaton, nodding towards the pictures. 'I thought you'd like to have a look.'

'Thanks,' said Beth, as convincingly as she could.

'There's no rush,' Caroline told her and turned to leave.

Beth nodded and watched as her colleague pushed open the door leading to the larger open-plan offices beyond. Through the glass partitions she could see most of the office occupants leaving for lunch. A couple of them looked across at her and waved. She returned the gesture then glanced down at the photos once more.

The baby in its crib.

The mother and father leaning over it, smiling down proudly.

Beth stuffed the pictures back inside the paper wallet and pushed them away from her, getting to her feet and snatching up her handbag.

She shoved the photos into the drawer of her desk, shutting them out of sight. She'd seen enough. She could feel the tears welling up, the prickling sensation around her eyes.

Enough.

She strode out of the office.

Fourteen

'It's all right, Jennings,' Simon Parker said, quietly. 'You can leave us. Karen and I will be fine, won't we?'

Karen Gregson didn't speak.

She looked at Parker, then at Jennings, then contented herself with looking around the room.

The nurse hesitated a moment until Parker nodded towards him, a signal to vacate the room, which he did a little uncertainly.

Sunlight was pouring through the large windows of Parker's office, the warm rays glinting off the polished wood of his desk. He watched as one of the beams lanced across Karen's legs. She looked down at it for a moment then tried to brush it away.

'I can open a window if you're too hot,' Parker said, getting to his feet.

She didn't answer.

He regarded her appraisingly for a moment. The exterior appearance of a patient was sometimes an indication of their true mental state. Not so with Karen it appeared. She was dressed in a white T-shirt and faded jeans, her small feet pushed into a pair of trainers. Her blonde hair was pulled back and fastened in a ponytail which swung like some furry pendulum every time she moved her head sharply from side to side. She looked curiously vulnerable.

'When we've had a talk, you'll be shown to your room,' he told her, glancing down at his notes then at Karen once more.

Still no answer.

'I'm here to help you, Karen,' Parker continued. 'But for me to help you, *you* have to help *me*. You have to talk to me. Tell me what you're feeling. I want to help you. You know that, don't you?'

She was gazing at one of the cracks in the paintwork on the wall behind his desk now, her blue eyes shining like electrically powered sapphires.

'My name is Simon Parker,' he told her. 'You can call me Simon if you want to.'

She smiled at him.

Jesus, those eyes.

Parker felt as if she'd looked through his soul. Seared right into him with those blue orbs. For a moment he held her gaze, almost relieved when she lowered her eyes and began picking at a piece of frayed cotton at the bottom of her T-shirt.

'You told the last doctor who saw you that you heard voices,' he continued. 'What kind of voices?'

She teased a loose thread free and held it between her index fingers.

'What did they say to you?'

She smiled at him once more.

'Did they tell you to kill your children?'

There was an intensity in her stare which Parker found almost hypnotic.

The smile never left her face. So angelic. So full of warmth.

'Mind your own fucking business, you nosey cunt,' she said, that beaming smile undiluted by the venom of her words.

'Do you still hear the voices now?' Parker asked, unfazed.

'What if I do?' she said, the smile finally disappearing. 'What's it got to do with you?'

'*Do* you hear them?'

'Sometimes.'

'Do they still say the same things?'

She returned to pulling threads from her clothes.

'Do you like hearing the voices, Karen?' he wanted to know. 'Are they people you know?'

'I can't tell you that,' she murmured. 'They told me not to.'

'Did they say what would happen to you if you did?'

She shook her head.

'I can make the voices go away, Karen.'

She regarded him impassively.

'Do you want them to go away?'

'They told me about *you*,' Karen said, flatly.

'What did they say about me?'

'They told me not to trust you.'

'Can you hear them now?'

She lowered her gaze and stared at the floor.

'Are they speaking to you now, Karen?'

She laughed and Parker was surprised what an infectious quality there was to the sound. Her whole face seemed to light up as she uttered such a joyous sound.

'They wouldn't let you see them,' she told him.

'You *see* them too? Do the people you see speak to you? Are they the ones you hear?'

'They're not always people.'

'What are they, then?'

'They could be anything. Any shape. They could be here now.' She laughed again. 'You could be one of them.'

'If I was one of them I wouldn't have told you not to trust me.'

'*They* don't trust *you*.'

'Why?'

'They didn't give me a fucking reason,' she hissed.

'Do *you* trust them?'

'I don't trust anyone. I couldn't even trust my own children, how can I trust *them*?'

'But you trust them enough to do what they tell you, don't you?'

She regarded him balefully.

'Did they tell you to kill your children?' he persisted.

'They weren't my children,' Karen told him. 'I knew what they *really* were.'

'And what was that, Karen?'

She pulled more threads from her T-shirt.

'If they weren't your children, what were they?' Parker continued, careful to control the tone of his voice.

'Have you got any children?' she finally asked, conversationally, turning those piercing blue eyes upon him once again.

'No,' Parker said, dismissively.

'Why?'

Because my wife is infertile.

'My wife and I are happy as we are,' he lied.

'Do you plan to have them sometime?'

Parker swallowed hard.

'Children are wonderful,' she said, enthusiastically.

'Weren't *your* children wonderful, Karen?'

'They weren't *my* children, I told you that,' she snapped.

'Then whose were they? You carried them both. You gave birth to them, you looked after them at the beginning.'

'I was told to.'

'Who by? The voices?'

'I didn't know what they were at the beginning, I didn't know what I had to do.'

'Until the voices told you?'

She smiled.

'You'd make a good father,' she told him. 'You've got kind eyes.'

Parker held her gaze for a moment then got to his feet and walked to the edge of his desk, perching on it, looking down at her.

A good father.

'Perhaps we should talk again tomorrow, Karen.'

She smiled up at him.

'All right, Simon,' she whispered, her grin spreading, her amused chuckle finally developing into a raucous laugh.

This time there was no warmth in the sound, merely a spiteful hollowness.

Parker felt himself fixed in the unwavering gaze of her piercing blue eyes and the hairs at the back of his neck rose.

She reached out and touched his wedding ring.

'Say hello to your wife for me,' she said, grinning.

Fifteen

The room was twelve feet square, bare but for a single bed, a small bedside cabinet, a table and a chair. There was barely enough room to accommodate Frank Jennings and Karen Gregson as they stepped inside.

Karen looked up towards the single window in the wall, sunlight filtering through the thick Perspex sheet. The surface of the plastic was covered in scratches and one corner looked as if someone had attempted to lever it free. Paint round the frame was chipped and peeling.

On the bed was the hold-all with which she'd entered the hospital. She looked at Jennings as if seeking permission to cross to the bag. He nodded and smiled, watching her as she unzipped it.

He gazed raptly at the outline of her buttocks, taut and shapely beneath the constrictions of her tight jeans.

As she began pulling at the contents of the bag he curled his key chain slowly around his fist, let it uncoil then repeated the procedure.

'Put your things in there,' he told her, pointing to the bedside cabinet.

He moved closer to her, inhaling, enjoying the scent she gave off. A clean, freshly washed smell.

He reached into the bag and pulled out her toothbrush and some soap. These he placed beside the bed, watching as she carefully pushed her clothes into the cabinet, arranging them as neatly as the tiny space would allow. He could see the outline of her bra through the material of her T-shirt.

Very nice.

She was on all fours now, pushing more clothes into the cabinet.

Jennings reached into the bag and handed her two or three pairs of knickers, sliding one thumb over them as he passed them to her.

They were soft beneath the hard pad of his thumb and he could smell their delicate fragrance.

How tightly did they cling to her crotch?

She reached out to take the undergarments from him.

What would they smell like after she'd worn them for a day? What pleasing scent would he detect, then?

As he handed them to her, his fingers brushed hers and she seemed to recoil sharply.

Jennings found himself staring into those wide blue eyes.

You could drown in those fucking eyes.

She averted her gaze as she straightened up, moving a couple of paces back from him, bumping into the chair in the process.

Jennings stood looking at her, still curling and uncurling the key chain around his fist. For interminable seconds he watched her then he turned and walked out, locking the door behind him, glancing back into the room through the spy-hole.

He could see her sitting motionless on the edge of the bed, looking round, hands gripping her knees.

When he inhaled he could still smell her.

'Is she OK?' asked Damian Wilks.

Jennings nodded.

The two of them headed back down the corridor towards the large metal door separating the Secure Ward from the rest of the hospital, and Wilks watched as his companion locked it.

'How long will she be here?' Wilks asked.

'Karen Gregson? Christ knows,' Jennings told him.

'How long are patients usually kept in Secure?'

'Ask one of the consultants. I don't know how long

she's going to be here.'

'Which was she? Mad, bad or sad? You said that—'

Jennings cut him short.

'I know what I said,' he snapped.

'So?'

'I don't know her well enough yet,' Jennings said, smiling.

But I'll make fucking sure I do.

He had the key chain wound so tightly around his fist his knuckles were white.

Sixteen

By the time Lucy got back to the house, the sun had banished the last of the rain clouds from the sky and now hung there defiantly, bathing the ground in a warm blanket. Drying the earth swiftly, it also helped to create an uncomfortable humidity. Lucy felt her T-shirt sticking to her back as she fumbled in her pocket for the key.

She pushed open the front door, quickly crossing the small hallway and jabbing the numbers on the wall pad in the sequence she'd been instructed to prevent the strident ringing of the alarm invading the prized silence.

Lucy headed for the staircase, the steps creaking protestingly as she climbed. The house felt welcomingly cool inside, a pleasing contrast to the heat of the sun. She ran a hand through her long red hair, wiping perspiration on her jeans.

As she reached the top of the stairs she paused, glancing across the landing first at the door of her own room then at the other doors facing off from the small landing.

The door of Beth and Simon's room was open slightly.

54

Lucy hesitated a moment then walked across to it, pushing it with one fingertip. The door swung open and she stepped inside.

The bedroom was large, dominated by a big double bed. Lucy smiled, crossed to it and lay down, gazing up at the ceiling, allowing her hands to sweep back and forth over the duvet. She sat up, peering round.

There was a portable TV on a wooden unit to the right of the bed, below it some books, a few small ornaments. A framed wedding photo of Beth and Simon commanded pride of place on one of the shelves.

On either side of the bed were matching cabinets. Perched on one was a clock radio, on the other a telephone. She wondered which side of the bed was Beth's.

For long moments she sat on the edge of the bed then, finally, she swung herself off and crossed to the large dark wardrobes opposite. Lucy pulled on the double doors and looked inside.

The stuff inside belonged to Simon. She saw suits, shirts, ties, sweatshirts and T-shirts, all hanging on their own separate hanger. She pushed the doors closed and pulled open the next set.

Beth's stuff.

Lucy ran her eyes across the array of clothes there.

All carefully arranged, neatly displayed and hung with almost military precision, a vast range of skirts, blouses, jackets and dresses in every style and colour imaginable. Lucy put out a hand and ran it along the line of clothes, brushing her fingertips against the different materials. Leather, cotton, silk. She reached up and pulled a red silk shirt from its hanger, holding it up against herself, checking her reflection in the full-length mirror on the back of one of the wardrobe doors.

She sought a skirt to match the blouse and picked out a short black one.

Smiling, she began pulling at her own clothes, tugging

them free, tossing them unwanted on to the bed. Clad in just her panties she watched her reflection as she pulled on the blouse and skirt. They fitted perfectly.

Lucy grinned and peered down into the bottom of the wardrobe to see a dizzying array of shoes.

There were court shoes, most with high heels. Short boots, long boots. Trainers. She even spotted an ancient and scuffed pair of platforms, now coated in a thick layer of dust.

She selected a pair of high-heeled black suede shoes and slipped her feet into them.

Again a perfect fit.

She and Beth could have been twins.

She studied the figure which looked back at her from the mirror.

Twins.

Like fuck.

Lucy pulled off the skirt and blouse, replacing them on their hangers, putting them back with the same care with which they'd originally been placed there.

She spotted a black crushed velvet dress and pulled it from its hanger, tugging it over her head, sliding into the figure-hugging material.

She smiled at her reflection briefly then turned towards the bedside cabinets, sliding open the top drawer of the one on the right.

There were more T-shirts, folded neatly this time. Sweatshirts. Leggings. Every drawer was full it seemed.

She crossed to the other cabinet and performed a similar search.

The top one was filled with stockings and tights. Black and grey mainly. There were a couple of suspender belts in there. Some socks, all neatly balled up in pairs.

The next drawer was stuffed full of knickers. Every colour and style imaginable. She smiled. How many pairs could you wear in a week? Lucy dug down deeper through the undergarments until her fingers brushed against something firm.

Cylindrical.

She lifted the vibrator into view, her grin broadening.

Lucy ran a finger over the fake phallus, tracing the contours of its white plastic shape, finally twisting the bottom slightly. She heard the low buzz as it hummed into life and she closed her hand tightly around it for a second before switching it off and pushing it back amongst the piles of knickers.

Your little toy, Beth.

She wondered what else her sister had hidden.

The bottom drawer was full to the brim with neatly folded sweaters. Lucy snaked her hand beneath the garments and was rewarded for her persistence.

She found a manilla envelope and pulled it free, feeling its weight. She loosened the flap and upended it.

Photos spilled out, scattering on the duvet.

Lucy picked two or three up and studied the images before her.

Beth as a child.

Beth in her Communion dress.

How fucking touching.

Seated there on the edge of the bed, wearing her older sister's dress and shoes, Lucy flicked rapidly through the pictures. Some were in colour but most were black and white, many of them faded or dog-eared.

Beth playing on a beach somewhere. She was young in the picture. Barely ten years old.

There was one of Beth and Simon. They both looked so different. He had long hair and a moustache. Beth was looking lovingly at him.

Lucy found one of herself.

Tucked away at the bottom of one of the piles, she guessed she must have been about six when it was taken. There were other children in the shot, all of them smiling happily at the camera.

Not Lucy.

She was looking skyward as if she'd spotted something as yet unseen by the others.

She sifted through the rest of the pictures disinterestedly.

Beth and the old Labrador they used to have.

Beth and her first bicycle.

Beth.

Beth.

Lucy tossed the pictures aside.

Beth and their parents.

Lucy looked at the picture intently.

There were more of their dead parents. Many more.

She gathered the pictures together hurriedly, stuffed them back into the envelope and pushed it back into the drawer.

She was about to push the door shut when she noticed another pile of papers.

Bound only by an elastic band and a paper clip, these sheets were barely visible towards the front of the drawer but Lucy reached down and pulled them out.

Letters.

Love letters, perhaps.

She pulled one free.

' "Dear Mrs Parker," ' she read aloud. ' "With reference to your visit of 29th May, I . . ." '

These were no love letters.

She glanced at the heading on the notepaper.

THE WADE CLINIC, HARLEY STREET.

Lucy read on, mouthing the words silently as she read.

Words like infertility began to appear with increasing regularity.

She looked at another of the letters.

The heading was the same.

She spotted the words 'fallopian rupture' and, further on, 'ectopic pregnancy'.

The recurrent word throughout all of them seemed to be 'regret'.

What had Beth said to her?

'I can't have children.'

Lucy flicked through the remaining letters then carefully replaced them, closing the drawer.

She slipped out of Beth's dress and pulled on her own clothes once more, hanging up the dress and replacing the shoes in approximately the same place. As she turned away from the wardrobe she heard a sound from outside and peered through the window.

When she saw its source she smiled to herself.

Pulling on her trainers she hurried out of the room.

She didn't want to miss this opportunity.

Seventeen

'Puerperal psychosis,' said Parker, defiantly. 'One of the most acute cases I've ever seen.'

'And you're sure of that?' Dr Flynn wanted to know.

'She's exhibiting all the classic signs,' Parker told him. 'She talked about hearing voices, even seeing figures. Her mood swings are violent and there's evidence of paranoia, possibly even schizophrenia.'

'There's nothing in her medical background to indicate why she should be so susceptible to such an acute attack,' Flynn said, flicking briefly through Karen Gregson's file.

'You know as well as I do that there are no contributory factors to this illness,' Parker said, a little sharply. 'Christ, over 4,000 women a year are admitted to psychiatric hospitals with some form of post-natal disturbance. They're not all latent manic depressives, are they?'

Flynn regarded his younger colleague warily for a moment then ran a hand through his snow white hair.

59

'Did she give you any idea of why she killed the children?' he asked, finally.

'I didn't press her too much,' Parker told him.

'Is that part of the *new* approach? Let the patients take things in their own time.'

'It's got nothing to do with any *new* approach, Doctor Flynn. I don't profess to have the secret to some revolutionary method of dealing with patients.'

'But your methods are different? Certainly different to mine?'

'I practise the way I was taught, the same as you. It's just that the methods I was taught are different to those *you* were taught.'

'Better?'

'I didn't say that.' Parker was finding it difficult to contain his irritation. 'Anyway, I didn't think we were here to discuss the relative merits of our individual working methods. I'm more concerned about Karen Gregson.'

'Any suicidal tendencies?' Flynn asked.

'Not as far as I could tell. The psychosis seems to be homicidal, all her anger is projected not internalised. That's why she attacked her children.'

'Was she lucid?'

'Very much so. Like I said, there were the usual mood swings, one minute she seemed able to talk, the next she became apathetic.' He raised his eyebrows. 'She seemed more interested in me than in her own problems. She kept asking *me* questions. She said the voices had told her about me.'

'What have you prescribed?'

'Lithium Carbonate.'

'I'm not sure I would have used Lithium. What was wrong with Haloperidol or Stelazine?'

'She's not breast feeding.'

'Obviously,' Flynn said, smiling sardonically.

'I wouldn't have prescribed Lithium if she'd been breast feeding. Do you want me to change the medication?'

'Certainly not, Simon, if you feel that Lithium is right then by all means continue with it,' Flynn said, sarcastically.

'It was the drug *I* felt would suit her best.'

'Well, who am *I* to argue with your opinion? Perhaps the use of Haloperidol is a little old fashioned now. It was always good enough in the old days.' He chuckled humourlessly.

Parker regarded his colleague with little short of contempt.

Ha, fucking ha, you patronising old bastard.

'Why do you think the psychosis was so much more violent the second time?' Flynn asked. 'She didn't suffer from it after the birth of her first child.'

'If you check the records,' Parker said, nodding towards the file, 'there is evidence of depression after the birth of the first child. She was treated by her GP for what he thought were the usual baby blues. He put her on valium for six months. As you know, if there's been some form of mental disturbance after the first child then the woman increases her likelihood of experiencing a worse form of post-natal psychosis by one in ten when she has another.'

'I was aware of those statistics, Simon,' Flynn said, sharply.

There was an uneasy silence, finally broken by the older man.

'Do we know anything about the husband?' he asked.

'Is that relevent?' Parker wanted to know.

'A troubled relationship might well have contributed to the psychosis. If she was already unhappy or disturbed then this may just be an extension of some deeper problem.'

'There's no correlation between puerperal psychosis and emotional disturbance, you know that,' Parker said, dismissively. 'Women from the happiest marriages can be as badly affected.'

'So, what about the father of Karen Gregson's children?' Flynn persisted.

'He disappeared shortly after the birth of the first one.'

'So he knows nothing of their deaths?'

'I doubt it. I don't know. I don't really care,' Parker snapped. 'I'm a psychiatrist, not a detective. What happened to the father of those children isn't important to me. What becomes of their mother *is*.' Parker looked at his watch. 'Now if we're finished, I've got my ward rounds to do.'

Flynn regarded him silently, his ruddy cheeks apparently glowing even brighter.

'I'll expect regular reports on Karen Gregson,' he said, finally.

'You'll get them, just like you get reports on all my other patients,' Parker said, irritably.

'We'll speak again, Simon,' said Flynn and turned his attention to the pile of papers in the tray on his desk.

Parker sat bewildered for a moment then got to his feet and headed for the door, he paused there a second longer then was gone.

Flynn looked up towards the closed door, his eyes narrowed. He gripped his pen more tightly for a second then threw it down angrily.

Eighteen

As Lucy stepped out into the back garden she heard the roar of the lawnmower even more clearly. The smell of freshly cut grass wafted through the air on the gentle breeze and she walked slowly down the narrow pathway leading from the back door of the house to the fence at the bottom of the garden.

Flowers were in full bloom on either side of the path but

Lucy paid them little heed, her attention was fixed ahead.

On the figure pushing the mower back and forth.

She smiled as she ran appraising eyes over him.

He certainly looked older than seventeen.

That was what Beth had said, wasn't it?

He was about five seven, three or four inches taller than Lucy herself, dressed in cut-off jeans and trainers. His body was sheathed in sweat, which glistened in the sunshine. There was very little muscle there, she noted, just a soft sheen to his flesh. Sweat had soaked into the waistband of his jeans, darkening the material. Lucy allowed herself a look at his crotch, smiling as she inspected the bulge there.

'I hope you're getting paid for that,' she said, raising her voice over the steady drone of the mower.

Mark Hennessey glanced in the direction of the voice, his look of surprise almost making Lucy laugh aloud.

He took his hand off the orange lever on the mower's handle and peace suddenly descended.

'Hello,' he said, a little sheepishly. 'I couldn't hear what you said.'

'I said I hope you're getting paid for doing that,' she repeated, nodding towards the lawn. 'Pushing a mower around in this weather.'

'I promised my mum and dad I'd do it,' Hennessey told her. 'A sort of surprise for them when they get back.'

'Where are they?' Lucy wanted to know.

'They're on holiday in Spain for a week,' he told her, wiping his forehead with one hand.

'How come you didn't go with them?'

'It's not really my scene. Besides, I've got revision to do for exams.'

'This looks like a strange kind of revision,' Lucy told him, running approving eyes over his torso.

Hennessey was aware of her probing gaze and looked at the ground, his cheeks colouring slightly.

'Your name's Mark, isn't it?' Lucy continued.

'Yeah, that's right. How did you know?' he enquired.

'My sister told me. Beth Parker, she's my sister.' Lucy jabbed a thumb in the general direction of the house.

'I can see the family resemblance,' he said, trying not to make it too obvious that his interest seemed to be in her breasts. Unfettered by a bra, beneath the thin material of her T-shirt he could see the dark points of her nipples pushing against the cloth.

She saw the colour spread across his cheeks once more.

'I'm staying with her for a little while,' she told him. 'My name's Lucy.'

'Hi, Lucy,' he said, awkwardly. 'Nice to meet you.'

She smiled broadly at him, allowing her own gaze to stray to his groin. She saw the unmistakable beginnings of an erection pushing against his cut-offs.

Obviously he liked what he saw.

'You look like you could do with a break,' she said. 'Fancy a cold drink?'

The expression that crossed Hennessey's face was a combination of surprise and delight.

'I saw some orange juice in Beth's fridge,' Lucy continued.

'Yeah, that's fine. Thanks,' he stammered.

'Back in a minute,' she said and headed back towards the house.

Hennessey watched her as she walked, her long red hair stirred by the breeze, the denim clinging tightly to her buttocks. He could feel the stiffness in his groin growing. He moved closer to the fence, hoping to hide it from her when she returned. Perspiration was still running from his forehead and he reached into his pocket for a handkerchief, mopping the moisture away, aware of that aching erection pressing more firmly against his jeans.

A moment or two later, Lucy headed back up the path with a glass of orange juice in each hand.

She handed one to him and watched him take two or three large swallows.

'Thanks,' he said. 'I needed that.'

64

She sipped her own drink and fixed him in an unwavering gaze.

'So, what are you studying?' she asked eventually. 'You said you were studying for exams.'

'I'm doing A levels in English and History,' he told her. 'I want to be a teacher.'

Lucy raised her eyebrows.

'I used to fancy one of my teachers,' she said, smiling.

Hennessey's cheeks turned an even deeper shade of crimson and he took a long swig from his glass. He wiped his mouth with the back of his hand and looked at Lucy, aware that his cheeks were burning.

'How long are you staying with your sister?' he wanted to know.

'I don't know yet. I moved out of my place in London. I got fed up with it.'

'What did you do there?'

'This and that. Odd jobs. Whatever paid.'

He nodded slowly.

'You said your sister told you my name,' Hennessey said, finally.

'That doesn't bother you, does it?' Lucy asked, feigning concern.

'No.'

'She told me about all the neighbours around here. It looks like you're the only one not in a wheelchair.'

He smiled.

'Well, the only one close to *my* age, anyway,' she continued.

'How old are you?' he asked, his cheeks darkening once again. 'Not that I'm being nosey but, I'm sorry . . .'

'I'm twenty,' she said, cutting short his flounderings.

He sipped at his drink, averting his gaze momentarily.

'So, what does everyone do for fun around here?' Lucy asked.

'They cut the grass,' he said, chuckling, happy when he saw her laughing too.

'Or study,' she said, a slight edge to her voice.

Hennessey didn't pick it up.

'What about you?' she asked. 'What do you do for fun?'

'I've got a motorbike, a Harley Davidson FXSTS Springer Softail. One of my mates, his dad runs a bike shop, he lets me rummage around for spare parts and that. It's taken me two years to build. I just love fiddling with mechanical shit, excuse my French.' He coloured again.

'I love motorbikes. A guy I used to know had one, he used to take me out on the back of it. God, it used to make me feel so horny.'

She looked directly at him.

'All that vibration,' she purred, smiling to herself as she watched him shifting position uncomfortably. 'Are you going to take me for a ride one night?'

He could only nod.

'Well, I'd better let you finish doing the grass,' she said.

He downed what was left in his glass and handed her the empty receptacle, trying to control his quivering hand.

As he passed her the crystal she brushed the back of his hand with her fingertips.

He tried to swallow but it felt as if his throat was full of chalk.

'Nice to have met you, Mark,' she said, quietly.

'Yeah, you too, Lucy. Thanks for the drink.'

He watched as she headed back up the path, turning halfway.

'Don't forget,' she said, smiling. 'I want that ride.'

Nineteen

Beth heard the scream as she stepped into the hall.

She pushed shut the front door behind her and wandered across to the sitting room.

There was another scream from inside.

It was followed by a gunshot.

Beth pushed open the door.

There was crying now.

Lucy glanced round briefly and looked at her sister before returning her attention to *Cape Fear* which was running on the video.

'I didn't expect you home so early,' Lucy said, watching as Robert De Niro slipped handcuffs on to Jessica Lange.

'I can tell,' Beth hissed.

Lucy was stretched out on the sofa wearing just a pair of white panties and a vest T-shirt. There was an ashtray propped on the arm of the sofa beside her, a couple of plates and a half-empty glass lay on the carpet.

'This has nearly finished,' Lucy said, her eyes still fixed on the screen. She took a puff of her cigarette.

Beth regarded her younger sister angrily for a moment then stalked across to the television and jabbed the Off button.

'What the hell are you doing?' Lucy rasped. 'I was watching that.'

'How long have you been lying around here?'

Lucy shrugged.

'A couple of hours,' she said. 'What's the big deal?'

'Can't you put some clothes on?'

'It's hot in case you hadn't noticed. I'm more comfortable like this.'

'And what if Simon had come home early instead of me?'

Lucy grinned.

'It might have brightened up his day,' she chuckled.

Beth shot her an angry glance.

'You were supposed to be looking for a bloody job,' she snapped.

'Chill out, Beth,' Lucy said, wearily. 'If you'd come home at your normal time you wouldn't have found me like this. What are you doing home so early, anyway?'

'Not that I have to justify it to you but my boss has got a meeting for the rest of the afternoon, he said I might as well leave early.'

Lucy raised her eyebrows and swung herself upright on the sofa, tucking her legs beneath her.

'Nice work if you can get it,' she said, rubbing one little toe.

'Talking of work. What happened at the Job Centre?'

'I've got two interviews tomorrow, actually. Bar work. Happier now?'

'I'll be happy when you've *got* a job. I'm warning you, Lucy, don't push me too far.'

Beth turned and headed out of the sitting room.

Lucy followed her into the hall.

'I'll get one of the jobs, don't worry about it,' she said.

If I go to the interviews.

'I need some money anyway, you know,' she persisted.

Beth headed out into the kitchen, turned the cold tap and filled a glass with cold water. She leaned against the sink and took a long swallow hoping that the cool fluid could dampen her anger as well as her thirst.

Lucy sat down on one of the kitchen chairs, studying Beth's back.

'I met Mark Hennessey this morning,' she said finally.

Beth turned to look at her.

'Why were you talking to him?' she wanted to know.

'He was cutting the grass, he looked like he needed some company. I was just being friendly.'

'I bet you were,' Beth hissed.

'He says he's got a motorbike, he said he'd give me a ride sometime.'

'Stay away from him Lucy,' snapped Beth.

'I wasn't doing any harm.'

'He's seventeen, for Christ's sake. Isn't he a little young for you?'

'He's cute.'

'I'm *telling* you, stay away from him.'

'Don't you ever get fed up with the big sister routine, Beth. Why the fuck don't you stop preaching at me? It's my life.'

'Maybe, but this is *my* house and while you're in it you do as *I* say. Got it? If not, then get out. Now get dressed, I don't want you lying around half naked.'

'Why, scared Simon might see me? What's wrong, Beth. Frightened he'll like what he sees?'

Beth pushed past her.

'Go and get dressed, you little slag,' she hissed. 'And I want this fucking house cleaned up by the time I get back.'

She slammed the front door behind her as she left.

Lucy smiled to herself and padded out into the hall. She heard Beth revving the engine of the Astra, then the muted squeal of spinning tyres as she reversed quickly.

'Fuck you,' murmured Lucy and wandered back to the sitting room.

Twenty

Damian Wilks turned over his cards and grinned broadly.

'Twenty,' he announced, triumphantly, jabbing his finger at the two kings lying before him.

Frank Jennings nodded and flipped over his own cards.

'Pontoon,' he said, pushing the ace and the queen towards the astonished Wilks.

'I don't believe it,' the younger man muttered, slumping back in his chair. 'You've won every single hand.'

Jennings scooped up the broken matchsticks in the centre of the table and pulled them to the large pile he had already accumulated.

'That's two hundred and fifty thousand you owe me,' he said.

'Will you take a cheque?' Wilks said, smiling.

Jennings shuffled the cards then pushed the deck towards his younger companion.

'Here,' he said, getting to his feet. 'Have a game of Patience. Even *you* can't lose at that? I'm going to have a walk round.'

'I'll come with you.'

'No, you stay here. I don't feel *that* sociable.'

You never do, thought Wilks, watching as the older man stepped outside the room, closing the door behind him.

It was almost eleven thirty and Brackley Heath was as quiet as a grave. Every now and then as he walked, Jennings heard what sounded like snoring, sometimes a muted sob floated on the stale air. But otherwise, the place may as well have been deserted.

He turned left out of the Staff Room and headed towards

Ward 6, his footsteps echoing on the polished floor. Another half-hour and his shift, like Wilks', would be over.

He could go home.

The thought didn't exactly fill him with joyous expectation.

It was as quiet there as it was here.

He opened the door to Ward 6 and walked in.

The silence was eerie.

Jennings walked slowly between the two rows of beds, the curtains of each bed drawn around it.

As he passed he could hear breathing, sometimes laboured. Occasionally the deep even breaths of a sound sleeper. He heard snores too.

He crossed to one of the windows, checking that it was securely fastened. He knew it was but this was part of his ritual and he rarely deviated from it. Jennings had always been a man of habit, able to adapt to rigid regimes.

He'd been like that even before he'd joined the army.

He'd spent four years in the Parachute Regiment. His mother had been so proud of him. His father probably would have been too if Jennings had known who he was. He couldn't even remember what the man looked like. There had been photographs dotted around the house once but, after he'd walked out on her, Jennings' mother had destroyed all the evidence of his existence. Jennings had been three when that had happened and all his questions about his father from that point on had been met either with stony silence or with a clip round the ear.

Jennings had shared that same house with his mother until her death eleven years earlier.

Even during his short marriage, he and his wife had lived there. She'd fucked off with some other bloke after six months.

Bitch.

If he found her *or* her fucking fancy man he'd cut both their throats.

Being alone didn't bother him, he'd always felt at home with his own company and, every month he took a trip down to London and walked the area around King's Cross. There were plenty of women there to satisfy his needs and he had plenty of money.

He was better off alone. He needed no one.

He passed through the ward, locking the door behind him as he emerged into another corridor.

Turning right he pushed open the door of the dayroom and wandered in without switching on a light, relying on the light of the moon and that filtering in from the corridor.

The air still smelled of stale cigarettes and perspiration but Jennings barely noticed. On the two or three tables in the room the boardgames that occupied some of the patients during the day were still spread out. He passed a Monopoly board and moved one of the pieces to a different square.

'Do not collect two hundred pounds,' he murmured, smiling to himself.

Behind him, housed in a wall receptacle, covered by a Perspex sheet, the television glared blindly out at him like a sightless eye. He saw his own reflection in the dead grey screen for a moment, then turned away as if the image displeased him.

He stood motionless in the room for a moment longer, the silence gathering around him, then he turned and left, locking the door behind him.

His wanderings brought him to the Secure Ward.

From beyond the heavy metal doors that separated the Secure Unit from the rest of the hospital, no sound seemed able to escape. Those beyond were as much prisoners of the silence as of their rooms. He took a key and unlocked the door, walking in.

There were doors on either side of him but he passed them, heading for the last on the right.

Jennings could feel his heart thudding a little more

72

heavily against his ribs as he reached for the slide of the observation slot. He pulled and pressed his face to the slot, peering in through the darkness.

Karen Gregson lay sleeping, the covers drawn up tightly around her neck despite the warmth of the night.

Jennings paused a moment longer before slipping a key into the lock of the door and moving slowly inside, quietly pushing the door shut behind him.

He could hear her breathing.

So softly.

Jennings moved nearer to the bed and stood over Karen, looking down impassively at her face, studying every line and contour. He reached out one hand, his fingers hovering inches from her smooth cheek, his hand trembling.

He kneeled beside the bed, moving as silently as he could, knowing that he would not disturb her. She'd been given 20mg of Thorazine only two hours earlier, she would not stir.

Jennings gently pulled down her covers, rolling them further down, trying to control his own breathing. He could feel the beginning of an erection swelling in his trousers.

She was wearing a long nightdress but as he pulled the covers further down, he could see that it had ridden up to reveal her legs.

Beautiful legs.

The hem had stopped just above her knees.

He moved closer, inhaling deeply, like a wine connoisseur savouring some vintage bouquet.

He was leaning across her now, inches above her stomach. He could smell the musky odour between her legs.

Between her legs.

He pushed the nightdress up, carefully, gently, until he saw that she was wearing nothing beneath.

Jennings studied the softly curled pubic hair which

73

covered her mound and he leaned closer, drawing deep breaths now.

His penis was throbbing, constricted by his trousers, and it was all he could do to control his breathing, but he hovered there like a man worshipping at an altar, his eyes fixed on that triangle of light hair.

If only he could taste her.

His gaze moved to her thighs, down to her knees, her calves, her feet.

So beautiful.

He pulled her nightdress down and pulled the covers around her neck then struggled to his feet, his erection almost painful.

She stirred in her sleep, her lips parting slightly.

Soft lips.

Jennings walked out and locked the door behind him, gazing back at her through the observation slot.

His breathing was harsh but there was a thin smile on his lips.

So beautiful.

He closed the slot.

Twenty-One

Beth Parker slid closer to her husband, nuzzling his chest, smiling as she felt his arm slip around her shoulder.

She lay there for a long time, feeling the warmth of his body against hers, her eyes fixed on the portable television at the foot of the bed but the images not registering. The multi-coloured shapes were the only light in the bedroom and the corners of the room were in deep shadow. It looked as if someone had sprayed them with black ink,

Beth thought, as she stared blankly at those puddles of darkness, tiring of the television.

Beside her, Parker moved occasionally, his eyes fixed on the screen. He began stroking her hair, his hand moving with a robotic rhythm as he continued to scan the swiftly moving images before him. The screeching of car tyres seemed to fill the room as Gene Hackman pursued the speeding elevated train through New York. Parker didn't know how many times *The French Connection* had been on but he was beginning to feel he knew this route better than Hackman himself.

Beth began pulling gently at the hairs around his navel, raking her nails gently across his belly.

'Is something on your mind?' he said, without looking down at her.

'What makes you think that?' she said, softly.

Parker chuckled.

'Just an educated guess,' he said.

'As a matter of fact there is,' Beth told him.

He reached for the remote control and jabbed the volume button, the screech of tyres gradually diminishing to a whisper.

'What is it, Beth?' he asked.

'It's Lucy, need you ask?' she told him, wearily.

'What now?'

'She's been talking to Mark Hennessey.'

'Is that such a crime?'

Beth sat up, pulling away from him.

'I know what she's like, Simon,' she snapped, irritably. 'Ingratiating herself with *our* neighbours, making herself at home.'

'What do you expect her to do? She is staying here, after all.'

'And you blame me for that?'

'I don't *blame* you for anything, Beth. She's your sister, you said you'd rather have her here than on the streets.'

'Now I'm not so sure.'

Parker regarded his wife impassively for a moment, the images from the television screen reflected in her eyes.

'Then throw her out,' he said, finally.

Beth looked at him in surprise.

'Is that the reasoned answer of a logical man?' she said, smiling.

'No, it's the answer of a man who doesn't want to see his wife upset,' Parker told her.

He held out an arm, an invitation for her to slide close to him once more. She accepted the offer willingly.

'I'm scared of what she'll do,' Beth told him. 'Everything she's been involved with in the past she's destroyed. She doesn't care about anyone except herself.'

'That hardly makes her unique, does it?'

'I can't trust her, Simon. I *daren't.*'

'No one's asking you to.'

She looked up at him.

'But I . . .'

He silenced her protestations with a kiss, feeling her respond fiercely as his tongue probed over the hard white edges of her teeth and sought the moist warmth beyond.

Beth ran her hands over his chest, feeling one of his fingertips tracing a path down her spine, gliding gently, sending shivers through her.

He cupped her buttocks in both hands and pulled her closer, his penis stiffening, swelling as it pressed against her belly.

She rolled on top of him, straddling him, reaching beneath her to grasp his erection, holding it firmly and using it to brush the tip of her own swollen clitoris.

Parker felt the moisture there, saw the pleasure on her face. He leaned forward and cupped one breast in his hand, taking the nipple between his teeth, tugging gently on it until the fleshy bud stiffened even more. He sucked avidly, transferring his attention to the other, hearing Beth gasp as he switched back and forth from one sensitive tip to the next.

She slid down his body, kissing his chest and stomach until she reached the bulbous head of his penis. Pausing for a moment she licked the tip then took the glans into her mouth, coating it with saliva, working her mouth up and down his shaft, happy with the low grunts of satisfaction he uttered. Those sounds intensified as she gently stroked his testicles with the tips of her fingers, feeling him raise his hips in response.

Beth moved slowly up to kiss his chest then onward and crushed her lips against his, her own passion now as fevered as his.

He gripped her waist, pulling her further up his body, sliding down the bed until her slippery cleft was above his face. She lowered herself on to his waiting tongue and stifled a gasp of pleasure as his tongue probed across her moist lips, flicked upwards to tease her clitoris then slipped into that hot, silky place between her legs.

She gripped her own breasts, pulling hard at the nipples as the feeling of warmth between her legs seemed to spread across her thighs and belly.

Her breathing was harsh and loud now but she made no attempt to silence herself, the pleasure was too great.

She felt his tongue pushing more deeply, felt it swirling around her clitoris and she ground her damp pubic hair against his lips, her pleasure now reaching a peak.

Her body shuddered, bucking three or four times with the force of the orgasm that swept through her and she threw back her head and let out a cry of pure delight.

The sensations seemed to last for an eternity but, as they subsided she rolled over on to her back, her face sheathed in perspiration. She lay back and spread her legs wide, seeing Parker guiding his throbbing erection towards her slippery cleft.

Beth waited for the new sensation, a smile on her face.

When he slid into her it was all she could do to stop herself shouting aloud.

Lucy heard the sounds and gritted her teeth.

Sounds of pleasure.

Beth's pleasure.

She heard them both, trying to disguise the noises, trying to mask the exhortations of joy.

Lying naked on top of the bed, Lucy gazed at the ceiling and listened.

She closed her eyes when she heard muted words, heard Beth gasp that she was coming.

Lucy pressed the headphones of the walkman closer to her ears and stabbed the Play button.

The roaring music seemed to fill her head.

'You will die, when I say, you must die . . .'

It obliterated the sounds of pleasure.

'You coward, you servant, you blindman . . .'

Beth's pleasure.

'Why am I dying? Hell, have no fear . . .'

She turned up the volume until it hurt her ears.

Twenty-Two

'I think he's gorgeous,' said Caroline Seaton, pulling a Silk Cut from the packet and pushing it between her lips. 'If he'd asked me to go with him for a drink I'd have gone.' She lit the cigarette and took a drag, blowing out a stream of blue-grey smoke.

'Apart from the fact that I'm married plus he's my boss I don't think that would have been a very good idea,' Beth Parker said, running a hand through her hair.

'Well, I'd have gone,' Caroline repeated. 'Married or

not. It's only a drink, Beth. It can't hurt.'

Beth raised her eyebrows.

'And what about the next time?' she said. 'When it's lunch. Then dinner and *then* what? Once things like that start they usually only lead one way.'

'So what?' Caroline said, dismissively. 'He fancies you.'

Beth smiled and shook her head.

'I can't believe you, you're practically trying to talk me into it,' she chuckled. 'If I was going to have an affair it wouldn't be with David Manning and *not* just because he's my boss.'

'Who *would* it be with?' Caroline asked, excitedly. 'Go on, tell me. If you could have an affair with anyone and you knew that Simon wouldn't find out, if you knew you could get away with it. Who would you do it with?'

'It wouldn't be anyone specific but he'd have to have special attributes,' Beth said, chuckling.

'Like what?'

'A ten-inch dick.'

Both women laughed, Caroline almost toppling off the edge of Beth's desk where she was perched somewhat precariously.

'What about you?' Beth wanted to know. 'Who would you choose?'

'The Chippendales,' Caroline told her. 'All of them.'

'One after the other, or in combinations of two?' Beth laughed.

The two women dissolved into fits of giggling.

They were still laughing when the door to the outer office opened and David Manning walked in.

He smiled broadly when he saw them laughing, his grin widening as he saw Caroline slide from Beth's desk and smooth creases from her skirt. She snatched up her cigarettes and held them behind her back like a teenager who's been caught smoking by a teacher.

'Can I share the joke?' Manning asked, smiling.

'Just girl-talk,' said Beth.

'You'd be disgusted, Mr Manning,' Caroline added, still giggling.

'Now I'm intrigued,' he said, looking first at Caroline then at Beth.

'I'd better get back to work,' Caroline said and headed for the door, waiting until Manning's back was to her before pursing her lips at him, blowing an exaggerated kiss and pushing an index finger between her lips as far as the second knuckle.

Beth was forced to bite her lip to prevent herself cracking up again.

Caroline winked and disappeared back towards her own desk.

'Can I have a word with you, Beth, please?' Manning said and walked through into his own office.

Beth got to her feet and followed him.

'If it's about what just happened,' she said. 'I'm sorry but we. . .'

'Don't apologise,' he said, smiling. 'It's nothing to do with that. It's nice to see people having a laugh at work, better than walking around looking miserable. No, this is more important. There's a meeting of managers from the largest dealerships in London tomorrow, it's expected to go on for a couple of days and I have to be there. Can you book me a room at the Mayfair Hotel?'

She nodded.

'Well, two rooms, actually,' he added. 'They're both to go on the company account. Will it be a problem for you to come with me? It's only a couple of nights.'

Beth looked surprised.

'I didn't think you needed *me* there,' she said.

'I'm sorry to spring it on you at such short notice but there will be a lot of work to be done. I need you there, Beth. It's very important.'

She hesitated a moment then nodded again, slowly, almost imperceptibly.

'I'll take care of it now,' she told him and pulled the

80

office door shut.

She wandered back to her desk and sat down staring at the phone, tapping one finger on the desk top.

'Shit,' she murmured.

It was then that the phone rang.

Twenty-Three

The scream was deafening.

Within the confines of the small room the volume seemed even more devastating, the explosion of sound all the more startling because of its source.

It didn't seem possible that a young woman of such slight build and appearance was capable of making so shrill and piercing a sound.

It was as if Karen Gregson's vocal chords had been wired to amplifiers.

The scream reverberated for long seconds then gradually died away.

Sitting cross-legged on her bed, dressed in jeans and a faded denim shirt she smiled at Simon Parker, gently running a finger over the sole of a bare foot.

He found his gaze held by her searing blue eyes.

They almost glowed.

'Are the voices still there?' Parker asked, riveted to her unblinking stare.

'I think I scared them off,' Karen said, smiling happily.

'Is that how you usually scare them off?'

'They'll be back soon.'

'What were they saying to you today?'

'They told me to get out of here.'

'Do you want to leave, Karen?'

'I don't fucking care,' she said, flatly, the smile disappearing. 'What do *you* want anyway?'

'I want to help you, you know that.'

'Nobody's ever helped me in my fucking life. Why should *you* want to?'

'That's what I'm here for.'

'You mean it's your job? You don't want to help me because you care about me, you only do it because you have to. You help all the fucking loonies in here.'

There was a vehemence in her tone that surprised him but he tried not to show it.

'Why do you bother?' she continued. 'They'd be better off dead. Fucking half-wits. Do you speak to them the way you speak to me? They don't listen to you.'

'How do you know that, Karen?'

'I was told.'

'By the voices?'

'Maybe.'

'But I thought you didn't trust them. Why listen to what they say if you don't trust them? Why believe what they tell you when you think they lie?'

'I *don't* trust them.'

'You trusted them enough to kill your children when they told you to. Why did you believe them then?'

'Does your wife like children?' she asked, her tone softening, the smile returning to her lips.

Christ, not again.

'Yes,' Parker said, quietly.

'But you don't have any. Why?'

'I told you once before, we're happy without them at the moment.'

Liar.

'Will you have them one day?'

He nodded.

She held him in her gaze, like a moth drawn to the glow of a torch.

'When the voices told you to kill your children, did they

82

tell you how to do it?' he wanted to know.

'How old is your wife?' Karen asked, running a hand through her hair.

'Twenty-six,' Parker informed her, hiding his frustration and impatience with practised professionalism.

'That's a good age to have children. She'll still be young when they've grown up.'

Parker swallowed hard.

'You wouldn't want to be too old either,' she continued, smiling. 'You'll be too tired to play with them otherwise. A father should play with his children.'

Her expression darkened suddenly, her tone hardening.

'I was left alone with my children,' she hissed. 'No one helped us. No one played with them.'

'What about their father?'

'Useless bastard, he did nothing. I hardly ever saw him, unless he wanted sex or money, not that I had much of that to give him. He used to piss away his dole money the day he got it. The thing is, he could be nice when he wanted to be.' She smiled wistfully, shifting position on the bed, drawing her legs up beneath her. 'He used to tell me he loved me, usually after we'd had sex. He was good in bed. He used to spend ages kissing me, licking me. All over my body.' She held Parker captive in that unblinking gaze. 'He used to make me so wet. Sometimes he only had to touch me once and I'd come.'

She lowered her gaze.

'That all stopped after I had the children,' she hissed.

'Is that when the voices started, after you had the first child?' Parker asked, his voice low.

'They said I was wrong to have a child. Wrong to have *his* child. They told me all about the child.'

'What did they tell you?'

'They said it had *his* eyes. I knew they were right. They both had his eyes.' She looked at Parker once more. 'That was why I cut them out and fed them to the dog.'

The smile that spread across her face was one of pure joy.

83

'*You've* got lovely eyes, Simon,' she said, softly.

Twenty-Four

Mark Hennessey smiled delightedly as he opened the front door and found Lucy standing there, her finger still pressed against the buzzer.

She stepped back as he grinned at her, returning the gesture.

She was wearing the same jeans he'd first seen her in, tight and threadbare in places, the denim clinging to her legs and buttocks like a second skin. Tucked into them was a thin white shirt. The top three buttons were undone and through the almost diaphanous material, Hennessey could clearly see the dark outline of her nipples.

'Hi, I'm not disturbing you, am I?' Lucy said, smiling.

Hennessey coloured slightly and coughed.

'No, I was just reading,' he told her.

'Anything interesting?'

He shook his head.

'Do you want to come in?' he offered, cautiously, as if fearing the invitation would cause her to leave.

'I thought you'd never ask,' she told him and headed into the hall.

Hennessey closed the door behind her, his eyes again inspecting the tight curve of her backside as she stood before him looking none too discreetly around the hallway.

The place was well maintained, spotlessly clean and festooned with so many pictures it was almost impossible to see the wallpaper in the hall and leading up the stairs.

Lucy moved closer to the nearest of the pictures and glanced at it.

It was Venice. She recognised the canals, having seen *Don't Look Now* several times.

'Who's the artist?' she wanted to know, glancing at other pictures, most of which were watercolours. The majority of them were cities. Landmarks. Historical monuments from around the world.

'My mum collects them,' Hennessey told her. 'Her and Dad travel a lot, they usually buy a couple of them wherever they go. I reckon it makes the house look like a travel agent's.' He chuckled at his own joke.

'How come you don't go with them?' Lucy wanted to know, tracing a finger over a sketch of the Vatican.

'I used to when I was younger but, like I told you, I've got to study for my exams. They didn't mind leaving me. No doubt they'll come back with an armful of pictures from Spain. We'll have to move to a bigger house if they don't stop collecting them.'

Hennessey walked through into the kitchen.

'Would you like a drink?' he asked. 'Tea, coffee, something cold?'

'Whatever you're having,' Lucy said, glancing at a brightly coloured painting of the Spanish Steps in Rome. She followed him into the kitchen.

'If I'm interrupting your revision I can go,' she told him, watching as he fumbled in the fridge for a can of Sprite, which he handed to her with a glass.

'It's OK,' he told her. 'Anyway, I'm sick of reading about the Battle of Waterloo. Do you want to come through into the living room?' He hesitated a moment then wandered through. Lucy followed.

The record player was on quietly in the background and she smiled approvingly at his choice of music.

'The Scorpions, isn't it?' she said, listening to the music.

'It helps me concentrate,' he told her, smiling. He beckoned her to sit down but she shook her head, crossing

85

instead to the marble fireplace, glancing at the photos propped on the mantelpiece.

'These are your parents,' she said, a statement rather than a question. 'And this must be you.' She picked up the picture of a baby and chuckled, looking at Hennessey who turned a deeper shade of scarlet.

'I think my mum just leaves it there to embarrass me,' he said, feeling his cheeks burning.

Lucy laughed and replaced the photo.

She sat down opposite him and he watched as she rolled the can of Sprite across her forehead, enjoying the touch of the cool can against her warm flesh. He swallowed hard as he saw her press the can to her chest.

The sudden chill against her skin caused her nipples to stiffen and Hennessey found his gaze drawn to those swelling buds, watching as they pressed more urgently against the material of her shirt.

Lucy looked at him and smiled, wondering just how much redder his cheeks could go before they ignited.

'Are you sure I'm not disturbing you?' she said. 'It's just that I get so bored being at Beth's alone all the time and you did say it was OK to call round. I was worried in case I might be disturbing you. I mean, with your mum and dad away, you might have been up to *anything*.' She smiled.

He shook his head.

'No such luck,' he said.

'I thought you might have asked your girlfriend round. I didn't want to burst in while you were in the middle of things.'

He lowered his head slightly.

'Not much fear of that,' he told her. 'I haven't got a girlfriend at the moment.' He sipped nervously at his drink, avoiding eye contact with her.

'All alone, eh?' she said, smiling. 'I know the feeling. I haven't had the chance to meet anyone around here yet. Well, apart from you.' She caught his gaze and held it. 'I think my sister and her husband forget I'm in the house some nights. I can hear them fucking, even with the doors closed.'

Hennessey shifted in his seat, feeling the first stirrings of an erection pushing against his jeans.

'They make such a bloody racket,' Lucy continued. 'Moaning and groaning and all I can do is lay there and listen and I've only got my fingers for company.' She smiled. 'I get so horny some nights I think I'm going to scream.' Lucy sipped at her drink. 'Do you know what I mean?'

He could only nod, conscious now of the stiffness he felt sure she must be able to see, anxious to relieve the aching in his groin.

Lucy stood up, sweeping a hand through her long red hair, her own cheeks now flushed.

'Mark,' she said, quietly, smiling at him. 'There's something I want.'

He cleared his throat.

'What is it?' he wanted to know.

She smiled and walked towards him.

Twenty-Five

'It's beautiful,' said Lucy, her voice hushed as if in reverence.

The Harley Davidson Softail stood proudly in the garage, the piece of tarpaulin which Hennessey had pulled from it now discarded on the floor.

'And you built this yourself?' Lucy continued, running her hand over the handlebars then the petrol tank.

'Well, more or less,' Hennessey told her, proudly. 'The main frame was there, I just added bits and pieces,

87

painted it and cleaned it up.' He stood back, watching as Lucy walked around the machine, which gleamed in the cold white light of the fluorescents flickering in the garage ceiling.

She stroked the tank, the metal feeling cool against her palm, then the seat, smelling the heady aroma of leather strong in her nostrils.

Hennessey watched her, his erection still uncomfortably constricted inside his jeans.

Lucy snaked out one slender leg and slid on to the seat, moving back and forth on it, making herself comfortable. She gripped the handlebars, closing her fingers around the throttle, rubbing herself gently against the leather until she felt a pleasing friction against her clitoris.

'Can I start it up?' she asked, looking at Hennessey.

'Just a minute,' he said and crossed to a switch nearby on the wall which he flicked on. 'Extractor fan,' he informed her. 'We don't want to suffocate.'

She grinned and flicked the ignition switch.

The powerful four-stroke engine first purred then roared and she felt the bike begin to vibrate as she twisted the throttle. She looked across at Hennessey and grinned, forcing the rev count up, the sensations between her legs becoming more intense. She could feel her own excitement growing now, the sticky moisture warm between her thighs.

Hennessey moved closer to the bike, the roar of the engine almost deafening inside the small garage. He saw Lucy shuffling back and forth on the seat, the vibrations coursing through her as the bike hummed. Her cheeks were flushed, her lips parted slightly.

She suddenly snapped off the ignition, the roar dying quickly.

When she spoke her breath was a low pant.

'It's great,' she gasped, still straddling the machine.

'You said you liked motorbikes,' he reminded her.

'Did I tell you why?'

'You said they made you horny,' Hennessey said, his own voice now rasping in his throat.

She caught his wrist and pulled him towards her, snaking out her free hand to grab the back of his neck, pulling his face to hers. Their lips crushed together and she pushed her tongue into his mouth. Hennessey responded cautiously at first then with more vigour as he felt her hand pulling at his jeans, forcing the popper open, tearing at the zip.

She used both hands to pull them over his hips, tugging his underpants with them, freeing his swollen erection.

He stood motionless before her, immobile beneath her appraising stare, his jeans around his ankles.

She looked at his penis, hard and erect, the slippery glans almost level with his navel, the stiffened organ virtually touching his flat belly.

Lucy slid off the bike and hurriedly pulled off her own jeans, her eyes never leaving Hennessey's face. He looked as if he was in a trance and she felt convinced that this was the first time he'd seen a woman naked. As she slid her jeans off to reveal she wore no knickers beneath, Hennessey groaned audibly. She kicked off her trainers then pulled her shirt free tossing it aside, standing proudly before him, the moist heat between her legs feeling as if it was filling every pore of her body.

He stepped out of his own jeans and pulled his T-shirt off, his hands quivering slightly.

Lucy kneeled before him, her face level with his throbbing penis.

Hennessey was finding it hard to control his breathing and, as he felt the warm wetness of Lucy's mouth envelop the head of his penis, he gasped aloud. The sensation was indescribable, her tongue sliding around his glistening glans, her mouth enveloping his stiff shaft.

Lucy knew that he wouldn't be able to stand much of this treatment but the speed of his orgasm surprised even her.

He grunted loudly then moaned, a guttural rasping sound deep in his throat, pushing his groin towards her, forcing more of his shaft into her mouth.

She felt the first two spurts of the thick, oily fluid splash on to her tongue, felt his body quivering madly as he climaxed. She swallowed quickly, the taste strong on the back of her throat. Sliding one hand up his thigh she lifted her head up and clasped one fist around his pulsing erection, sliding it swiftly up and down the rigid length, coaxing more of the thick, white fluid from him. She kept rubbing, allowing him to send the warm cascade over her chin and breasts. Some of it ran down over her pumping hand, dripping to the dusty floor beneath.

She moved back slightly and smiled up at him.

Hennessey's cheeks were scarlet and he lowered his gaze, as if reluctant to meet hers.

'I'm sorry, I . . . ' he muttered.

She gripped his hand and pulled him down to the tarpaulin with her, laying back on her elbows, her feet pressed against the floor, her legs open wide.

'Now you do it to me,' she said, softly, watching as he kneeled between her open legs, inhaling the musky scent of her slippery cleft, inspecting every fold and crease of her glistening sex.

He lowered his head and she pushed her hips forward to meet the first tentative, exploratory, probings of his tongue, raising and lowering herself so that he grazed her swollen clitoris with his mouth.

She snaked out a hand to keep him there, rubbing his mouth against her, his loud grunting mingling with her own gasps of pleasure.

His movements were unpractised but effective and she felt that feeling of warmth begin to spread across her thighs and lower belly.

Lucy lay back, cupping her own breasts, thumbing the erect nipples, her climax building rapidly now.

She felt his tongue sliding over her clitoris, probing

deeper into her vagina to stir the moisture there and when she felt that beautiful sensation begin to sweep over her she gripped his head and ground herself against his mouth.

Lucy came with a loud moan, a smile spreading across her face.

A smile of pleasure.

And triumph.

She looked down at Hennessey and grinned.

Twenty-Six

'Penny for them,' said Parker, looking at Beth.

She didn't answer, merely sat gazing blankly at the television screen.

Lucy, stretched out on the sofa also glanced round at the sound of her brother-in-law's voice. She looked at Beth, saw her expression then returned her attention to the television.

'Beth,' Parker persisted.

She looked at him.

'Sorry,' she said, apologetically. 'I was miles away.'

'I gathered that. You have been since you got home. Is something wrong?' Parker wanted to know.

'I was just thinking about this trip to London,' she murmured.

About sharing a hotel with David Manning.

'It's only a couple of nights, it'll be OK,' Parker assured her.

'Yeah,' murmured Beth, distractedly.

'I suppose that's one of the perils of having such an important job, isn't it?' Lucy offered, her eyes still riveted to the television.

Beth caught the edge to her voice.

'Talking of jobs,' she said, irritably. 'What happened about those two you were supposed to be going for?'

'They'd already filled the positions,' Lucy told her without looking round.

'How convenient,' Beth said, angrily.

'It's not my fault, Beth. I tried.'

'Next time try a bit harder. I told you, you're not lazing around here at our bloody expense indefinitely.'

Lucy shook her head but still didn't pay her older sister the courtesy of even a cursory glance.

Parker looked at the two young women, thought about saying something, then thought better of it.

'What have you been doing all day anyway?' Beth asked Lucy.

The younger girl shrugged.

'I went to the Job Centre again,' she lied.

And paid a visit to Mark Hennessey.

'There's nothing about,' she continued.

'There is if you look hard enough,' Beth insisted.

Lucy ignored her.

I found something today.

She smiled to herself.

'I told you, I'm trying,' she said, her gaze never leaving the flickering images on the screen.

Beth rubbed her eyes and yawned.

'I'd better go and pack my bag,' she said.

'That sounds pretty final,' Parker chuckled.

Beth smiled too.

'I don't know why Manning wants me with him,' she said.

'It's an important meeting you said,' Parker offered. 'He obviously can't manage without you.'

Or he just wants to get me alone for a couple of days.

Beth looked at Parker and smiled thinly.

Maybe you're flattering yourself. Who says he fancies you?

'I'm sorry I had to spring it on you at such short notice,' she continued.

'Don't worry about it,' Parker said. 'It's not *your* fault.'

Lucy shook her head almost imperceptibly.

Mr and Mrs Fucking Perfect.

'You might even enjoy yourself,' Lucy said.

'Yeah, a couple of days without having to do the washing-up,' Parker said, smiling. 'Make sure you drink the mini-bar dry, and what you can't drink, bring home.'

'It *is* supposed to be work, Simon,' Beth chuckled.

'Two days. It'll fly,' he said, quietly. 'And don't worry about anything.'

Not even David Manning?

'We'll manage without you,' Lucy added, finally turning to look at her elder sister.

'I bet you will,' Beth said.

Lucy smiled.

'And don't worry, Beth,' she said, running a hand through her hair. '*I'll* take care of Simon.'

Twenty-Seven

'She's only been here three days and you want to release her from the Secure Ward. Do you think that's wise?'

Dr Marcus Flynn stopped walking and looked at Parker who halted in the corridor and turned to face him, seeing the disbelief and something approaching incredulity on the features of the older man. His ruddy cheeks seemed to have turned even more crimson than usual. To Parker, it appeared that dozens more tiny blood vessels beneath the older doctor's flesh were bursting, colouring his face.

'Have you really thought about this, Simon?' Flynn continued, finally.

Parker exhaled.

'I'm not talking about releasing Karen Gregson from the Secure Ward,' he said. 'Far from it. All I said was, I thought she might benefit from contact with some of the other patients. Needless to say, she'll have to be closely supervised at all times.'

Flynn raised his eyebrows quizzically then started walking again, moving alongside his younger companion.

'Another of your revolutionary ideas, is it, Simon?' he said. 'A more modern approach to the problem?'

Parker saw that the bait was being dangled but refused to rise to it.

'I think it will do her good,' he said, sharply.

'But what about the other patients?'

'We're talking about a young woman who's suffering severe puerperal psychosis, not a raving axe murderer.'

'She did kill her children, in case you've forgotten.'

'I hadn't forgotten.'

'She's dangerously disturbed.'

'No more so than many of the schizophrenics in the wards. Karen Gregson has displayed no sociopathic behaviour, there's no reason to think that allowing her to mix with other patients will be detrimental to her *or* to them.'

They entered Ward 4.

There were five or six vacant beds amongst the twenty or so in the ward. Two staff members busied themselves attending to the half a dozen patients who remained there. Most had already left for the dayroom.

The ward was populated by some of the hospital's older inhabitants. Men and women whose ages went from fifty upwards. Most had been in and out of psychiatric hospitals most of their lives. Some had known nothing else but institutionalisation from birth.

Parker stopped beside the first bed and smiled at its

occupant, a man in his early seventies who was continually clenching and unclenching his fists.

'Good morning, Brian, and how are you?' said Parker, smiling.

Brian Reece looked straight past him, hardly lifting his head.

Parker checked the notes attached to the clipboard at the bottom of the bed, making a note to decrease Reece's medication. He noticed a photo standing on the old man's bedside table. It showed a young woman holding a baby.

Parker picked up the photo and studied it more carefully.

'Is this your grandson?' he asked, pointing at the child.

Beautiful child.

Reece looked at the picture then at Parker, his eyes blank.

'He's a lovely lad,' Parker said, replacing the picture.

Reece stared straight ahead, hardly noticing when the two consultants moved on.

'I'm not keen on this idea about Karen Gregson,' said Flynn as they approached the next bed. 'You don't know enough about her yet to be sure of her reactions to other patients.'

'Any aggressive feelings she had were externalised against her children,' Parker said, irritably. 'There's no reason to expect any more violence. She hasn't displayed any homicidal tendencies since she was admitted.'

'It's a risk.'

'Then don't authorise it,' Parker snapped.

Doreen Frayne was doing a jigsaw puzzle when the two men arrived at her bedside. She had the pieces laid out on the table across her bed but seemed to have made little progress with it. A dozen or so pieces were joined together in the centre but, other than that the tray was a jumble of multi-coloured segments.

The picture would eventually show the coronation of Queen Elizabeth II. An event which had happened the same year Doreen was admitted to Brackley Heath. She was now into her sixty-fifth year.

Parker helped her with some of the jigsaw then watched as she pulled the pieces he'd assembled apart again, spreading them around with the rest of the scattered sections.

She smiled at him and he smiled back.

He and Flynn moved on.

'Are you willing to take responsibility for her if I authorise release from the Secure Ward?' Flynn wanted to know.

'I'm only asking for two hours a day, less if I feel she can't cope,' Parker said. 'She's a young woman, she shouldn't be in here.'

'She should be where she can be helped,' Flynn countered.

'I agree and I think allowing her to mix with some of the other patients *will* help her.'

'She's to be strictly supervised at all times.'

'I wouldn't want it any other way, for Karen's sake.'

'You're taking a big risk, Simon, and so am I by agreeing to this. If anything goes wrong then I can do nothing.'

'I accept that.'

'It could mean your job.'

Parker regarded his colleague angrily.

'Nothing *will* go wrong,' he said.

'You sound very sure. I just hope you're right.'

Twenty-Eight

Beth handed the porter a couple of pound coins and smiled at him as he laid her small suitcase on the bottom of the bed. He pointed out where the mini-bar was, informed her that should she need any more information about the Mayfair Hotel then she could find it in the Directory of Services, then smiled his practised smile and left.

She heard his soft footsteps echoing away as he walked back up the corridor towards the lift, then she crossed to the window and peered out into Berkeley Street, looking down on a couple of taxis parked outside the main entrance of the hotel, their drivers in animated conversation with one of the blue-coated doormen. Every so often she would hear laughter drifting up on the warm air. She moved back to the bed and unlocked her case, lifting items out.

She hadn't packed much, after all, how many clothes could she wear in two days? A couple of blouses, one of her suits, two skirts and a pair of trousers. She'd also pushed in some leggings and a T-shirt just in case she did get the chance to have a wander round the shops. After all, Oxford Street was only five minutes' walk away. Somehow she doubted it, though.

Manning had said that the next couple of days were going to be busy. That suited Beth, at least it meant there wouldn't be too many opportunities for them to be alone together.

Imagination working overtime again?

She opened the wardrobe and began hanging up her

clothes, draping blouses over the padded hangers.

Manning himself had driven down earlier that morning, telling her that he was due to have breakfast with some clients and that there was no need for her to be present for that. Beth had been relieved. She'd caught the train down, travelling first class. What the hell, the company were paying. It had also saved the problem of travelling to the capital with Manning.

What were you worried about?

She carried her meagre supply of toiletries into the bathroom and set them out on the glass shelf beneath the mirror, catching sight of her reflection in the process.

Beth ran a hand through her long hair, checking the image that stared back at her.

So what if Manning fancies you. Do you blame him?

She smiled and stuck her tongue out at her reflection, wandering back into the bedroom to continue unpacking.

Why are you scared if he does?

She took a couple of grapes from the fruit bowl on the table by the window and popped them into her mouth, chewing as she hung up her remaining clothes.

Afraid you'll give in if he makes a pass?

She administered a swift mental rebuke and closed the wardrobe, putting her case on the ottoman at the foot of the bed.

Beth checked her watch and saw that it was approaching lunch-time. Her stomach rumbled as if to remind her of this fact. Manning had asked her to meet him in the bar at one o'clock. He'd said they'd have a sandwich before the meeting began at two. One of the conference rooms had been hired for that purpose.

She had enough time.

Beth crossed to the phone, pressed 9, then jabbed out the number she wanted.

'It's only me. It's about quarter to one, I just thought I'd let you know I got here OK. Give me a ring tonight, I'm in room 226. Love you.'

Lucy stood beside the phone listening as the message came in.

She waited for the answerphone to record Beth's words then watched as the call counter registered a flashing red 1.

Lucy pressed Rewind and then Play.

' . . . *Give me a ring tonight* . . .'

Lucy pressed Rewind.

'. . . *ring tonight* . . .'

She looked down at the answerphone.

' . . . *Love you* . . .'

She jabbed Rewind once more.

'*Love you* . . .'

Lucy pressed Erase.

The call counter registered zero.

She walked away.

Twenty-Nine

Simon Parker hit the brakes as he rounded the corner, seeing the tractor pull out ahead of him.

'Shit,' he murmured.

The bloody thing was moving slow and the country road was too narrow to allow Parker to overtake safely. He eased off the accelerator and crawled along behind the tractor, the needle of his speedometer barely reaching twenty.

Another car pulled in behind him, its driver as impatient as Parker for the tractor to move aside but there were no turn-offs ahead for a good mile or so. Parker knew, he used this road to drive home most days.

He tapped agitatedly on the wheel as he drove, his mind already spinning, his exasperation at being trapped behind this ponderous vehicle now growing. He'd felt irritable enough when he'd left Brackley Heath.

Bloody Flynn.

Dr Marcus bloody Flynn.

Just the thought of his older colleague was enough to cause Parker a grunt of dismay.

'This could mean your job.'

Fucking old bastard.

As far as Parker was concerned, with careful supervision, Karen Gregson could only benefit from contact with other patients, keeping her locked up with her own twisted thoughts for company was not helping her. She needed something to occupy her mind, to counter those thoughts.

'You'll take full responsibility for her.'

Of course he would, she was his fucking patient, wasn't she? Flynn had seen to that.

The old bastard *wanted* him to fail. Wanted to prove that his *methods* were unsound.

Bastard.

So, Flynn was worried about Parker taking his job, was he? Well, fuck him, he might take it just for the hell of it.

Parker smiled to himself, relieved also to see that the tractor was turning left on to a dirt track. He pushed down on the accelerator and sped past the farm vehicle.

'This could mean your job.'

Flynn's words echoed inside his head as he drove, repeating endlessly like a stuck record.

When he finally spotted his house he spun the steering wheel hard to the right and sent the car careering across the street, slamming on the brakes as he came to a halt in the driveway.

He remained sitting there, waiting for his anger to subside, trying to push thoughts of Flynn out of his mind and, gradually, the image receded.

Eventually, Parker reached on to the back seat for his briefcase then hauled himself out of the car, locked the door and headed for the front door.

'Hello, Mr Parker.'

The shout made him turn and he saw Mark Hennessey hurrying by.

Parker waved then fumbled for his key.

He wished Beth was at home. Tonight he felt like talking and she was always ready to listen. It was one of the things he loved about her.

He'd barely pushed the key into the lock when the door was opened from the inside.

Lucy smiled at him and pulled the door wider.

'I saw you pull up,' she told him.

As Parker entered he smelled food. A delicious aroma of roasting meat.

'Something smells nice,' he said, putting down his briefcase.

'I cooked us a meal,' Lucy told him, disappearing back into the kitchen.

Parker watched her go, smiling as he saw how elegantly she walked on her high heels, the tight black mini-skirt she wore hugging her slim buttocks.

He recognised the shoes and skirt.

They were Beth's.

He followed her through into the kitchen and paused in the doorway.

The table had been laid and there were two candles at either side, waiting to be lit. He saw a bottle of wine, too.

'What's the occasion?' he asked.

'It's only a meal, Simon,' Lucy said, stirring one of the pots on the cooker.

'With candles and wine?' he said.

Lucy turned and smiled at him.

'I did tell Beth I'd look after you, didn't I?' she said, quietly.

Parker grinned.

'Have I got time to get changed?' he wanted to know.

'Five minutes. I don't want it to spoil.'

'I didn't even know you could cook.'

Her smile broadened.

'You'd be surprised what I can do,' she chuckled.

Thirty

Beth Parker closed her eyes and sank lower into the bath, allowing the scented water to lap around her neck.

The steam rising from the water had clouded on the mirrored tiles of the bathroom and Beth reached out with one finger and drew her name in the steam, chuckling to herself.

She ran both hands over her face and sighed contentedly, feeling the stiffness leave her muscles, particularly her neck.

The main meeting that day had lasted more than five hours and she'd taken copious notes for Manning, sent a number of faxes and used the hotel's facilities to type up three memos, as well as an agenda for the following day. Some of the other directors had their secretaries with them too, but Beth had found little time to speak to them, they'd all been kept busy. The word redundancy had been mentioned a few too many times for comfort but Beth felt sure that it referred to management. She hoped Manning wasn't likely to lose his position. If he lost *his*, odds on she would lose *hers*.

She tried to push such thoughts from her mind, concentrating instead on luxuriating in the bath.

Beth lifted first one leg then the other from beneath the foam layer which covered the surface of the water, watching as the bubbles and soap trickled down her shapely legs.

She massaged her own shoulders gently, the stiffness drifting away as if carried by the warm water.

She thought about Simon.

About Lucy.

She wondered what Lucy was doing. If Simon was home yet. Glancing at her watch she decided that he would be by now. She might wander out for a walk later, just a brisk stroll around the West End. It was a long time since she'd seen the lights of Piccadilly. She and Simon had spent three days in the capital not long after they'd met, staying at a little hotel in the Bayswater Road, walking and exploring, doing the things tourists usually did. Beth thought that there were probably many English people who had seen less of their capital city than most tourists. How many Londoners had been round Buckingham Palace or Madame Tussauds? The visitors were usually foreign.

She and Simon had discovered many wonderful little restaurants which the casual visitor usually missed. It had been a blissful few days, one of the few times they'd had anything approaching a holiday.

Perhaps she'd nip out this evening for an hour or two, try to rediscover some of those delights.

By the time she got back, Simon would be calling her.

Her thoughts were interrupted by a knock on the door.

She guessed that it was the maid to turn the bed down. Beth hadn't left the Do Not Disturb sign out, so she could just walk in if she wanted to. Beth waited for the sound of a key in the lock but it didn't come.

Instead there was another knock.

Beth hauled herself out of the bath, pulled on the monogrammed bathrobe and padded, dripping, to the door.

'Mrs Parker?' said the uniformed young man who stood there.

103

She nodded, noticing that he was pushing a small room-service trolley. On it she saw an ice bucket containing a bottle of champagne, some chocolates and a large bunch of red carnations.

The young man smiled at her and wheeled the trolley into the room. Beth watched as he laid the flowers on the bed and lifted the bottle of Moët from the ice bucket.

'It's OK, I'll open it,' she said.

He smiled again and exited with what seemed like undue haste.

Beth crossed to the table and saw a note lying there. She opened the small envelope and took out the card.

Simon must have sent them, she thought, beaming. He must have ordered them and . . .

She read the card.

Thanks for your hard work. Table booked for nine.
David

They were from Manning.

Beth sat down on the edge of the bed, reaching out to touch the carnations, the cellophane wrapping crunching beneath her fingers.

Table booked for nine.

She glanced at the glowing red digits of the radio alarm clock.

7.49.

What the hell was he playing at?

Thirty-One

Simon Parker poured himself another glass of white wine then refilled Lucy's glass. She smiled across the table at him, the warm glow of the candles softening her features, making it appear that her skin was luminous. The yellow light picked out the auburn colour of her hair. It was very striking.

Parker sat back in his chair and looked at Lucy and she was aware of his appraising gaze. She flicked one hand through her hair then took a sip of her wine, twisting the glass gently by its stem, rolling it between her index finger and thumb.

'You should cook when Beth's here,' Parker said. 'I'm sure she'd appreciate the help.'

'I doubt if Beth would appreciate *anything* I do, Simon,' Lucy told him.

'Come on, it's not that bad.'

'Isn't it? You've seen the way she is with me, you've heard the way she speaks to me. You think that's going to change just because I cook a few bloody meals?'

'You do tend to rub each other up the wrong way, I'll give you that,' Parker said, smiling.

'It's always been the same. Ever since we were kids. She's always hated me.'

'If she hated you, she wouldn't have let you stop here.'

Lucy shrugged and sipped more wine.

Parker topped it up.

'She didn't really *want* me here,' Lucy continued.

'If she didn't want you then you'd be out by now. You know Beth, she's too strong-willed for that. If she didn't

105

want you here, Lucy, you'd have been on your way days ago.'

'And what about you, Simon? What do you think about it all?'

He shrugged.

'It was Beth's decision whether you stayed or not,' he said, refilling his own glass. 'You're *her* sister. I left it up to her.'

'Does it bother you that I'm here? It's *your* house.'

'It's *our* house. Mine and Beth's. She doesn't have to ask my permission before she does anything.'

'I wouldn't want to cause any trouble between you, I mean, if you wanted me to go I would.'

Parker shook his head and smiled.

'I am trying to find a job, Simon,' she told him. 'Beth doesn't seem to believe me though. I thought maybe something like a nanny or . . . ' She caught his gaze and held it. 'I'm sorry, I didn't mean to mention anything to do with kids.'

'Why not?'

'Well, I know how much you wanted them and with Beth . . .'

She allowed the sentence to trail off.

Parker sucked in an angry breath.

'What the hell are you going on about, Lucy?' he snapped, reaching for his glass.

'Beth can't have kids, can she?' Lucy said, softly.

'No, she can't,' Parker told her, sharply.

'She said how much you both wanted them. She said she knew how much it hurt you especially.'

'Really? And when did she tell you all this?'

'Not long after I got here,' Lucy told him, watching as he poured himself more wine. He'd already drunk most of the bottle.

'It's true, isn't it?' Lucy continued.

'What? That Beth can't have kids? Yes, it's true.'

'No, that you're hurt because she can't.'

106

Parker exhaled wearily.

'I accept it,' he said. 'I've accepted the situation. I've got no choice, have I?' There was an edge to his voice Lucy wasn't slow to pick up.

'But you don't like it?'

'Lucy it's none—'

'—Of my business?' she continued.

'Look, whether I like it or not, it's nobody's fault,' Parker snapped. 'Beth can't have children. It's as simple as that.'

'I feel sorry for you.'

'Don't.'

He downed more wine.

'Does Beth know how angry you are?' Lucy persisted.

'I'm not angry,' he rasped.

'You *sound* angry, Simon.'

'I don't mean too. You just asked me a question and I'm answering it. I wanted kids. We both wanted kids. We can't have them. Simple as that. End of story.' He brought his glass down hard on the table top, his breathing harsh now. 'But it doesn't make living with it any easier. I see people walking around with their kids or pushing them in prams.' He swallowed hard. 'I wouldn't be human if I didn't wish that could be me one day, but I know it can't be and all the wishing in the world isn't going to change things, is it?'

Lucy studied him a moment then reached out and touched the back of his hand, smiling when he didn't pull away from her.

Parker looked down at her slender fingers against his flesh then across into her brown eyes.

He moved his hand gently and finished what was left in his glass. Picking up the bottle he saw that it was almost empty.

'There's another one in the fridge,' she told him.

Parker smiled humourlessly.

'Good,' he murmured. 'Why don't you get it?'

He watched her as she walked across the kitchen to the

fridge, his gaze settling on her slim legs. As she turned back to face him he looked away, taking the bottle from her as she approached and pouring himself another glass. He didn't usually drink wine and it was making him feel lightheaded.

What the hell.

He topped up Lucy's glass and raised his own in salute.

She reached out and gently touched his hand again.

This time he didn't move it.

Beth looked around as she sipped her Perrier and noted that, apart from herself and David Manning, there were just four diners inside Overton's restaurant in St James's Street.

A young couple was seated away to their left, the woman giggling loudly as she watched her companion eating oysters from the shell and, close to the restaurant entrance, there were two single tables. A man in his fifties sat at one, at the other a younger man in a sweater and jacket who was eating with what seemed almost unnatural haste.

The place had been quiet all night and without even a hint of music the silences had sometimes been uncomfortable.

At least they had for her.

Manning seemed unconcerned by the bouts of tranquillity, barely interrupted by the comings and goings of waiters. Now he sat over his coffee gazing down at the brown fluid as if seeking something within the cup.

Beth had to admit he looked smart. He wore a dark blue Armani suit, black shirt and blue tie. It looked reserved without being sombre and it fitted perfectly. Tailor-made she guessed.

The meal actually hadn't been the ordeal she had anticipated. They'd spoken mostly about work, what had gone on that day. Manning had told her about some of the other conferences he'd been to, how they'd dragged on for up to a week sometimes. He'd discussed restaurants with her, even asked about Simon once or twice. He seemed fascinated by the fact that she was married to a psychiatrist.

And he'd mentioned children.

She'd changed the subject as quickly as possible and, either taking the hint or tiring of the subject, Manning hadn't mentioned it again. There had been a particularly long silence after that. One broken by the arrival of the waiter with the coffee.

Beth spooned sugar into hers and stirred.

'This was one of my wife's favourite restaurants,' Manning said.

Beth looked up, surprised.

'We used to eat somewhere different every time we were in London,' he continued. 'She had a diary – *The Londoner's Diary*, I think it was called – and it had a list of restaurants at the front. We decided to work our way through the list.' He smiled wistfully. 'A different place every time.'

'I'd heard you were married, well, divorced,' Beth offered, surprised that her boss had opened up so unexpectedly. 'Office gossip.' She shrugged. 'Things get around. When you took over, it was one of the rumours we heard.'

'What else did you hear?'

'That you were a hatchet man.'

'That's what they say about *all* new bosses.'

'That you were a workaholic.'

'Maybe.'

She sipped her coffee.

'So, did the real thing turn out to be worse than the rumours?' Manning wanted to know.

'Much worse,' Beth told him, smiling.

Manning laughed. A bright, infectious sound.

'How long were you married?' Beth enquired.

'Six years. Next Tuesday would have been our

109

anniversary,' he confided. 'Strange, I could never remember things like that when we were together.'

Beth looked at him as he sipped his coffee, his gaze focused on something unseen beyond their table.

'*She* used to say I was a workaholic,' he mused. 'Never at home, always more concerned with what went on in the office than the house.'

'Do you think that's what broke the marriage up?' Beth asked.

'It didn't help, I can see that now but it wasn't the only problem. There were a couple of – how shall I put it? – a couple of indiscretions on both our parts. I was away from home a lot, she got fed up with being alone. I suppose it was almost inevitable.'

'You mean affairs?'

'There isn't really a pleasant word for it, is there?' he shrugged. 'We were both to blame. We were too young. I don't think either of us knew what we wanted out of the marriage. I knew how to be successful at work but not as a husband.'

'Who ended it?'

'It was a mutual decision. I left. We'd had a couple of big rows. She was hot tempered. I told her it was her Celtic temperament.' He smiled. 'She was Irish, you see. I still think about her when I hear the accent.'

'Do you see her at all?'

He shook his head.

'We've spoken once or twice on the phone but not at any length. She's living with someone else anyway.'

'Did she find out about your affairs, then?'

'One of them. That was why *she* went out and had one. Tit for tat, I suppose. I don't really blame her.' He downed what was left in his cup and called the waiter over. 'Do you want a liqueur?' he asked Beth but she declined, sipping her Perrier as Manning ordered a brandy. He pushed his cup aside then looked at Beth.

'You remind me of her,' he said. 'Except she had long

blonde hair insted of brown like yours. Otherwise there are lots of similarities. *She* was very attractive too.'

Beth held his gaze for a moment, then lowered her eyes.

She shifted uncomfortably in her seat.

When she looked up again his eyes were still on her.

The brandy arrived and Manning thanked the waiter, holding the glass balloon in his hand and warming the amber liquid. He took a sip.

His eyes never left Beth's face.

Thirty-Three

Parker couldn't remember the last time he'd been drunk.

He wasn't paralytic as he'd been on a few occasions in the past, but his head was spinning enough to make him seek refuge in the sitting room, where he slumped into one of the chairs, grinning inanely but wishing that the lounge would stop whirling around him. He gripped the arms of the chair as if to stop this imagined spin.

How much wine had he drunk?

A bottle? Maybe two?

Fuck it. Who cared?

A tiny voice inside his head, barely noticeable, warned him that he'd feel like shit in the morning, that this was unprofessional for one thing.

Fuck it. There were plenty of aspirins in the house.

The tiny voice reminded him he was going to need them.

Lucy joined him in the sitting room, kicked off her shoes (*Beth's shoes*)

and sat on the sofa opposite him, drawing up her slender legs beneath her, pulling up the hem of her skirt

111

(The hem of Beth's skirt)
an inch or two to reveal a little more smooth thigh.

She smiled at Parker.

'Are you going to be OK?' she asked.

'I'm fine,' he told her. 'It usually only takes one drink to get me pissed. The tenth one.' He chuckled at his own quip. 'When I was a student, I used to drink Guinness and Lucozade, at least when I got pissed I had the fucking energy to crawl back to my digs.' He laughed again, more loudly this time. 'But I always knew when I'd had enough. I used to throw up, fall over and hit a policeman.'

Lucy chuckled.

'I think I'd better make you a coffee,' she said, getting to her feet.

Parker merely nodded and watched as she left the room.

He closed his eyes and once again wished that the room would stop revolving.

The foyer of the Mayfair Hotel was deserted when Beth and David Manning walked in. The receptionist behind the desk smiled briefly at them then continued with her work.

'Will you join me for a drink, Beth?' Manning asked, turning towards the bar.

She hesitated.

'Just one,' he insisted. 'I hate drinking alone.'

Leave it. Just go to bed now.

'Just one?' she said.

He nodded.

One drink. Where was the harm?

Against all her better judgement, she shrugged then said: 'All right. Thanks.'

They walked through into the bar.

Parker was asleep by the time Lucy came back into the sitting room.

She stood in the doorway for a moment gazing at him, listening to his low, steady breathing, then she crossed to his chair and set down the cup of black coffee.

She brushed his leg with hers as she stepped back and Parker opened his eyes, blinked myopically and groaned.

'Your coffee,' Lucy said, motioning towards the cup.

'I think I'd better get to bed,' he said, wearily, and dragged himself upright, swaying uncertainly for a moment.

'Sure you can make it all the way up the stairs?' Lucy chuckled.

He smiled back at her.

'See you in the morning,' Parker said and headed for the door. 'By the way, Lucy, it was a lovely meal. Thanks.'

She held his gaze for a moment longer then sat back on the sofa, listening as he climbed the stairs.

Lucy took a drag on her cigarette.

She'd give him five minutes.

As the lift bumped to a halt, Manning stepped back to allow Beth inside then he walked in behind her and jabbed the button marked 2.

The doors slid shut and the lift began to rise.

Beth leaned against the back wall of the car, hands behind her back.

'I've thoroughly enjoyed tonight, Beth,' said Manning.

'So have I,' she told him.

The lift bumped to a halt at the first floor but no one got in.

Manning waited a moment then pressed 2 again.

He smiled.

'Beth. . .'

The lift reached the second floor and she stepped out swiftly.

Was this it? Was he going to make a pass at her now?

She dropped her room key but Manning stooped to pick it up before she could react.

113

He pressed it into her palm, his hand brushing against hers.

Beth looked at him and they locked stares.

Manning smiled.

Thirty-Four

Parker didn't bother to fold his clothes, he merely pulled them off and let them drop, finally sitting down on the edge of the bed in just his underpants.

He sucked in a deep breath, held it, then exhaled slowly, cradling his head in his hands. The sensation that the world was turning that little bit faster than normal had slowed somewhat. He'd found it relatively easy to stand on one leg to remove his jeans. He just felt so bloody tired.

If Beth could see him now.

He grinned stupidly.

Sitting here in his underwear wondering whether or not to lay down in case he imagined the bed was twirling beneath him.

He could almost hear her laughter inside his head.

What he did hear was the creaking of the stairs as Lucy ascended slowly.

Parker was grateful for her concern, she obviously thought that he was already asleep and she was doing her best not to wake him. Although the squeaking complaints of the steps were not helping her. He could hear her reach the top of the stairs and silence descended for a moment.

He heard footfalls crossing the landing and raised his head.

The soft steps were approaching his own door.

He looked at the door and saw it open a crack, that crack

widening until he saw Lucy standing there looking in at him.

She seemed unphased by the fact that all he wore was underpants. In fact, she advanced into the room and Parker noticed that she was carrying Beth's shoes in her hand.

'I just thought I'd check you were all right,' she said, moving to the side of the bed.

'Yeah, I'm fine,' he told her, smiling.

'I brought these back, too,' she said, holding the high heels up.

(*Beth's high heels*)

'I borrowed them.'

'I'd noticed.'

'We take the same size but these have cut into my foot,' Lucy told him.

As she spoke she raised her left foot and rested it gently on his thigh.

'See the mark,' she whispered.

Parker nodded almost imperceptibly, looking first at Lucy's face and then down at her foot, the sole warm against his thigh. She flexed her toes and he saw the pinkish-red line on her instep.

She smiled as he traced it gently with the tip of his finger, finally running the smooth digit over each of her toes in turn.

Parker felt a warmth spreading across his groin, and as Lucy clenched her toes on his thigh, he felt the beginning of an erection pressing against his underpants. It was impossible to disguise the growing bulge and he sucked in a sharp breath as she moved her foot higher, resting the tips of her toes against his hardening penis.

The short skirt she was wearing had ridden up, slipped upward on her smooth thighs, and when Parker looked up again, he could see the soft white material of her panties. She pulled the skirt a little higher, still balancing on that one slender leg, pressing her toes more urgently

115

against his shaft now.

'Lucy . . .' Parker began, his voice low. 'Don't. . .'

She took her foot away and stood motionless before him, her eyes fixed on his erection, her own breathing now more shallow, harsher.

She unzipped the skirt, let it fall and stepped out of it in one fluid movement, standing there now in just her panties and blouse.

He watched as she began to unbutton the blouse.

'Lucy, stop it,' he said, trying to force some authority into his voice, standing up so that he was looking straight at her.

'Why?' she wanted to know, still undoing the buttons.

'Just stop it,' he repeated, aware of the ache in his groin.

She pulled the blouse open and Parker saw her breasts.

The nipples were already erect.

He shook his head gently as she took a step towards him and pressed herself against him, feeling his erection crushing against her stomach.

She snaked one hand across his belly and he moaned as he felt her nails rake his skin gently before plunging further, gliding over the waistband of his underwear.

Her fingers enveloped his shaft and squeezed gently, her thumb slipping over his swollen glans, smearing the clear liquid there over the sensitive flesh.

'Do you really want me to stop?' she said, taking a step back.

He nodded.

'Leave it,' he grunted, his breath coming in gasps.

'You still haven't told me why,' she said, smiling, her own face flushed, her own breathing hard.

She hooked her thumbs into either side of her knickers and pulled them down, sliding them over her thighs and knees, kicking them aside.

Parker allowed his gaze to travel over her body, finally returning to her face.

She met his gaze and held it, taking a step forward.

116

He could smell her perfume and that strong musky odour of her sex. In the light cast by the bedside light he saw tiny droplets of moisture glistening between her legs.

'Simon,' she whispered, hoarsely. 'Come on.'

He stood motionless.

She reached out for him.

It was then that the phone rang.

Thirty-Five

Beth looked at her watch as she waited for the phone to be answered.

11.46 p.m.

Even if Simon was in bed it was unlikely he'd be asleep.

She lay back on the bed, just one of the bedside lamps lit. It created deep, impenetrable shadows in the corners of the room.

Still the phone rang.

Perhaps he was in the shower.

Perhaps something had happened and he couldn't get to the phone.

Perhaps. . .

'Hello.'

She recognised his voice and smiled.

'Did I wake you up?' Beth said, softly.

'Beth?'

'Who were you expecting?' she chuckled.

'I'm sorry . . . I. . .'

'*Did* I wake you up?'

She thought he sounded flustered and confused.

'I feel like shit, I have done all night,' he said, quickly.

'I'll let you get back to bed then. I just wanted to see if you were all right.'

'How's it going?'

'I'll tell you when I get back. You go back to bed. I love you, Simon.'

'I love you too,' he croaked, his voice rasping.

He hung up.

Beth looked at the buzzing receiver for a moment longer then replaced it gently on the cradle, her brow furrowed into a frown.

She flicked off the light and stretched out on the bed but it was a long time before she slept.

Parker turned away from the phone and glared at Lucy.

'What the fuck are you playing at?' he grunted, his head clearing somewhat.

She sat naked on the edge of the bed watching him.

'I love you, Beth,' she said, scornfully. 'But I've got to go now because Lucy's with me.'

'Get out of here, Lucy,' he snapped.

'If she hadn't rung you'd have done it, wouldn't you?'

'Just get out, now,' he said, more forcefully.

'She wouldn't have found out, Simon.'

'And what the hell do you think she'd do if she could see you now?'

Lucy shrugged.

'What would she say if she could see *you*?' she chided. 'Don't tell me you didn't want it, Simon.'

'Get out.'

'If that phone hadn't rung you would have fucked me and you would have *loved* it. I could make you feel so good. Ten times better than Beth does.'

'I doubt it.'

'And what if she does find out what happened tonight?'

'Nothing *did* happen.'

'Beth doesn't know that.'

'If she thought you'd tried it on, she'd throw you out.'

Lucy chuckled.

'It takes two, Simon. Do you think she's going to believe you were completely innocent?' She picked up the blouse and draped it around her shoulders.

'She knows I wouldn't . . .' He allowed the sentence to trail off.

'Does she? Does she know you *that* well?'

'Get the fuck away from me, Lucy, before *I* throw you out of the house,' he snapped.

'If you even think about it I'll tell Beth what happened tonight.'

'*Nothing* happened tonight.'

'By the time I've finished, I'll have Beth believing we did things together even *you* couldn't imagine.'

'She'd never believe you.'

'I can be very persuasive.'

She picked up the rest of the clothes and turned towards the door.

'If you change your mind, Simon,' she said, smiling, 'I'm only across the landing. And just remember what I said.'

'Don't try to blackmail me, Lucy,' he rasped.

'Goodnight, Simon,' she said and left the room.

Parker slammed the door behind her.

Thirty-Six

Frank Jennings had been standing motionless over the sleeping form of Karen Gregson for more than twenty minutes, staring down at her, allowing his gaze to travel over every part of her exposed body.

He had pulled down the covers and pushed them off

119

the end of the bed, then he had carefully pushed up her nightdress towards her breasts.

Karen had not stirred.

Jennings moved closer, kneeling beside her, inhaling deeply, catching the scent of her flesh, the musky aroma that came from between her legs. He bent closer to her pubic mound and allowed his chin to brush against her softly curled hair but still he did not touch her.

There were buttons from the neck to the breast of the nightdress but, at the moment, Jennings was content with what he saw.

So beautiful.

His erection was already throbbing hard against his trousers but he did not attempt to release it. Even the exquisite ache brought with it a heightened pleasure, his own reluctance to touch her adding to the entire delight which seemed to fill his veins like fire.

A bead of perspiration trickled down his face as he moved to the foot of the bed and stared lovingly at her small feet.

Only now did Jennings lean forward and allow his flesh to meet hers.

He snaked out his tongue and slowly licked into the crevice between her first two toes, running his tongue over the smooth nail. He moaned softly to himself then took her big toe in his mouth sucking gently.

So gently.

Tasting her.

God, there was so much more to come.

He repeated the procedure with her left foot. Taking each toe into his mouth lovingly, sucking it for a moment or two before passing to the next.

He licked the sole of her foot then flicked his tongue over her instep and ankle.

Jennings could feel his penis rubbing almost painfully against his trousers now.

Karen remained motionless, her Thorazine-induced

sleep suiting Jennings perfectly.

He got to his feet and walked across the small room to where she had left her clothes. Jennings picked up each of the items one by one, rubbing the material with his fingertips. Her jeans, her T-shirt, her denim shirt. Her knickers.

He held this last garment with particular delicacy, inspecting the flimsy material. There was a faint scent of perspiration there and he inhaled, his eyes closed.

He turned the cotton panties inside out and pressed the gusset to his face, flicking out his tongue to press against the cotton at the place where he knew her vagina had been. He sucked at the material wishing he could taste her there. Jennings noticed one or two pubic hairs nestling in the material and he touched them as if they were precious stones, sniffing deeply one more time before replacing the knickers with the rest of the clothes.

He walked back to the bed and looked down at Karen again.

So beautiful.

His eyes were fixed on her pubic mound, the place that had been hugged so tightly by those flimsy knickers.

Should he taste her now?

He kneeled again and placed his nose a fraction of an inch from her vagina, drawing in deep breaths.

The aroma was intoxicating and he drank it in and savoured it.

For brief seconds he looked up at her face.

Her beautiful face.

He could see the steady rise and fall of her chest too, her breasts still hidden from view beneath her nightdress.

He still had that delight to come.

Jennings was having difficulty controlling his own breathing, such was his excitement, but he knew that he must retain his self-control. At least for the time being.

He pulled Karen's nightdress back down then drew up the sheet around her neck again, standing a moment longer to look down upon her sleeping form.

For now he would wait.

There was plenty of time.

He crossed to the door of her room, slipped out quietly and locked it, taking one final look through the observation slot.

He could hear her breathing softly.

So softly.

Jennings smiled to himself.

He didn't have much longer to wait.

When he drew in breath he could still smell her.

Not long now.

Thirty-Seven

As Lucy gripped the sheet more tightly, she felt Mark Hennessey's movement become more urgent, his breathing become more laboured.

She pushed back her bottom to meet his impatient thrusts, a smile on her flushed face as she felt the swollen stiffness of his erection sliding backward and forward inside her slippery cleft. Lucy reached back with her right hand and stroked her clitoris, hastening her own climax, knowing that Hennessey wouldn't be able to control himself much longer despite the fact they'd been through one frenzied bout of coupling already that morning.

Lucy heard him moaning, little grunts of pleasure and muffled words as if he was encouraging himself, urging himself on to his next climax.

The sheets were already damp with perspiration and she clawed at them with increased ferocity now, her finger stroking quickly on her clitoris, in time with his thrusts.

Lucy felt the orgasm sweep through her and she yelled out her pleasure, bucking hard against him, her red hair whipping around her face like writhing snakes.

The sensations subsided slightly and she was only vaguely aware of Hennessey's continued probings, his loud gasps as he gripped her hips and sought the release he wanted so badly.

Lucy pulled forward, away from him, and lay down on her back, smiling up at him, her face inches from his bloated, glistening penis.

'What are you doing?' he panted, exasperatedly.

'There's plenty of time,' she purred, pulling him close to her, one hand cupping his swollen testicles.

She kissed him deeply and felt him respond almost savagely, rubbing against her, the moisture on his penis smearing against her belly and matted pubic hair.

He looked at her, enraptured.

Lucy ran a hand through her hair and clasped both hands behind her head.

'When are your parents back?' she said, gazing at the ceiling.

'A couple of days,' he told her.

'You'd better put these sheets through the washing machine before they get back then,' she chuckled.

Hennessey nodded.

'I suppose all this will have to stop, then?' she continued, a note of mock concern in her voice.

'What do you mean?'

'You and I. Once your parents are back we'll have to stop seeing each other.'

'Why?'

'Well, they probably wouldn't approve of me and, besides, if they speak to Beth about me she'll probably tell them I'm bad news.'

'It's none of her business.'

Lucy shrugged.

'I probably won't be able to stay much longer anyway,'

she said, lifting herself up on one elbow and sliding closer to him.

One of her breasts brushed his chest, the hard nipple grazing his flesh.

'Where are you going?' Hennessey wanted to know.

'Beth told me to get a job. I haven't been able to so the only money I've been able to give her is my dole money and I don't get any more of that for two weeks.'

'She wouldn't throw you out, would she?'

'You don't know my sister,' Lucy said, stroking his chest.

'All because of money?' he said, almost incredulously.

She nodded.

Hennessey swallowed hard and looked longingly at her.

'How much do you need?' he wanted to know.

'Does it matter? Where am I going to get it, anyway?'

'My dad keeps some money in his safe here in the house, you know, for bills or for emergencies, in case he can't get to the bank. I could let you have some of that if it'll help.'

Lucy smiled at him then kissed him lightly on the lips, her right hand stroking across his belly then down to his penis.

'Would you do that for me?' she said, softly.

Hennessey nodded.

'I think there's about a hundred in there,' he told her.

'That should be enough for now. I can pay you back,' Lucy offered.

'I'll tell my dad I had to pay for some text books or something, he won't mind.'

Lucy kissed him.

'Do you want me to get it for you now?' he asked, breathlessly.

'It can wait until I go,' she purred. 'We've got other things to do, haven't we?' She closed her hand around his hard shaft and began to rub gently.

Hennessey closed his eyes as the pleasurable sensations

became more intense.

Lucy looked at him indifferently, her hand working expertly on his penis.

A hundred pounds.

She straddled him, rubbing the bulbous head of his penis against her swollen vaginal lips.

That would be enough for now. She'd be back for more.

Lucy sank down slowly on his penis, the sensation causing her to grunt in pleasure. She began to slide up and down his shaft.

He'd do anything for her, she knew that now.

She ground herself harder on to him, seeing his body tense.

Her own breathing became harsher and she gripped his hands as the pleasure grew.

Hennessey raised his hips, trying to push more deeply into her, desperate for release.

Lucy kept up her steady rhythm.

One hundred pounds to start with.

It had been easier than she'd anticipated. She smiled down at him as he began to climax.

Thirty-Eight

As she dropped her overnight bag on the hall floor, Beth breathed a deep sigh.

Home at last.

She smiled to herself.

The conference had finished half a day earlier than anticipated or at least her part in it had. Manning had suggested she go home early. Another reward, he had told her, for her hard work.

Like dinner?

The house was silent. No sound of music coming from the sitting room. The blare of the television set was conspicuous by its absence. She wondered if Lucy was out in the back garden. Lying in the sun probably, she thought, walking into the kitchen.

There was still washing-up in the sink and Beth muttered under her breath, glancing out of the window.

The back garden was empty. No sign of Lucy.

Beth was partly relieved that her younger sister wasn't in but that relief was tinged with irritation too. If Lucy had gone out then she'd forgotten to set the alarm.

Forgotten or not bothered?

Beth shook her head, filled the kettle, then wandered back into the hall, picking up her bag and making her way upstairs. She'd unpack, shower, then have a cup of tea. She was glad of the peace. Since Lucy had moved in, it seemed as if the house wasn't their own.

The stairs creaked protestingly as Beth climbed them. She wondered where her sister was. Working?

The thought was far fetched enough to be comical.

Beth glanced towards the door of Lucy's room.

Working? Fat bloody chance. She didn't. . .

Beth frowned, catching sight of something on the bottom of the bed, visible through the open door of the guest room. It was an item of clothing, wasn't it? A skirt?

She walked into the guest room.

Her skirt.

The black garment had been tossed unceremoniously on to the unmade bed. There were other clothes on the bed, some on the floor. She recognised a white blouse belonging to her. An orange sweater. Jesus Christ, even the knickers lying on the floor near her feet looked familiar. Beth stooped to pick them up and saw that they were indeed hers.

On the chair beside the bed, partially hidden beneath a pair of Lucy's jeans, was a silk shirt Beth also recognised

126

as her own.

'Borrow what you like,' she muttered, irritably under her breath. 'Borrow everything in my bloody wardrobe!' She snatched up the clothes angrily, grabbing at the silk shirt.

The chair on which it had been thrown toppled over and Beth picked it up angrily, banging one leg against the bedside cabinet in the process.

The door to the cabinet swung open, the duffel bag inside falling out, the top slightly open.

What else had Lucy borrowed? she wondered. Had she hidden clothes in here, too?

Beth reached for the duffel bag and set it on the bed, glancing around the room. It was a bloody tip. Tapes, clothes, even sweet papers and cigarette ends had been discarded wantonly. Beth gritted her teeth and tugged at the opening of the bag.

She saw the knife first.

Beth swallowed hard, her anger subsiding quickly into bewilderment and shock.

What the hell was this?

She reached in and took out the double-edged blade, hefting it, the light gleaming on the razor-sharp edges. Beth found that the breath seemed to have caught in her throat. She laid the knife down, her gaze fixed on the lethal-looking instrument.

What the hell did Lucy want with a weapon like that?

Beth pulled the bag wider and slid her hand in more cautiously, wondering just what the hell else her sister had hidden inside.

More knives?

Something even more potent?

She saw the small plastic bag and prodded it tentatively with her finger, finally lifting it up, cupping it on the palm of her hand.

Beth saw that it was sealed.

She pressed the bag between her finger and thumb,

testing the consistency. It wasn't sugar, it was too fine for that, besides, some of the powder was discoloured, brownish in fact.

'Oh God,' Beth murmured, her mind gradually wrestling with what appeared to be the truth. She shook her head.

Surely not.

Even Lucy wouldn't be *that* fucking stupid, would she?

Would she?

Beth squeezed the bag once more, trying to break the plastic, and then she reached for the knife. Christ, it was obvious, she'd seen them do it enough times in films.

She took the razor-sharp blade and made a tiny nick in the bag. Some of the white powder spilled on to her palm.

Beth wet the tip of one index finger, dipped it in the powder, then pressed it to the tip of her tongue.

The chill, the cool numbness she tasted were enough to convince her.

It was cocaine.

She'd never taken it but at a party when she was barely eighteen, she'd met a friend who had. Beth hadn't been tempted when it had been offered but she had tasted it and that taste had been distinctive enough for her to remember it, and this powder she tasted now was the same.

'Jesus,' she muttered, her anger growing. 'Jesus.'

She roared it at the top of her voice, hurling the bag across the room where it burst, the white powder falling like thick dust.

She picked up the duffel bag and flung that too, her rage now all enveloping.

Enough was enough.

Thirty-Nine

'Why not now?' Lucy said excitedly, propping herself up on one elbow.

Mark Hennessey gazed up at her.

'Come on,' she persisted. 'Let's do it. Now.' She was already swinging herself off the bed, reaching for her jeans and sliding them on.

Hennessey watched as she pulled them up tight over her smooth buttocks. She stepped into her trainers and began fastening her blouse.

'Well, are you going to take me for a ride on this motorbike or not?' she said, looking down at him, at his naked body.

He smiled and nodded, dressing with equal haste.

Lucy moved up close behind him, sliding a hand around his waist.

'I told you motorbikes make me horny,' she whispered in his ear. 'Take me somewhere quiet.'

Hennessey could only nod expectantly.

They hurried off down the stairs.

Beth sat on the edge of the bed for what seemed like an eternity.

She was staring across the room at the dusting of cocaine which had spattered the wall and carpet opposite.

Should she wait for Simon to get home to tell him?

Ring him?

Ring the police?

Wait and confront Lucy?

She got to her feet angrily.

There was no need to wait for anyone.

Beth *knew* what she had to do.

She looked down at the knife laying on the bed.

Hennessey twisted the throttle on the Harley, a comforting roar filling the garage. He nodded to Lucy and she pushed open the wooden garage door, stepping aside as he rode past her, bringing the bike to a halt as she pushed shut the door. She clambered up behind him, snaking her arms around his waist and squeezing tightly.

He turned and looked at her, saw her eyes widen expectantly through the visor of the black helmet she wore, her long red hair trailing out behind her.

Hennessey guided out the bike into the street, the roar filling the air, a cloud of exhaust fumes billowing out from the twin tail pipes of the machine.

Lucy held him tighter, her laughter drowned by the thundering engine.

Within two minutes they had reached the main road, Hennessey coaxing even greater speed from the bike.

Away to their left, less than fifteen minutes' ride, he guessed, there was a range of low hills densely planted with trees. He reached round and tapped Lucy's shoulder, pointing in the direction of the hills.

She nodded excitedly and gripped on to him more tightly as the bike accelerated.

All the drawers were empty now.

Everything Lucy had brought with her was scattered around the room, hurled angrily by Beth as she'd emptied the drawers.

Now she began gathering the clothes up, pushing them unceremoniously into the duffel bag, her face twisted with rage.

The knife she left until last.

130

Forty

It was like flying, thought Lucy. The bike roared along doing almost seventy, the wind whipping past her on both sides, tossing her hair in all directions, flapping it around her face. The Harley hummed with power beneath her and she gripped more tightly to Hennessey, who shifted on his seat, his body hunched over the handlebars.

Lucy slipped one hand from his waist to his thigh and began stroking gently, allowing her probing fingers to glide across to his groin where she squeezed his growing erection, gripping more tightly until she felt it swell even more.

The steady vibration of the motorbike seemed to fill every fibre of her body, starting between her legs as she ground herself more tightly into the seat.

They had left the main road about three minutes before, turning into an area of countryside with fields stretching away on both sides of them.

The brilliant yellow glow of corn in a field to her right was dazzling and the high stalks bowed and bent in the wind.

To their left a tractor was moving slowly backward and forward, its sound drowned out by the roar of the Harley's engine. A noise which seemed intrusive in the harmony of the countryside.

Hennessey had slowed down slightly now, the bike bumping heavily over one or two pot-holes in the road but the suspension made the impacts only marginally uncomfortable.

Lucy could feel the sunshine beating down on them. It

was hot inside the helmet, as if someone were pumping warm air inside. She needed to take it off, to breathe fresh air. She felt perspiration beading on her forehead and a rivulet ran down her face.

The tractor driver looked across as they sped past but didn't acknowledge them, more concerned with his own work.

There were farm vehicles in some of the other fields too. Lucy could see a combine harvester trundling along in a field to her left, the massive piece of machinery looking like some kind of prehistoric life-form chewing up the corn, spewing it out in neat bales at the back.

A wood lay up ahead and Lucy nudged Hennessey in the ribs and pointed towards it.

He understood.

The road was narrowing, turning left and right with increasing frequency now but he guided the Harley with ease and skill, the powerful machine negotiating each curve effortlessly.

Lucy giggled and slipped one hand down the front of Hennessey's jeans, her hand closing around his erection.

He slapped at her shoulder, an indication to stop, although the gesture was hardly performed with conviction.

He glanced quickly over his shoulder at her.

'Pack it in, Lucy,' he shouted over the roar of the bike but she merely laughed and continued to squeeze his shaft.

The road bent sharply to the right and they took the curve with ease, turning out into a stretch of straight road which was little more than a dirt track flanked on either side by high hawthorn hedges. The track was deeply rutted by the passage of farm vehicles, the deep trenches cut by such heavy machinery now baked hard by the summer sun. The bike skidded once or twice as Hennessey guided it over these ruts but he handled the Harley with admirable skill and strength.

The bushes seemed to be closing in on them as the track narrowed, huge expanses of green rising fully six feet, meeting in places above them to form a thorny canopy.

The sun, now poking through this canopy at intervals, dappled the bike and its two riders, some of the warmth of the blazing orb dissipated by the arcing hawthorn.

The spiky greenery was so close in places that Lucy could feel the sharp barbs brushing against her as the bike sped along. She was relieved when the track began to widen once again. The hedge receded also, as if the canopy of green had retracted back into the raised banks flanking the thoroughfare.

The wood was less than a mile ahead.

Hennessey turned to smile briefly at her, feeling her light touch on his thigh once again.

The urgency to reach the wood, anywhere they could step off the bike for a while now seemed paramount in his mind. When her hand strayed yet again to his stiff penis he could think of little else.

He worked the throttle.

The tractor reversed from a gap in a hedge to the right.

The Massey-Ferguson rumbled backward across the dirt track, blocking it completely, no more than twenty feet ahead of the speeding bike.

It loomed like some huge red painted roadblock, filling the narrow track, filling Hennessey's view.

The driver of the tractor could do nothing and the last thing Hennessey saw was the look of terror that flashed across the man's face.

The bike was doing sixty when it hit the tractor.

The Harley ploughed into the side of the farm vehicle, slamming Hennessey into the side of the tractor close to the cab door.

The front of the bike dipped sharply and Lucy screamed as she was catapulted through the air like a human cannon-ball.

She struck the glass of the tractor cab and crashed

133

through it, slamming into the driver and knocking him from his seat, but such was her momentum, she continued through the cab, landing with a thud on the other side of the tractor.

Hennessey was lying close to the bike, the rear wheel of which was still spinning madly. He was trying to lift himself up on one elbow, trying to see through the splintered Perspex of his visor, wondering why it looked as if someone had coated the inside with red paint. Blood was running freely down his face and neck, dripping from the rim of the helmet. When he tried to crawl he felt excrutiating pain flood both legs and turned to see that one ankle was turned inwards at an impossible angle, almost ninety degrees in the opposite direction.

He saw that his left leg was broken just below the knee, a thick jagged piece of bone protruding through jeans soaked in blood. He wondered what the reddish-brown fluid was running from the centre of the riven bone then realised it was marrow.

Seconds before he passed out he wondered what had happened to Lucy.

She lay face down, unmoving, legs splayed, arms by her sides.

As the driver of the tractor tottered from his cab he saw her, saw her red hair matted with blood, saw the puddle of the crimson liquid spreading out slowly around her head, spilling into the hardened ruts.

Her helmet was cracked in three or four places, and as he staggered closer, he saw something pink bulging through the smashed helmet. Something that pulsed and throbbed rhythmically.

It took him a few seconds to realise it was part of her brain.

Forty-One

'Jesus Christ,' murmured Simon Parker, gazing at the dusting of cocaine on the wall and floor of the bedroom. 'Where did you find it?'

Beth told him.

'God knows how much more of it she had with her,' she snapped. 'Or what she did with the rest. That's not all.'

Beth reached for the duffel bag and slid her hand inside, carefully pulling out the double-edged blade.

Parker took a step closer, inspecting the vicious-looking weapon.

He shook his head almost imperceptibly.

'I should use this on *her*,' Beth rasped.

Parker sat down on the edge of the bed beside his wife, his eyes still fixed on the gleaming steel.

'Perhaps it was meant for us,' Beth said.

'Oh, come on, Beth, that's ridiculous.'

'Is it? Then what was she doing with it?'

'She hitched a lot, perhaps she wanted it for protection.'

'And the cocaine?'

'Do you think she was dealing?' he wanted to know.

'Maybe that's why she had to get out of London. Perhaps she thought she'd start again around here. I just hope to God we've stopped her in time.' Beth pushed the knife back into the duffel bag.

'I gave her free run of this house, Simon,' she said, bitterly. 'I came close to believing she might just manage to get on with her life without fucking it up again.' Beth smiled grimly. 'I trusted her. If it wasn't so stupid, so pathetic, it might even be funny.'

'So now what?' he asked.

'I'll leave her bag outside, I don't want her in this house again,' Beth said. 'I don't want to see that little bitch ever again.'

Beth got to her feet and snatched up the skirt, *her* skirt, she'd found lying on Lucy's bed.

'She took this from my wardrobe,' Beth announced.

'I know,' he said, quietly.

She wore it last night when she cooked me dinner.

'Even *these* are mine,' Beth raged, holding up the pair of knickers she'd found nearby. 'I know I told her she could borrow my things but . . .' She allowed the sentence to trail off.

Parker merely sat silently, watching as Beth paced angrily back and forth.

'Was she here last night, Simon? Was she in the house with you?' Beth wanted to know.

He nodded.

'As a matter of fact, she cooked dinner for us,' he said.

Beth glared at him.

'Did anything happen between you?' she demanded.

'Beth, don't be ridiculous . . .'

'Did anything happen?' she yelled, her fury surprising Parker.

'No.'

But if the phone hadn't rung when it did then. . .

'Did she come on to you?' Beth persisted.

'She tried.'

'Did you fuck her, Simon?'

'Beth, you should know better than that.'

'I know *her*. Did you fuck her?'

'No.'

She held his gaze, her anger practically uncontrollable.

'Tell me the truth, Simon,' she hissed.

'I *am* telling you the truth, Beth.' He got up and moved closer to her. 'She tried it on but I didn't want to know. Nothing happened, I swear to you.'

136

Thanks to your phone call.

'I should have known she'd try it,' Beth said. 'When I knew I had to spend some time in London, I should have known.'

Downstairs, the doorbell rang.

Beth spun round, heading for the stairs, her face dark with anger.

Parker followed.

'That'll be her, little slag's forgotten her key, I bet,' Beth stormed, she took the steps two at a time, Parker a fraction behind her.

Beth heard the doorbell ring again as she reached the hall.

She gritted her teeth and wrenched open the door, the anger raging within her.

The policeman who stood at the door seemed unmoved by her angry expression.

'Mrs Beth Parker?' he said.

She was silent for a second.

Parker joined her in the hall, slipping an arm around her waist as he, too, faced the uniformed man.

'Yes, I'm Beth Parker,' she finally said.

'You are the sister of Lucy Morton?' the constable persisted.

Beth nodded, watching the policeman's expression soften.

'I'm afraid there's been an accident,' he said, quietly. 'Your sister was involved.'

Forty-Two

The room was less than twelve feet square, equipped with just a worn two-seater sofa, a couple of wooden chairs and a chipped table which supported a small lamp. The lamp was lit even though the fluorescents overhead blazed, buzzing softly like bloated houseflies.

Beth sat in the room picking at one fingernail, listening to the muffled sounds coming from beyond the door of the room. The room was tucked away just off a ward, close to the main reception area of St Angela's Hospital. It was the largest hospital within a twenty-mile radius, located roughly a mile from the centre of Oakley, and despite having been ravaged by the usual government spending cuts, it was still highly regarded by the residents of towns around it.

The policeman had told them that Lucy had been brought in at around seven thirty.

Beth looked at her watch.

10.18.

She continued picking at her nail for a moment longer then got to her feet and tried pacing back and forth as efficiently as she could in such a cramped area.

She'd read the posters on the walls about rabies and AIDS more times than she cared to remember.

Jesus, how much longer before they heard something?

No one had been in to speak to them since they'd arrived. Even the nurse who'd shown them to the room had disappeared and not returned. They didn't know how badly Lucy was hurt, the nature of her injuries, how it had happened, where. They knew nothing.

Beth sat down again and drew in a deep breath, smelling the stale air, the usual combination of disinfectant and

(*and what? What was that other odour? Urine? Polish?*)

pain?

Did pain have a smell?

Did illness exude an odour?

Beth ran a hand through her hair.

Was Lucy dead?

For one shameful moment she found herself wishing that she was.

'*Your sister's dead, your problems are solved.*'

So simple.

She swept the thought aside, angry with herself for even allowing it into her mind.

She got up, walked around the small table, sat down again.

The door opened and she stood up again.

Parker pushed his way in, his teeth gritted in pain as he held two plastic cups of coffee he'd got from the vending machine in the main reception.

'Shit,' he hissed, setting the cups down and blowing on his fingertips. 'Any news?' he asked, looking at Beth who merely shook her head.

Outside they heard movement but it passed. There was the squeaking of a gurney wheel. Parker heard two nurses talking and poked his head out.

One of them gave him a curious glance then walked on.

He thought about stopping them, asking them if they knew anything but finally ducked back into the room and reached for the coffee cup, wincing as he felt the heat once again.

'How much longer are they going to leave us in here?' Beth said, irritably.

Parker sat down beside her and reached out, closing one hand over hers.

She looked at him and Parker saw confusion in her eyes,

conflicting emotions. And the trace of a tear.

'How much longer?' she whispered.

As if in answer to the question, the door of the room opened and a tall man with curly brown hair walked in. He smiled at them happily, his hands dug into the pockets of the white coat he wore.

'Mr and Mrs Parker,' he said. 'I'm sorry we've made you wait so long.'

They both rose.

'My name is Doctor Christopher Leighton,' he announced. 'I was on duty when your sister was brought in, Mrs Parker.'

'How is she?' Beth wanted to know.

Leighton motioned to the chairs.

'You might want to sit down,' he said.

'Is it *that* bad?' Beth asked.

'I'm afraid it is,' he said, seating himself on the edge of the low table. 'There was massive damage to the head and neck, we can only assume she was thrown from the motorbike.'

'Motorbike?' Beth said in bewilderment.

Parker, too, frowned.

'The driver was badly injured too,' Leighton continued.

'Is Lucy dead?' Beth asked, flatly.

Leighton clasped his hands together and swallowed hard.

'Technically, yes,' he said.

'What the hell is that supposed to mean?' Parker snapped. 'She either is or she isn't.'

'We've got her in intensive care. She's on life support.'

'Oh Jesus,' murmured Beth.

'I'm very sorry,' Leighton said. 'If there *is* any consolation to be found from this it's that the injuries to her lower body were minor.'

'What difference does that make if she's brain dead?' Parker wanted to know.

Leighton looked puzzled.

'Considering her condition—'

'What are you talking about?' Beth interrupted, irritably.

The doctor looked straight at her.

'I thought you knew,' he said, quietly. 'Your sister is four months pregnant.'

Forty-Three

'It's impossible,' Beth said.

'I can assure you it's not,' Leighton insisted. 'Your sister is pregnant. We performed an ultra sound scan. The foetus seems to be perfectly healthy, undamaged in the accident.'

'Four months?' Parker said, softly. 'But wouldn't it have shown? She didn't look pregnant.'

'Some women can go for the full nine-month term and never even realise that they're pregnant, Mr Parker. It's not uncommon.'

Beth held up a hand to silence the two men.

Her mind was spinning.

'Lucy's dead but her baby is alive,' she said.

Leighton nodded.

'As long as she's on life support, her body will continue to function, the foetus will continue to develop,' the doctor explained.

Beth got to her feet.

'This is insane,' she murmured.

She felt faint. Nauseous.

What the hell was happening?

'How can you be sure that the baby will survive?' Parker wanted to know.

'Obviously, under the circumstances, there's no

141

guarantee of that,' Leighton told him. 'But, as I said, if Miss Morton's bodily functions are maintained by machinery then there's no reason why the child shouldn't remain as normal as any other growing foetus.'

'And when the nine months are up?' Beth asked.

'It will be possible to deliver the child by caesarian section,' Leighton told her.

'I can't get a grip on this,' Beth said, sitting down again. 'How can you be sure Lucy is dead?'

'There are many different tests to certify brain stem death and we've conducted all of them since your sister was admitted.'

'What are they?' Beth wanted to know.

'Well, Mrs Parker, it depends whose definition you use but it all amounts to the same thing.'

'How many bloody definitions are there?' Beth snapped.

'The Harvard Medical School established a list of criteria in 1968, so did the Duquesne University Law School. We use the World Medical Association criteria.'

'Which are?' Beth enquired.

'Well, obviously there are many different factors to be discussed but . . .'

'Just the short version will do,' Parker said.

'There are four main criteria to establish brain stem death,' Leighton continued, reeling off the facts as if he'd memorised them the previous night. 'The first is a total lack of response to external stimuli. Secondly, an absence of all spontaneous muscular movement, notably breathing. Part of this test is to switch off the respirator for three minutes to see if the patient breathes unaided.' He sighed. 'Thirdly, an absence of reflexes. For instance, there must be no contraction of dilated pupils if light is shone on them. We also do tests for corneal reflexes.'

'What kind of tests?' Beth wanted to know.

'The eyes are touched with probes,' the doctor said. 'We also pour drops of iced water into the inner ear to test for

142

ocular response. The gag reflex is used too. The back of the patient's throat is touched and any reflex is watched for.'

'And fourth?' Parker said.

'EEGs are taken every two hours,' Leighton said.

Beth shook her head slowly.

'Electroencephalograms, they test for brain-wave patterns, or, in this case, unfortunately, the lack of them,' the doctor said, apologetically.

The three of them sat in silence for a moment, an uncomfortable stillness resting in the room.

Beth inhaled, held it, then let the breath out.

'And all these tests have been done?' she said, finally.

Leighton nodded.

'There was nothing we could have done for her, Mrs Parker. She was dead when we got her,' he said, quietly. 'It's a miracle the baby wasn't killed too.'

Beth looked at Parker and then at Leighton.

'You said she was in intensive care,' Beth said. 'I want to see her.'

'Beth, why?' Parker asked. 'There's nothing you can do.'

Beth shot him a warning glance and he almost recoiled at the vehemence in her tone.

'I want to see her, *now*,' she snapped.

Forty-Four

It looked like a scene from a Frankenstein movie, Beth thought, glancing around the room.

There was just one bed but it was surrounded by all manner of electrical machinery and paraphenalia. Most of the machines had wires running from them, those wires connected to Lucy. There were four separate drips set up

143

alongside the bed, Beth could see the fluid from them running along thin pipes into Lucy's arms. The steady blip of an oscilloscope and the low pumping of a respirator were the only sounds to break the silence inside the room.

As they prepared to enter, Leighton handed each of them a white surgical mask which they pulled across their mouths and noses.

Beth stood motionless as Leighton opened the door of the room and ushered them in.

Parker turned and held out a hand to beckon her forward.

She took it and moved inside.

Lucy's eyes were closed. For some reason Beth had expected them to be open. She moved closer to her younger sister and looked down at her.

Lucy's head was heavily bandaged, those portions of skin not covered by gauze were blackened with bruises or scored with lacerations. Her lips were parted slightly, showing that two of her lower front teeth had been shattered, one torn free of the gum. There was a thick droplet of blood congealing there. Beth swallowed hard and ran her gaze over the rest of her sister's body, her eyes fixing on Lucy's midsection.

'*The baby is still alive.*'

Beth moved closer, reaching out a hand, touching Lucy's arm.

The flesh was cool, white as milk and waxen.

'These tests you did on her,' Beth said, not taking her eyes from Lucy. 'Are they foolproof?'

'Performed together, yes.' Leighton said.

'There's no way she could be alive?' Beth persisted.

The doctor shook his head.

Beth reached out and laid her hand gently on Lucy's stomach.

Parker watched her closely.

She stroked Lucy's belly.

'*The baby is still alive.*'

144

'Is there any chance of her recovering?' Beth wanted to know. 'Even partially?'

'None at all.'

Beth felt dizzy again but not from shock, not from seeing her sister in this condition. Her mind was spinning from the thoughts tumbling through it.

She should be feeling sorrow.

She wasn't.

She wanted to feel pain.

She couldn't.

Parker crossed to her and slipped an arm around her shoulder.

'I can leave you alone with her for a while if you'd prefer,' Leighton offered, his voice muffled by the mask.

Beth shook her head.

'There's nothing you can do for her now, Beth,' Parker said, quietly.

'I know,' she said, unconcerned.

'What's the next step, Doctor?' Parker wanted to know. 'Do you switch her off?'

'You can't,' Beth blurted. 'You'll kill the baby.'

Parker looked at her, only his eyes showing over the mask.

'A decision must be made within forty-eight hours,' Leighton informed them.

'By whom?' Parker wanted to know.

'By one doctor from this hospital and two independent consultants from another.'

'And what about us? Don't we get a say?' Beth said, angrily.

Leighton exhaled deeply.

'No, Mrs Parker, I'm afraid you don't,' he informed her. 'The decision must be made on a medical basis, the quality of life must be considered, the time taken to maintain care for your sister. There are many things to be considered. I realise how hard this is for you and I can only say I'm sorry.'

'You *can't* switch her off,' Beth said, angrily. 'You can't kill that baby.'

PART TWO

'. . . I'm inside, open your eyes.
I'm you. Sad but true . . .'

                      – Metallica

'. . . all that live must die,
Passing through nature
to eternity.'

                 – *Hamlet* Act 1 Scene ii

Forty-Five

The radio was only on for the time checks. It was on every morning from seven thirty until eight thirty while Beth and Parker readied themselves for work. Vacuous ramblings from a DJ interspersed with equally inconsequential pop songs added a background and little more.

Beth got to her feet and eased down the volume on the radio, returning to the table in the kitchen and her coffee.

She hadn't slept much the previous night and when she had that sleep had been fitful and light. She'd dreamed that she had seen Lucy standing beside a fire holding a child in her arms, preparing to throw it in. Beth could remember running towards her younger sister in her dream but never quite closing the distance between them. The rest was hazy. She thought she'd probably woken up after that.

'Are you OK?' Parker asked, looking across the table at her, at the dark rings beneath her eyes.

She smiled.

'I'm fine,' she said. 'Just tired.'

'Look, I can stay with you if you want me—'

Beth cut him short.

'Simon, I'm not going to have a nervous breakdown,' she chuckled.

'I know that, but with Lucy being dead . . .'

Again she interjected.

'You expect me to be sorry for that?' she said, flatly.

The indifference in her tone startled Parker.

'I don't care, Simon,' Beth continued.

He studied her carefully, seeing that her face was set in hard lines.

Was it bravado? Was she trying to convince herself she was unaffected by Lucy's death?

'I know what you must be feeling,' he said, softly.

'Don't talk to me as if I was one of your bloody patients,' she snapped. 'You *don't* know how I'm feeling. What do you think this is, Simon? The prelude to the *real* mourning? You know what I was like when Mum and Dad died. *That* was genuine.' She fixed him in an unflinching stare. 'Lucy's dead, the only thing keeping her out of a box is a couple of hundred thousand pounds worth of machinery. And I don't care. The only thing I care about is that child.'

'Why?'

'Because those doctors have no right to kill that child and if they decide to switch the machines off, that's what they'll be doing. They have to keep her on life support for the sake of the baby. If it survives it'll be the only good that's ever come out of her miserable bloody life.'

Parker regarded her almost warily for a moment then got to his feet, walked around the table and kissed her.

'Don't tell me *you* haven't thought about it, Simon?' Beth said quietly.

'About what?' he asked, puzzled.

'If the child is born it's going to need a home, parents. We . . .'

He held up a hand to silence her.

'Beth, you're being ridiculous,' he snapped. 'Are you going to sit around for five months waiting for them to deliver that child, switch off Lucy and then expect them to hand the baby to you? There's all sorts of legal red tape involved, things we couldn't even imagine.'

'She never wanted that child.'

'How do you know that? You didn't even know she was pregnant.'

'I bet she didn't even know who the father was.'

150

'Beth, she's four months pregnant, don't you think that if she'd wanted to get rid of it she'd have done it earlier?'

'How, Simon? Where was she going to find the money to pay for an abortion?'

'By selling those drugs she had,' he insisted.

Beth shook her head.

'You're crazy to even think about having her child when it's born,' Parker continued. 'Forget about it, Beth. We've both gone through enough pain already.'

'So are you telling me that if they offered us the child you'd refuse it?' she asked.

'What do you mean *offered* it? It's not a bloody cigar, it's a human being.'

'Would you refuse it?' she persisted.

'It's not going to happen, Beth.'

'Answer me, Simon,' she snapped, angrily.

He held her gaze.

'Would you refuse to take the child?' Beth asked again, her voice low and surprisingly calm.

'No,' he said, wearily.

Beth smiled.

'It's what we both want, you know that,' she told him.

'Beth, please don't get fixated on this child, you—'

She interrupted angrily.

'I told you, I'm not one of your bloody patients, don't tell me not to get fixated. It's something worth thinking about.'

'There are too many obstacles,' he insisted. 'The doctors might decide to switch Lucy's life support off. The child might die anyway and, even if it does make it, what gives you any more right to it than the next person?'

'I'm her sister and I'll tell you something else. She *owes* me that fucking child.'

Parker hesitated a moment longer then headed for the hallway where he picked up his briefcase and car keys.

Beth followed him out into the hall.

'Please, Beth,' he said, touching her cheek with his fingertips. 'Don't allow yourself any more pain over this.'

151

She kissed him gently on the lips, then watched him as he walked to his car, climbed in and drove off.

Beth pushed shut the door and stood against it for a moment, then she headed upstairs to change.

She should be at the hospital before ten.

Forty-Six

'Any problems?' said Simon Parker, glancing first at Karen Gregson who was seated in one corner of the dayroom, then at Frank Jennings who stood beside him.

Jennings shook his head, his eyes also on Karen.

She looked so beautiful.

'She's been fine, so far,' he said.

'How is she interacting with the other patients?' Parker wanted to know.

'A couple of them have spoken to her,' Jennings told him. 'She seems OK.'

Parker smiled and looked at Marcus Flynn.

The older man shook his head.

'Two hours in the dayroom hardly vindicates the decision to allow her out of isolation, Simon,' he said, dismissively.

Parker ignored the remark.

'I don't want her stressed or overtaxed,' he said to Jennings. 'Give her another hour and then take her back to her room.'

Jennings nodded.

'I'll speak to her later today when I've finished my ward rounds,' Parker added.

As he watched, Karen Gregson, seated at one of the old wooden tables in one corner of the dayroom, had a pack of playing cards in front of her and she seemed reasonably engrossed in a game of Patience, ignoring those in the room who wandered close to her or those who squabbled over other games in other parts of the room. She sat serenely contemplating the cards, her blonde hair drawn back to reveal her finely chiselled features.

'It's far too early to get excited over her progress,' Flynn muttered.

'It's better therapy for her than being alone twenty-four hours a day in her room,' Parker said, his eyes still on Karen.

Another patient, a young woman he recognised as Jane Owen, was approaching the table where Karen sat.

Jane was a couple of years younger than Karen, a plump, long-haired individual whom Parker had seen two or three times as an outpatient. Her own GP had finally recommended that she be treated at Brackley Heath on a short-stay basis, her family unable to cope with her manic depression. The depressive side had finally manifested itself most vehemently when she'd tried to kill herself, using a broken glass. The scars were still visible on her large forearm, the cuts made from the elbow towards the wrist.

Jane had meant business.

Parker knew that most suicide attempts were half-hearted, the clichéd 'cry for help'. With wrist slashing the cuts were usually made horizontally across the wrist close to the hand, this ensured lots of bleeding but the relative certainty of survival provided help was at hand soon enough.

The more determined suicides cut vertically, opening both the radial and ulnar arteries. Unless help came within seconds, death was relatively certain.

Jane Owen had slashed her arm from the elbow to the palm of her right hand.

She'd lost three pints of blood and the use of her thumb but, much to her initial annoyance, she'd survived.

Parker watched her sitting down beside Karen, peering at the cards. He wondered about moving over to them, asking Jane to move on but, after all, he wanted Karen to mix with others and here was that chance.

Karen looked at the newcomer and smiled. Jane was content to watch as she played.

'Just watch her,' Parker said, turning towards the door of the dayroom. He motioned to Flynn, holding the door open for him.

The older man hesitated a moment, watching the two young women seated at the table. They were talking now. He saw Karen Gregson laughing.

'I'll be along in a moment, Simon,' he said and stood back as Parker walked off up the corridor.

'What medication has Doctor Parker prescribed for Karen Gregson?' Flynn asked Jennings.

'She's on 20mg of Lithium carbonate, 10mg of diazepam and 20mg of Thorazine,' Jennings said, reeling off the medicines.

'Cut the dosages by half,' Flynn said.

'But Doctor Parker hasn't said . . .'

Flynn cut him short.

'*I'm* telling you, Jennings,' he snapped. 'Cut the dosages by half. I'll discuss this with Doctor Parker now. Just see that it's done.' And he was gone.

Jennings shrugged and began walking slowly around the dayroom.

He smiled as he got closer to Karen Gregson.

She really did look so beautiful.

He couldn't wait for the night to come.

He mouthed her name as he approached the table.

Flynn found Parker waiting in the corridor for him.

'I've got some work to do, Simon,' the older man said. 'I'll let you continue your rounds alone, if you don't mind.'

Good. Leave me in peace, you interfering old bastard.

154

'I wondered why you'd bothered joining me in the first place,' Parker said.

'I'm as interested in the welfare of Karen Gregson as you are. I just wanted to see that your revolutionary techniques were paying dividends.'

Parker heard the scorn in the older man's voice but chose to ignore it.

'I'll carry on then,' he said and walked off.

Flynn watched him go, a thin smile on his lips.

He headed off towards his own office.

There was something he had to do.

Forty-Seven

Beth walked briskly through the main reception of St Angela's, glancing only briefly at the other visitors to the hospital.

There was a coffee shop off to her left and she saw a number of patients sitting around in dressing gowns talking with visitors. To her right were half a dozen wheelchairs lined up as if in some kind of bizarre car park. The occupant of one was being helped back to the mobile seat by an intern who was practically carrying the old man.

Beth reached the lifts and pressed the Call button, standing motionless as she waited for the car to arrive. As she stood gazing up at the flashing numbers distractedly she was aware of a presence beside her and she turned.

The boy couldn't have been more than ten, his right arm held across his chest by bandages and Beth saw that the lower part of the limb was encased in plaster.

'I fell out of my bedroom window,' the boy said,

155

cheerily, raising the injured arm as far as he could, brandishing it as if it were some kind of trophy. 'I was shooting birds with my air rifle and I slipped. Mum said it served me right. She said it was God's way of getting me back for shooting the birds.'

He smiled wistfully and allowed Beth to step into the lift ahead of him.

'And what do *you* think?' she asked him, smiling.

'I think I shouldn't have been sitting on the window-sill,' he told her.

Beth chuckled.

'Which floor do you want?' the boy asked, already having jabbed the button he required.

Beth told him.

'Intensive care's on that floor,' the boy said, as the lift rose. 'My dad says that the people in there don't usually come out.'

'I'm sure some of them do,' Beth said.

'But they're very ill, aren't they?' the boy persisted.

Beth nodded.

'Do most of them die?' he wanted to know.

'I suppose some do.'

Like Lucy.

The boy shrugged as the lift reached his floor, then waved with his good arm and skipped out of the lift, the doors sliding shut behind him. Beth shook her head, smiling to herself. Kids.

What the hell would you know about kids?

Her smile faded as she reached the top floor, stepping out into the solitude of the reception area. There didn't appear to be anyone around so Beth headed straight for the room where she knew Lucy would be.

She passed a door and glanced in, noticing a man seated next to the bed of a woman in her mid-forties. The woman was hooked up to drips in both arms and Beth noticed that there was a catheter by the side of the bed, the bag filled with dark fluid. The man sitting beside the bed was reading a book but he looked up briefly as Beth passed, seeing her but only sparing her a cursory glance. He returned to his book and Beth walked on to the door she sought, pausing a moment before pushing it open.

Why feign sorrow?

She swallowed hard.

Frightened someone will see you're not as devastated as you're supposed to be?

Beth pushed the door.

No one cares how you feel anyway.

The room was silent but for the slow rhythmic thud of the ventilator as it pumped oxygen into Lucy's dead lungs.

Beth crossed to her sister and looked down at her face, the skin still criss-crossed by cuts, coloured by bruises. Her eyes were closed. Beth was grateful for that at least.

She reached out a hand slowly and touched Lucy's cheek.

The flesh was cold.

Beth withdrew her hand quickly, wiping her fingertips against her jeans as if to remove some kind of contagion.

She glanced at the drips beside the bed, watching as the droplets of fluid trickled down the pipes before being swallowed up into Lucy's veins.

For what seemed like an eternity, Beth gazed at her sister's ravaged features wondering why she felt no sorrow, almost ashamed at first that she was untouched by the younger woman's plight.

It wasn't in her to be a hypocrite.

She looked down towards Lucy's belly, hidden beneath the single sheet that covered her.

Covered the baby.

Beth found that her hand was trembling slightly.

The baby.

She reached out with infinite slowness and rested her hand on Lucy's belly.

On the baby.

She was still standing there when the door opened.

157

Forty-Eight

The nurse who entered the room was a little older than Beth, her white uniform so clean it seemed to glow. The paleness of her skin seemed to match the stark brilliance of what she wore.

Beth pulled her hand away from Lucy's stomach, feeling her own cheeks burn briefly, like some naughty child caught in the act of committing some misdemeanour.

She stepped away from the bed, forcing a smile for the nurse, who crossed to the bottom of the bed and consulted the first of a series of charts pinned to the clipboard there.

'It's my sister,' Beth blurted, feeling as if she had to explain her presence somehow.

'I'm very sorry,' said the nurse, a genuine warmth in her tone.

Beth watched her as she began moving around the bed, checking the drips, noting the levels in each container.

The steady thump of the respirator filled the room.

'You can speak to her if you want to,' the nurse said. 'A lot of them do.'

Beth looked puzzled.

'You can speak to your sister,' the nurse repeated. 'Even though she can't hear you. Not *here* anyway.'

Beth stood back, sitting down on the chair at one side of the bed.

'I speak to them all the time, you know,' the nurse continued. 'It helps if you do, it stops you thinking about them as just pieces of meat.'

'Isn't that what they are?' Beth said, flatly.

158

'They're still patients to me and they're here to be cared for as long as they're in my charge,' the nurse told her.

'I don't know how you stand it,' Beth said.

'I enjoy it, most nurses will tell you the same thing. At least in IC you've got two, maybe three tops, to look after, you get closer to them.'

'Even though they're dying?'

'They don't *all* leave here in boxes, you know.'

Not like Lucy.

'There's a sixty-five per cent recovery rate for patients who've spent time in IC. They're not all like your sister.'

'But why bother with her?' Beth wanted to know, watching as the nurse rearranged the sheet beneath Lucy.

'I told you, she's still in my care while she's in here,' the nurse said. '*She* needs me even more.'

'Even though she's dead.'

The nurse nodded.

'My husband's a porter here,' she continued. 'He works in the morgue most of the time and yet he can't understand how I can do *this* job.' She chuckled. 'At least some of mine *walk* out of the hospital. None of *his* ever have.'

'How long have you been a nurse?' Beth enquired.

'Six years and I wouldn't change it for anything in the world.' She continued her duties almost mechanically, it seemed to Beth, moving from each piece of machinery to the next, taking readings, making notes. 'When my son was born I said I'd give up work but we needed the money and I couldn't wait to get back here. I've been in IC for the last eighteen months. My mum looks after my son until I get home.'

Beth nodded.

'Have you got any children?' the nurse asked.

'No,' Beth said, a little sharply.

The nurse finished her final task then replaced the clipboard on the end of the bed.

'There'll be a doctor round soon but you can stay if you

159

like,' the nurse said.

'I need to speak to Doctor Leighton,' Beth said.

'I can page him for you if you like,' the nurse said, heading for the door.

'I'd appreciate that.'

The nurse smiled that warm smile again and opened the door, preparing to leave.

'Sit with her,' she said, nodding towards Lucy. 'Like I said, if you talk to her she'll hear you, somewhere.' She smiled again. 'I'll get Doctor Leighton.' And she was gone.

Beth got to her feet again and crossed to Lucy's bedside, one hand touching the drips that led into her sister's arm.

How easy to pull them free.

Her fingers tightened around them.

So easy.

'What would you say to me if you *could* hear me?' Beth whispered, her eyes fixed on Lucy's waxen features. 'You bitch.'

She looked down at Lucy's belly once more.

The baby was still growing inside.

Beth sat down and waited for Leighton to come.

Forty-Nine

Frank Jennings stood behind Karen Gregson for a moment, watching her as she turned her cards. She seemed barely aware of his presence.

'What are you staring at?' Jane Owen asked him, glancing at her own cards.

'Who's winning?' Jennings asked, seating himself on the other side of the table from the two women.

'It's a friendly game,' Jane told him, scratching the side

of her face with a stubby finger.

He looked at Karen and smiled.

I know nearly every inch of you.

'Don't you want to join in?' she asked him.

I know how you smell.

Jennings nodded.

I know how you taste.

Karen shuffled the cards and dealt three hands.

I know how you feel.

She looked across at Jennings and he felt himself ensnared by her gaze.

Jesus, those eyes.

'You don't usually hang around in here,' Jane observed, sorting her cards. 'That young bloke does, whatever his name is.'

'Damian,' Jennings told her.

'Yeah. He's all right, he is,' Jane chuckled.

'Fancy him, do you?' Jennings enquired.

'No,' Jane snapped, defensively. 'I was just saying.' She laid down her first card.

'Your turn,' Karen said, her voice soft, almost lost in the babble of conversation inside the dayroom.

Jennings looked at her and she smiled at him.

Did she know?

He shifted in his seat, aware of the beginnings of an erection stirring inside his trousers.

Did she realise that he came to her in the night? Realise and welcome his advances?

She continued to smile at him.

Was there complicity in that gesture?

He laid down a card, picked up another, his mind more occupied with thoughts of Karen than of the game before him.

Jane grabbed at the discarded pile and snatched up the card, flinging one of hers away.

Jennings watched as Karen did likewise. It was as if she moved in slow motion. Every movement so exquisite it

161

deserved to be studied and revered.

He longed for the night when he could touch her again, inhale the glorious scent of her body. His erection grew stronger as his thoughts ran wild.

Soon he would take her fully. While she slept. He would strip her, push those slim, smooth legs apart and he would slide into her.

The image in his mind was almost unbearable.

Karen looked across at him.

You want me to, don't you?

Jennings swallowed hard.

He was *sure* now she knew of his nocturnal visits.

And yet how could that be? She was sedated. Dead to the world. Only her unconscious state had given him the opportunity to indulge his fantasy.

How *could* she know?

'Gin,' shouted Jane, laying down her winning hand. She punched the air in triumph.

'Well done, Jane,' Jennings said, smiling benignly.

'Don't patronise me,' she hissed at him, her eyes blazing.

Jennings got to his feet.

'Come on, Karen, I've got to take you back to your room,' he said.

'Leave her alone,' Jane muttered, angrily.

'It's all right, Jane,' Karen told her, getting to her feet and standing obediently beside Jennings.

She looked at him and smiled.

'I'm ready,' she murmured.

Jennings swallowed hard and nodded.

She walked out ahead of him.

'Cunt,' murmured Jane as Jennings passed her.

He ignored the remark, more concerned with watching the contours of Karen Gregson's buttocks as she walked ahead of him.

*

162

What had seemed like an eternity, Beth realised, had actually been less than fifteen minutes. She stood up as Dr Leighton entered the room but he gestured for her to remain seated.

She'd watched as he'd checked some things which were attached to Lucy, covering the same ground, it seemed, as the nurse before him. He'd expressed his sorrow once again at what had happened to Lucy but Beth had been more concerned with the news he had for her.

Two doctors from a nearby hospital were to come to St Angela's the following day. They and a senior consultant from the hospital's own neurology unit would decide whether or not Lucy's life support was to be switched off.

He kept mentioning words like retarded, phrases like 'right to life' or 'dignified death' but, through this verbal fog, the only word which glowed with any luminosity to Beth was the word baby.

She asked what time the meeting was scheduled for and he told her three the following afternoon.

He asked her if she had any questions regarding Lucy's condition.

She didn't.

She asked that he call her as soon as a decision had been reached, watching as he scribbled down her phone number.

She left hurriedly.

Leighton paused for a moment, the only other sound apart from his own quiet breathing was that of the respirator.

He folded the piece of paper with Beth's number on it and pushed it into his pocket.

As he turned to leave the room he caught sight of something dark outside the window. A shape which cast a shadow.

Leighton saw that a large crow had alighted on the window ledge outside the room. It peered in at him with its cold black eyes for a second then stalked from one end

163

of the sill to the other.

Bloody things, he thought, he'd always been told they meant bad luck.

It turned and watched him for a second longer then flew off.

Fifty

Simon Parker woke to find he was alone in bed.

He groped to his right-hand side but, instead of the warm flesh he normally felt, he touched only the cool cotton of the sheet.

He sat up, trying to see his watch in the darkness, unable to manoeuvre it into the light. He looked at the glowing red digits of the radio alarm and groaned when he saw the time.

3.11 a.m.

'Beth,' he mumbled, listening through the stillness for any indication of where she might be.

Silence.

Parker swung himself out of bed, pulling on his underpants, trudging across the landing towards the head of the stairs. As he descended he heard movement below him.

There was a light shining beneath the kitchen door and he made for it, pushing the door open, seeing Beth sitting at the table there, hands cupped around a mug of tea.

'Are you OK?' he asked, rubbing his eyes.

She nodded.

'I didn't mean to disturb you,' she apologised.

'You didn't. How long have you been down here?'

'About an hour. I couldn't sleep.'

164

'You should have woken me up.'

'There's tea in the pot,' she told him, hooking a thumb over her shoulder.

'Thanks but the idea of bed is more appealing than tea at the moment,' he told her, wearily. 'What is it, Beth?'

'Do I need to tell you?'

He shook his head and sat down opposite her.

'By this time tomorrow we'll know whether or not they're going to switch off Lucy's life support,' Beth continued.

He ran a hand through his hair.

'We'll know if they're going to kill that child or not,' she insisted.

'Beth, for Christ's sake . . .'

She interrupted him and Parker was surprised at the vehemence in her tone.

'I know,' she snapped. 'You're sick of hearing about it.'

'It's consuming you,' he protested.

'Don't start giving me your professional bullshit, Simon. You'll be telling me next it's becoming an obsession.'

'I think it's gone beyond that.'

'What the hell do you expect me to do? How do you expect me to react? If they switch off Lucy, they kill that child.'

'What does it matter if they do? It's Lucy's child. Not ours.'

'But it could be ours.'

'Beth, give it a rest. How many times do we have to go over this. There's no way you're going to be given that child even if it manages to survive. It'll be taken into care.'

'And given to someone who's had their name on a fucking waiting list for years.'

'It'll be given to people like us. People who want a child but can't have one. I told you before, there's too much red tape involved in this kind of thing. They can't just hand the child over to you.'

'But it wouldn't be *mine*. It would be *ours*. Don't you

165

want that any more, Simon? Have you resigned yourself to living without kids? Well, maybe you have but *I* haven't. I want that child.'

'The chances of it surviving are slim anyway, stop torturing yourself, for Christ's sake. Haven't you been through enough already?'

'Yes, I suppose you're right. After all, it is *my* fault we can't have kids of our own, isn't it?'

'Drop it, Beth,' he said, the first hint of irritation creeping into his voice.

'It's all right for you, Simon. You don't have to live with it, the knowledge that you're not whole. I don't even feel like a real woman sometimes. I'm the one who has to carry that with me. Not you.'

'You talk as if you're the only one who's missing out. *You* can't be a mother. *You* can't have children. Did you ever stop to think how *I* feel? I'm the one who's married to a barren woman,' he hissed.

He saw her face darken.

Immediately he regretted his words.

'I'm sorry, Beth,' he said, quickly. 'I didn't mean that.'

He saw the tears form immediately in her eyes, saw the knot of muscles at the side of her jaw throb.

'You bastard,' she whispered, her voice cracking.

He got to his feet, crossed to her.

'Keep your fucking hands off me,' she rasped.

He stood his ground.

'I'm sorry,' he said, quietly. 'I didn't mean that.'

'But you still said it.'

She got to her feet and pushed past him. He heard her footfalls on the stairs.

'Beth,' he called after her.

She didn't answer.

'Shit,' he snarled and brought his fist slamming down on the table top.

The mug she'd been drinking from toppled over, rolled, then fell to the floor where it shattered, cold tea spilling over the carpet.

He closed his eyes and stood, head lowered, in the middle of the room.

From upstairs he could hear her crying.

He stood motionless, his breath coming in short gasps, then he sat down where Beth had been sitting, his head cradled in his hands.

'I'm sorry,' he whispered, his words echoing around the silent room.

From upstairs, the sound of crying continued.

Fifty-One

Karen Gregson turned the cards slowly, glancing at the columns that she'd already laid on the table before her.

Red eight on black nine.

She'd slept fitfully the previous night, her dreams vivid. She had dreamed of her children. For the first time since their deaths she had seen them in her dreams. They came to her as they looked after she'd finished with them. Their eye sockets empty, the glistening orbs gouged from them with the fork she'd used. The bulbous spheres dangling by bloodied optic nerves with the older child. Crimson had flowed down their cheeks like red tears, dripping from those vivid gashes.

They had reached out for her and she'd woken screaming.

But as soon as she'd slipped back into sleep they had come again.

Black four on red three.

One of them held the fork that had been used to tear the eyes free and Karen had found herself helpless, unable to escape them as they lowered over her.

Black ten on red jack.

Then they had pushed that fork into her eye, prizing the orb from the socket, spilling blood and clear fluid down her cheek.

Red six on black five.

She sat back in her seat, her brow greasy with perspiration. The noise in the dayroom seemed more intense than usual, the chattering much louder. So many voices crowded in upon her like living things which filled the air, crushing her like verbal bricks stacked around her.

They were walling her in with their voices.

She gritted her teeth.

Black eight on red seven.

The noise seemed to be building.

'Hello, Karen.'

The voice startled her and she looked round to see that Jane Owen had joined her. The younger woman was wearing a brightly coloured T-shirt which, unfortunately, only served to emphasise the size of her ample breasts. A hair band, used to push back her curly black hair, made her face look even chubbier than it already was.

Karen looked at her indifferently and continued with her game.

Red six on black five.

The voices were still crowding around her, pushing in more tightly, making it hard for her to breathe, and now Jane was right next to her, sucking the oxygen from the air.

Karen looked into her eyes.

They bored back into her.

Red five on black six.

The sound of the voices was deafening now.

'Shall we have a game like we did yesterday?' Jane said.

Karen tried to suck in a breath but felt as if her lungs were constricted.

'You'll get bored playing that by yourself all the time,'

Jane persisted.

Black on red.

Still the voices.

Black. Red.

Karen clenched her teeth.

'Here, give me the cards, I'll deal,' said Jane, reaching for the pack, trying to grab the rows of cards laid out before Karen.

Black on black on black.

'Look, you've messed it up now, anyway,' Jane said.

Stop the voices.

Jane was reaching for the cards again.

Red on red.

Karen shook her head.

Red. Red. Red.

'Come on, Karen,' Jane protested.

'Leave them,' Karen hissed.

From across the dayroom, Damian Wilks saw the two young women and got to his feet, walking slowly towards them.

He saw Jane grab for the cards.

'Come on,' she snapped.

'Leave them alone, you fat fucking bitch,' Karen snarled.

'Fuck you then.'

Wilks quickened his pace.

Red. Red. Red.

Karen looked directly into Jane's eyes.

Those eyes. They stared back. They accused.

They knew.

She'd seen those eyes before a million times.

In her dreams, in her nightmares.

In the faces of her children.

Jane held Karen's gaze.

Wilks was running now, anxious to reach the table.

'Fuck off,' Jane said.

Karen looked into those eyes and grunted.

Stop looking at me.

Karen snatched up the Biro which lay on the table and rammed it with incredible power into Jane's left eye.

There was a loud plop, as if someone had burst a water-filled balloon, the sound immediately drowned out by a scream of agony as Jane clutched at the Biro which was still protruding from her eye. Blood was pouring down her face, splashing on to the table. On to the cards.

Red on red.

The thin tube of ink, ruptured by broken shards of plastic, burst and spilled dark fluid into the stream of crimson.

Karen sat staring as Jane fell backwards off her chair, the pen sticking out of the riven orb, blood and ink pouring from the wound.

Other voices were raised now. Screams. Shouts.

Karen stood up, as if to escape the noise.

She felt strong arms envelop her as Wilks grabbed her but she didn't resist.

She couldn't see the eyes, that was all that mattered.

Jane wasn't looking at her any more.

Somewhere she heard an alarm bell, heard footsteps running close by.

Karen allowed herself to be wrestled away.

The wall of noise around her was growing higher, tighter.

Faces were turned towards her.

More eyes.

But not *those* eyes.

As she was dragged from the dayroom she could still hear Jane screaming.

But at least she couldn't see her eyes.

Simon Parker looked down at Karen Gregson, studying her features. She looked so tranquil. He swallowed hard as he saw there were still drops of blood on her denim shirt.

He kneeled beside her bed, the only piece of furniture in the restraining room.

She was heavily sedated. He lifted her eyelid slowly and shone his pen-light into the eye, studying the pupillary reflexes.

'I warned you this would happen,' the voice behind him said, mockingly. 'You should have listened, Simon.'

Dr Marcus Flynn stood at the door of the room, arms folded across his chest.

Parker gritted his teeth.

'I can't understand why,' the younger man said, quietly. 'The dosage of drugs hasn't been changed.'

Flynn shot Frank Jennings a warning glance and Jennings merely lowered his gaze.

'I said she wasn't ready to be integrated into the ward,' Flynn persisted. 'You did say that you would take responsibility for this.'

'What do you want, my fucking resignation?' Parker shouted, rounding on the older man. 'If you want it you can have it.'

'I think we need to discuss this matter more fully,' Flynn said. 'Be at my office in ten minutes.' He walked away.

Parker clenched his fist, his breath coming in short gasps.

'Did you see what happened?' he asked Damian Wilks.

'Not what started it,' the nurse told him.

Parker gently lifted Karen's other eyelid and shone the pen-light on her eye.

'I want her checked every half-hour,' he said, straightening up.

Jennings nodded and he and Wilks walked out.

Parker turned to follow them.

'Simon.'

He spun round when he heard his name.

Karen spoke it slowly.

Parker shook his head.

She couldn't be conscious. He'd personally given her 30mg of Thorazine only twenty minutes earlier.

He took a step back towards the bed.

Her eyes were open.

'Jesus Christ,' Parker murmured.

She turned her head and looked at him.

'Simon, don't let them kill the child,' she said, softly, a beatific expression on her face.

'What child?' he said, his voice a low whisper.

She smiled at him.

'Lucy's child,' she said and closed her eyes again.

'Karen,' he said, agitatedly. He shot out a hand as if to try and rouse her from this drug-induced slumber.

He pulled her eyelids up again.

She didn't stir.

When Parker stepped away from her he was trembling.

Fifty-Two

There were three blades, each one about two inches long, double-edged and razor sharp.

Beth could see them by pulling back the plastic flaps that masked the cylinder of the waste-disposal unit.

She peered down the black maw, recoiling slightly from the rancid stench that rose from the hole. Pieces of food stuck to the blades, hardened and rank. Stagnant water was puddled beneath the glistening cutting tools and she saw pieces of kitchen debris floating there.

The bloody thing had been working intermittently for the last two days. Stopping and starting, not digesting the waste pushed into it, sometimes spewing the rancid matter back up into the sink. Beth knew that it sometimes jammed, pieces of potato peel gumming up the mechanism, and she wondered if that was the problem now.

172

She'd already tried prodding the inside of the blade-filled cylinder with a knife but that had proved fruitless, in fact, at one point, she'd thought she'd lost the knife in there.

In addition to the wall switch, a switch beneath the sink turned the machine on and off, and she'd been careful to check that this red switch hadn't been knocked accidentally, causing the waste disposal to pack up, but everything seemed to be in working order. Why then did she only get a series of metallic screeches or groans from the bloody thing when she turned it on?

Beth knew she'd have to unlock it by hand.

She pulled on the rubber gloves more tightly, steeled herself against the rank odour and pushed one hand tentatively into the yawning black mouth of the waste disposal.

As she delved deeper she felt the dripping edges of the blades.

What if it started up now?

The mere thought of those churning blades catching her hand made her withdraw the probing appendage immediately.

Don't be stupid. It was turned off. Nothing could happen.

She swallowed hard then pushed her hand inside once more, groping around, up to her elbow in the wide black cylinder which seemed to swallow her arm as easily as it digested scraps.

She could feel something blocking the pipe at the bottom. A thick flux of half-decayed foodstuff which seemed to have congealed around the mechanism.

Beth pushed and pulled at the odorous mess, trying to free it.

One of the blades brushed against her forearm, the razor-sharp steel cold against her flesh.

The stench coming from the unit was almost intolerable but she persevered, feeling some of the thick coagulated matter come free in her rubber-covered fingers.

Another blade brushed her arm, nicked the flesh.

Any further and her arm would be stuck. Held as far as the elbow by the unit.

One more blob of mess came free and she realised she'd nearly freed the central ring of blades. The spiral should be able to turn without too much trouble.

If only she could twist it.

If only. . .

The ringing of the doorbell almost made her shout aloud.

She pulled her arm free of the waste-disposal unit, noticing that the slight nick below the crook of her elbow was bleeding slightly.

As she walked towards the front door she pulled off her rubber gloves, tossing them on to one of the worktops, smelling rubber on her hands.

She wiped them on her jeans in an effort to remove the smell, reaching for the door-handle with one latex-scented hand.

David Manning stood on the doorstep.

Beth looked surprised even though she tried to hide it.

'I heard about your sister,' he said. 'I just wanted to say how sorry I was. I hope you don't mind me calling round like this?'

'No. Thank you for coming. Will you come in?' she asked, still somewhat taken aback by his sudden appearance.

Manning shook his head.

'I won't stop, I really just wanted to tell you to take as long as you need. Don't rush back to work until you feel you're ready. I know how you must feel, my father died about nine months ago. It gutted me.'

She smiled thinly.

'We might find it hard to manage without you, Beth, but we'll try,' Manning told her, smiling.

She grinned too, aware that her cheeks were flushed.

Beth was aware of his eyes on her breasts, an appraising glance which ran the length of her body.

'Are you sure you won't have a coffee?' she persisted.

'I'd better get back.'

'Another time, perhaps?' she murmured, wondering why she'd said it.

'I'll take you up on that,' he told her, turning and heading for his car. 'You take care now,' he called as he climbed behind the wheel of the Jag.

She watched him as he drove off, finally closing the front door.

Beth stood against it for a moment, eyes closed.

'Come in for a coffee,' she said aloud. 'What the hell are you doing?' She smiled to herself.

She was heading back towards the kitchen when she heard the crash upstairs.

Fifty-Three

Beth hesitated for a moment then looked up towards the landing. Whatever the noise was, it had come from further back in the house, from one of the bedrooms.

Beth climbed the stairs, her mind still occupied with Manning rather than with what damage awaited her upstairs.

The steps creaked under her weight as she climbed and when she finally reached the landing, she looked round at the closed doors that faced her.

By the sound of the crash and the accompanying thud, whatever had fallen was reasonably heavy.

She crossed the landing to the bathroom and peered inside.

Everything seemed to be in place.

She moved to their bedroom.

Again, nothing had been moved or fallen. Beth checked in the en suite bathroom, too, but there was no sign of a disturbance.

She walked back across the landing to the door of Lucy's room.

What had once been Lucy's room.

Beth turned the handle and pushed.

The door wouldn't open.

She pushed harder.

It still wouldn't budge.

What the hell was going on? Was the lock jammed?

She put all her weight against it, irritated now.

The door swung open at last and she stumbled inside.

Beth kept her hand on the handle, lifting it up and down, checking the mechanism. It seemed to move easily enough. She couldn't see why it should have stuck but she made a mental note to put some oil on the mechanism and also on the hinges.

The bed had been stripped, the sheets already consigned to the washing machine. Lucy's belongings, meagre though they were, had been put in a cardboard box in the garage.

Beth looked slowly around the room, eyes alert for any signs of disturbance.

She noticed that there was something missing from one of the bedside cabinets.

Moving around the bed she found that the photograph of her mother and father had fallen to the floor.

That had caused the thud she'd heard.

As Beth picked it up she noticed that the glass in the frame was shattered.

No. Shattered was the wrong word.

It was pulverised.

The glass had been smashed so badly it was like powder. It looked as if someone in heavy boots had been leaping up and down on the picture continuously. Pieces of broken glass had gouged through the picture itself, in places cutting it so badly it was impossible to make out her parents' features.

Even the frame was cracked.

As she held the shattered photo a piece of glass fell to the ground, bouncing at her feet like a crystallised tear. More fragments were scattered for several inches round about.

Beth sighed. The bedroom window was slightly open to allow some freshness in. A breeze must have dislodged the picture, caused it to fall.

And yet the breeze didn't seem strong enough to knock over a picture in such a heavy frame. It would have taken a gale to dislodge this portrait.

Beth gazed out into the garden, at the trees in the Hennessey's garden.

The branches were motionless, almost frozen in the still air.

There *was* no breeze.

Beth looked at the picture once again and frowned.

She closed the window, aware again of how still the air was.

Somewhere in the garden she could hear a bird calling but it wasn't the shrill whistle of a sparrow or starling, it was a lower, guttural sound. Intrusive in the calm day.

Perched in the branches of the tree at the bottom of the garden she saw the source of the raucous noise.

One of the largest black crows she'd ever seen glared at her.

Fifty-Four

'They could close us down for this,' Flynn shouted, angrily. 'You're bloody lucky Karen Gregson didn't kill her. As it is Jane Owen will lose the sight of her eye.'

'*I'm* lucky Karen didn't kill her?' Parker said, incredulously. 'Do you think I wanted this to happen?'

'You couldn't wait, could you? Couldn't just let things take their course, you had to rush it, didn't you? I warned you that Karen Gregson should be kept in seclusion.'

'So you've kept telling me,' grunted Parker.

'God alone knows what the authorities will make of this,' Flynn continued.

'It wouldn't be the first time an accident had happened here and you know it.'

'But this wasn't an accident, we're not talking about someone tripping and falling down some stairs. We're talking about attempted murder.'

Parker shook his head exasperatedly.

'So I was wrong,' he snarled. 'Which do you want first? The written apology or the resignation?'

Flynn walked back behind his desk and sat down in the large leather chair there. He drummed agitatedly on one arm with his fingertips.

'There will be repercussions, Simon, I can't help that,' he said.

'And I said I'd take the responsibility,' Parker reminded him.

'I feel that your methods—'

'Will you shut up about my methods, for Christ's sake,' Parker roared. 'There *isn't* any new method. I'm not trying to undermine your authority here and I certainly don't want your fucking job.'

'I could dismiss you on the spot for speaking to me like that,' Flynn said, pointing an accusatory finger at his young colleague.

'Then do it,' Parker said, defiantly.

'There will have to be an enquiry into what happened,' Flynn continued. 'I want the views of the other consultants on this, in the meantime I can see little alternative but to consider some form of additional therapy for Karen Gregson.'

'Such as?'

'If there is no radical improvement in her condition

within a week then I will recommend a course of ECT.'

'Jesus Christ, put her in a time machine and take her back fifty years first. ECT is hardly used these days and certainly not in cases of puerperal psychosis,' Parker raged. 'When was the last time it was used at this hospital?'

'Ten or eleven years ago,' Flynn told him.

'More like thirty or forty. Even the most acute forms of depression can be treated with drugs now. There's no need to strap electrodes to someone's head any longer.'

'I expected that sort of reaction from you, Parker. Well, I'm afraid that is my recommendation for Karen Gregson unless there is a marked improvement in her condition within the next week.'

'But she's *my* patient.'

'Only for the next week.'

'Why were you so eager for me to take her in the beginning?' Parker demanded.

'I told you at the time, I felt your methods might be useful in dealing with her case. Obviously I was wrong.'

Parker got to his feet, his heart thudding hard against his ribs as he fought to control his anger.

'Karen Gregson will remain in seclusion for the remainder of her stay here,' Flynn added as Parker turned and headed for the door. 'I still want regular reports on her progress, if there *is* any.'

Parker wrenched open the office door.

'Just remember, Simon,' the older man called. 'You had your chance.'

Parker slammed the office door and stalked off up the corridor.

Flynn sat back in his chair, a victorious smile on his lips.

He waited a moment then picked up the phone and jabbed one of the internal numbers, waiting until he heard a voice at the other end.

'It's Doctor Flynn,' he said. 'Tell Jennings I want to see him in my office immediately.'

Fifty-Five

Beth muttered to herself as she heard the phone ring, reluctant to leave the recalcitrant waste-disposal unit when she felt she was so close to freeing the last of the rancid matter from it. Nevertheless, she pulled one gloved hand from the cylinder and crossed to the phone, brushing her hair back with her clean hand.

She picked up the receiver.

'Hello,' she said.

Silence.

'Hello,' Beth repeated.

There wasn't a sound at the other end, not even an occasional hiss of static, just deathly, impenetrable silence.

She held the receiver to her ear a second longer then replaced it.

Wrong number maybe.

The smell from the disposal unit seemed to be worse but Beth wrinkled her nose and persevered, pushing her arm deeper into the blade-filled cylinder until she was in as deep as the elbow. She felt something thick and putrid between her thumb and forefinger and tried to pull it away from the base of the turning blades but it wouldn't budge.

The phone rang again.

'Shit,' hissed Beth and walked over to it once again.

When she pressed the receiver to her ear for the second time there was no sound at the other end.

'Very funny,' she said into the mouthpiece, as if expecting some kind of reaction from the other end. Kids mucking about, perhaps.

She slammed the receiver down.

She'd barely reached the sink when the phone rang again.

Beth stared at it for a moment as it continued to ring.

And ring.

She took a step towards it.

The ringing continued for a moment then seemed to slow down, the sound dying as if all the power were being sucked from the machine. The loud ringing degenerated into a barely audible buzz.

Beth snatched up the receiver.

She could hear something this time.

Breathing?

She told herself it was interference on the line and flicked the cradle.

Beth replaced the receiver and reached for the pad and pen close by, making a note to call the telephone company. Perhaps there was some kind of fault on the line, she ought to get it checked out. She wondered if she could phone out. The way the phone had seemed to lose power bothered her. Perhaps there had been a cut in power somewhere on the grid.

She jabbed the digits of her work number and waited.

It was ringing. There didn't appear to be any problem.

Still, she'd get it checked, anyway.

The phone was still ringing. She wondered why no one was answering. The main switchboard was manned by three women, surely they couldn't be *that* busy.

She pressed down on the cradle, dialled again and waited.

Waited.

There was a harsh burst of static, so loud she held the phone away from her ear, then she heard voices. Distant and barely recognisable, as if they were coming to her through her dreams.

She heard fragments of words, realised she must have a crossed line.

'. . .kill the bastard if I. . .'

'. . .time will come . . . then he's a dead man . . . listening. . .'

There was silence for a second.

Were the callers aware of her presence?

The voice that came next bellowed down the phone so loudly she almost dropped the phone.

'LET HER FUCKING DIE, YOU SELFISH CUNT . . .'

Beth jumped back, horrified. She slammed the receiver back on to the cradle and stood back, panting, her eyes riveted to the phone.

What the hell had she overheard?

She crossed to the kitchen table and sat down, feeling a little faint. The odour from the waste-disposal unit made her nauseous and she clamped her jaws together firmly until the feeling passed.

She'd wait a few minutes then ring the phone company. There was obviously something wrong and she wanted it sorted out quickly.

The phone rang again.

Beth merely stared at it.

The ringing echoed around the kitchen.

She felt overwhelmed by a sudden deep-rooted fear, a reluctance to pick up the receiver.

The ringing was deafening.

Perhaps if she left it long enough it would stop, but could she stand that continuous strident sound?

Ringing.

Pick it up.

It's only a bloody phone.

She crossed to it quickly and snatched up the receiver.

'Hello,' the voice at the other end said.

'Hello.'

'Mrs Parker? This is Doctor Leighton from Saint Angela's hospital.'

For long seconds the name didn't register, then she seemed to grip the receiver more tightly.

'I'm sorry,' she said, her heart still pounding.

'I thought you should know immediately,' Leighton continued. 'About your sister.'

Beth swallowed hard, her blood racing more swiftly through her veins.

'What decision did they reach?' she asked.

'They felt that the baby's right to life was stronger than your sister's right to die. I'm sorry that . . .'

Beth smiled triumphantly, glad that Leighton couldn't see her expression.

'So Lucy's life support will be kept on?' she said.

'Until the baby can be delivered. Then, I'm afraid, that will be it.'

Beth grinned even more broadly.

'I'm very sorry about your sister, Mrs Parker,' the doctor continued.

I'm not, Beth thought.

'Thank you for calling,' she said. 'I appreciate it.'

'If you need to know anything then please don't hesitate to get in touch,' he reminded her. 'We'll do our best for the baby now.'

She thanked him and hung up. It was all she could do to suppress a shout of delight.

The child would live.

Suddenly, the crossed line, the faulty phone didn't seem so important.

She glanced across at the waste-disposal unit and shook her head.

It could wait.

She had more important things on her mind now.

183

Fifty-Six

Parker peered through the observation slot in the door of the seclusion room, watching Karen Gregson.

She was sitting on the bed, her back pressed against the wall, hands clasped around her knees. It seemed as though her eyes were fixed on something in front of her but there was nothing else in the room except the bed.

'How's she been?' Parker asked, never taking his eyes off her.

'Quiet,' Damian Wilks told him.

'Open it up,' said Parker, jabbing a finger at the door.

Wilks selected a key and did as he was instructed.

'I'll come in with you, Doctor,' he said.

'No need. I'll call you when I've finished,' Parker told him.

'I was told not to let anyone in unaccompanied except Doctor Flynn.'

'Told by whom?'

'Mr Jennings, the senior nurse.'

'Where is Jennings?'

'I don't know.'

'I need to speak to Karen Gregson alone. Stand outside the door by all means but if you come in with me she'll clam up and it's difficult enough getting her to talk as it is.'

'But what if she—'

'If she what? Decides to attack me? I'll worry about that, Wilks. She's here because she's suffering acute puerperal psychosis, she's not a female version of the Yorkshire Ripper. Now open the door.'

Wilks hesitated a moment then did as he was told,

pushing the door open.

Parker stepped inside the room and pushed shut the door behind him. He crossed to the bed, running appraising eyes over Karen.

She was barefoot, her legs drawn up on to the bed, small hands hugging her knees. When she saw him she smiled.

'How are you feeling, Karen?' he asked, crouching beside the bed.

'When can I get out of here?' she wanted to know.

'Not for a while. We want to make sure you're well enough before—'

'You want to know why I stabbed the fat bitch in the eye, don't you?'

'If you want to tell me.'

'She was staring at me.'

'Did the voices tell you to stab her? The same ones that made you kill your children?'

She didn't answer.

Parker eased himself down on to the floor and sat cross-legged before her, watching as she began running a finger between her toes.

'You said something to me the other day about a baby,' he began. 'A child.'

'Lucy's child,' she said, smiling.

He felt the hairs on the back of his neck rise.

'That's right. Did the voices tell you about Lucy's child too?'

She didn't answer.

'Do you know anyone called Lucy?' he persisted.

She looked directly at him.

'Do you know who she is, Karen?'

'What the fuck does it matter to you?' she snapped, her features hardening. 'You're always asking me questions.'

'Don't you like me asking you questions?'

'Why do you want to know so much about me? What makes *me* so fascinating? You should be dealing with the fucking loonies in here, not bothering with me.'

185

More mood swings, he thought.

'What do you know about Lucy's child?' he asked.

She didn't answer, merely smiled, that softness returning to her expression.

'What did the voices tell you about it?' he persisted.

'Your wife wants the child, doesn't she?'

'Did the voices tell you that?'

His skin was crawling, as if millions of tiny insects were scurrying across the flesh.

Karen Gregson was silent.

Parker got to his feet, aware of how cold it was inside the room. He crossed to the door, saw Wilks look in at him through the observation slit.

'I hope she'll be happy with the child,' said Karen and he felt as if fingers were plucking at the back of his neck again.

She turned and looked at him, her smile serene.

'You'll make a wonderful father, Simon,' she whispered.

Fifty-Seven

He sat at the kitchen table, head slumped back against the wall, the beginning of a headache gnawing at his skull. Parker reached up and began to massage his own shoulders gently, anxious to dispel the growing tension.

'Did you hear what I said?'

He looked at Beth who was gazing at him with a hint of irritation in her expression.

'About Lucy, yes, I heard you,' he replied.

'I thought you might have a little more to say about it,' she murmured.

'What do you want me to say, Beth? I'm glad they're

186

keeping her alive? I'm glad that in five months or less they'll be pulling the plug? Is that what you want to hear?'

She regarded him warily.

'I'm afraid I can't quite share your enthusiasm for Lucy's death.'

'You knew what she was like.'

'That doesn't mean I have to applaud because they're switching off her machine as soon as they've delivered the baby.'

The pain was getting worse.

'I don't care about Lucy, just the baby,' Beth told him.

'You've already told me that a dozen times,' he said, wearily.

How did Karen Gregson know about the baby?

'Beth, how much did you know about Lucy before she came here? Her friends, where she went. Things like that,' he wanted to know.

She shrugged.

'I only know what she told me,' Beth said, flatly.

Could Lucy and Karen Gregson have met somewhere? Could she have been pregnant then?

'Why?' Beth wanted to know.

'Just curious,' he said.

How the hell could Karen have known about the baby?

Beth regarded him indifferently for a moment, watching as he continued to massage his own neck.

'Do you want me to do that for you?' she asked, her tone softening.

'I thought you'd never ask,' he said, smiling, watching as she got to her feet and walked around to where he was sitting. He leaned forward, feeling her hands kneeding his shoulders and neck. He sighed appreciatively.

Should he mention what Karen had said?

Beth continued with her expert manipulations.

Parker decided not to say anything.

'I'm going back into work next week,' she told him.

'So soon?'

187

'Well, as you keep telling me, I'm not sorry Lucy's dead, why be a hypocrite about it? Besides, I get bored at home on my own. I don't suppose there's any chance of you taking a couple of days off?'

'Not now.'

'I didn't think there would be.'

'Come on, Beth, you know it's not that easy. I can't just walk in and tell Flynn I'm taking two or three days off. They need time to rearrange rotas, re-assign consultants to my patients.'

'I get the point,' she said, irritably.

There was a long silence as Beth stood behind him, still massaging gently.

'I'm going to speak to Doctor Leighton tomorrow,' she said, finally. 'I want to know where we stand with guardianship of Lucy's baby once it's born.'

'Beth, for Christ's sake—'

She cut him short.

'I know it doesn't matter to you, Simon,' she snapped, pulling away from him. 'But this baby means everything to me.'

'Beth, don't build your hopes up,' he said, imploringly. 'You don't even know if it will survive.'

'Doctor Leighton said they'd do everything they could for it.'

'I'm sure they will but there are so many dangers,' Parker insisted.

'It might be a slim chance but it's better than no chance at all. It's better than the chance you and I have got of having a baby of our own. You know that can never happen. At least Lucy's child would give us something. Why can't you see that?'

'Don't you think I do? I'm just asking you to be realistic. The baby's chances are fifty-fifty and even if it survives, the odds on us being given custody are hundreds to one. I can only see pain in this, Beth, one way or another.'

'And what do you think I'm feeling now?' she blurted.

'What do you think I've been feeling ever since I found out I couldn't have children? Do you think it could be any worse? We've got one last chance and *I'm* not letting it go. If you don't want to support me, that's fine but I'm telling you, Simon, I'm not giving up. I want that child and I'll have it. With your help or without it.'

She turned and walked out of the kitchen.

He rose, prepared to follow her but then heard her footfalls on the stairs.

Parker sat down again, his head still throbbing.

He glanced out of the kitchen window to see that night was sliding across the land, forcing the dying sun from the sky. Darkness was brewing and he felt as if some of it was seeping, uninvited, into his soul.

Images flashed through his mind with savage rapidity.

Lucy.

Karen Gregson.

The baby.

He could picture Beth holding a child.

Lucy's child?

Parker exhaled deeply and sank forward on to the table, the headache now pounding inside his skull.

The only accompaniment to his thoughts was the steady ticking of the wall clock. He glanced up at it.

9.47 p.m.

He could hear Beth moving around upstairs.

Parker got the feeling it was going to be a long night.

189

Fifty-Eight

Damian Wilks felt cold. The stone corridors of Brackley Heath always made him shiver, especially at night. It was as if the grey stonework were draining all the warmth from those who passed by.

As he walked he could hear his own footsteps echoing in the stillness, the only other sound that of the wind outside. It whipped around the building, rushed through the branches of the trees close to the great grey monolith, and occasionally rattled the windows in their frames.

The only good thing about night duty was that it was normally quiet but, other than that, he hated it. It involved living a kind of vampiric existence. Sleeping during the day then rising with the onset of evening, and it usually messed up his body clock for at least a week afterwards. He was glad he was required to do nights only one week in every month. There were some nurses who did nights permanently but Wilks could never understand how they adjusted.

There were more suicide attempts during the hours of darkness, too.

He'd only had to deal with one during his time at Brackley Heath, but one was enough.

The man had been old, in his early seventies, and he'd cut his throat with a razor blade.

One of the other patients had alerted staff. By the time Wilks found the man, he'd staggered up and down the ward spraying blood from his gashed throat over a wide area and over most of the other patients in the dormitory.

Wilks had managed to prevent himself from vomiting.

At least until he reached the toilet, anyway.

The old man had died long before the ambulance arrived.

Wilks came to the end of the corridor and turned to his left, towards a flight of steps.

He was about to descend when the lights flickered and died.

The stairwell and the corridor behind him were plunged into impenetrable darkness.

'Shit,' murmured Wilks, grabbing the banister, careful not to overbalance and trip on the top step.

He waited a moment and the lights came back on.

Perhaps it was the wind, he thought. As he descended he could hear it gusting with ever increasing ferocity around the building. Maybe it had brought down a power line somewhere close by.

He was halfway down when the lights went out again.

He overbalanced, his foot slipping off the edge of a step. Wilks gripped the handrail more tightly, stumbling a few more steps and only just managing to remain upright.

The lights came back on again.

He looked up at the banks of fluorescents in the ceiling and muttered something to himself.

The tubes of light emitted a soft buzz.

Wilks hurried to the foot of the stairs, not wanting to fall should the electrics decide to go haywire again.

He wondered if the lights were being affected all over the hospital or just in the East Wing, where he was now. He'd have to report the fault of course. He was due to meet up with Frank Jennings at the dayroom in another ten minutes, he'd tell the older man about the faulty lights.

Wilks set off down the corridor to his right, once again aware of the steady tattoo of his own footsteps.

An emergency door lay ahead.

He selected the key from his chain to open it.

The lights went out again.

'For fuck's sake,' muttered Wilks, irritably. He could

barely see his hand in front of him. The only light permeating the cloying umbra surrounding him came from a window at the top of the stairs.

Dull grey light crept through from outside and lit up about half of the stairway.

Wilks looked up at the dormant fluorescent, waiting for it to come back on again.

It didn't.

He heard a shout somewhere off to his left, probably from one of the dormitories. One of the patients disturbed by the sudden darkness. Wilks made a note to check as soon as the lights came back on.

If they did.

Muttering to himself he fumbled for the key to the emergency door and tried to slot it into the lock, having to feel his way.

The key slipped and fell from his grasp.

He dropped to his knees, scrabbling around in the darkness.

The lights came back on and Wilks snatched up the key angrily.

The wind was howling madly now, screaming around the building like a wild thing.

He shivered. The bloody heating must have been affected as well as the lights, he thought. There was a radiator directly opposite him and yet it was freezing in the corridor.

Don't tell me the bloody thing has broken too.

He crossed to it and pressed his hand against the metal.

'Jesus,' he hissed, pulling away his hand sharply.

The radiator was red hot. He glanced down at the temperature dial and saw that it was twisted round to maximum.

Then why was it so cold in the corridor?

He was still wondering when the lights went out again.

Fifty-Nine

Jennings was heading towards the Secure Ward when he heard the scream.

It was hardly an uncommon sound at night in Brackley Heath. Screams, sobs, shouts and any combination of the three were practically guaranteed at some time during the hours of darkness. One of the patients dreaming probably.

But this sound had a searing quality to it that stopped him dead.

He waited a second or two, listening to the sound of the wind raging around the building.

The second scream seemed to mingle with a particularly powerful gust of wind, combining together to form one deafening ululation.

Jennings turned swiftly to his left, towards the dormitory from which the sound had come.

The curtains around most of the beds were open, many of the patients sitting up, some of them already climbing out of bed.

Jennings muttered under his breath as he saw this scene of potential pandemonium unfolding before his eyes. There was already a low chorus of murmuring which was growing in volume.

He looked around, trying to locate the source of the scream.

He didn't have to wait long.

The sound seemed to fill the room, reverberating around the high-ceilinged room and drumming in Jennings' ears.

193

He scanned the faces, most of which were turned towards him.

'Nurse,' someone nearby called.

He ignored the call, moving further into the dormitory, pulling open curtains as he went until every bed in the room was exposed.

Outside, the wind was reaching gale force proportions, slamming the branches of nearby trees against the windows with a force that threatened to shatter the glass.

'Someone woke me up,' said a voice beside him.

'And me,' another added.

'Who screamed?' Jennings said.

No one answered.

'Someone woke me up,' the voice next to him persisted.

'It was the noise that woke you,' Jennings told the man who was standing before him in a pair of faded pyjamas.

'No, it was before that,' the man told him. 'Someone tapped me on the shoulder.'

'Someone shook me until I woke up,' another man said.

Jennings spun round.

'Who screamed?' he called once more.

Again his question was met with silence.

'All of you get back into bed,' he said, moving quickly from bed to bed, ushering the more reluctant back to the warmth of their sheets.

After all, it was cold in the dormitory.

'I want to know who woke me up,' the man in the faded pyjamas said as he clambered back into bed.

Jennings ignored him and continued from patient to patient, cajoling, reassuring.

Eventually they all returned to their beds and he prepared to flick off the lights, gazing one last time at the puzzled faces fixed on him.

'Go back to sleep,' he called.

Night lights burned, their dull yellow light barely penetrating the darkness. He noticed one of them flicker then glow more brightly.

There was a sudden crack to his right, so loud it sounded like a gunshot, and he spun round to see that a tree branch had smacked against one of the windows. The spidery twigs seemed to clutch at the glass for a second before slipping back into the blackness beyond.

Jennings stood in the doorway watching the room, looking for any sign of movement, wanting to be sure that all his charges were settled before he moved on.

At the end of the dormitory he saw the curtains flutter slightly.

'Oh Christ,' he murmured. He'd told them to stay in bed. What the hell were they . . .

The curtains by the bed opposite moved.

Then those next to it.

On both sides of the dorm the curtains by the beds flapped simultaneously, as if someone were walking past them, creating a gentle draught.

Jennings wondered whether one of the windows had broken, allowing a breeze into the ward.

He watched as the cotton screens rippled, the breeze that stirred them running the full length of the dorm.

Jennings felt a sudden icy chill envelop him. A coldness so intense he sucked in a deep breath. It was as if someone had injected liquid nitrogen into his veins.

Then the feeling passed.

The curtains hung still in the dorm.

The only sound was the raging of the wind outside.

He closed the dormitory door and turned back into the corridor, intent on reaching the Secure Ward.

As he walked the lights above him flickered slightly.

Jennings looked up, muttering to himself.

He turned a corner and found himself facing the door to the Secure Ward.

That door was standing wide open.

Sixty

Grey light leaked from the end of the corridor, feebly forcing its way in through the window at the top of the stairs.

Damian Wilks turned and headed towards this island of light, wondering how much longer the fluorescents were going to be off. He thought about hitting one of the emergency buttons but realised it would be pointless, probably even dangerous.

Yes, it might alert someone to the fact that the electrics in the hospital seemed to be up the shoot but it might also cause panic amongst the patients.

Instead he stumbled towards the bottom of the stairs, his hand still throbbing from where he'd touched the red hot heater.

Red hot. And yet the corridor was still icy cold.

Perhaps it was just the wind or the electrics were . . .

A shadow fell across him.

He saw the dark outline and realised it came from the top of the stairs.

Someone was standing there, silhouetted against the dim outline of the window.

Standing motionless looking down at him.

Were they looking? It was impossible to see the eyes, difficult even to make out a shape.

'Jennings?' he shouted up at the figure that seemed to be part of the darkness. Like a portion of the umbra had detached itself.

Perhaps his older companion had encountered similar problems on his own rounds and had come looking for

196

Wilks to tell him that the power was on the blink.

The figure at the top of the stairs didn't move.

Could it be a patient?

Wilks began climbing the steps, moving cautiously in the gloom, his eyes never leaving the black shrouded figure which remained immobile before him.

Even as he drew closer he couldn't make out the features.

Where the hell were the lights?

The wind thrashed against the building, threatening to dent the stone walls.

Ahead of him, the figure didn't move.

He could trace the outline more clearly now against the window although the blackness outside didn't help.

'Jennings?' he called again, realising that this surely couldn't be his colleague. If it was, he would have answered.

Wilks was halfway up now.

The figure took a step to the left, away from the window.

Wilks shivered, his breath frosting in the air before him.

Jesus, it was getting colder.

It had to be a patient. One of them must have left the dorm.

And yet how could that be, all the dorms were locked?

Wilks tried to quicken his pace but it felt as if his legs had been plunged into deep freeze. Every step was an effort.

He could barely see the figure now, it had been swallowed by the darkness once again.

He heard footsteps moving away from him, moving down the corridor.

All the doors down there were locked, he'd checked them himself. The figure had nowhere to hide.

Wilks reached the top of the stairs and heard the footfalls echoing away down the corridor.

And all the time that bone-numbing cold enveloped him like a freezing blanket.

Could it be an intruder? he thought. Had someone broken into the hospital?

197

He could hear breathing ahead of him as he strode along the corridor.

Whoever was in the passageway with him had nowhere to run.

The lights flashed back on with almost blinding brilliance.

The corridor was empty.

Wilks looked around.

He was alone.

The doors to his right, his left and ahead of him were all locked with the keys which he himself carried and there was no way the figure could have slipped past him going back the other way.

'What the hell is this?' he murmured.

The wind screeching wildly outside sounded like distant laughter.

He had to find Jennings.

Sixty-One

Frank Jennings slowed his pace as he approached the open door. Through it he could see the Secure Ward.

Only as he reached the door did he accelerate slightly, checking the door of each room carefully, glancing through the observation slots and studying each of those housed within.

He left Karen Gregson until last.

In the restraining cell, she was sleeping soundly.

Jennings turned away and headed back to the main door.

How the hell had it been opened? He had the only key amongst the night staff. The only other men authorised to carry keys to this part of the hospital were the consultants.

He checked the alarm next to the door but found it untampered with.

Shaking his head he pushed shut the door and locked it.

It was as he was checking the alarm again that he heard footsteps behind him.

Spinning round he saw Wilks running towards him, his face pale and greasy with perspiration.

'Have you been near this door?' Jennings snapped, jabbing a finger at the offending partition.

Wilks shook his head.

'I've been checking out the East Wing like you told me to. Why?'

Jennings waved a hand dismissively.

'What the hell's wrong with the lights?' Wilks asked.

'It must be this bloody wind. It could have brought a power line down somewhere close by. Good job it hasn't affected the alarms.'

Wilks wondered about mentioning the figure he'd seen.

Or thought he'd seen.

'What's the matter with *you*?' Jennings snapped.

'Nothing,' Wilks told him, wiping sweat from his face.

'I bet you were shitting yourself when the lights went out, weren't you?' Jennings chuckled.

Wilks didn't answer.

The two men set off back down the corridor towards the small room which passed for a staff room. Jennings paused to check the locks on a nearby window.

Something smacked against the glass, startling him.

Tree branch, he thought, angry with himself for allowing Wilks to see him jump.

But that couldn't be. The nearest tree was twenty feet away.

Jennings cupped his hands around his eyes and looked out into the darkness, squinting in an effort to penetrate the tenebrious gloom.

From where he stood he could see over part of the

hospital's gardens, the heavy cloud cover parting momentarily to spill some dull light on the neatly manicured lawns.

At first Jennings thought the dark shape was shadow.

It was close to the edge of the lawn, moving away towards some hedges on the left.

Shadow, he told himself.

The shape had been cast by deviations in the light, the silhouettes of trees and hedges.

'What is it?' Wilks wanted to know.

'Nothing,' Jennings said, stepping away from the window.

Wilks moved towards the glass but his older companion grabbed his arm and pulled him away.

'I said it was nothing,' he snapped.

Wilks pulled loose and they walked back towards the staff room, the younger man wishing that this night would come to an end. He glanced at his watch and saw that the second hand wasn't moving.

'Shit, what's the time?' he asked.

Jennings glanced at his own watch.

'I don't know,' he muttered, irritably. 'My bloody watch has stopped.'

Both men looked at their timepieces.

The hands of both were frozen at 12.49 a.m.

Sixty-Two

Beth drifted in and out of sleep, unable to catch more than twenty or thirty minutes' at a time.

She rolled on to her back and stared at the ceiling, her eyelids heavy but determined not to close, her mind insistent that she be denied the peaceful oblivion of restful sleep.

Beside her, Parker slept, and she rolled over and watched him in the gloom of the bedroom, studying his face then the rhythmic rise and fall of his chest.

She'd been sleeping when he'd come to bed but, despite his attempts to move around quietly, he'd woken her. However, Beth had given no indication of this, merely lain still and waited for him to settle down beside her.

She continued to gaze at him.

Why didn't he share her enthusiasm for the baby?

Maybe because it isn't his.

But it could be his. Could be *theirs*. Beth had been considering every option in her mind. She would visit their solicitor, see if there were any precedents for such a case. Surely, as Lucy's only living relative she must have some kind of prior claim on the unborn child. More so than a stranger. Why should someone else take this child that would mean so much to her?

And to Simon too.

Why wouldn't he admit how much he wanted a child?

That child.

She lay still, listening as the wind screamed around the house.

She closed her eyes, wanting to sleep, wishing she could seek refuge in the oblivion of sleep, but it would not come.

Beth moved closer to her husband, feeling the warmth from his body, hoping that it would drive away the chill she felt seeping through her. Through the room.

She shivered and pulled the duvet tighter around her neck.

Parker stirred slightly in his sleep and, for a moment, she thought she'd woken him but he merely rolled on to his back, his breathing still even.

She looked across at the glowing red digits on the radio alarm.

12.49 a.m.

Beth frowned.

It had to be later than that. She felt as if she'd been in bed for hours.

She reached out for her watch and squinted at the hands in the gloom.

12.49.

She muttered to herself. She'd have to reset the alarm, they'd oversleep otherwise.

There was a clock in the spare room.

(*Lucy's room.*)

She'd reset the timepieces against that.

Moving as quietly as she could, Beth slipped out of bed and pulled on her dressing gown.

God, it was freezing. The heating switched itself off at midnight. It must be considerably later than 12.49 for the house to be this cold.

The sky, filled with bloated black and grey clouds, gave no indication of what time it might be. There was certainly no promise of dawn in those forbidding heavens. She guessed it must be around two.

Beth padded out of the room, muttering to herself when a board creaked loudly beneath her. She glanced back towards Parker but saw that he was still asleep. She hurried across the landing towards the door of the spare room.

She was about to enter when she heard a sound from downstairs.

Beth froze, her ears attuned to the noise, homing in on it like a bat's radar.

It came from directly below her.

From the sitting room.

She heard a scratching sound, like fingernails on wood, then the groan of door hinges.

Beth stood motionless, her heart hammering madly against her ribs.

She heard footsteps crossing the hall beneath her. Tentative, cautious movements designed for stealth.

Beth turned as slowly as she could and, placing one bare foot gingerly in front of the other, she crept towards the wooden ballustrade and peered over the landing, down into the black maw of the hallway.

She could see nothing but she could still hear those footsteps moving quietly across the hall.

There was more scratching.

Fingers on wood.

Beth ran to the bedroom as quickly as she could, her throat dry, her eyes bulging in their sockets. She shook Parker, leaning close to him.

He woke suddenly, found himself looking into her staring eyes.

'Simon,' she rasped, her breath coming in gasps.

'What's wrong?' he groaned, trying to force the drowsiness from his mind.

She jabbed a finger towards the landing, her hand shaking madly.

'Beth, what's wrong?' he said, gripping her shoulders, his own concern now growing.

She tried to swallow but couldn't, the words caught in her throat and emerged as a hoarse whisper.

'I think there's someone downstairs.'

He sat up, swinging his legs out of bed, his mind spinning.

Stay calm.

He didn't even bother to pull on his dressing gown, just scurried, naked, to the bedroom door, his ears alert for any sound.

'Call the police,' he said, trying to keep his voice low.

She scrambled for the phone beside the bed and snatched up the receiver.

'Oh God,' she whimpered. 'The line's dead.'

She flicked the cradle furiously.

Maybe she'd been wrong.

He would have to check.

He snatched up the vase on the unit near their bed. It

was tall and slim but heavy, Waterford crystal. A wedding present.

It had become a weapon.

'Stay here,' she gasped, seeing him approach the bedroom door.

'Keep trying the phone,' he told her, moving further out on to the landing.

'Simon.'

He gripped the vase like a crystal cosh, his heart pounding hard.

He swallowed hard, prepared to cross the landing.

It was then he heard the first unmistakable footfall on the bottom step.

Someone was coming up.

Sixty-Three

Parker thought that the rational part of his mind would hold his fear in check. He expected, naively, that his educated, logical mind would force the doubts away and tell him loudly that the noise he heard was settling boards.

But the panic-override button which he expected to be automatically pressed inside his supposedly logical mind never kicked in.

He felt fear unlike he'd ever known before.

There was someone coming up the fucking stairs.

Someone had broken into their house,

(Christ knows how they'd by-passed the alarm)

stumbled about downstairs and now they were heading for the first floor, and all Parker had to defend himself was a fucking crystal vase.

Should he move closer to the head of the stairs and meet the intruder?

Should he duck back into one of the other rooms and take the interloper by surprise?

His mind was spinning, his heart thudding madly against his ribs.

Think.

He took a step forward and slapped at the light switch.

The staircase was empty.

No one was climbing inexorably towards him.

No intruder was trekking towards the first floor.

'Jesus Christ,' Parker sighed, swallowing hard and relaxing his grip on the vase so much he almost dropped it.

He peered over the banister into the hall.

It too was empty.

'Simon.'

He turned to see Beth crouching on the end of the bed staring at him.

He held up a hand to signal to her that everything was fine.

'Is the phone still out?' he wanted to know.

She stabbed a few digits.

'It's working,' she called back.

'Bloody phone company, that's all,' he said, by way of explanation.

She swung herself off the bed and scurried across to join him, slipping one arm through his. When he looked at her he saw how pale she was.

'I heard someone down there, I know I did,' she whispered.

'It must have been the wind,' he told her, moving towards the top step, the vase still clutched in his hand.

As if to reinforce his theory, a particularly savage gust struck the house.

Parker made his way down the stairs, crossing the hallway quickly and pressing the four digits which silenced the alarm that had been tripped by his appearance. He looked at the key pad.

Beth wandered down after him, pulling her dressing gown more tightly around herself.

She felt cold.

'What's wrong?' she wanted to know, seeing how intently Parker was looking at the control pad of the alarm.

'The zone light for the sitting room is still on,' said Parker.

The alarm was tripped by sensors, one located in each downstairs room. These corresponded to zones on the main control pad and if anyone broke in, the room into which they gained entry would be illuminated on the main pad.

The red zone light for the sitting room was flashing.

It meant that someone was in that room.

'Stay here,' he said to Beth, moving towards the closed door.

Again she tried to pull him back but he shook his head, waving her back, leaning against the door, his ears alert for the slightest sound.

There's no one in there.

His mind screamed it at him.

He closed his hand over the door handle and pushed it down gently.

Open it.

He hesitated a moment longer.

Beth took a step back.

And if there is someone in there . . .?

He pushed open the door, shoving hard so that it swung back on its hinges.

Parker snapped on the lights.

The room was empty. He crossed quickly to each of the windows. None had been tampered with.

'It must be an electrical fault with the alarm, we'd better get it checked out,' trying to disguise the note of relief in his voice.

Beth started to giggle.

'What's wrong?' he said as he turned to face her.

She could only chuckle and point at him.

Then Parker began to laugh too, the chill enveloping him.

No wonder he was cold. In his haste to confront the intruders he'd neglected to put on any clothes. Not even his robe. Stark naked, he stood in the centre of the sitting room clutching the vase.

'I don't know which would have scared them most,' Beth laughed pointing at him. 'The vase or you.' She looked at his groin.

Parker was laughing now. Loudly, almost uncontrollably.

He wondered if it was relief.

They headed back upstairs, still chuckling, and as he pulled her close to him, he felt the warmth of her body against him.

'I wouldn't have known which weapon to use on them,' he said, smiling broadly.

Beth was giggling like a schoolgirl, tears coursing down her cheeks.

They slid into bed side by side, holding each other tightly.

Outside, the wind continued to roar angrily around the house.

Sixty-Four

'What are *you* doing here?'

Beth heard the voice as she locked the Astra, and turned to see Caroline Seaton approaching.

'That's a nice greeting,' Beth said, smiling. 'I was expecting maybe "Hello, Beth, nice to have you back" or "You're looking well, Beth".' She chuckled.

'You know what I mean,' Caroline said, touching her arm. 'I didn't expect you back so soon, none of us did.'

The two women headed across the car park towards the main building, the first hint of rain in the air making them quicken their pace.

'I wasn't doing anything at home,' Beth said. 'I thought I might as well be here where I'm useful to someone, instead of moping around the house.'

Hardly moping.

'I'm sorry about what happened to your sister,' Caroline told her as they entered reception and headed for the lifts.

Beth merely nodded almost imperceptibly.

Should she mention the baby?

'She was your only family, wasn't she?' Caroline persisted.

'Yes.'

The lift bumped to a halt at the floor they wanted and the two women stepped out.

'Listen, Beth, I know it's the worst cliché anyone can come out with at a time like this, but if there *is* anything I can do . . .' Caroline allowed the sentence to trail off.

'I'm fine, Caroline, really. Thanks anyway,' Beth said, her smile genuine.

Why shouldn't it be? This was no brave front. This was for real.

'I just think I'll be better back here, with people around me,' Beth continued.

'I'll see you for lunch,' Caroline said, wandering off towards her desk.

Beth passed through into the inner office and sat down at her desk. She sighed, caught sight of her reflection in the blank VDU screen then switched the machine on.

She got to her feet and crossed to David Manning's office, knocking gently on the door. A voice beckoned her in.

As she stepped in, Manning's face clearly reflected his surprise.

He got to his feet.

'Beth, I wasn't expecting you for a week or so,' he said. 'Are you all right?'

'I'm fine,' she told him.

'You shouldn't have rushed back.'

'I wanted to come back.'

'Well, we've just about managed to cope without you but it's been a struggle,' he laughed. His tone changed then, softened. 'If you find it's too much for you then just go home again. Take as long as you want, I said that at the beginning.'

'I appreciate that but I can't stay locked away forever, can I?'

'What's the news on your sister?'

Beth shrugged. 'They can't do anything for her, I'm afraid.'

'How long will they leave her on life support, if you don't mind me asking?'

'I don't know,' she lied.

'It must have been terrible for you, I'm very sorry.'

Beth smiled weakly.

'I just thought I'd let you know I was here,' she said before wandering back out to her desk.

There were memos in her trays, computer printouts, hand-written notes. She decided to open the mail that had just been set down on her desk.

Next Beth pressed a button on her computer and the screen lit up, words flashing across it.

She tapped in her password while she glanced at the mail. After a second or two the screen flickered again and Beth glanced at it.

She frowned.

One word had appeared, repeated dozens of times in endless rows across the screen.

LUCY

Beth frowned and sat back from the screen.

What the hell was this?

She pressed Delete, then went in again.

It flashed up again. Spreading across the screen with alarming speed like some electronic rash.

LUCY LUCY LUCY LUCY LUCY LUCY LUCY LUCY LUCY LUCY LUCY

Beth tapped in Override and waited.

The screen remained blank.

All that Beth could see was her own reflection in the glass.

She waited.

Still nothing.

And waited.

She typed in Access.

Blank screen.

She was about to reach for the phone to call maintenance when the screen flickered into life again and she was relieved to see the main menu flashing before her.

She shook her head and began her work.

Hallucinations? Maybe someone had been messing about with the machine.

She smiled and started typing.

Beth was so immersed in her work that she did not notice the time slipping by.

Caroline popped her head around the door of the outer office and tapped the face of her watch.

'Come on, you,' she said, reproachfully. 'God, I hate conscientious workers.'

Beth chuckled and switched off her unit. Picking up her bag and jacket, she followed Caroline out.

Had she looked back she may well have seen the light on the VDU screen.

The letters came slowly this time. One by one, as if tapped out by fingers unfamiliar with a keyboard.

L
The keys were not moving.
U
The letters flickered brightly.
C
They were like tiny strobes on the blank screen.
Y

```
      L
L  U  C  Y
      C
      Y
```

Sixty-Five

'When was the last time you heard the voices, Karen?' Parker asked, sitting back in his seat, his eyes never leaving his patient.

Karen Gregson didn't answer him; she merely stared past him as if gazing at something behind his left shoulder.

'Did they speak to you last night?' he persisted.

'I don't always hear them,' she said, continuing to look beyond him. 'I know they're there but I don't always hear them.'

'Are they speaking to you now?' he wanted to know.

Karen shook her head.

'Can I ask *you* a question?' she said, finally fixing her gaze upon him, turning those soft blue eyes towards him as if they were sapphire searchlights.

'Of course you can,' he said, excited that she was opening up more.

'Do you blame your wife for not being able to have children?' she said, inquisitively, a slight smile on her face.

Parker swallowed hard, attempting to hide his shock but finding it impossible.

'What makes you say that, Karen?' he asked, his voice low.

'I wondered if you were angry with her, after all, it is *her* fault, isn't it? She's the one who can't conceive.'

Parker felt the hairs rise on the back of his neck.

Those fingers were plucking away again.

'What makes you think my wife can't have children?' he wanted to know.

'She can't, can she?'

There had to be some kind of association here, he thought. Karen had been obsessed with her own children. This was an extension of her paranoid feelings. *She* had no children, she couldn't bear to think of anyone else with them.

Simple, eh?

He studied her closely, aware that her eyes never left him.

'Do you blame her for it?' she continued. 'I mean, it's not as if she could ever have one, is it? A ruptured fallopian tube is serious and the infection she had too.'

Parker frowned.

Explain that away.

He sat forward on his seat.

This was more than a lucky guess. She was *too* specific.

But how could she know?

'Did the voices tell you this about my wife?' he wanted to know.

She shook her head.

'Do you blame her for it, Simon?' she persisted.

'No, I don't,' he snapped.

'Don't get angry with me, you said I could ask you a question.'

He got to his feet and began pacing the room slowly, his mind spinning.

'Did the voices tell you to say that about my wife?'

She shook her head again.

'I just wanted to know,' she told him. 'How do you feel about having to go through the rest of your life without children because your wife can't have them? You wanted children, didn't you, Simon? You both did, but you were trying to be brave, you were trying to protect your wife, make her feel that you weren't angry with her, but you *are* angry, aren't you?'

The knot of muscles at the side of his jaw pulsed.

'Children can be wonderful,' she said.

'Then why did you kill *yours*?' he snapped, angry with himself for using such a harsh tone.

'They weren't *my* children,' she said.

'Then whose were they?'

She smiled crookedly at him.

He held her gaze.

'Whose children were they, Karen?' he persisted, his patience running out.

'Do you believe in God, Simon?' she said, softly.

The question caught him unawares.

He hesitated a moment then nodded stiffly.

'My children came from God,' she told him, smiling serenely. 'They are *His*.'

'Then why kill them?'

'I saved them. I stopped them growing up in such a terrible world.' She chuckled. 'Don't you think it's strange that God can't look after the rest of the world and yet he decides to bring two more children into it? And he chose *me* to bring them into the world.'

'And did God tell you to murder them?'

She shook her head.

'*They* told me and they were right,' she said.

'The voices told you to kill them?'

Karen nodded.

'You haven't told me yet who these voices belong to,' he reminded her.

Karen Gregson lowered her gaze, her eyes fixed on the

mattress beneath her.

'Tell me how the voices know about my wife and me,' Parker persisted.

She looked up at him and the smile that spread slowly across her lips sent a shiver down his spine.

'There's a new voice now, Simon,' she said, softly. 'And she's angry.'

'Who does the voice belong to, Karen?' he asked.

She sat back and closed her eyes.

'Karen,' he repeated, moving a fraction closer.

Still she didn't move.

Thirty minutes passed before Parker got to his feet and left the room. He looked back through the observation slot then hurried off to his office.

There was something he had to do.

Sixty-Six

'What the fuck is it with this place?' snapped Frank Jennings. 'Has someone been slipping speed into the bedtime drinks?' He slumped down into his chair in the staff room, needing to relax before he went off duty, and reached for the mug of tea Damian Wilks pushed towards him. 'Eleven patients reported that they were woken up in the night by someone pulling at them, grabbing their shoulders or something. Perhaps we ought to give them all Mogadon.'

'Eleven?' Wilks mused.

'I'm surprised it wasn't more.'

'I had nine reports,' the younger man said.

Jennings frowned.

'Exactly the same thing,' Wilks went on. 'They said

214

they'd been woken up in the middle of the night by someone shaking them, three or four said someone had whispered in their ears, told them to wake up.'

Jennings shook his head.

'They'll all be at it tonight, once one starts they'll all be playing the bloody game,' the older man hissed.

'Twenty patients in one night report being woken up, what the hell is it?'

'They're crazy, that's what it is. Have you forgotten where we are? Did any of them say who woke them up? It wasn't the Devil or God, was it?'

'Three or four said it was a young girl.'

'They reckon they saw her?'

Wilks nodded.

'Same here,' Jennings told him. 'At least five of them told me that a young woman had woken them in the night.'

Wilks frowned.

'It's one of the other patients for Christ's sake,' snapped Jennings. 'One of the silly bastards is having a game. It happens all the time.'

'And you think it'll happen again tonight?'

'I'd bet money on it.'

He took a swig of tea and reached for his cigarettes.

Parker flicked through the first of the large tomes on his desk, a pen and paper close by. He found the section he sought and ran his finger down the page until he found what he wanted.

' . . . Two days after the birth of her child, thirty-two-year-old Gillian was intercepted when she began hammering the baby's head. "It's the wrong shape. It's too long," she explained . . . ' Parker read aloud, his voice gradually receding to a whisper then to silence as he scanned the words before him.

Usually there is an acute onset with a complete change of personality overnight.

He scribbled something on his piece of paper.

'I had to have an anaesthetic because the baby wasn't breathing well. The following day I was ill in the form of hearing imaginary voices talking to me.'

Karen's voices.

But who was the new one? Why was she angry?

These ill patients are confused and muddled by bizarre thoughts.

(Like thinking they had given birth to God's children?)

The patient lives in her own fantasy world removed from reality.

Parker exhaled deeply, chewed the end of his pen and continued reading.

She may ask the same question a dozen times over.

(Like Karen Gregson?)

Often there is some slight evidence of reality and word association.

Parker pushed the first book away and reached for the next one, flicking through quickly, scanning the pages anxiously.

Often the sight of a particular person triggers off a whole imaginary sequence.

(Was *he* the trigger?)

Parker slammed shut the book angrily, reached for another and continued his search.

There had to be an explanation somewhere. Some evidence to back up his theory about Karen Gregson's puerperal psychosis, or at least the new stage it had reached.

The answer was here somewhere, he was sure of it.

Wilks looked round as he heard the knock on the staff-room door. The patient standing there was a small, middle-aged man with prematurely white hair.

He raised his hand, like a child in a classroom, as if to attract the nurse's attention.

'What is it, George?' Wilks asked, smiling.

'C-c-c-could you c-c-come, with me, p-p-p-lease,' George Casey stammered, finally, the effort involved

216

apparent on his gaunt face.

Wilks got to his feet and crossed to the door.

Jennings shook his head and watched as his companion joined the patient.

'Just d-d-d-down here,' George said, leading the younger man along the corridor.

They turned a corner and Wilks stopped in his tracks, his eyes widening.

'Jesus Christ,' he murmured then, recovering his voice, he shouted, 'Jennings, come here, quick!'

Some mothers are convinced they are being poisoned, or that they have a religious mission.

(The children of God.)

Parker pushed the book away from him and shook his head.

These were all things he knew. Incidents he'd read about before. He understood, as much as any psychiatrist, what puerperal psychosis did to the sufferer, but something else was troubling him. Something peculiar to Karen Gregson's case.

Some of the things she'd said to him, there would have been no way of her knowing them unless she'd been told; but who could have told her?

How could she have known about his and Beth's inability to have a child?

How did she know that Lucy was pregnant?

The phone rang.

'Parker.'

It was Jennings on the other end, speaking quickly, almost incoherently.

Something about the West Wing.

Something important.

Parker said he'd be there immediately.

The books remained open on his desk.

The stench in the corridor was overpowering.

217

Parker raised one hand to his mouth as he approached, his eyes scanning what was before him.

'When did you find this?' he said, quietly.

'Five minutes ago,' Jennings told him, standing back, as if reluctant to move closer.

'How many of the patients have seen it?' Parker wanted to know.

'It's hard to say,' Jennings told him. 'Three or four. I'm not sure.'

'And you never saw it until Casey pointed it out? How the hell could you miss it?' Parker wanted to know.

'It wasn't here this morning, Doctor Parker, I swear to you,' Wilks told him. 'It's been done in the last ten minutes.'

'That's impossible,' whispered Parker, his eyes fixed ahead, his gaze filled by what he saw.

The letters on the wall were at least six feet high.

FREE ME

They were written in blood.

218

Sixty-Seven

Beth parked the Astra and stood beside it for a moment, looking up at the huge concrete and glass edifice that was St Angela's hospital. The rain clouds that had been gradually darkening the sky were reflected in the glass of the structure and seemed to give it an appearance of mournfulness. A grey hue that mirrored Beth's mood.

She walked briskly across the car park to the main entrance, narrowly avoiding an elderly man in a wheelchair who was being pushed by a younger companion. They both looked at Beth, who marched ahead through the main reception towards the lifts.

It was as she drew closer to the lifts that she saw a familiar figure.

When the figure turned to face her, she smiled.

'Hello, Mrs Parker,' Mark Hennessey said, balancing as best he could on his metal crutches.

Beth looked at his face. It was still criss-crossed by scars, some of which would never disappear. His left ankle was still heavily bandaged and there was a plastercast on his right leg. He moved with practised ease on the crutches, despite an occasional pained look which crossed his face if he put too much weight on the right leg.

There were some plastic-covered seats nearby and Beth steered him towards those, watching as he unhooked himself from the crutches and sat down heavily beside her, wincing slightly.

'I'm sorry about what happened,' he said, refusing to meet her gaze. 'I mean, about Lucy and. . .'

'It wasn't your fault, Mark,' she told him.

'She was on *my* bike.'

'Don't blame yourself, Mark.'

He stared at the floor for a moment.

'What are they going to do with her?' he wanted to know. 'I heard she was on life support.'

'They'll keep her on it until the baby is born,' Beth told him.

'Baby?' he said, shocked. 'I didn't know she was pregnant.'

'Nor did anyone else.'

'Oh my God,' he murmured. 'Whose is it?'

'It doesn't matter. No one knows that either. Why, Mark? Did you and Lucy have sex?'

He blushed and nodded.

Surprise, surprise.

Beth touched his hand gently.

'When do you go home?' she wanted to know.

'At the end of the week,' he said.

Beth got to her feet.

'You take care, I'll see you when you get home,' she told him. 'And, Mark, don't blame yourself for what happened to Lucy. If it hadn't have been you it would have been someone else.'

She turned and headed for the lift.

He watched her step inside, saw the doors slide together and the floor numbers begin to light up as the car rose.

Beth stood alone in the lift, leaning against the back wall, waiting for the appointed floor. When it came she walked out into the reception area, nodded to the duty nurse and headed up the corridor towards Lucy's room.

She hesitated before entering, much as one would pause at the door of someone who was sleeping even though Beth knew there was no fear of waking Lucy.

Ever.

She pushed the door and walked in.

The antiseptic smell inside seemed even stronger than

220

usual and it was particularly warm. So warm in fact that a thin film of condensation had formed on the windows.

Beth sat with Lucy for almost forty-five minutes, not really sure why she had come.

To check on the baby?

She enquired on the way out about the child's health and was told that it seemed to be progressing well under the circumstances.

Beth was happy about that.

The rain clouds were preparing to spill their load as she climbed back into the Astra and started the engine. She glanced in her rear-view mirror, realising that she was able to see the windows of Lucy's room.

Had she looked more closely, she may have seen the outline of a figure peering out from behind the steamy glass.

A figure that stood motionless.

Watching her.

Sixty-Eight

'There must be an injured patient somewhere in the hospital,' said Dr Marcus Flynn, eyeing first Jennings then Wilks who stood before his desk.

'No injuries were reported,' Jennings told him. 'All the patients have been confined to their wards for the time being, the other duty nurses are checking them thoroughly.'

'Are you sure it was blood?' Flynn continued.

'Definitely,' Parker added, still standing with his arms behind his back. He was staring out across the front lawns of Brackley Heath. He watched as two visitors wheeled an elderly patient down a pathway, disappearing behind a row of conifers.

An uneasy silence descended, the ticking of the wall clock the only sound in the solitude.

Wilks shifted uncomfortably, lowering his gaze slightly.

Jennings remained ramrod straight, as if he'd been called to attention.

Old habits died hard.

It was Flynn who finally broke the silence, sighing wearily.

'Well, gentlemen,' he said. 'What's done is done, I'm not looking to blame someone.'

That makes a fucking change, thought Parker.

'I'm only concerned with the welfare of the patients and how this might affect them.' He looked at Parker. 'First that business with Karen Gregson attacking the other woman and now this.'

Parker thought about turning around but then decided not to rise to the bait.

'Just clean it up,' the older man added, dismissively.

'That's already been taken care of,' Jennings added.

Flynn waved them away and the two nurses left the room. Parker remained where he was, staring out of the window, watching as a slight breeze set the conifers waving.

'At least this is one thing you can't blame on me or my methods,' he said, sardonically.

Flynn chose to ignore the remark. 'Do you have any idea how it might have happened?' he asked.

'None at all. If it *was* a patient then it doesn't conform to any kind of behaviour I've ever seen consistent with mental disorders of *any* kind.'

'Your extensive knowledge of the field leads you to that conclusion, does it?' Flynn said, acidly.

'What are *your* theories on it, then?' Parker snapped, turning to face the older man.

'You said *if* it was a patient. What are you trying to imply?'

'I'm not trying to imply anything, I'm just trying to look at the whole bloody thing logically. Those letters were at least six feet high. For one thing, it would need a lot of blood to draw letters that size, there was none anywhere except on the wall. No splashes, no drops. Nothing. It would also require time. I'm just looking for explanations.'

'And?'

'I don't have one,' Parker muttered.

'You surprise me, Simon,' Flynn said, smiling thinly.

Parker shot the older man an angry glance.

'Have you made any further progress with Karen Gregson?' Flynn wanted to know. 'And, by the way, it might interest you to know that Jane Owen has lost the use of that eye. I wouldn't blame you for feeling a little responsible for *that*.'

Parker clenched his fists behind his back.

Should he tell Flynn about his latest conversation with Karen?

About the fact that she knew things concerning him it was impossible for her to know?

Perhaps Flynn would come to the same conclusion as Parker.

Flynn was still looking at him.

'Have you made any further progress?' the older man persisted.

'The psychosis seems to be more or less under control,' Parker said. 'She's spoken of a possible reason why she killed her children.'

'Delusionary?'

Parker nodded.

'So tell me,' Flynn demanded.

'She thinks they were God's children.' He continued to tell the older man what else Karen Gregson had said about her dead offspring.

Tell him what else she said.

'That's not unusual,' Flynn said.

'I know that. I've read of other similar cases. One

woman thought that she was Eve, her husband was Adam and their baby was an angel. Many of the sufferers attach some kind of religious importance to their children. Some are killed to prevent them being exposed to evil forces which the mothers are convinced are waiting to take them.' Parker ran a hand through his hair.

'So you know why she killed her children?'

'That's only part of the reason.'

'But it's more than we had when she was first admitted.'

'The nature of the psychosis is changing. It isn't internalised any longer.'

Tell him about the conversations.

Flynn frowned.

'She's making *me* a part of her psychosis,' Parker announced.

'In what way?'

Tell him.

'She's begun exhibiting symptoms that are obviously allied to puerperal psychosis but which I've never seen before.'

'Such as?'

Parker sucked in a deep breath and walked around the desk until he was facing Flynn across it. The younger man leaned forward on to the oak-topped cabinet, propping himself on his fists.

'I think she may be telepathic,' he said, flatly.

Flynn didn't speak, he merely sat back in his chair and gently pressed his fingertips together, regarding Parker over the steepled digits.

The younger man stepped away from the desk waiting for his colleague to speak.

Had he made a mistake mentioning his theory?

'Telepathic,' Flynn said, quietly, as if he were using the word for the first time. 'What evidence do you have to support this?'

'It's just an idea,' Parker told him.

'Those afflicted with psychological problems aren't

224

usually blessed with psychic gifts, Simon,' Flynn said, a slight smile on his lips. 'What makes you think she's telepathic? Have you been doing card tricks with her?'

'She's told me things about me it would be impossible for her to know,' Parker snapped. 'Things only *I* could know.'

'How do you know she hasn't picked them up from staff members?'

'Because I don't talk about my private life to the staff here. There's no one here I have enough respect for to share my private life with.' He looked straight at Flynn.

'So what's Karen Gregson been saying?' Flynn demanded.

'I'd rather not discuss it.'

'If it forms the basis for your rather wild claims, Simon, surely it's important enough.'

'It's important to me. It's nobody's concern but mine. I'm only interested in how she could possibly know these things. I am offering the possibility that some form of telepathy could be the next stage of the psychosis.'

Flynn shook his head dismissively.

'So you *know* for a fact that it couldn't happen?'

Parker glared at his older colleague.

'I'm afraid that your ideas are a little grandiose, Simon,' Flynn said. 'I've never read or seen anything linking puerperal psychosis to telepathy.'

'So because you've never experienced it before, you dismiss it?' snapped Parker. 'If Fleming had dismissed mould cultures we wouldn't have penicillin now. It's the same principle. Jesus, you're so fucking blind.'

'Get out of here,' Flynn said. 'I've heard enough.'

'You're terrified I might be right, aren't you? Afraid of what might be the truth?'

Flynn sat forward. 'If you believe this theory, prove it,' he said, challengingly.

Parker nodded.

'I'd be happy to,' he said, his tone softening. 'But I need

225

your help.' He held Flynn's gaze. 'And it isn't going to be pleasant.'

Sixty-Nine

As Beth pulled the Astra into the short driveway of the house she saw the light burning in the sitting room.

She smiled, thinking that Simon must have got home before her. He must have parked the car in the garage. Her smile faded slightly as she wondered if she should tell him she'd been to the hospital. If she mentioned the baby again they'd probably end up having an argument about it and Beth didn't want that.

She still found it hard to understand why he didn't share her enthusiasm, though. But she knew that, in time, he'd come round to her way of thinking.

The logical answer, the *only* one as far as she was concerned, was for them to have Lucy's child when it was born. To hell with the bureaucratic red tape he'd spoken of There had to be a way of getting the child. Surely no one was more deserving of it than she. Could anyone have suffered so much pain over an inability to bear children of her own?

He would see her point of view eventually.

She swung herself out of the Astra and locked it.

It was later than she'd thought and the sky was darkening rapidly. She wondered how long Simon had been home, if he'd cooked them anything. If not they could always get a takeaway.

She glanced towards the sitting-room light, smiling as she saw the comforting glow it gave off. The house looked welcoming. It was a refuge for them after what had gone on in the last few weeks with Lucy. And, more importantly, it was *theirs* again.

Another light came on, this time in one of the bedrooms.

Beth fumbled for her key and turned it in the lock.

The door wouldn't move.

She withdrew the key, wondering if she'd selected the wrong one but saw that she hadn't.

The hall light flashed on.

'Simon,' she called, trying the key once more.

He obviously hadn't heard her.

She called more loudly this time, agitatedly twisting the key in the lock.

From inside the house she heard music. Loud, strident music. Not the kind of thing either of them usually listened to.

They had a ghetto blaster in the kitchen; Simon had bought it for her two years ago as a birthday present. The music was coming from that but it sounded as if the volume had been cranked up to maximum.

She banged the door with her fist, tiring of the stuck key.

'Simon,' she shouted.

The hall light went off.

He must have walked through into the kitchen or sitting room without hearing her, she mused.

Beth bent down and peered through the letter box, trying to catch sight of him.

As she pushed the brass slot the sound of the thunderous music seemed to flood out, stabbing into her ears. She remained in her crouched position, seeing that light was indeed flooding from beneath the closed sitting-room door. She could also see that the kitchen door was shut. And yet, even from behind the closed door, the music was deafening. It drilled into her head incessantly, the shrill scream of guitars and thunder of drums threatening to put cracks in the wall.

No wonder he couldn't hear her calling him.

Beth straightened up and tried the key once more.

227

It turned easily in the lock and she froze in surprise as the door swung open.

The music seemed to envelop her, closing around her like some cacophonous python, filling her head, surrounding her. She strode towards the kitchen, determined to shut off that infernal din.

She called Simon's name as she pushed the door but even her own exhortations were drowned out by the music, the vocalist's words rising above the thundering rhythm:

'. . . *On the eve of destruction, a reign of terror rules the streets* . . .'

Beth winced as the sound pierced her ears.

'. . . *When the heads start rolling, the Devil comes to let it bleed* . . .'

Beth hit the Off button.

Silence.

Beth stood staring at the ghetto blaster for a moment, a hint of irritation in her expression.

'Simon,' she called, heading back towards the sitting room.

There was no answer.

She pushed open the door and walked in.

As she did, the light went out.

Beth muttered in surprise as the room was plunged into darkness and she stood for a moment, blinking, trying to accustom herself to the gloom.

She reached out and slapped on the main light, which flickered weakly for a moment then also went out.

The lamp on the television, the one that had been glowing originally, burst back into life, but now the glow it gave off seemed cold and forbidding, unlike the warm welcoming luminescence it had emitted as she'd pulled up.

She glanced round.

Perhaps Simon was upstairs, she'd seen a light go on. She turned on her heel and headed for the stairs.

The landing light glowed brightly for a second then went out.

Beth slowed her pace slightly as she reached the halfway point of the stairs.

She called his name again, not so loudly this time.

The landing light flickered then settled into a sickly orange glow.

As Beth reached the landing, it went out.

She hadn't realised how dark it was up there. All the doors leading off from the landing were closed; there was very little natural light left to brighten the area.

She reached out for the light switch and pressed it, flicking it repeatedly.

Nothing happened.

'Funny joke, Simon,' she called. 'Ha, ha! There, can you hear me laughing?' There was an edge to her voice. Irritation and something else.

Anxiety?

Fear?

The landing light flashed back on, brightly, forcing Beth to shield her eyes momentarily from the brilliance.

She sucked in an exasperated breath and moved towards their bedroom.

It was in darkness.

There was no sign of Simon's clothes anywhere, nothing to indicate that he'd even been home then gone out again.

Then who'd turned the bloody ghetto blaster on?

The landing light went out again.

'Christ,' she hissed. It had to be some kind of electrical fault.

The fuse box was in a cupboard beneath the stairs. Beth turned and headed back towards the steps.

The landing light was now flashing on and off so quickly it resembled a strobe. She looked up at it, wincing.

As she reached the top of the stairs the ghetto blaster roared into life once more.

She tutted, the sound lost beneath the thudding power spewing from the kitchen.

Electrical fault.

Beth hurried down the stairs, anxious to silence the music again.

'. . . *They pray for your eternal damnation . . .*'

It seemed even louder.

'. . . *They pray for your soul to keep . . .*'

She hit the Stop button hard, ejecting the tape, turning it over in her hand.

There was writing on it, faded pencil letters in a hand she recognised.

Face the fire - The Scorpions

It was Lucy's handwriting.

Seventy

Beth was still gazing at the tape when she heard the rapping on the front door.

What now?

She passed through the hall, glancing up towards the landing as if expecting the light to flash on once more, but the upper floor remained in darkness.

She pulled open the door, a look of surprise crossing her face.

The man who faced her was in his early fifties, short and balding, heavily wrinkled but also deeply tanned. He smiled, even though his mouth seemed to curl downwards rather than up as he did so.

Beth smiled back at Ted Hennessey.

'Hello, Beth,' he said. 'I hope I'm not calling at a bad time.'

She shook her head, coughed and finally managed to speak.

'No, of course not. Come in, Ted,' she said, stepping back and ushering him inside. He wiped his feet exaggeratedly on the mat and entered.

'I saw your car outside when we got back from the hospital. We've been to see Mark,' Hennessey told her. 'I said to Val that we ought to pop in. She said that we should leave you in peace for a while longer but, well, you know me, I wanted to see if there was anything we could do.'

Beth led him through into the kitchen where he seated himself. She filled the kettle and switched it on.

'Mark said he'd seen you at the hospital,' Hennessey continued.

Beth nodded. 'He said he'll be out by the end of the week, that's good news.'

Hennessey smiled. 'He's a strong boy.'

Beth milked and sugared two mugs, dropped in tea bags, then turned to face her neighbour.

'Beth, about your sister, I just wanted to say how sorry we are.'

Beth nodded almost imperceptibly, turning to pour boiling water into the mugs.

'It must have been a terrible shock for you,' Hennessey resumed.

No, actually it was a relief.

'Mark blames himself for the accident.'

'I told him he shouldn't,' Beth said, stirring the tea.

'It hit him hard. He told us they were close.'

Beth, her back to Hennessey, swallowed hard.

'What exactly did he tell you?' she wanted to know.

'He said that he'd been seeing your sister for a while. He told us she'd been round a few times while we were away.'

231

Beth gritted her teeth.

Little bitch.

She crossed to the table and set down a mug of tea in front of Hennessey, seating herself opposite.

'Look, if you'd rather I didn't talk about it . . .'

'No,' she said, cutting him short. 'Please go on. You said Mark and Lucy were close.'

'He's a good kid, a bit of a loner – Val worries about him spending so much time on his own. I think he went a bit overboard on your sister. All that attention from a pretty girl.' Hennessey chuckled.

'What else did he say?'

Hennessey sighed, wearily.

'He said he lent her money.'

'How much?'

'One hundred pounds.'

'Jesus Christ!'

'Did you know about it?'

Beth shook her head.

'I've got a safe in the house, he took it from there.'

'Oh, God, Ted, I'm sorry. I warned her to stay away from Mark, I . . .'

He raised a hand to silence her.

'There's no problem, Beth,' he told her, smiling. 'I think Mark was infatuated with her. He'd have given her anything if she'd asked. I'm not here to ask for the money back, you know.'

Beth sighed.

'She had no right doing that,' Beth said, angrily.

'I said, it's not a problem. That's the least of my worries. You've lost a sister and our son was badly hurt – what's a hundred pounds compared to that?'

Beth didn't answer, merely cradled her mug in her hands.

'I came round to find out how you and Simon were coping, not to tell you I wanted a hundred quid,' Hennessey continued.

232

Beth smiled at him.

'We're fine,' she said, quietly.

The kitchen light flickered slightly.

Beth glanced up at it and tutted.

'Electrical problem?' Hennessey enquired.

She nodded.

'Even the waste disposal is playing up,' she told him.

'Would you like me to have a look at it for you? I'm no handyman but yours is the same model as ours, I think. What's wrong with it?'

'I think it's jammed, there's some muck at the bottom that seems to be making it stick.'

Hennessey got to his feet and crossed to the sink, aware as he drew nearer of a pungent odour. He lifted the plastic lid of the unit and the smell intensified.

He waved a hand in front of him and wrinkled his nose.

'Is it switched off?' he enquired.

Beth nodded, indicating that the wall switch was in the Off position.

Hennessey rolled up the sleeve of his shirt and pushed his arm down into the dark maw of the disposal unit.

'You don't have to do this, Ted,' Beth said.

'I'll get it fixed for you. Besides, I like getting my hands dirty; I did spend twenty years in engineering you know. I miss dirt under my fingernails.' He chuckled.

Beth watched as he pushed his arm down as far as the elbow and began rummaging around in the rancid mess at the bottom of the blade-filled cylinder.

Above them, the kitchen lights flickered once again.

233

Seventy-One

Parker pulled open the door of the Peugeot, sliding swiftly behind the wheel as he felt drops of rain falling more quickly now. They spattered on the windscreen and he watched them for a moment, trickling down like molten glass beads.

In his rear-view mirror he glimpsed the light still burning in Flynn's office.

They would do the test on Karen Gregson tomorrow at ten, that was what he had agreed, somewhat grudgingly.

Old bastard.

Parker started his engine.

Flynn was terrified of being proved wrong, that was what scared him about the test. Parker smiled to himself. If he could prove that Karen Gregson was telepathic, then Flynn would have to admit he was wrong.

And if she was?

He guided the Peugeot into the long drive which led away from Brackley Heath towards the main road. Trees lined both sides of it, lowering darkly over the muddied drive, the lower branches of some snatching at the car as if trying to sweep it up into their dense foliage.

Telepathy.

Could it possibly be the next stage of the psychosis? Had he stumbled upon something more important than even *he* realised?

Perhaps it wasn't confined just to Karen Gregson. Maybe *all* women who suffered such an acute form of puerperal psychosis eventually exhibited this gift.

Gift?

234

Well, tomorrow Flynn would see that she did indeed possess this ability.

Parker slowed down as he drew closer to the main road. The lights lighting the thoroughfare glowed a sickly yellow in the growing gloom. He glanced to his right and left, squinting closely through the rain-spattered glass.

The road was generally busy during the day but at this time of the evening traffic was usually pretty light.

The dashboard clock told him it was 7.34 p.m.

Rain hammered hard on the roof and sides of the car, beating out an incessant tattoo.

He would show Flynn tomorrow, he thought, smiling.

And if you're wrong?

What other explanation could there be for her knowledge? How could she possibly know about Lucy's child and the things that had happened. How could she know about Beth's inability to bear children?

Telepathy had to be the answer.

He swung out into the road.

It *had* to be the answer.

All he heard was a loud blaring which he recognised as a hooter.

The motorbike shot past him doing ninety, engine roaring, the driver and machine moulded into one dark shape in the growing gloom.

Parker hit his brakes, thought for one terrible instant he was going to hit the bike, but then the machine roared away into the deepening darkness.

He could just make out its red tail-light disappearing in the distance.

'Fuck it,' hissed Parker, his mind spinning, his hands gripping the steering wheel so tightly it seemed he might tear it from the column.

He hadn't seen the bike.

The rain had obscured his view. The rain and the darkness. He'd seen no headlight either.

'Fuck,' he snapped again, trying to slow the speeding

235

pace of his heart as he drove on. The road had looked deserted for a good five or six hundred yards in either direction.

Bloody rain.

He sucked in a deep breath and drove on, the rain hammering even more heavily against the windscreen. Parker wiped condensation from inside the screen; outside the wipers were barely able to cope with the downpour. He slowed down, aware that he seemed to be the only car on the road. Anyone with any sense was home by now, he reasoned.

Except that motorcyclist, wherever the hell he'd come from.

Parker could feel his hands trembling slightly.

He drove on.

Dr Marcus Flynn watched as the Peugeot pulled away, its tail-lights gradually disappearing in the sheets of rain. But the older man remained where he was, looking out into the gloom, as if seeking something in the growing darkness.

An answer. But to what?

He'd agreed to the test on Karen Gregson the following morning purely and simply because he was sure that Parker would be proved wrong in his assumptions about the young woman.

The arrogant little bastard.

If she did indeed show telepathic traits then Parker would become unbearable. News of his discovery might leak out into the psychiatric community as a whole. He would be hailed as a ground-breaker or whatever other hackneyed phrase the press chose to pin to him.

Flynn knew that he couldn't allow that to happen.

And if he *was* right about Karen Gregson?

The ability to read minds?

To discover men's deepest thoughts, even those they would not voice themselves.

Flynn shook his head.

236

How much could she tell him about what went on inside his mind?

Could she probe memories, too?

Flynn swallowed hard.

This test *had* to fail.

Seventy-Two

'What have you been putting down here, Beth?' asked Ted Hennessey, screwing up his face as his fingers sank into something soft and rancid.

He withdrew his hand from the waste disposal, dark matter dripping from the digits.

'Leave it, Ted,' Beth said, apologetically. 'I'll call someone out in the morning to have a look at it.'

'*Nil desperandum,*' he chuckled, wiping his fingers on the tea towel she offered. 'Have you got a torch?'

She nodded and retrieved one from a cupboard beneath the sink, passing it to Hennessey, who stood over the unit and directed the beam down into the murky depths.

The light reflected off two of the gleaming blades nestling at the bottom of the cylinder. He could see two more higher up, grime encrusted but still razor sharp. A mass of soggy matter was caked around the base of the central spiral, the piece of the machine that actually moved when it was in operation.

'I can see what it is,' Hennessey said, passing the torch back to Beth.

She watched as he pushed his hand into the black hole once again.

Above them the lights flickered and Beth glanced up at the fluorescent strips, which were glowing brightly at both ends. They looked as if all their power had been sucked to either end.

Hennessey twisted something inside the cylinder and smiled.

Again the lights flickered, more brightly this time.

On. Off.

'Just about . . . there . . .' Hennessey murmured, his face wrinkled with the effort.

One of the fluorescents crackled loudly.

'Got it!' Hennessey shouted triumphantly.

The lights flashed more vividly.

He pulled his arm free of the waste disposal, something thick and gelatinous held between his fingers. It was dripping rancid fluid into the sink and the stench was appalling.

Hennessey brandished it before him like some kind of surgeon presenting a tumour he's just removed.

'You shouldn't put tea bags down there, Beth,' he said, looking around for somewhere to dispose of the rotting bag.

She pointed to the dustbin and he threw it away, turning back to the waste disposal and flicking the wall switch on.

The machine started up immediately, blades swirling wildly, a loud grinding noise accompanying the turning metal.

'As good as new,' said Hennessey, smiling, raising his voice over the churning blades.

He flicked the switch to Off and then turned on the tap, allowing water to wash down the dark hole.

'Thanks, Ted,' Beth said.

'A bloody plumber would have charged you a fortune to fix that,' he informed her, the water still running. 'Best thing to do now is clean it out, let the water wash over it for a while.'

The water drummed on the stainless steel of the sink as Hennessey pushed his hand back into the unit.

'If you give me that cloth, I'll wipe it round, make sure there's no other crap left inside.' He pointed to a dishcloth lying on the draining board.

He took the cloth from her with his free hand, his left still pushed into the cylinder. He rubbed the lower blades with his thumb, brushing away some more sticky muck.

Hennessey turned back towards the machine.

There was a loud roar as it started up.

For long seconds he froze, his eyes fixed on the wall switch.

OFF.

And yet the waste disposal was working. The blades were turning.

Hennessey's eyes widened in terror as he realised what was happening, and then the moment that seemed to have frozen suddenly melted away.

He screamed in agony and fear as the slashing blades cut into the flesh of his hand and forearm, slicing deeply, the fingers twisted and drawn into the very mechanism. He tried to pull free but it was as if some carnivorous beast had seized his arm and would not let it go.

Beth shrieked too as she saw blood fountain upwards from the mouth of the disposal unit, spewing up like crimson paint, spattering Hennessey then spreading across the sink.

Despite the fact that his arm was wedged tightly into the unit, the blades turned with relative ease, slicing open muscles and cutting through veins. Above the grinding sound Beth heard the more strident cracking of bone and then a sickening crunch as two of his fingers were pulped by the machinery.

Hennessey tried to pull away, his face already white, his eyes bulging madly in their sockets.

White hot agony shot up his arm as he felt another finger, or at least what remained of it, being crushed.

Fresh gouts of blood spurted up from the unit and portions of flesh and splintered bone were also hurled forth.

Beth, fighting her own nausea, saw a fingernail skitter across the sink as the disposal unit continued to swallow up Hennessey's arm as far as the elbow.

She slapped wildly at the wall switch but it was already off.

The lights flashed madly around them but all she was aware of were the high-pitched screams of Ted Hennessey as he fought to pull himself free of the machine.

She tried to help, clasping her arms around his waist and tugging, tearing him away from the machine which was macerating his arm.

Hennessey sagged to his knees, the hungry machine still gripping his arm but then, with one final effort, he wrenched free, the movement accompanied by another deafening scream.

He went sprawling across the kitchen floor, blood spouting from what remained of his arm.

Beth saw the ruined appendage and it was all she could do to stay conscious.

The arm had been almost stripped of flesh in places, huge chunks of muscle torn away to expose the ulnar and radial bones. She saw veins hanging free like bloated worms, spurting blood on to the floor. What remained of the fingers poked upwards, the digits crushed, splintered bone, pulped flesh and blood all churned together like some reeking porridge.

Hennessey lay on his back, the mutilated arm held away from him, blood spreading across the kitchen floor.

Beth didn't know whether he was unconscious or not. She prayed for his sake that he was.

The waste disposal unit was silent. Unmoving.

She saw blood and strips of flesh smeared around it and put a hand to her mouth.

Hennessey was twitching slightly, his lips moving soundlessly.

The coppery odour of blood mingled with a strong acrid stench of urine and she saw the dark stain spreading

240

across the front of his trousers.

On shaking legs, Beth bolted from the kitchen to the hall, snatching up the phone, hitting three nines as fast as she could.

The lights in the kitchen were still flickering, flashing above Hennessey like strobes.

He raised the pulverised arm once again, blood still jetting from the savage wounds.

And he began to scream.

Seventy-Three

At first Parker wasn't sure which house the ambulance was outside. Only as he drew closer did he realise it was his own.

He stopped the car in the middle of the road, swung himself out from behind the wheel and sprinted towards the house, glancing across at the motionless emergency vehicle, its blue lights turning slowly and soundlessly in the gloom.

Lights were on in the windows of other houses up and down the street, figures silhouetted against some of them, trying to see what was happening. Trying to determine who was being carried to the waiting ambulance.

'Beth,' Parker murmured, speaking her name over and over again as he ran.

Please God let her be all right.

He saw a policeman standing by the door of the house and the uniformed man blocked his way as he tried to push by.

'Let me through,' Parker snarled. 'This is my house.'

The policeman regarded him quizzically for a moment.

'I'm Simon Parker. What's happened to my wife?' he blurted.

The policeman stepped to one side but only allowed sufficient room for Parker to squeeze through with him.

The psychiatrist glanced into the kitchen and saw the blood.

So much blood.

'Beth,' he called, frantically.

'Mr Parker . . .' the policeman began but Parker shook him off.

'Where is she?' Parker demanded.

'She's all right.'

Parker blundered into the sitting room and saw Beth sitting by the fireplace, a WPC standing over her.

Beth rose to her feet when she saw him, her face tear stained.

She ran to him as he spoke her name, feeling his arms close around her reassuringly. Parker felt her sobbing against his chest, her tears wetting his shirt.

He saw that there was blood on her hands.

'What happened?' Parker blurted, holding her tightly to him.

The WPC stood by, watching them.

When Beth didn't answer him, Parker looked across to the uniformed woman.

'There was an accident,' she said, softly. 'A neighbour of yours.'

Parker looked blank.

'A Mr Hennessey,' the WPC continued.

'The waste disposal,' Beth sobbed. 'It nearly took his arm off.'

Parker held her more tightly.

An ambulanceman entered the room and looked at Parker and Beth.

'We're ready to go,' he said and the WPC nodded.

Parker turned to look at the other man.

'Can I see him?' he asked.

242

'He's sedated,' the ambulanceman said. 'His wife's with him. She's going with him to the hospital.' And he was gone.

'Will he be all right?' Beth blurted.

'You rest, he's being well cared for now,' the WPC told her.

Parker stepped away from his wife towards the hallway. He looked out to see the rear doors of the ambulance being closed. The emergency vehicle pulled away, driving a few yards silently before starting its siren.

The uniformed officer who'd been standing in the doorway said something to Beth about a statement then, joined by the WPC, he left.

Parker turned and saw the blood that had sprayed across the kitchen floor. Great arterial gushes of it which also spattered the cupboards and wall in places.

What in God's name had happened?

He sucked in a deep breath, his stomach turning slightly at the sight of so much crimson.

Beth hovered around the doorway but couldn't enter the kitchen.

'You go and sit down,' he told her. 'I'll clean this up.'

He looked again at the blood, some of it now congealing into sticky puddles.

'It can wait,' she said, her voice cracking. 'I don't want to be left alone.'

He crossed to her and held her tightly, her body shaking.

As they stood there in the hallway, Parker could smell the coppery odour of the blood, still strong in the air.

Despite the fact that they were standing close to a radiator, he felt as if someone had injected iced water into his veins. He too shivered.

Seventy-Four

Beth lay on her side, eyes fixed on the glowing red digits of the clock radio.

She watched as the numbers changed every minute, each moment of time seeming to stretch into an eternity.

1.39 a.m.

Beside her, she could hear Parker's low even breathing.

She felt safe with that sound. She felt safe with *him*. He'd cleaned up the mess in the kitchen, even the thought of what had happened to Ted Hennessey making her feel queasy. She closed her eyes tightly but all she saw was the image of him falling back, away from the waste disposal unit, blood spurting from what was left of his fingers and from the savage lacerations that ran from his fingertips to his elbow.

Beth opened her eyes as if that simple action would banish the vision but it was seared on to her retina, stamped there like some obscene brand. Even the red digits of the clock seemed like glowing streaks of blood.

They'd had a phone call from Val Hennessey about ten o'clock to tell them that Ted was sedated but stable.

Beth had apologised, as if she felt personally responsible for the incident.

She rolled on to her back, staring at the ceiling.

How had it happened?

The electrics in the house had been playing up but the waste disposal had been switched off. She was certain of that.

Could she have been mistaken?

Could Hennessey have set it going by mistake, touched

244

something inside the mechanism?

That *had* to be the answer.

And the flickering lights?

Electrical fault.

The cassette blasting out music?

It must have been left on without anyone realising.

With one of Lucy's cassettes in it.

Beth sat up, running a hand through her long hair.

Lucy's stuff had been put in the attic, bagged up and put out of sight. How had one of her tapes come to be in the ghetto blaster?

It could have been there for weeks; no one noticed.

Beth wasn't sure whether she was even convincing herself with some of these explanations. But if her answers weren't the right ones, then what *were*?

What other possible explanation could there be for some of the bizarre incidents that had occurred in the past few days.

Ever since . . .

She swallowed hard.

Ever since Lucy's death.

Coincidence. It had been a traumatic time. She was trying to attach too much importance to a series of unrelated coincidences.

Unrelated?

'Are you OK?'

The voice startled her and she spun round to look at Parker.

'Shit,' she murmured.

'Am I that frightening?' he said, sleepily.

She bent down and kissed him on the forehead, moving closer to him, feeling his arm snake around her shoulders.

'Did I wake you up?' she wanted to know.

'I wasn't asleep,' he told her. 'I've only been dozing since we came to bed. I keep thinking about Ted Hennessey.'

'You were lucky, you weren't here to see it,' she told him.

'First Mark, now Ted, that family must be jinxed.'

Beth moved closer to him.

'Ted was talking about Lucy before the accident,' she said. 'He told me she'd been seeing Mark, that they were close.'

'Did she mention anything about it to you?'

'I'd told her to stay away from Mark, she was hardly going to tell me she was sleeping with him, was she?'

'How do you know she was?'

'I know *her*. Ted said that Mark thought a lot of her. He was probably infatuated with her. She'd have used that to the full. I bet she had him so far around her little finger he didn't know what time of day it was.'

She mentioned the money he'd given her.

Parker listened patiently, his arm still clasped tightly around Beth's shoulder.

'Simon,' she began softly, 'so many strange things have happened since Lucy died . . .' She allowed the sentence to trail off.

She wondered whether she should tell him about the incident at work the other day with her VDU but then decided not to.

'All these strange things happening around us,' she continued.

'What are you trying to say, Beth?'

'I don't know,' she sighed, exasperatedly.

Parker sighed too, sucked in a deep breath.

'There have been incidents at the hospital too,' he said, almost reluctantly. 'Electrical problems, patients complaining of being woken in the middle of the night by someone – a young woman. One of my patients . . .' He wondered whether it might be wise to stop there.

Beth propped herself up on one elbow, looking down at him.

'What about her?' she demanded.

'You remember I told you about her when she was first admitted? She'd killed her two children, ripped out their eyes and fed them to a dog. It's the most acute case of its kind I've ever seen.'

'What's this got to do with what's been happening here?'

'Nothing, I'm sure of it but, just lately, Karen Gregson has been asking me questions about my life. About *us*. She asked me how I felt about *you* not being able to have children.'

Beth looked shocked.

'But how could she know that?' she wanted to know.

'She knew we couldn't have children, she even knew the reason. She knew things which only Lucy could have known.'

They looked at each other in the gloom, both motionless.

'I don't understand,' Beth said, finally. 'How *could* she know?'

'I think it's a form of telepathy, that's the only answer. We're doing some tests on her tomorrow so I should know more then.'

'And all this has started happening since Lucy's death too?'

Parker nodded.

'Could what's happening here and what's happening at the hospital be linked?' she enquired.

'How? It's impossible. It's just coincidence.'

That word again.

'And what if it isn't?' Beth asked.

'It *has* to be. There's no other logical answer for it.'

'Why does it have to be logical, Simon?'

'If I think you're trying to say there's something supernatural involved here then perhaps I'd better book you a room at Brackley Heath.' He smiled thinly.

'Don't laugh at me,' she snapped, pulling away angrily. 'I'm trying to understand this.'

'Beth, all of these things, everything that's happened, they have a logical answer. It's just a matter of finding it.'

'And what if you're wrong?'

He shrugged.

'I won't be,' he told her. 'Telepathy, auto-suggestion, paranoia, psychosis, thought transference. There are so many possible answers to everything that's been happening and all of them can be explained rationally and scientifically.'

'*All* of them?'

He nodded.

'The things that have been going on are probably our own reactions to the events of the last few weeks, they've been pretty traumatic, after all. The mind reacts in strange ways.'

'Don't talk to me like one of your bloody patients, Simon,' she snapped.

'So what do *you* think, Beth?' he said, irritably. 'That the house is haunted? And haunted by what? Lucy?'

She didn't answer, merely swung herself out of bed and padded across to the bathroom.

He exhaled deeply and rubbed his face with both hands.

What about the six feet tall letters drawn in blood, smartarse? Which part of your fucking mind was responsible for those?

He heard the toilet flush, saw Beth heading back towards the bed.

'It's cold,' she said, quietly, slipping into bed beside him.

They lay motionless for a long time, each occupied with their own thoughts.

The silence was broken by Beth.

'These tests you're doing on Karen Gregson,' she began. 'What if it isn't telepathy?'

'Beth, it has to be.'

'What if it isn't?'

He had no answer.

Her words hung ominously in the chill night air.

Coincidence?

Parker reached for her hand, but when he touched her flesh he found it was ice cold.

He turned and looked at her face.

248

She was staring blankly at the ceiling.

The silence closed in on them like a shroud.

Seventy-Five

Frank Jennings kneeled beside the bed, his breathing low and harsh, his gaze never leaving the face of Karen Gregson.

Her lips were slightly parted and Jennings traced their soft outline with his prying stare, studying every inch of her flesh.

He could feel his erection throbbing inside his trousers and, with his right hand, he loosened the zip and freed his swollen organ, gripping the hard shaft in his hand so tightly it made him wince.

He never took his eyes from Karen Gregson.

Outside, the wind was blowing through the trees, stirring the branches gently. The sound seemed to mirror Jennings' own breathing, which he was finding increasingly hard to control as his excitement grew. He released his grip on his penis and moved closer to Karen, his face only inches from hers. So close he could feel the warmth of her skin.

Jennings leaned across her and licked her lips with his tongue, allowing it to probe beyond into her mouth, rubbing against the hard edges of her teeth.

Still she did not stir.

He pulled her sheets down and gazed at her body for a moment before pushing her nightdress up her legs. Past her knees, over her slim thighs.

His excitement was almost uncontrollable now.

Jennings pushed the material that last few inches and

sucked in a deep breath as he looked down upon her pubic mound. Studying the tightly curled light hair there.

He bent his head within an inch or two and inhaled the musky scent, pushing her thighs gently apart, using his right index finger to stroke through her downy hairs. He felt the soft contours of her vaginal lips then pushed gently, feeling his fingers sink into the liquid smoothness of her cleft.

He kept his fingers there for what seemed like an eternity, enjoying the moist pliability of the flesh against his own probing digits.

Then, slowly, he withdrew those fingers, lifting them close to his face, seeing them glisten in the half-light, drawing the aroma deep into his nostrils.

Jennings pushed the fingers into his mouth and tasted them.

As he did, he felt his penis throb and it was all he could do to prevent himself ejaculating.

He sucked at his fingers, enjoying her flavour, smearing the slippery fluid around his lips.

When he looked down at her, Karen's eyes were still firmly closed. She hadn't stirred.

Jennings grinned.

So beautiful.

He stood up, his penis hovering a few inches from her face.

Jennings began to masturbate.

The alarm bell shattered the silence, the strident ringing echoing through the stillness of the hospital, hammering inside his ears.

He grunted, pushing his erection back inside his trousers, the alarm seemingly growing louder. He heard first one bell, then two and they built in volume until it seemed as if every one in the place was clanging away madly.

'Shit,' hissed Jennings and bolted from the room, locking the door swiftly behind him before hurtling down the corridor.

Already shouts were beginning to join the sound of the alarm, swelling to a wild cacophony of sound.

Was it a fire?

A breakout?

What the hell was going on?

He turned a corner and saw Damian Wilks running in his direction.

'What's happening?' Jennings shouted.

Wilks didn't answer.

The lights in the corridor flickered then went out.

In the darkness, the clanging alarm bells seemed even louder.

'Turn the fucking things off,' snapped Jennings, bumping into his companion in the gloom.

He pulled the large torch from his belt and flicked it on, the broad beam cutting a swathe through the blackness.

He and Wilks headed off in opposite directions.

As Jennings passed through the Secure Ward he didn't stop to look in on Karen Gregson.

Had he bothered he would have seen that her eyes were open, staring at the ceiling as if focused on something which only she could see.

She was smiling.

Seventy-Six

Parker turned on to his side and let out a weary breath. Sleep still eluded him in all but five-minute spells. Even when he dozed it was a light sleep, broken by the slightest sound or movement.

He lay there for several minutes then carefully swung himself out of bed, looking back to check he hadn't woken

251

Beth. She lay on her back, her chest rising and falling evenly. Parker pulled on his jeans and padded out of the bedroom, cursing the creaking boards on the landing as he approached the head of the stairs. He paused, took one look back and then, satisfied that she was still sleeping, he made his way downstairs.

It was cold in the kitchen, and as he stood waiting for the kettle to boil he could hear the wind whipping around the house.

It sounded like someone wailing.

Like the disembodied voice of some unhappy spirit?

He smiled to himself and shook his head.

Bullshit.

He poured hot water on to the tea bag and stirred it around, watching the colour spread.

All they needed now was clanking chains and the cliché would be complete.

He'd read some novel about ghosts once, *Haunting, Haunter*, some shit like that, he couldn't remember exactly. It had all the classic ingredients of the ghost story. The old house, the strange sightings.

Bullshit.

He was surprised that Beth had even mentioned it, found it difficult to fathom that she was actually willing to expect a supernatural explanation for what had been going on around them just lately.

So, bigshot, what's your answer?

He sat down at the kitchen table, cupping the mug of tea in both hands, watching the steam rise.

Beth was right. All this *had* started happening since Lucy's death and yet . . .

Coincidence.

He took a sip of his tea.

Lucy. Karen Gregson.

There couldn't be a link between them, it wasn't possible.

So how did Karen know what only Lucy could have known?

252

He exhaled deeply.

Well, come on, you're the one with all the bloody answers.

It was as he'd said, a form of telepathy.

Except that even Lucy didn't know precisely *why* Beth was unable to have children. Or did she? Had Beth mentioned it?

So many questions.

How strong was this telepathic power? Did it extend to auto-suggestion as well?

Parker sat back on his seat suddenly feeling useless, he was getting into areas about which he knew little or nothing. He was used to dealing with the logical part of the mind, with the psychological workings of that most specialised organ. Not the subconscious and what lay beyond it.

He drained what was left in his mug and crossed to the sink to wash it up.

As he stood there he thought back to what it had looked like a few hours earlier. The stainless steel spattered with Ted Hennessey's blood, tiny fragments of bone sticking to the blades along with lumps of ravaged flesh.

More blood on the floor.

Parker closed his eyes tightly for a second, as if to drive the vision from his mind.

It was as he opened his eyes he heard a sound from beyond the kitchen.

A scraping. Muffled. Barely noticeable.

The wind?

It was coming from inside the house.

From the sitting room.

Parker moved quickly but quietly from the kitchen, paused in the hall and listened.

Again the scraping.

He was sure now that it came from the sitting room.

What are you waiting for?

He crossed to the door and paused again, listening, straining his ears for any sound beyond the wooden partition.

For interminable seconds he stood there then, finally, he pushed the door open.

Parker slapped at the light switch but nothing happened. The room remained in darkness. He muttered under his breath and flicked repeatedly at the switch.

Only blackness.

There was a little natural light coming in from the hallway but barely enough to illuminate the inside of the sitting room. He glanced to his right, to the door which led to a cupboard under the stairs housing the fuse box.

Something must have blown.

He left the sitting-room door open and turned to the cupboard, pulling it open, kneeling beside the bank of switches.

Sure enough, one was down.

He pushed it up then scrambled to his feet and flicked the switch again.

This time the room was bathed in light.

He could see everything.

'Jesus,' he murmured, his voice cracking.

He was so intent on staring into the room, he never even noticed the figure approaching him from behind.

Then the hand closed on his shoulder.

Seventy-Seven

With the sound of the alarm bells stilled, the corridors of Brackley Heath seemed to be filled with a chorus of shouts and screams instead.

The lights had been restored too and Frank Jennings stalked back and forth checking each of the alarms which, moments earlier, had been ringing so loudly.

'They don't look as if they've been tampered with,' he said, irritably.

'All the wards were locked,' Damian Wilks told him. 'There's no way any of the patients could have set them off.'

'Turner and Harding said it was the same in the East Wing,' Jennings offered. 'Nothing touched. No security breaches.' He stood with his hands on his hips and shook his head.

'Power overload?' Wilks offered.

'It had to be,' Jennings agreed. 'I'm going to check out the back-up generator.'

Wilks looked blank.

'The reserve power should be cutting in as soon as something goes wrong with the main system,' Jennings told him. 'You and the others, get these bloody patients settled again, will you?'

He disappeared around a corner.

Parker shouted in fear and surprise as he felt the hand on his shoulder.

He spun round, his heart thudding madly against his ribs.

His reaction startled Beth, who let go of his shoulder and jumped back.

'Fuck it!' gasped Parker. 'You scared the shit out of me.' He swallowed hard.

'I heard someone moving about down here,' Beth told him.

He nodded.

'I couldn't sleep, I got up,' he told her.

She looked beyond him, into the sitting room, the lights glowing brightly inside.

As she stepped forward, Parker held out an arm to keep her back.

'What's wrong, Simon?' she demanded.

'I don't know,' he said, quietly, taking a step inside the

255

room, the skin on his arms prickling.

What he'd seen initially was still there.

The auxiliary generator was housed in a brick building roughly ten feet square, about a hundred yards from the main hospital. A gravel path protected on one side by thickly planted conifers and on the other by a privet hedge led down to the outhouse.

As Jennings trudged down the path he could hear the gravel crunching beneath his feet.

The wind whipped around his face, unexpectedly cold. The trees, buffeted by this strong breeze, bowed towards him as he walked, the branches rattling.

As he drew closer he fumbled in his pocket for a key-ring and found a large iron key which unlocked the padlock on the door.

The lock was well oiled but despite that Jennings found it difficult to turn the key.

He cursed under his breath as he struggled to loosen the padlock.

'Come on, you bastard,' he murmured.

Behind him he heard gravel crunching.

Wilks must have followed him out to the generator.

'Help me with this,' he called, his voice almost lost in the wailing wind.

No answer.

Jennings continued wrestling with the lock, the footsteps coming closer.

He finally turned the key and pulled the padlock away, turning round triumphantly towards the direction of the footsteps.

The path was empty.

He was alone.

'My God,' whispered Beth.

'Tell me I'm not seeing things,' Parker mumbled, his eyes darting around the room.

There were six pictures on the walls of the sitting room, a couple of expensive copies of military paintings which they'd bought in an art shop, two sketches which they'd picked up at a car boot sale and a drawing of each of them, done by a pavement artist in Rome while they'd been on honeymoon.

Every one of the pictures had been turned around to face the wall.

As if someone had carefully lifted them off their hooks, reversed them and then left.

Neither of them spoke.

Beth moved first, crossing to a print of Meissonier's *1814* which hung over the fireplace. She lifted it down then turned it to face the right way.

Parker watched as she did the same with the other pictures, leaving their own sketches until last.

As she touched the first she hissed loudly.

'It's freezing,' she said, prodding the metal frame.

Parker joined her and pressed his finger to the frame, withdrawing it hastily when he felt the severity of the cold.

Beth watched as he pulled a handkerchief from the pocket of his jeans and lifted down the first sketch.

He didn't replace it immediately but took down the second drawing too.

Behind each of them, scratched into the paintwork of the wall as if with the tip of a blade, were two words:

FREE ME

Seventy-Eight

As he stepped from the car, Parker felt the light drizzle and, for a moment, considered raising his face towards it in the hope that the rain would revive him.

He'd had two hours' sleep the previous night and that was a somewhat overgenerous estimate, he thought. After the episode with the pictures, he and Beth had returned to bed but neither of them had slept much. Hardly surprising really, he considered.

They'd hardly spoken about it that morning over breakfast. It was as if not mentioning it would somehow erase it from their memories.

Parker had checked behind the two sketches and found that the scrawled words were still there.

He'd driven to work with the radio on almost at full blast in an effort to keep him alert, the loud music perhaps an attempt to blow away his lethargy.

Now he pulled his briefcase from the passenger seat, locked the Peugeot, and headed towards the main entrance of Brackley Heath.

In the drizzle, silhouetted against a sky the colour of wet concrete, the hospital looked a forbidding sight. Its dark walls towering over him menacingly. He saw figures moving at the many windows that fronted the building, some pausing to stare out at him as he made his way to the doors. One of the figures waved and Parker waved back. He couldn't make out the man's features from so far away but he raised his arm in acknowledgement of the gesture.

He hurried his pace, anxious to be inside before he got soaked. The drizzle was little more than a curtain of moisture but it swept persistently across the land, driven by a light breeze.

The blue and white van with Electricity Board markings was parked close to the main entrance and as Parker entered, he saw two men in blue overalls heading towards him. One peeled off to the left and wandered down one of the corridors, the other passed through the main doors and set about retrieving some tools from the van.

Parker continued on towards his office, wondering what the engineers were doing here.

There were two or three patients in the corridor, one of whom he recognised. A middle-aged woman called Barbara Oakes who was one of his patients. She'd lost her husband and two sons in a car accident over a year ago, forced to sit in the twisted wreckage of the vehicle with the mangled corpses of her family while the fire-brigade cut her free.

She'd been clutching the severed head of her youngest boy when the firemen had finally pulled her out.

After more than a dozen operations to repair her own smashed legs, Barbara had been admitted to Brackley Heath suffering from extreme depression. Social workers had feared a suicide attempt and recommended her admittance.

She was a pale-looking woman who always looked as if she needed a good night's sleep,

(*Parker knew how she felt*)

but this particular morning she seemed more haggard than usual.

'Why do they keep waking us up in the night, Doctor Parker?' she said, crossing to him, accompanied by two other women he didn't recognise. One was chewing constantly on the nail of her left index finger.

'It's happened for the last four nights now,' Barbara told him. 'We just get to sleep and then they wake us up.'

'Who wakes you?' Parker wanted to know.

'We never see them,' the woman chewing her nail said.

259

'It's all wrong,' the other one added.

Parker, angry with himself, suddenly found himself looking at the women and thinking of the three witches from *Macbeth*, but he pushed the thought quickly to one side. He administered a swift mental rebuke and stood listening to their complaints.

'They get angry when we don't sleep then they come and wake us every night,' Barbara Oakes continued.

'And usually at the same time,' the second woman added.

'We never see them,' the third concluded, still chewing her nail.

'So who do you think it is that wakes you up?' Parker wanted to know.

'Alarms went off last night,' the third woman told him. 'The noise was dreadful.'

'And the lights,' the second woman told him.

'But we were already awake by then. They'd disturbed us,' Barbara said.

Parker frowned.

Lights and alarms going off. Maybe that explained the presence of the Electricity Board.

'The lights are always going on and off at night,' the second woman persisted. 'Flashing. On then off. It's terrible.'

'What time did this happen?' he wanted to know. 'Can any of you remember?'

'About two o'clock, I think it was,' Barbara told him.

Around the same time the lights were playing up at home?

Parker swallowed hard.

Coincidence?

'We were already awake though,' Barbara went on. 'They'd woken us up before that.'

'But we never see them,' the second woman offered. 'They just touch our shoulders, shake us, whisper to us to get up. I didn't even know we had them here.'

'Who?' Parker asked, increasingly bemused.

260

'They wake us all, everyone on our ward,' Barbara told him indignantly. 'It's a disgrace.'

'You'd think they'd know better,' the woman chewing her nail said.

'But they're very gentle,' Barbara added. 'Never rough. That's what surprised me. I didn't think we had any lady nurses here.'

Parker looked puzzled.

'We haven't,' he said, softly.

'Well, Doctor Parker, I think you're having a joke with us then,' Barbara said. 'It's always a woman who wakes us up. Always a woman.'

'And none of you has ever seen her?' Parker said, looking at each of the women in turn.

'Never,' the second woman insisted.

'I've heard her once or twice,' Barbara told him.

'No respect,' the third woman offered.

'Well, the young are like that, aren't they?' Barbara agreed, shaking her head. 'The one who wakes us up is young. No respect.'

'How old do you think she is?' Parker wanted to know.

Barbara looked pensive for a moment then shrugged.

'She can't be more than twenty,' she told him.

Parker looked at each of them in turn.

'No respect,' Barbara repeated.

Seventy-Nine

Beth Parker folded her notepad as she left David Manning's office, glancing briefly at the hastily scrawled shorthand which criss-crossed the page like hiero-glyphics. She made her way back to her desk and sat

261

down, glancing at the screen of her computer.

There had been no repetition of the incident of a few days ago, no more strange words appearing on the display unit, and she shook her head dismissively as she thought about it.

Strange, though.

A haunted display unit.

She smiled to herself.

Simon was right, deep down she knew it. Her talk of a possible haunting was ludicrous, although she was aware how easy it was to be dismissive of such a thought in the airy, brightly lit solace of the office.

A pile of mail lay on the corner of her desk and she reached for it, flicking through the envelopes and internal memoranda.

One of the envelopes was marked BRITISH TELECOM.

Each department's bills were notarised in the post room and logged before being delivered by whoever was doing the post that day. Each telephone call was itemised, ostensibly to prevent abuse of the company's phones by employees. The company didn't like too many private calls being made on their time and at their expense.

Beth opened the envelope and scanned the itemised sheet.

There were at least six pages.

She frowned, scanning the numbers carefully. The columns reading across told her the time and duration of each call, and the number reached.

The first half of page one displayed the usual batch of business calls; she recognised most of the numbers and, indeed, the majority of the calls had been made from her phone on Manning's behalf. She saw a number of calls that he'd made himself; there were even some to his home number.

She smiled. Obviously, restrictions on private calls didn't apply to management.

The smile faded as she looked at the second sheet.

The read-out was practically identical to the first sheet; all that varied was the duration of the calls.

And they were all made to the same number.

Every single one.

Beth ran a finger across the rows of numbers, her frown deepening.

She checked the times of the calls.

08.24

09.03

Could someone have been using her phone before she got to work?

03.19

Who the hell was using the phone at *that* time of the morning?

04.46

A nightwatchman?

05.32

But why her phone. If it was a security guard, there were plenty of phones on the ground floor.

06.15

Beth studied the rest of the times.

She flipped over on to the next page.

It was identical.

The duration of the calls varied between one minute and forty minutes.

14.25. Duration of call 39 minutes 21 seconds.

Beth shook her head.

She scanned the other times.

15.34.

That was a shorter call.

18.47

She shook her head.

It looked as if calls had been made virtually every ten or fifteen minutes.

As she studied the rest of the read-out, she saw that some of the calls to the mysterious number dated back to two weeks ago.

This had to be the phone company's mistake.

She totted up the calls quickly.

This wasn't possible.

Two hundred and twenty-six calls in the past two weeks, and all to the same number.

She checked the number.

It didn't look familiar but she could see that it was local.

Realising the quickest way to discover who the number belonged to was to simply dial it, Beth picked up the receiver and jabbed out the digits, waiting as she heard the ringing at the other end.

It was answered on the third ring.

'Hello,' said an efficient-sounding voice. 'Saint Angela's hospital.'

Beth put down the phone.

Eighty

Christ, those eyes.

Simon Parker gazed into the pools of brilliant blue and felt as if he were floating.

He held Karen Gregson's gaze for as long as he could.

It felt as if she were looking into his mind. He wondered if he should grip the edge of his chair to prevent himself being sucked across the desk by the sheer magnetic power of her stare.

Those eyes.

She was dressed in a faded black sweatshirt, jeans and trainers. Unremarkable. Her blonde hair was tied back, she wore no make-up and yet she seemed to give off an aura that was practically visible. Parker studied every curve of her features and, possibly for the first time since she'd been admitted, he realised how very beautiful she was.

She was smiling slightly.

Beside Parker, Dr Marcus Flynn also watched her, separated from her, like Parker, by the width of the desk.

Frank Jennings stood at the door like some kind of sentry, his gaze flicking towards the two psychiatrists then back to Karen.

The room was empty but for the four occupants, three wooden chairs and the small desk. A single fluorescent tube buzzed in the ceiling. The curtains were drawn, shutting out the drizzle which was still sweeping across the countryside like a dirty veil.

The silence inside the room was almost palpable, closing around them like an invisible blanket.

'We need to ask you some questions, Karen,' Parker said.

She continued to smile.

'Do you mind?' Parker continued.

'No, Simon,' she said, softly. 'What do you want to know?'

'Do you know who this is?' he said, motioning towards Flynn.

She shook her head.

'My name is Doctor Flynn,' the older man said.

'What do I bloody care?' snapped Karen, her smile disappearing.

Flynn sat back in his seat and glanced at Parker.

'We need your help,' the younger man said.

'Why should I help *you*?' she demanded.

'Because we care about you.'

'No one's ever cared about me,' she snarled.

'Did the father of your children care about you?' Flynn wanted to know.

'I haven't got any children,' she told him.

'You *did* have.'

'I never had any children, you stupid old cunt,' she

rasped, turning her angry gaze upon Flynn.

'You had two, you know you did,' Parker interjected.

'You killed them both,' Flynn added.

'They deserved to die,' she told him, flatly.

'Why?' Flynn wanted to know.

'They weren't my children anyway. How many fucking times do I have to tell you?'

'You told me they were God's children,' Parker said.

'What difference does it make who they belonged to? They weren't mine.'

She got to her feet, leaning menacingly across the desk towards the two men.

Jennings took a step forward but Parker waved him back.

'Why are you so interested in my fucking children?' Karen hissed.

'You said they weren't yours,' Parker reminded her.

'You know what I mean,' she snapped.

'How do you know they were God's children?' Flynn enquired.

She sat down.

'I just know,' she murmured, the rage draining from her voice. Then she looked directly at Flynn, the smile returning to her lips.

'Simon wants children but his wife can't have them,' she said.

Parker coloured slightly feeling Flynn's gaze upon him.

'Can she, Simon?' Karen said, softly.

Parker looked at his colleague and nodded almost imperceptibly.

'How did you know that, Karen?' Flynn wanted to know. 'Did someone tell you?'

She merely smiled.

'Does Doctor Flynn have children?' Parker asked.

Karen shrugged.

'Brothers, sisters?' the younger man persisted.

A small notepad lay on the desk in front of Flynn. He

266

pulled it towards him and scribbled something, then pushed it towards Parker.

ONE BROTHER, DIED THREE YEARS AGO.

Karen looked impassively at the older man.

'Do you know if he has any brothers or sisters, Karen?' Parker persisted.

'How would I know *that*?' Karen said.

Parker exhaled deeply.

'You know things about me,' he said, wearily. 'What do you know about Doctor Flynn?'

Flynn shifted uncomfortably in his seat.

'This is ridiculous,' he whispered to Parker.

'Tell me what you know about him, Karen,' Parker continued.

She merely sat smiling at Parker.

'Why is your wife afraid of fire, Simon?' she said, quietly.

Parker swallowed hard.

'What makes you think she is, Karen?' he wanted to know.

'Her parents died in a fire.'

Flynn scribbled IS THAT TRUE? on the notepad.

Parker nodded, not taking his eyes off Karen.

'She suspected Lucy, didn't she?' Karen continued.

Parker didn't answer.

'She's always hated her, hasn't she?' Karen insisted. 'And now she wants her baby.'

Parker was silent.

'This is proving nothing,' said Flynn, irritably.

'Shut up, you old bastard,' snarled Karen, vehemently.

'Take her back to her room, Jennings,' snapped Flynn and the nurse took a step forward.

Parker watched as Jennings hooked one arm through Karen's and guided her towards the door.

'I can walk on my own, I'm not a fucking cripple,' she rasped.

'Lucy,' Parker said softly, as Karen reached the door.

She turned and looked at him, the softness returning to her features.

He felt that all too familiar chill ripple along his spine.

Karen smiled at him.

Jennings ushered her out of the room and closed the door behind him.

'What a bloody waste of time,' snapped Flynn. 'What did all that prove?'

Parker didn't answer.

'Telepathic,' the older man snorted. 'The woman is displaying the classic symptoms of acute puerperal psychosis, nothing more. It was there to see, the mood swings, the anger, the disorientation. Not helped by your questioning, I might add. And what was all this nonsense about her telling me if I had brothers and sisters or children? What were you expecting her to say?'

Parker got slowly to his feet.

'What she said about my wife,' he murmured. 'It was all true. There was no possible way she could have known that other than . . .' He allowed the sentence to trail off.

'Telepathy?' Flynn snorted. 'Why couldn't she read *my* mind?'

Parker had no answer.

Why?

'When she was leaving, I called her Lucy,' he said, his voice still low. 'The name of my dead sister-in-law. She turned when I said it. She answered to that name.'

'Perhaps you mentioned the name during the conversation and she was simply reacting to it. The name might have acted as some kind of psychological trigger,' Flynn said, dismissively. 'I'm afraid I'm not convinced, Simon. This telepathy theory doesn't hold water.'

'I told you, she knew things about my wife she couldn't possibly have known,' the younger man snapped.

'I've only got your word that they're true.'

'Are you calling me a liar?'

'I think you're too involved in this case. I think that you

268

would interpret her answers any way you wished as long as they backed up this absurd theory of yours about Karen Gregson being telepathic.' He headed for the door.

'Then what's *your* answer?' Parker rasped, angrily.

'I don't have one yet,' Flynn said, opening the door. He paused and looked back at Parker. 'Reading your mind, telling you things she has no way of knowing, answering to the name of your dead sister-in-law.' The older man grunted indignantly. 'You'll be telling me next she's possessed.'

Parker heard the scornful laughter as the door was closed.

He gritted his teeth and brought his fist crashing down on the desk top.

Eighty-One

The hands of the wall clock seemed to be crawling, Beth thought as she glanced across the office yet again. It felt as if the morning had lasted an eternity.

The phone bill lay close to her arm, accusingly. It seemed to glare up at her every time she looked down.

Manning was out for the day at a meeting, he'd told Beth she could leave early if she wanted to but she didn't feel like spending too much time at home alone. It gave her time to think.

About Lucy.

About the baby.

About the phone bill.

She shook her head and glanced down at it once more. There had to be a fault on the line; she decided she'd call in BT to check it out.

Perhaps she'd visit the hospital later in the day.

Why?

Beth ran a hand through her hair.

To look at Lucy?

She squinted at the display screen in front of her, felt the beginning of a headache building at the base of her skull.

Stay away from the hospital.

She wondered if she'd visit, speak with Dr Leighton, find out about the baby's progress. Surely there was someone there who could tell her if they'd received so many phone calls in such a short space of time and . . .

(*it was a hospital, they got hundreds of phone calls every day*) if the caller had made their identity known.

And the source of their call? Get real.

Beth sat back from the screen and exhaled wearily.

'Are you coming to lunch?'

The voice startled her and she looked up to see Caroline Seaton standing there, pulling her coat on.

Beth looked blankly at her.

'Watch my lips,' said Caroline, smiling. 'You come get lunch now,' she said slowly, exaggerating every word.

Beth managed a smile too but shook her head.

'I'm up to my ears in it, Caroline,' she said, waving a hand over her desk. 'Manning's left for the rest of the day.'

'Even more reason to have a long lunch then.'

'I want to get this stuff finished.' She shrugged. 'Sorry.'

'If there's one thing I hate, it's conscientious workers,' said Caroline, grinning.

Beth held out her arms.

'Just call me dedicated,' she said, smiling.

'See you later,' Caroline called. 'Do you want me to bring you back a sandwich?'

'No thanks.'

'Go on then, starve yourself too,' Caroline said then she was gone.

Beth sat motionless for a moment, only the low hum of

her display unit breaking the relative silence of the office. Everyone else had left for lunch, it seemed. She sat staring at the screen a moment longer then got to her feet, fumbled in her bag for change, and headed off towards the vending machine down the corridor.

She could hear the odd voice in some of the other offices on the way but, otherwise, the building was quiet.

Beth fed coins into the machine and got herself a cup of coffee, carefully carrying it back to her desk.

She saw the writing as she sat down.

In glowing green letters it flickered with almost unbearable brightness.

THE CHILD WILL DIE

Beth swallowed hard and pressed the Erase key.

The words disappeared.

Then reappeared.

THE CHILD WILL DIE

She sat staring at them for a second longer then snatched up the phone and dialled quickly.

'Hello, Saint Angela's hospital,' the voice said.

'Can I speak to Doctor Leighton, please?' Beth said, watching the screen constantly.

'He's busy at the moment,' the voice told her. 'I can try paging him for you.'

'Yes, please.'

Beth waited.

The words disappeared from the screen.

Beth gripped the receiver more tightly.

'I'm afraid I'll have to get him to call you back, can I have your name and number, please, and can you tell me what it's in connection with?' the voice asked.

Beth gave her the relevant details, pausing as she came to the reason for the call.

Well, my computer's just told me my dead sister's baby is going to die, I wanted to see if it was right.

That was convincing, wasn't it?

Beth thought how ridiculous her reason for calling was.

271

The computer screen was still blank.

'Can you tell Doctor Leighton it's about my sister, she's in intensive care and . . .

(*she's dead but still carrying a child*)

I wanted to know if there was any progress.'

She hung up.

Beth kept her eyes on the screen, wondering if the letters were going to reappear.

They didn't.

She took a sip of coffee and waited.

The phone rang and she snatched up the receiver.

Leighton had been quick.

'Hello, Beth Parker.'

Silence.

'Hello.'

The line went dead.

Beth put down the receiver.

The phone rang again, loudly at first but then the tone seemed to die, to fade.

When she picked it up there wasn't a sound, not even a hiss of static.

As she replaced it again she saw that her hand was shaking.

Come on, get a grip.

The phone rang again.

Beth looked at it but didn't pick it up.

It continued to ring.

She reached out, her hand hovering over the receiver.

And ring.

She snatched it up and pressed it to her ear.

'Hello.'

'Could I speak to Mrs Parker, please?' said the voice at the other end. 'This is . . .'

'Doctor Leighton,' she said, recognising his voice.

'I got a rather strange message,' Leighton said. 'You wanted news about your sister. I'm afraid . . .'

Again she cut him short.

272

'I know there's no change, it was the baby I was concerned about,' Beth told him.

She heard Leighton sigh.

'I did promise to inform you if there were any developments, Mrs Parker, and, as far as we can see, the child is still doing as well as can be expected.'

'Thank you. Look I'm sorry to bother you,' she said, apologetically. Beth put down the receiver and sat back in her chair.

Christ, she felt stupid.

Forget about the baby, forget about Lucy.

And the writing on the screen? The phone calls?

She shook her head. There had to be some kind of electrical fault somewhere.

Forget it.

The phone rang again.

Probably Leighton, wondering why she'd cut him off so abruptly.

She picked it up.

'Hello.'

'Keep away from my fucking baby, you bitch.'

Beth dropped the phone, the words ringing in her ears, her eyes bulging wide.

The voice was Lucy's.

Eighty-Two

Parker watched as she paced back and forth agitatedly, her face pale and drawn. Beth finally turned to face him.

'I'm telling you, Simon, it was *her* voice,' she said. 'It was Lucy.'

He swallowed hard.

273

Go on, tell her it's impossible.

'I'd know her voice anywhere and I swear to you it was her,' Beth repeated.

'How could it have been?' he said, trying to sound as calm and unmocking as possible.

Why not tell her about what Karen Gregson had said?

'Lucy's dead. You know that,' he continued.

'Then explain that phone call,' she challenged.

Go on then, smartarse, you're supposed to be the one with the answers.

'There has to be a logical answer,' Parker said.

'Why?' Beth stormed. 'Why does there always have to be a logical answer? Christ, Simon, I've heard that before, remember?'

'So what are you saying? What do *you* think is going on?'

'You told me yourself that strange things had been happening at the hospital as well, things you couldn't explain.'

'Not yet.'

'Are you frightened?'

He looked puzzled.

'You seem so intent on proving all this is psychological,' she said. 'Are you frightened to admit there could be something supernatural involved?'

'Do you know how ridiculous that sounds?' he said, mockingly.

'Don't patronise me,' she shouted. 'You say it's psychological. Could something psychological have turned those paintings in our sitting room round, carved words into the paintwork, made over two hundred calls from my office to Saint Angela's hospital? It wasn't something psychological that almost tore off Ted Hennessey's arm.'

'It was an electrical fault.'

'The bloody machine was turned off at the socket,' she bellowed at him. 'No electrical fault could have caused it

274

to start up on its own.' She regarded him angrily. 'You told me yourself that that Gregson woman had been saying things to you which she couldn't possibly have known herself. Things only Lucy could have known.'

Parker sat back in his chair and frowned.

'Perhaps it's some kind of possession,' Beth offered.

Parker smiled.

'Flynn said the same thing today,' he told her. 'After my attempts to prove Karen Gregson was telepathic had failed. He was taking the piss, Beth. Karen Gregson's not possessed, she's just a very disturbed young woman.'

'Who happens to know things about you and me that only my dead sister could possibly have known,' Beth added.

Parker had no answer.

He got to his feet and crossed to the drinks cabinet where he poured himself a large vodka.

'What's been happening here and at Brackley Heath,' he began, 'goes against everything I've ever been taught, everything I've ever read. Christ, it goes against every rule of common sense. Look at what we're saying here, Beth. Our house is being haunted by your dead sister whose spirit has simultaneously possessed one of my patients and is speaking and acting through her.' He ran a hand through his hair. 'Jesus Christ, it sounds even more fucking ludicrous when you say it out loud.'

'Then explain it, Simon,' she said, quietly.

'I can't,' he roared and she recoiled from the vehemence in his tone.

He poured himself another drink, his back to her.

'I *can't* explain it,' he said again, his voice more subdued. 'Not in my terms anyway. Not in ways that I understand.'

'Can you admit the possibility that it might be true?' she asked, cautiously.

'That Lucy is somehow haunting us? That Karen Gregson is possessed by her?' He shrugged. 'I don't see

275

how that can be. That sort of stuff belongs in horror films, Beth.' He shook his head, a forced smile on his face. 'I mean, our house isn't built on a Red Indian burial ground, a murderer didn't live here before us, unspeakable acts of Satanism weren't performed in our kitchen and, as far as I know, none of the staff at Brackley Heath has ever vomited green bile over priests or masturbated with crosses.' He laughed but there was a bitterness in the sound.

Beth regarded him coldly.

'I'm glad you think it's so funny, Simon.'

He rounded on her. 'What the fuck do you want from me, Beth?'

She headed for the door.

'Some help,' she hissed and slammed the door behind her.

Parker downed what was left in his glass, looked at the bottle, then poured himself another.

'Fuck it,' he snarled.

As he lifted the glass he noticed his hand was shaking.

Eighty-Three

Parker didn't know how many he'd drunk. Half a dozen. More? Who cared? He downed what was left in his glass and rose somewhat unsteadily to his feet, crossing to the drinks cabinet again but this time pausing before he lifted the vodka bottle.

That's it. Get drunk. That'll solve a lot won't it?

He put down the bottle and sucked in a deep breath. His head felt as if it had been wrapped in gauze, his eyelids heavy. When he exhaled he could smell the liquor on his own breath.

Jesus Christ, what was happening?

Here in the house and at Brackley Heath there were things going on which he had no answers for, and that was what worried him. All through his life, his mind had been trained to look for the rational answers. To seek the logical solutions. And a voice inside that clouded mind told him the answers to these problems were logical, but that voice was becoming more and more indistinct as time passed. Another voice was apparent now. A dissenting one which shouted that what was transpiring was *not* logical. Could *not* be explained away by psychological reasoning. What was happening may well be out of the realms not only of his experience but also of his understanding, and he didn't like that. Parker hated not being in control.

And this particular situation was rapidly becoming uncontrollable.

There had to be an answer somewhere.

A haunting?

It couldn't be. It wasn't . . .

Logical?

He crossed to the two sketches of himself and Beth on the wall and lifted each one down in turn.

Behind each, those words were still visible.

FREE ME

They seemed to have faded slightly, like healing scratches on skin, but they were still clearly visible.

He replaced the sketches.

FREE ME.

The same words that had been scrawled on the wall at Brackley Heath, but there in letters six feet high. In blood.

Free who? From what?

A patient could have scrawled the words on the hospital wall.

Maybe.

But here, in the house?

Parker shivered. It was cold in the sitting room. The central heating had switched itself off thirty minutes before. The air itself seemed to be cooling.

He crossed to one of the radiators and put his hand on it.

There was still warmth in the metal.

Then why was it so bloody cold in the room?

Wasn't that what happened during hauntings?

Perhaps Lucy's ghost was sucking all the warmth from the air.

He smiled to himself.

All they needed was clanking chains, that was all that was missing.

He shuddered.

Jesus, it was getting colder. Noticeably and rapidly colder.

It felt as if he was standing in a deep freeze.

Parker saw the goosebumps rise on his flesh, felt the chill tightening around him. When he exhaled, his breath frosted lightly in the air.

He shook his head.

'Shit,' he murmured, his teeth chattering, his whole body trembling now. He crossed to the rear windows and drew the curtains across. Then to the front, peering out into the dimly lit street.

At first he didn't see it, hidden in the deep shadows away from the sodium glare of the street light, but squinting through the blackness, Parker looked more closely.

A figure was standing at the bottom of their short driveway.

The figure was staring at the house.

Eighty-Four

Parker shook his head, as if trying to clear the fuzziness that had dulled his brain.

It wasn't a figure he was looking at. It was a shadow.

Wasn't it?

He traced the outline with bleary eyes.

A shadow. It had to be.

A human being couldn't stay so still for so long. This shape was completely immobile.

Was it a burglar watching the house?

No way. A burglar wouldn't risk being seen. This figure was close enough to the street light to be identified.

And yet . . .

If it was a shadow, where was it being cast from? He could see nothing nearby. No tree which could cause such a shape. Such a human shape.

Parker moved even closer to the window to get a better look, then suddenly stepped to one side and switched off the lamp. It was dark inside the house now and he squinted harder at the shape.

Still it didn't move.

The chill inside the room seemed to intensify. Parker felt himself shivering almost uncontrollably now, his eyes still fixed on that black shape in the road.

It moved.

He swallowed hard as he realised it was moving towards the house.

It was difficult to see *how* it moved. Much of the shape was still in darkness, he could only make out the top half. The human shape. The rest of the figure seemed to be a

279

part of the impenetrable blackness, a fragment of it which had somehow become detached from the umbra and was now moving independently.

He listened for footsteps but heard none. All he could detect was the soft hissing of a breeze through the trees nearby.

The figure was in the driveway now.

Parker swallowed, wondered what to do. Should he wrench open the front door and confront this visitor?

The drink had fortified him somewhat but not perhaps to that extent.

It grew colder.

The figure was now on the path, heading for the front door.

The nearer it got, the colder the air became.

Parker gritted his teeth, finding it almost impossible to move in the numbing chill. It was as if his muscles and bones had been filled with ice.

He leaned closer to the window, peering through the glass so that he could trace the route of the figure.

The dark shape was within feet of the front door now.

Parker moved slowly towards the hall and found that he could move a little more easily, but still every step was an effort and the numbing cold spread through his body as if pumped by a freezing heart.

He moved across to the front door.

Outside he heard a rattling sound.

The sound of glass.

Something had knocked over one of the milk bottles.

It rolled back and forth for a moment as Parker forced his way towards the door, to the spyhole in the centre of it. If he could reach the porch-light he would be able to see through the spyhole, be able to see the face of the visitor.

There was a dull thud against the front door, as if something heavy had pressed its weight against the wood. Not thrown itself forcibly, merely leaned against the partition.

280

Parker was in line with the light switch now.

He reached out a hand and flicked it on.

Nothing happened.

Darkness remained.

He flicked wildly at it, one eye pressed to the spyhole.

He could see nothing in the darkened porch.

Angrily, without realising what he was doing, he reached for the handle and pulled it down sharply, tugging the door open.

It flew back an inch or two then slammed hard against the chain.

Cursing, Parker slipped the chain free and pulled the door wide.

A gust of icy air met him.

Nothing else.

The porch was empty.

The shape was gone.

He glanced down and saw that one of the milk bottles was, indeed, rolling gently back and forth, the sound of glass on concrete creating a strident rhythm.

Bending over, Parker hurriedly stood it upright, then he took a couple of steps outside, glancing around. Unable to see anything in the gloom. There was no shape. No figure. Nothing.

He wiped a hand across his chin, his breath coming in low gasps, his heart thudding hard against his ribs.

There was a heavy dew on the grass but he could see no footprints in it and there were no wet marks on the concrete of the path. He stepped back inside the house and quickly locked and bolted the door, leaning against it and drawing in several deep breaths.

Trick of the light?

Or of his own mind?

The chill which had been so intense was beginning to disappear rapidly. Parker felt the air warming again. He had stopped quivering.

Relieved, he sighed, relaxing slightly.

Then he heard the scream from upstairs.

Eighty-Five

Parker took the stairs two at a time, stumbling as he reached the top, almost falling. He shot out a hand to steady himself, spinning round, dashing in the direction of the scream.

He could hear Beth sobbing as he threw open their bedroom door, his head still spinning.

She was sitting up on the bed, still dressed, tears coursing down her face.

'What's wrong?' he gasped, grabbing her, pulling her close to him.

She threw her arms around him, hugging him tightly, unable to speak. He felt her body shaking, felt her tears wetting his shirt.

For what seemed like an eternity they remained in that position in the darkened bedroom, Parker holding on to her as if his life depended upon it. He murmured words of comfort to her and, finally, she eased back slightly and looked at him, her eyes swollen and puffy, the veins in the whites standing out starkly.

'Beth, what happened?' he asked.

'Oh God, I dreamed . . .' she began, her voice cracking. 'It was so real.' Her breath was coming in gasps. 'It was as if it was happening *here*, in front of me.'

He kissed her forehead, wiped tears from her cheeks.

'I must have dropped off when I came up here earlier,' she continued. 'It was so vivid.' She was still having trouble controlling her breathing. 'I saw a woman, in the dream . . . She was pushing a baby in a pram.'

282

'Beth, just try to forget it,' he urged but she pressed on regardless, shaking her head, as if speaking about what she'd dreamed would somehow wipe it from her mind.

She swallowed hard.

'She was in a garden,' Beth continued. 'She was a young woman, younger than me. It was sunny, a beautiful day. I saw her lift up the baby, she was smiling at it all the time. It looked so happy. Then she sat down and put the baby on the ground, just let it crawl about for a minute or two, then she lay down beside it but she took something out of her pocket. It looked like a fork.'

Fresh tears began to flow now but Beth continued.

'She cut its eyes out,' she blurted. 'I could see it so clearly. She dug the fork into its face and cut them out, scooped them out and the baby was screaming but all the time she was smiling. And the baby was screaming but it wouldn't die. I could see it with these big holes where its eyes had been, just full of blood and there was blood all over its face and body but it wouldn't die.' She was sobbing almost uncontrollably. 'And the woman just kept smiling and looking round, as if she could see me watching her. Like she knew I was there and I could see her face so clearly, as if she was in front of me now. Every detail.'

Parker held her tightly, stroking her hair.

'Was it Lucy?' he asked, quietly.

Beth didn't speak.

'The woman in your dream, was it Lucy?' he repeated.

She shook her head.

'I don't know who she was, it was someone I'd never seen before but I could see every detail of her face and it was so clear. She was about twenty-three or twenty-four, blonde, pretty, but it was her eyes, they were so blue. Almost hypnotic.'

Parker stiffened slightly.

'What else?' he asked.

'Thin lips, soft skin, high cheekbones.'

283

'Was her hair long or short?'

'Shoulder length.'

He nodded, feeling prickles at the back of his neck.

'But, Simon, it was her eyes. They seemed to bore right through me. They were so blue, so intense.' She pressed herself to him again and he held her tightly, trying to disguise the fact that he too was shaking.

The description was faultless.

He knew Beth had no way of knowing, but the details were unmistakable.

She had just given a perfect description of Karen Gregson.

Eighty-Six

'What do you mean, they're refusing to work?' stormed Dr Marcus Flynn, angrily.

Frank Jennings shrugged. 'Just what I said, Doctor, two called in sick, three are refusing to work.'

'This is preposterous,' snorted Flynn. 'I want them all back here before the end of the day or I'll sack the lot of them.'

'You can't do that, Doctor,' Jennings reminded him.

'Five of my staff go absent and there's nothing I can do about it? We'll see about that,' Flynn snarled. 'Why are they refusing to work?'

'It's only in certain parts of the hospital,' Jennings explained.

Parker looked on quietly, his eyes roving from one man to the other. He noticed that Flynn's cheeks, normally a vivid scarlet, had turned crimson. The contrast all the more striking because of his white hair.

284

'I asked *why* they were refusing,' Flynn repeated.

Jennings coughed self-consciously.

'Because of what's been going on here,' he said. 'The disturbances.'

Flynn shook his head.

'Is this anything to do with *you*?' he snapped, turning his gaze on Parker.

'What's that supposed to mean?' the younger man demanded.

'All this garbage you've been coming out with lately about telepathy, patients being woken in the night, alarms going off. Have you been talking to these men?' Flynn wanted to know.

'Don't be bloody ridiculous,' Parker said, angrily.

'How am I supposed to run a hospital with half my staff absent?' Flynn groaned. 'I want them back here, Jennings. By tomorrow at the latest.'

The nurse shook his head.

'No can do,' he said flatly. 'They won't come back. They're scared. So are a lot of the patients.'

'Of what?'

'Things have been happening, Doctor Flynn, you know that,' Jennings said.

'Lights going on and off, alarms ringing,' Flynn snapped.

'There's been more than that and you know it,' Parker interjected. 'The incident with the writing a few days ago, patients have reported being woken in the middle of the night repeatedly by someone they never see. I'm sure Karen Gregson's state of mind is something to do with what's been going on too.'

'How much of these incidents have you seen, Jennings?' he wanted to know.

The nurse hesitated, looked at Flynn as if for reassurance then spoke: 'I've heard footsteps, thought I've seen figures in the grounds at night.'

'For God's sake,' snorted Flynn.

'Have these incidents been centred around any particular part of the hospital?' Parker wanted to know.

Jennings shrugged.

'They've been pretty widespread but most of the complaints have been of things happening in the wards adjoining the Secure area,' he said. 'The corridors leading to and from it. Wards Three and Four.'

'What exactly have the patients reported?' Parker enquired.

'What you said, Doctor. Being woken in the night. Things have been taken also. Personal things. We thought there might be a thief on one of the wards but stuff's just disappeared. Photos, watches, books, but never any money.' He shrugged.

'It's been hidden somewhere,' Flynn interrupted.

'We searched every locker, anywhere stuff might have been hidden but we didn't find anything,' Jennings continued. 'Like I said, it's as if it just disappeared.'

'Half the staff are terrified of coming to work, patients are convinced they're being robbed. They're being woken in the night by people they never see, staff are hearing footsteps, lights are going on and off, alarms are being tripped for no reason and figures have been sighted in the grounds.' There was a disdain in Flynn's tone which matched his expression.

'We have to find an answer to all this,' Parker said.

'Very astute, Simon,' the older man said, mockingly. 'How do you propose to do that? Hold a séance?' He shook his head dismissively.

Parker looked coldly at him, holding his gaze.

'There *is* a way,' he said flatly.

Eighty-Seven

Beth didn't feel much like company that lunch-time. Occasionally she would drive to the lake if she felt in the mood for solitude, or sometimes just for a bit of peace and quiet.

It was a man-made feature about half a mile from where she worked. A waterway about seven or eight hundred yards wide in the centre of neatly manicured lawns. There was even a small pitch and putt course away to her right. She could hear several people on it, the sounds of their laughter intruding upon her mood. She wound up her window as if to shut out the sounds of merriment.

She felt tired. Sleep had been elusive the previous night and even when it had come, she had felt almost reluctant to surrender to it in case that dream returned.

That dream.

As she closed her eyes she could still see the dreadful images etched on her brain, as if stencilled there with a red-hot needle.

That face. *Those* eyes.

The blood.

Beth rubbed her face with both hands and turned up the volume on the cassette, as if the loud music would banish the unwanted recollections.

She gazed out across the lake. It was a popular location for watersports and, as she watched, a couple of would-be windsurfers were trying to make their way across a few yards of water but only with difficulty. Beth saw them laughing too.

Everyone was laughing.

The sun was shining but, despite that, she felt cold. A creeping, insidious chill that seemed to penetrate her every pore.

She'd had nightmares before (especially after the death of her parents) but never one as vivid as that of the previous night. Even the recollection was enough to make her shudder.

That face.

Had she seen the woman before? Surely it was impossible to dream so vividly about a person she'd never encountered.

Beth shook her head. She had another twenty minutes before she had to be back at work but even sitting amidst such beautiful surroundings she was unable to exorcise the demons of the previous night. She started the engine.

As she guided the Astra out on to the road, she passed a couple walking their dog. The animal looked at the car quizzically then dashed off in pursuit of a ball which had been thrown for it.

Beth found that the roads around the lake were relatively quiet, only a handful of vehicles passed her going in the opposite direction. It was the time of year for holidays, she reasoned, perhaps people were enjoying the sunshine at the seaside or abroad.

She and Simon had lived in the area long enough to know their way around with ease so Beth wasn't surprised to see the signs for a school on both sides of the road. It was a large comprehensive with an adjoining junior school, separated by a high privet hedge. There was also a fence around the perimeter of the playing field and the playground but, even so, as she drove by, she could see the children inside.

Their child would have come here.

If only. . . .

Lucy's child could when it was theirs, she told herself. The thought brought a smile to her lips but it faded quickly.

Lucy's child.

She slowed the car down, spotting a lay-by across from

288

the main entrance to the school. She could see three or four women standing around outside the gates, some with toddlers, one pushing a pram.

Beth pulled into the lay-by and stopped the engine. She sat gazing across at the waiting mothers, watching their numbers gradually increase. She reasoned that they had come to collect their children from the junior school.

There were about fifteen women gathered by now, some standing alone, others in groups, chatting as they waited.

The first of the children began to appear through the gates, some running to meet their mothers, others sauntering out unhurriedly.

They were no more than five or six.

She saw some walking hand-in-hand with their mothers away down the road, others headed for parked cars.

The woman with the pram stood motionless, watching the playground.

Beth studied the woman carefully, watching as she rocked the pram back and forth slowly.

There was something familiar about this woman, she felt.

Shoulder-length blonde hair, petite, dressed in jeans, a dark blue T-shirt and trainers.

Beth could only see her from the back.

Something familiar.

She stood there rocking the pram mechanically.

More and more children were flooding through the gates now but Beth kept her eyes fixed firmly on the blonde woman, who had barely moved other than to keep up that almost robotic rocking motion.

Why did this woman seem so familiar?

Beth swung herself out of the car and stood beside the vehicle, still watching.

She barely saw the red-headed boy run from the playground to join the blonde woman. He grabbed for her free hand and they set off down the road in the opposite direction, it seemed, from almost everyone else.

They were walking slowly and Beth could still only see the rear view of the woman.

She crossed the road and set off after her, walking briskly, wondering what she was going to say to the woman if she caught her up, if she managed to see her face.

'Excuse me but you look like someone in a nightmare I had.'

And yet Beth had only seen the back of her head.

The blonde hair, the slight, slim build.

She quickened her pace, almost bumping into a woman coming the other way.

That chill seemed to be intensifying. Beth shivered as she walked, drawing closer to her quarry.

The child was chattering away excitedly, she could hear him but the mother was silent, listening.

Beth was only feet away now.

That hair. That shape. So much like . . .

Beth reached out a hand and touched the woman's shoulder.

'Excuse me,' she said.

The woman turned.

Beth started.

The woman smiled back at her. Young. Early twenties. A rounded face, large ear-rings dangling from her lobes. She had high cheekbones

(*like the woman in the dream*)

and thin lips.

The eyes were brown.

'I'm sorry,' Beth said, apologetically. 'I thought you were someone I knew. Sorry.'

The woman smiled back.

Beth looked into the pram.

'I hope I haven't disturbed your baby,' she said.

'He'd sleep through a bloody war, he would,' the young woman told her, pulling the covers away from the baby's face.

Beth looked at the child's face and felt that chill deepen.

It felt as though her soul was frozen.

The child was beautiful.

So beautiful.

Sleeping.

Like the one in her dream.

'What happened to him?' Beth asked, her voice cracking, her gaze riveted on the baby's face.

'We think it was next door's cat, bloody thing,' the woman said. 'He was lucky.'

Beth felt her head spinning.

All around the child's eyes there were scratches.

As if something sharp had been dug into the soft flesh.

Eighty-Eight

It seemed to Parker as if time had momentarily frozen after he spoke, and he looked from face to face, studying the reactions of both Flynn and Jennings, waiting for either of them to respond.

'It's the only answer,' the younger man said finally, as if to reinforce what he'd already stated.

'Psychic investigators?' Flynn said quietly, his face still expressionless.

'What other choice do we have?' Parker offered. 'What other option?'

Flynn sat down and clasped his hands together in front of him.

'You're asking me to consider calling ghost hunters into this hospital?' the older man said, his voice still low but with an edge.

'They're not ghost hunters, for Christ's sake, they're

trained professional men and women,' Parker told him.

'Oh, of course, that makes all the difference then, doesn't it?' Flynn snorted. 'We wouldn't want just *anyone* running around here trying to catch our ghosts, would we?'

Parker eyed him angrily.

'There are phenomena here which need investigation,' he said. 'That investigation has to be done by the right people.'

'Do you think this hospital is haunted?' Flynn asked.

'I think there are things happening here that are unexplainable by methods any of us are used to dealing with,' Parker told him. 'Things out of our experience.'

' "There are more things in heaven and earth, Horatio, than are dreamt of in your philosophy",' Flynn said, smiling.

'Very poetic but it might just be true,' Parker added.

'And where do you propose to find these ghost hunters, Simon? The *Yellow Pages*?' Flynn sneered.

'Other hospitals in this area have been investigated,' Parker informed his colleague. 'I spoke to a friend of mine who works at Guy's. Even *they've* been the subject of an investigation.'

Flynn listened impassively.

Jennings, too, was staring intently at Parker as he talked.

'There's a society in London that specialises in this kind of thing, the Society for Psychical Research, they're based in Kensington. But they have contact with investigators all around the country.'

'And your *friend* told you this too, did he?' Flynn said, scornfully.

'What do they do?' Jennings wanted to know.

'I'm not sure of the mechanics of the investigation, we wouldn't know that until they got here, but I don't see that we have any other option than to let them investigate Brackley Heath.'

'Which other places around here have they tested?' Jennings wanted to know.

'Charwell Grange, it's about twenty miles from here,' Parker replied.

'I know it, I know a couple of the nurses there,' Jennings said.

'Then can you contact them and ask how we can reach these psychic investigators, Jennings?' Parker said.

'I thought you were the one who was the expert here,' Flynn interjected. 'Besides, if you know about the investigation of Charwell Grange, how have the names of the investigators escaped you? Where did you hear of this so-called investigation, anyway?'

'There was something in one of the local papers about it a year or so ago,' Parker said. 'This jogged my memory, the things that have been happening here.'

'And was anything discovered at Charwell Grange?' Flynn demanded.

'Not as far as I know.'

'Exactly. And nothing would be found *here* if I agreed to this lunacy.'

'What are you trying to say?' Parker snapped. 'That you're not going to allow this investigation?'

'Do you realise what will happen if any of this gets out? Can you even begin to comprehend what would happen to this hospital if the press got hold of a story like this?' Flynn stormed. 'I will not expose this hospital, its patients or its staff to ridicule. If you wish to look like a fool, Simon, that is your choice, I want no part of it.'

'Jennings, get in contact with those nurses at Charwell Grange,' Parker said. 'I want to find those investigators.'

'If you contact them I will have no choice but to ask for your resignation,' Flynn said, fixing the younger man in an unblinking stare.

'What are you frightened of? That I'll be proved right?' Parker snapped.

'I told you, I will not have this establishment turned into

a laughing stock,' Flynn repeated.

'What's it going to take to convince you?' Parker snarled. 'Patients have been reporting things for weeks now, even the staff have. What do you put it down to? Mass hysteria? We need help here.'

Flynn got to his feet and walked to the window, his back to the younger man.

'You've heard my final word on this,' said Flynn. 'These . . . *disturbances* started spontaneously, they'll die out just as quickly.'

'And if they don't?' Parker demanded. 'We've got patients here who are frightened to go to sleep at night, disturbed people being caused more distress and that distress will continue unless you do something about it, and calling in psychic researchers is the only way.'

Flynn didn't answer.

Parker waited for an indication that the older man was even listening but saw none.

He was about to say something when Flynn turned to face him.

'You have your ward rounds to complete, I believe,' he said, matter of factly, pulling a notepad towards him.

Parker glared at the older man for a moment, the knot of muscles at the side of his jaw pulsing angrily.

He turned and stormed out, slamming the door behind him.

Jennings also turned to leave.

'Jennings,' Flynn said. 'If you breathe one word of what was said in here this morning to anyone, I'll have you out of here before you can draw breath. Do you understand?'

The nurse nodded then ambled to the door.

Flynn heard his footsteps echoing away down the corridor.

He picked up his pen and began to write.

Eighty-Nine

The house was freezing.

Beth felt the chill in the air as soon as she stepped into the hallway. A bone-numbing cold which caused her to shudder.

Outside, the sun had disappeared behind a bank of grey cloud but it still wasn't cool enough to explain the lack of warmth inside.

She made her way directly upstairs, crossing the landing into the main bedroom and through into the bathroom, where she turned on the shower. The sound of the water spattering against the tiles and shower curtain quickly filled the room and Beth began removing her clothes, shivering as she did so.

It was just after three in the afternoon. Beth had driven back to work and told David Manning she felt ill. He'd immediately suggested she take the rest of the afternoon off, which she'd gratefully done.

She didn't know why but on the way home she'd driven past the school once more.

Perhaps she was hoping to catch sight of the blonde woman again.

The woman she had been so sure had appeared in her nightmare.

And the child?

She could still see the baby, the marks around its eyes. She could still recall vividly the baby in her dream, its eyes gouged out, the riven sockets clogged with blood.

Beth shook her head as if to drive the memory away.

She kicked off her shoes, sat on the edge of the bath and

finished unbuttoning her blouse, listening to the hypnotic sound of the pounding shower. The mirror was beginning to steam up as the water grew hotter and Beth reached over to dip a hand into the spray, satisfied that it was warm enough now.

She pulled off the rest of her clothes and stepped beneath the jets of water.

As she closed her eyes and allowed the warm water to bathe her body, she tried to push thoughts of the nightmare from her mind but it was as if the images had been etched on her eyelids.

The smiling blonde woman.

The baby with no eyes.

They were there constantly.

She opened her eyes.

Was she going insane?

Who else would follow a complete stranger along a street just because, from the back, they resembled a figure in a dream?

You're cracking up.

And the scratches around the baby's eyes?

Just like in the nightmare.

Coincidence.

What else?

Beth reached for the soap, muttering to herself as she felt the water temperature grow hotter. She adjusted the gauge.

Coincidence.

If she hadn't driven past the school she wouldn't even have *seen* the woman and her child.

The water was getting hotter.

Beth turned down the heat further.

She began soaping herself.

The shower cubicle was filling with steam.

The water was very hot now.

She reached for the dial and turned it all the way to Cool.

296

The jets that exploded from the shower head were scalding.

Beth screamed, felt her skin rise under the intense heat.

She jumped from the shower and sprawled on the bathroom floor, her flesh now pink from the heat of the water.

She scrambled to her feet, the room filled with steam. More water splashed from the shower but, when it touched her it was cold. As cold as the temperature gauge in the shower said it should be.

Tentatively, she thrust one hand beneath the spray.

Freezing.

Beth let out a deep sigh as she stood, dripping, by the shower.

Had she imagined that too?

She hesitated a moment then decided not to step back into the shower, reaching instead for her robe, which she pulled on hastily. She saw the mirror as she turned.

Covered by steam, the condensation had formed a diaphanous curtain across the glass.

Into that condensation was scrawled one word:

BITCH

Beth stared at it dumbfounded, then crossed to the mirror and, using the towel, wiped the condensation, and the word, away.

She stepped back, staring at the glass as if fearing the word might reappear.

For what seemed like an eternity, she stood gazing at her own reflection in the mirror, then she eventually walked out of the bathroom.

As she reached the bedroom she heard a door slam.

It was across the landing.

The door of the room that had been Lucy's.

For a second Beth hesitated, her heart pounding hard against her ribs.

Had someone got into the house?

She dismissed the idea and crossed the landing quickly, pulling open the bedroom door, looking inside.

Jesus, it was like a fridge in there.

Her breath frosted in the air as she exhaled, her eyes drawn to one particular thing in that room.

Beth took a couple of steps closer to the bed, her eyes widening.

She tried to swallow but it was as if someone had filled her mouth with chalk.

In the centre of the normally fastidiously smooth quilt was an indentation, as if someone had been lying there for some time.

Beth reached out one shaking hand and touched the indentation.

It was warm.

Ninety

Dr Marcus Flynn sat back in his chair and rubbed his eyes. As he stretched he heard his joints crack and he groaned. The wall clock opposite told him it was almost five thirty but he checked his own watch as if mistrusting the other timepiece.

He leaned back in the chair and closed his eyes.

Psychic Research.

What the hell did Parker think he was playing at?

Jumped-up little bastard.

Something brushed the back of his head, a light, barely noticeable ripple against his white hair.

He sat forward, hands clasped before him on the desk.

The series of events that had occurred lately at Brackley Heath were strange, there was no denying that. But the work of some supernatural force? He smiled to himself.

Again that tiny touch on the back of his head.

He put up a hand and brushed his hair back, thinking that some stray white locks must be causing the feeling.

Flynn hoped that Parker would keep his theories to himself, he didn't want talk like that circulating about *his* hospital. If the younger man *did* speak to anyone outside the hospital then Flynn would be forced to discipline him.

Put him in his place?

He felt another touch on his head.

A little heavier this time.

He spun round.

Nothing.

Again it came.

And again.

He raised a hand, brushed it through his hair and inspected the palm.

'Oh God,' he murmured.

His palm was stained with blood.

He felt frantically at the back of his head.

As he did he heard a faint thud on the desk in front of him.

A drop of blood had landed there and splashed across his pad.

It was followed by another.

Flynn got to his feet.

Several more droplets hit the desk.

He looked up.

A dark stain was spreading inexorably across the

ceiling. A dark crimson puddle which was being absorbed into the plaster like ink into blotting paper.

The blood was dripping from there.

He realised it was coming from the ward above.

As he rushed for the door he heard a scream.

It was joined by another. Then by shouts. By running feet.

As he pulled open his office door he saw Damian Wilks hurtling towards the stairs.

An alarm was going off.

The sounds all seemed to mesh into one unholy cacophony which filled Flynn's ears as he hurried up the stairs as fast as he could.

He heard more screams now.

A number of patients were crowded around the doorway of Ward 2 and Flynn watched as Wilks pushed them aside and disappeared inside. The older man followed.

The alarm was still clanging stridently. Voices were raised.

He saw the blood as he entered the ward.

It covered most of the floor, like a deep red lake emanating from one central source.

Gathered around the source were Wilks, Jennings and Parker.

Flynn could hear agonised screams.

It came from the centre of the huddle.

He saw legs thrashing about.

'She told her to do it,' someone shouted at him.

'We heard the voice too,' another bellowed.

Flynn pushed past them.

'What's going on?' he demanded.

Parker looked round, saw the older man, then returned his attention to the patient lying on the floor in the spreading pool of blood.

Wilks was gritting his teeth, feeling his stomach somersault.

'The ambulance is on the way,' Jennings barked, cradling the woman's head in his hands.

Flynn looked down and saw that it was Barbara Oakes.

'Tell her to leave me alone,' she screamed, holding both arms up towards Flynn.

It was then that he saw that both her wrists were cut. Although that was something of an understatement. They were destroyed. The flesh was torn away as far as the elbow on her left arm, veins and arteries exposed and spurting blood in all directions.

'She wouldn't leave me alone,' Barbara sobbed, brandishing her bloodied arms aloft.

'We heard her voice,' a woman offered.

'She called her names,' another said.

'How did this happen?' Flynn wanted to know.

Parker ignored his question.

'She must have been here a good thirty minutes,' Parker said, noticing the pallor of Barbara's skin too. 'Where's that fucking ambulance?'

'Who found her?' Flynn wanted to know.

'One of the other patients,' Jennings said.

'Why didn't they say anything earlier?' the older man wanted to know.

'She told us not to,' the first said.

'Who?' Flynn demanded.

'She told us to be quiet or she'd kill us,' the other added.

'Who is this woman who told you to be quiet?' the older man wanted to know.

'Tell her to leave me alone!' screamed Barbara Oakes.

'How could she do this?' Flynn shouted. 'You're supposed to keep all sharp objects away from patients, you know that.'

'I do,' hissed Jennings, and as he held one of Barbara's torn wrists, blood pouring down over his own hand, Parker pointed and rasped, 'She did this with her own teeth.'

Flynn didn't speak.

'How she did *this*, I don't know,' the younger man

301

persisted angrily. He pulled up Barbara's skirt slightly and Flynn saw more blood on her wrinkled thigh.

The words had been carved, quickly and expertly, into the flesh, as if with a sharp knife:

FREE ME

Parker shot him an accusatory glance.

'What's your answer now?' he snarled.

Ninety-One

Rain hammered against the windscreen of the Renault so hard that even with the wipers on double speed, Flynn had difficulty seeing through the glass. Combined with the lights of on-coming vehicles, it was practically impossible to maintain a reasonable speed. He drove slowly, carefully, squinting through the rain and gloom, his headlights cutting ineffectually through the blackness.

Wilks had travelled to the hospital with Barbara Oakes; other staff members had set about cleaning up the ward and settling the patients down for the night.

Parker had insisted on staying, talking to the other patients who claimed to have heard a voice telling Barbara to kill herself.

More evidence for his haunting theory, Flynn grunted.

He slowed down as he reached a bend in the road, checked his rear-view mirror.

Eyes were staring at him from the back seat.

He spun round, his heart thumping.

The car swerved and he turned back, fighting to regain control.

The eyes were gone from the mirror. There was no one on the back seat.

Behind a car was gaining.

The lights. It must, he reasoned, have been the lights of the approaching vehicle he'd seen reflected.

Angry with himself for allowing his mind to be tricked, he gripped the wheel more tightly and concentrated on the black road ahead.

There was a stretch of road coming up with no street lights.

Perhaps the rain had caused them to fail. He didn't know. All that was evident was that the road was particularly black and treacherous.

He eased off on the accelerator even more, muttering to himself as the car that had been behind him suddenly shot past and disappeared into the enveloping umbra. So dense was the blackness that Flynn couldn't even see the tail-lights of the car as it was swallowed up by the night.

There was no traffic coming in the other direction now. He was denied even the momentary relief their headlights offered.

It was like driving off the edge of the world.

He heard great splashes as the car ploughed through puddles and rain continued to batter mercilessly against the Renault.

He looked ahead, anticipating a stream of street lights.

There were none.

The road remained enveloped in darkness.

His headlights seemed to dim slightly then glow even more brightly.

Flynn muttered something to himself and flicked at the headlight switch. He was on full-beam.

Why were the bloody things getting weaker?

303

They went from a brilliant white light, to a dull yellow then to a sickly red.

He could barely see two feet ahead.

He glanced down at the dashboard to check there were no faults. Everything seemed to be working.

Except the lights.

He slowed down.

The darkness was closing in around the car like a black glove, threatening to crush it out of existence.

'Come on,' hissed Flynn, flicking at the lights angrily. He knew that he'd have to stop in a minute, visibility was non-existant.

He knew little enough about cars as it was. He certainly didn't fancy having to muck around under the bonnet on a deserted, darkened stretch of road on such a filthy night.

What was wrong with the bloody lights?

He was less than a mile from the centre of the town, how could it possibly be so dark? Off to his left he could see some lights flickering in houses but they were pin-pricks in the gloom.

Surely he wouldn't have to go too much further before he came to the welcoming sodium glare? Flynn picked up speed.

The headlights flashed back on again with almost blinding brilliance.

And there, pinpointed in the twin beams in the middle of the road, stood a woman.

Flynn shouted something and spun the wheel madly, sure he was about to plough into her.

As he slammed on the brakes, the car skidded on the wet surface, twisting fully ninety degrees, and Flynn's head snapped forward, smacking hard against the wheel.

The Renault hit the low bank that formed a natural safety barrier alongside the rain-drenched thoroughfare and, for one terrible second, Flynn thought the vehicle was going to rise into the air, propelled by its own speed and the bank's incline, but instead it slid back down and came to a halt on the road.

Flynn felt a tightness across his chest and he sucked in a deep breath, his mind now spinning, his head filled with images of that young woman he'd almost hit.

Or *had* he hit her?

She could be lying in the road at this very moment.

He scrambled out of his car into the blackness, the headlights illuminating his stumbling progress across the road, the torrential downpour soaking him in seconds.

There was no sign of the woman.

He staggered from one side of the road to the other, raising a hand to shield his eyes against the pelting rain. He could feel something warm running down his face, something throbbing just above his right eye. He guessed he must have cut his head when he slammed it against the steering wheel. But that seemed irrelevent now. All he could think of was the young woman he'd seen illuminated in his headlights.

The young woman in the jeans and T-shirt with the long red hair.

There was no sign of her.

He started back to his car, walking into the glare of the headlights this time.

There was someone in the passenger seat.

As he drew closer to the car he was sure of it.

Perhaps it was the young woman with the red hair.

Perhaps she'd climbed into his car when he'd got out.

Perhaps . . .

No, this woman wasn't a redhead.

Flynn slowed his pace, shielding his eyes against the blinding white lights of the Renault.

The rain. The lights.

He couldn't see properly.

He shook his head as he drew nearer the car.

The woman in the passenger seat was smiling at him.

Flynn narrowed his eyes, felt the cut on his head throbbing.

Yes, that was it, he had suffered a mild concussion. There could be no other answer.

And the woman in the passenger seat?

She was smiling at him.

A sweet, almost angelic smile as she brushed her shoulder-length blonde hair away from her face. Hair untouched by the rain.

He shook his head, able to see her more clearly now.

Yes, she was smiling.

Laughing. At *him*.

He could see the outline of her face and

(*She was laughing*)

her hair, even in the darkness

(*pointing at him*)

that seemed to fill the car.

He shielded his eyes from the harsh glare of the headlamps and looked into her eyes.

Karen Gregson was still laughing.

Flynn ran to the side of the car, slipping on the muddy verge beside the tarmac. He fell heavily, the rain soaking into his already sodden clothes.

He hauled himself upright, tugging at the passenger-side door.

His heart was hammering madly against his ribs.

The car was empty.

Ninety-Two

'I don't know how much more of this I can stand, Simon,' Beth said, anxiously.

He held her tightly as they stood in the doorway of the spare room gazing across at the bed.

The indentation was still there.

Parker didn't ask her if she'd been mistaken about the boiling shower-water, he didn't try to offer her reasoned explanations for the outline on the duvet.

He offered no answers because he had none.

'Come on,' he said quietly, guiding her away from the room, closing the door firmly behind him.

The chill that had filled the house earlier seemed to have dissipated somewhat but it was still cold within the building.

They sat together in the living room, on the sofa, holding each other tightly.

'Am I going insane?' she asked him, finally.

He shook his head.

'If you are then I am too,' he told her. 'I've seen the things you've seen Beth and more besides. What with the goings-on at the hospital too . . .' He allowed the sentence to trail off. He'd mentioned that one of the patients had tried to commit suicide but he hadn't mentioned the two words carved into her leg. And yet, logically, there was no reason for him to retain this information. They'd both suffered enough already. What was one more piece of mayhem going to do to them?

Could things get worse?

He hoped not.

Logic told him it could.

Logic.

He almost smiled.

What the fuck did logic have to do with anything that was happening either at their home or at the hospital?

'I know it's Lucy,' Beth said, quietly.

He remained silent.

She looked at him in bewilderment.

'Aren't you going to tell me not to be stupid?' she asked. 'That it's impossible? That Lucy's dead?'

Parker exhaled deeply and got to his feet, walking towards the drinks cabinet.

'The answer's not in that bottle, Simon,' she said, reproachfully.

He spun round angrily.

'You said you wanted help from me,' he snapped. 'Do you know how helpless I feel?'

'Join the club,' she retorted.

'Do you want to know what I really think?' he said, challengingly. 'The *real* answer to this bloody mess?'

She eyed him expectantly.

'It's the child,' he said. 'Lucy's child.'

Beth looked puzzled.

'Let the hospital switch off the life support for Lucy,' he said. 'Finish it, once and for all.'

'And kill the baby, no way,' Beth hissed.

He opened his mouth to speak but she cut him short.

'I want that child,' she rasped. 'I'm not going to let those doctors kill it. I thought you wanted it too.'

'Beth, how many times?'

'I won't let them take away that child,' she said, angrily. 'Lucy's child.'

'*My* child,' she bellowed at him. 'That child should be mine. She never wanted it. She wouldn't have wanted it if she'd been alive. I won't let them take it from me.'

They glared silently at each other.

The ringing of the phone cut through the stillness.

Beth got to her feet and walked past him out of the room.

Parker let out a weary breath. He finally crossed to the phone and picked up the receiver.

It was late for someone to be calling.

He looked at his watch and noticed that the hands were frozen at 10.46.

The clock on the mantelpiece had also stopped, the hands motionless at exactly the same configuration.

'Hello,' said Parker.

He recognised the voice on the other end immediately.

It was Flynn.

He sounded breathless.

Frightened?

'Simon, listen to me,' he said. 'Those psychic researchers you were talking about. Call them in. You have my full co-operation.'

Parker frowned.

'What made you change your mind?' he wanted to know.

'Just do it,' Flynn insisted.

Again that note in his voice.

Fear?

'I'll speak to Jennings tomorrow,' he said. 'He was going to find out how to contact them and . . .'

The line went dead.

Parker flicked the cradle.

Nothing.

Just the somnolent buzzing of a dead line.

He put down the phone and waited for it to ring again.

He was still waiting fifteen minutes later.

The younger man jabbed the digits that made up Flynn's number.

Nothing.

There was a buzz of static but nothing else.

Parker tried once more then hung up.

He turned to the drinks cabinet and poured himself a large vodka.

The phone rang again and he snatched it up.

'Hello.'

There was no sound on the other end, at least to begin with he thought he was listening to dead air.

Somewhere through the hiss and buzz he heard breathing.

Didn't he?

Low guttural breathing.

'Who is this?' he said, defiantly.

'You're all going to die,' the voice said suddenly.

It was female.

The line went dead once more.

Ninety-Three

Parker sat opposite Karen Gregson, their eyes locked. She barely blinked as she gazed at him and he found her continuous stare intimidating.

Don't show it.

'When are you going to let me out of this fucking place?' she said, suddenly.

'When you're better, Karen,' he told her, relieved that she had lowered that stare and was now gazing at the table top. 'When we've helped you.'

'How are you going to help *me*?' she sneered.

'If you talk to me I might be able to help.'

'I've done nothing *but* talk since I got here. I want to get out of here.'

'And where are you going to go?'

'Home.'

'Is that where you want to go?'

'I just want to get out of *here*. I've answered all your

questions, why are you keeping me here?'

'We can't just let you go, Karen, you know that. Anyway, like I said, I want to help you.'

'I'm not the one who needs the help,' she told him, irritably.

Parker narrowed his eyes slightly.

'Who does then?' he wanted to know.

She smiled at him, the gesture causing his flesh to prickle. There was no warmth there, only a kind of amused spitefulness.

'You and your wife,' she said, flatly.

'What makes you say that?' he enquired, trying to keep his voice even.

She got to her feet and began pacing the room, hands tucked into the pockets of her jeans.

'Why do my wife and I need help?' he insisted.

She turned on him, that spiteful malevolence still in her expression.

'To get what you both want,' she told him.

'And what's that?'

'A child.'

Parker exhaled wearily.

'Haven't you ever thought of leaving her, Simon?' Karen persisted, her tone softening. 'I mean, she's failed you, hasn't she? She hasn't given you the son you wanted.'

'What makes you think I wanted a son?' he asked, his voice low.

'Doesn't every man? To carry on the family name. That kind of thing?'

She was smiling almost pitifully now.

'She's failed you, Simon,' Karen said, flatly.

He wanted to slap her face. Strike her hard. Tell her to shut up. Everything he knew he couldn't do he wanted to do to this young woman.

Touched a nerve, has she?

'That was another reason she hated Lucy,' Karen said.

Parker didn't answer.

'Lucy had an abortion when she was fourteen, didn't she?' said Karen. 'Your wife paid for it. And even then she was jealous of Lucy. Because she could have children but your wife couldn't. That's why she wants Lucy's child, isn't it? She thinks that by taking Lucy's child she'll be able to give you the thing you want so badly too. But she's selfish, Simon. She wants that child for herself.'

Parker clenched his fists.

'She always had what she wanted, all through her life,' Karen continued. 'And now she wants a child so she thinks she's going to take Lucy's doesn't she?'

Parker got to his feet and headed for the door.

'She'll never get that baby, Simon,' Karen hissed.

He glared at her.

'I won't let her,' Karen continued, her face set in harsh lines once again.

'I'll kill her if she tries to take it,' Karen hissed.

Parker held her gaze.

'You'll all die,' she continued.

He unlocked the door and stepped outside.

'You're all going to die,' Karen bellowed after him.

He looked back at her through the observation slot.

Those words sounded familiar.

The phone call from the previous night.

Impossible.

She saw him looking at her and smiled at him.

'You're all going to die,' she said, more quietly.

Parker slammed shut the slot.

Ninety-Four

Beth saw Dr Leighton standing just inside the door of the casualty unit as she drew up and jumped out of her car.

He had called her at work less than twenty minutes earlier and asked her to come to the hospital as quickly as she could. He wouldn't, he'd told her, tell her the reason over the phone but he had emphasised the need for haste.

Beth had dashed out without even telling Manning.

She'd driven faster than she could ever remember doing before to cover the distance between work and St Angela's, her heart pounding hard throughout the journey, her mind spinning.

What the hell could be so important?

Was it Lucy?

The baby?

She locked the door of the Astra and sprinted across the car park towards the entrance where Leighton had now spotted her. She saw the pinched expression on his face and it caused her heart to race even more swiftly.

'I'm glad you came quickly,' he said as she reached him and he immediately turned and headed off down the corridor, Beth hurrying along beside him.

'What's happened?' she demanded.

'I don't know what caused the problem,' he began. 'Your sister's functions have been carefully monitored the whole time.'

They reached the lift and he jabbed a button.

'What's happened?' Beth repeated.

They stepped into the lift.

'The baby is in danger,' Leighton told her, flatly.

313

The lift began to rise.

'Oh God,' she murmured. 'How? What kind of danger?'

'We did an ultrasound scan, its standard practice at this stage of a pregnancy, regardless of a mother's condition. The results showed that the umbilical cord is dangerously close to the baby's throat.'

Beth listened with growing horror.

'But there was something else,' Leighton told her. 'We also test the amniotic fluid, I'm sure you're aware of that.'

'Amniocentesis,' Beth said.

He nodded. 'That's also standard to detect early signs of Down's syndrome but there's a new test we carry out. It's called cordiocentesis. It involves removing foetal blood from the umbilical cord.'

The lift bumped to a halt at the required floor and they stepped out.

Beth was even more aware of the antiseptic smell of the place than usual. They made their way hurriedly along the corridor towards the room where Lucy was.

'Just tell me what's wrong, Doctor,' Beth urged.

'We found blockages in the umbilical cord,' he said, pushing open the door and stepping inside.

Beth followed, looking down at her sister's motionless figure, surrounded by so many pieces of machinery, one of which was necessary to keep her lungs operating, another her blood pumping, and each required to keep her in touch with some semblance of life.

To keep the child alive.

'It appears that there's been a series of small haemorrhages in the umbilical cord. It's blocked off the blood supply to the foetus. The baby isn't getting enough oxygen.'

'Oh my God,' Beth murmured, looking down at Lucy's face then at her stomach, where *her* baby lay, helpless.

'What can you do?' she wanted to know.

'The only hope for the baby is to operate,' Leighton told her.

'Then do it.'

'The foetus is barely five months old, if we remove it from the womb the chances of it surviving are very small.'

'And if you leave it there it'll certainly die, that's right, isn't it?'

Leighton nodded.

'Operate, please, Doctor,' Beth said, imploringly.

'You must understand the risks to the child, Mrs Parker,' the doctor insisted. 'Even if we operate, even if we do manage to keep it alive, there are strong possibilities that the child will be damaged either physically or mentally. Possibly both.'

Beth clenched her jaws together until they ached.

Please don't die. Not now.

'If you operate there's a slim chance,' she said finally. 'Otherwise there's no chance at all.'

Leighton nodded.

She gripped his arm.

'Operate,' she said, staring into his eyes, her own filling with tears. 'Please.'

Leighton crossed to a phone on the wall and jabbed a couple of digits.

'I need OR Two immediately,' he said into the mouthpiece.

Beth didn't hear anything else, she was glaring down at Lucy's face, at the cold, waxen skin.

'You won't win, you bitch,' she murmured. 'Not *this* time.'

Ninety-Five

How could she possibly know?

How?

The question turned over and over in Parker's mind until he felt dizzy.

How could Karen Gregson know so much about himself and Beth, Lucy and the baby?

He ran both hands through his hair and let out a weary sigh.

Every logical, common-sense solution had been considered a dozen times but the answer was always the same.

There *was* no logic to the whole bloody case.

She *knew*.

Somehow she knew. End of story and Parker was beginning to despair of finding out *how* she knew.

When all possible answers have been exhausted, look for the *im*possible.

That was a quote, wasn't it? Some smartarse philosopher or writer had said it, hadn't they?

'Jesus Christ,' Parker murmured and got to his feet, pacing back and forth across his office.

And the options for the impossible?

Karen Gregson was possessed.

Unlikely.

She had some form of telepathic power.

If so, why was it limited to his mind alone?

Brackley Heath was haunted.

How much did anyone know about ghosts and what they were?

Parker stopped pacing for a moment feeling a weight of

hopelessness and desperation on his shoulders unlike anything he'd ever experienced before. He had run out of answers.

And he was frightened.

The phone rang.

He spun round and stared at it for a moment, reluctant to pick it up at first. Finally he crossed to his desk and lifted the receiver.

'Hello.'

'Could I speak to Doctor Simon Parker, please?' the voice at the other end said, cheerily.

'Speaking.'

'Doctor Parker, my name is Bill Hadley. I was asked to call you by a Mr Jennings. I understand you need our help.'

'I'm sorry, I'm not—' None of it seemed to be sinking in. Hadley cut him short.

'I'm head of a team of psychic researchers,' Hadley said. 'I believe you have some problems there.'

Dr Leighton had suggested she go home. He'd told her that they'd ring her as soon as there was any news.

Beth had chosen to stay.

She sat in the main reception, surrounded by other people. Some were patients, others visitors. A low burble of conversation filled the large foyer area and Beth found it preferable to the silence of the room into which she'd been shown by a nurse almost four hours earlier.

She'd stayed in that room for ninety minutes or more before the solitude finally drove her out to seek the company of others. Not to speak to them, just to absorb the comfort of their activity.

She cradled the plastic cup of coffee in her hands and watched as an elderly man in a faded dressing gown balanced a young boy on his knee. His grandson, Beth assumed. The older man was tickling the boy who was giggling excitedly.

317

At the vending machine a woman no older than herself was chatting with a man Beth presumed to be her husband. She saw the wedding ring on the woman's finger, saw her lean forward and kiss the man who turned and motioned to two young children who ran excitedly towards their parents. She watched the mother hug them.

Beth watched for interminable seconds, then she could stand it no longer. She got up and wandered back towards the room into which the nurse had shown her what seemed like an eternity ago.

She passed public phones on the way and again thought about calling Simon, telling him what was going on, but she shook her head.

What good would it do to tell him?

There was nothing he could do. It would mean two of them wasting time at the hospital instead of one.

She continued on past the phones.

Four hours.

How much longer would she have to wait?

Had the child died?

Were there more complications?

Beth tried to drive the thoughts from her mind.

Please God, don't let it die.

She reached the room, let herself in and sat down, shutting out the faint babble of conversation beyond.

Beth checked her watch against the wall clock. The ticking sounded thunderous.

She waited.

Parker guessed from the tone and pitch of Bill Hadley's voice that he was a young man. A little younger than Parker himself. He sounded affable and extremely interested in what the psychiatrist had to say.

'We'll need to speak to anyone who's come into contact with the phenomenon,' the investigator said.

'That'll be most of the people here,' said Parker, wearily.

'You let *us* worry about that, Mr Parker,' Hadley

318

reassured him.

'How many of you are there?'

'Three. We usually work together. It helps.'

Parker nodded.

'When can you get here?' he wanted to know.

'Tomorrow morning, it'll take us a while to get our equipment together and to set up. We might as well start fresh tomorrow.' A brief silence followed, broken by Hadley. 'There is one more thing I need to know, Doctor Parker. Has the phenomenon been confined to the hospital or have any of your members of staff or relatives of patients reported similar occurrences at their homes?'

Parker hesitated.

'Mr Parker?' Hadley persisted.

'Yes,' the psychiatrist said, finally. 'There have been *happenings* elsewhere.'

'I need as much detail as you have on those as well.'

'That shouldn't be difficult. They've been happening at *my* home.'

Beth got to her feet as she heard the door open.

Leighton walked in, his face greasy with perspiration, his skin pale.

Please God let the child live.

Beth took a pace towards him, not daring to hope.

'The operation is complete,' Leighton said.

'The baby?' Beth wanted to know.

'It's alive. Barely. We got to it just in time but it's in a critical condition. To be honest, Mrs Parker, I don't hold out much hope.' He looked apologetically at Beth. 'We disconnected the life-support equipment from your sister. I'm very sorry.'

Beth nodded gently.

'So she's dead?' she murmured.

'She was before. Now it's official.'

Beth turned away from him, anxious to hide the slight smile that crossed her lips.

319

'There's nothing more you can do here, Mrs Parker,' Leighton told her. 'My advice would be to go home, get some rest. We'll keep you informed of any developments.'

'Don't let it die,' she said, softly. 'Please.'

Parker had barely put down the phone after speaking to Hadley when the door of his office burst open.

He saw Damian Wilks standing there, his face flushed, his breath coming in gasps.

'Doctor Parker, come quick,' he panted.

The psychiatrist was already on his feet.

'It's Karen Gregson,' Wilks said. 'She's going berserk.'

Ninety-Six

He heard the sound as he reached the door leading to the Secure Unit.

An unrelenting chorus of shouting and screaming. Wild exhortations of rage and pain unlike anything he'd ever heard before.

Parker hurried through into the unit, following Wilks.

As they drew closer he could see Jennings standing outside the door of Karen Gregson's room, one hand braced against the thick door as if he feared she might come bursting through it.

'What happened?' Parker wanted to know, the sounds from inside the room ringing in his ears.

'One minute she was fine,' Jennings said, his face pale. 'The next, she went apeshit.'

Parker pushed the nurse out of the way and slid back the observation slot.

'She was on her own in there when it started,' Wilks added.

Parker watched as Karen Gregson hurled herself against the walls of the room. There was already blood on her hands, her fingernails broken and torn where she'd ripped at the concrete, as if trying to dig her way through.

As she turned towards the slot she saw him and flung herself at the door.

The shriek she released was enough to raise the hairs on the back of his neck.

Again she hurled herself against the door, hawked loudly and spat at the slot.

Parker was lucky to avoid the projectile glob of mucus that came flying towards him.

For fleeting seconds he looked into her eyes, which bulged so insanely they theatened to burst from her skull. The whites were criss-crossed by blazing red veins. He saw blood on her chin and lips and as she opened her mouth to bellow more hatred, he saw that she'd bitten her tongue.

She began pounding on the door.

Parker slid the observation slot closed and turned to Wilks.

'Go and fetch some Thorazine. And hurry,' he called as the nurse sprinted off down the corridor.

In one or two of the other rooms the screams and shouts of patients could be heard as, disturbed and frightened by the commotion, they added their own voices to the growing cacophony of sound filling the unit.

'You fucking scum,' Karen roared, her voice clearly audible through the thick door.

'And you're sure nothing was said to her, or done to her?' Parker asked, looking at Jennings. 'Something must have happened to trigger this kind of reaction.'

'No one touched her or spoke to her. She's a double-header, what the hell do you expect?' There was a vehemence in Jennings' tone that Parker didn't care for.

321

Wilks returned a moment later clutching a small bottle and a syringe.

Parker pushed the point of the needle into the fluid and drew 30mg into the hypodermic. He pointed it upwards and pressed the plunger to expel any air, then nodded towards the waiting nurses.

Jennings opened the door.

'Go,' said Parker and they rushed in.

Karen Gregson threw herself at Wilks and managed to grab his arm, diving her head down to sink her teeth into the side of his hand.

He screamed in agony as she bit through the flesh, his own blood mingling with hers as it dripped off his hand.

She kicked out with one foot and caught Jennings in the shin.

He dropped like a stone, clutching the injured leg but grabbing at Karen's flailing arms.

She raked his face with her nails, gouging skin away and leaving two raw furrows across his cheek.

'Bitch,' he hissed as she released her grip on Wilks and spun round to face Parker.

'I'll fucking kill you,' she bellowed at him.

Before any of them could move she launched herself at the psychiatrist, slamming into him with enough force to knock him off his feet.

He felt sharp nails clawing at his eyes.

Gripping the syringe in one hand, he grabbed at her hair with the other, tugging her backwards.

'Cunt,' she roared, still pummelling at him.

Jennings managed to get behind her, pinning her arms, holding her long enough for Parker to roll free, but even the nurse was surprised at the strength he felt in her small frame.

She shook wildly to free herself, turning her head to spit at him, a thick wad of mucus hitting him on the chin and hanging off like a thick gleaming tear.

Parker grabbed her left arm and ran the needle into the

vein nearest the crook of her arm, pushing down hard on the plunger, ensuring that all the Thorazine was expelled into her bloodstream.

She managed to jerk her arm wildly to one side and he was horrified to hear a loud crack as the metal broke, the end of the needle still embedded in her arm.

Blood was running freely from the puncture now but Jennings held on to her, wondering why it was taking so long for the drug to take effect.

Her strength was incredible as she writhed within his powerful grip.

'I'll kill you,' she roared at Parker. 'You and your cunt fucking wife.' She hawked loudly and spat at him again. 'You won't take my baby.'

Jennings felt her body stiffen, then relax slightly but he still held on to her.

Her gaze was directed at Parker.

'You won't take my baby,' she hissed, her struggles gradually diminishing.

Parker backed off a pace or two.

'I won't let you,' she gasped.

Parker dropped the broken syringe, watching as Karen Gregson finally slumped to the floor, her body twitching slightly.

'I'll kill you all,' she whispered, bubbles forming in the spittle that coated her lips.

She rolled on to her back, her eyes closed.

'Jesus Christ,' gasped Wilks, clutching his bleeding hand, staring down at her prone body, the broken needle still protruding from the swollen vein.

'I want her in Seclusion,' said Parker, breathlessly. 'And I want her watched.' He bent and plucked the sliver of steel from her arm.

As he did, her eyes flickered open briefly.

'You won't get my baby,' she croaked then closed her eyes again.

Parker backed off, shaking.

Ninety-Seven

Beth glanced across at the phone in the bedroom as she dried herself. She could hear the bathwater draining away in the bathroom, steam still hanging like thin white smoke in the air.

She pulled on a robe then sat down at the dressing table. As she began brushing her long hair, she noticed the dark areas beneath her eyes. She looked as if she hadn't slept for days.

Again her gaze strayed to the phone, as if she expected it to ring at any moment.

'I'm sorry, Mrs Parker, but the baby has died.'

She tried to force the thought from her mind, forced herself to banish such negative musings.

And yet, at five months, its chances were slim and she knew that.

She continued brushing her hair, finally running both hands through the silken tresses to fluff it up a little.

The clock on the bedside cabinet told her it was almost 9.25 p.m. But it felt as if the day had been going on forever.

She'd told Simon what had happened about the child, about Lucy. He'd seemed preoccupied, mentioning just a few words about Karen Gregson but little more. Beth had thought how pale he looked, how weary he'd sounded.

She got to her feet and went downstairs.

As she entered the sitting room she found him asleep on the sofa, the TV remote control still held in one hand.

He stirred slightly as she entered, blinked myopically and looked at her.

'I dropped off,' he said, rubbing his eyes.

'So I see,' she answered, smiling, sitting next to him.

Parker held out a hand and touched her cheek, feeling the smoothness of her skin beneath his fingertips.

Karen Gregson's words echoed in his head.

'I'll kill you. You and your cunt fucking wife.'

But he knew she couldn't. However, despite that knowledge he was unsettled.

Beth laid her head on his chest, stretching her slender legs out on the sofa.

'I'll see to the arrangements for Lucy's funeral tomorrow,' she said, feeling his heart beat.

'Are you going to be all right?' he wanted to know.

'She's been dead for the past six weeks, Simon. It's just a matter of burying her.'

He began stroking her hair.

'You make it sound so easy, Beth,' he said, quietly. 'Don't you feel anything for her?'

'Why should I?'

He had no answer.

Above them the floorboards creaked, as if there was a weight on them.

As if someone was moving slowly across the landing.

Parker raised his eyes.

The boards settling?

He waited a moment and the sound died away.

Beth also heard it and she sat up, glancing towards the ceiling.

'It's all right,' he told her, sounding none too convincing.

'Is it? I'm beginning to wonder if it's ever going to be all right again.'

He pulled her closer to him and silenced her protestations with a kiss.

Beth responded fiercely, her tongue pressing eagerly against his, her body shuddering as he slid one hand inside her robe and sought her left breast, kneading gently, squeezing the nipple until it stiffened.

She pulled at the buttons of his shirt, tugged at his zip in her anxiousness to release his rapidly hardening penis.

Parker held her other breast, bent his head to kiss the swollen pink buds, taking first one then the other in between his teeth as he flicked them with his tongue.

She was straddling him now, grinding her pubic bone against his erection and he felt the moisture between her legs, felt her holding his penis in her hand as she squatted over him, felt her rubbing the bulbous head against her hardened clitoris until, at last, she allowed herself to slide down its hard length. The contact brought a loud gasp from both of them.

She began to move rapidly up and down, her breath coming in deep racking gasps.

Parker barely noticed the crackling from the direction of the television set.

The sudden blur of interference that broke up the picture.

All he was aware of was the growing pleasure he felt and yet, despite the heat they were generating, he felt a creeping chill beginning to envelop his legs and feet.

Beth was moving faster now, gripping his shoulders to give herself leverage as she ground herself against him more frantically, feeling his penis sliding deeper with each downward movement of her hips.

Parker closed his eyes, as much to blot out the sight of the flashing television screen as in pleasure.

Beth gasped something which he didn't hear but, from the frenzied movements she was making and the tightening of her muscles around his shaft he knew she was reaching a climax.

He gripped her breasts, nuzzling against her nipples, his tongue sliding over each in turn.

She felt him thrusting upwards to meet her downward movements and it heightened her pleasure.

Her orgasm made her shudder wildly three or four times, her body quivering as the sensations subsided

326

slightly but she kept sliding up and down on him, wanting to prolong the pleasure, wanting to feel his climax too.

Parker opened his eyes and saw that the flashing on the television screen had stopped.

The chill he'd felt was leaving him.

He became even more aware of the pleasure building inside him.

As Beth clenched her muscles tightly around his penis he grunted and she smiled as she felt his fluid shooting warmly into her.

He grabbed her, pulled her to him as the orgasm swept over him and, for precious seconds, they were aware only of each other.

The moment seemed to stretch wondrously.

'I love you,' he whispered, kissing her lips gently.

When they finally uncoupled she looked down at the oily white liquid seeping from between her legs and smiled.

For the first time in weeks, the house seemed warm.

It remained that way for the rest of the night.

When they slept, they both slept dreamlessly.

The night passed without incident.

Ninety-Eight

Parker warmly shook the hand offered by the man facing him. A man a year or two younger than himself. Tall, well built and with strong features, his face was framed by a mop of curly hair which reached as far as his shoulders.

'I'm Bill Hadley,' said the younger man. 'These are my colleagues.'

He introduced a young woman with a pinched

327

expression and short dark hair as Sheila Carson and another young man, dressed in jeans and a T-shirt which bore the legend SAME SHIT, DIFFERENT DAY although the words were difficult to see because of the checked shirt he wore over it, as Clive Beeston.

'Before you say it,' said Hadley, brightly. 'I know we don't look like psychic investigators, you were expecting old farts in suits and glasses, right?'

'I didn't know what to expect,' Parker told him.

Frank Jennings eyed the trio suspiciously then glanced at Parker.

'What can we do to help?' the psychiatrist wanted to know.

'Well, once we get our equipment set up, the best thing you can do is keep out of our way,' Hadley chuckled. 'But, in the meantime, we need to see every area where sightings or manifestations have taken place and we need to speak to anyone here who's witnessed anything to do with the disturbances.'

'That's just about everyone here,' Jennings said.

Hadley smiled.

'Well, Sheila will need to talk to you all individually if that's possible. I know it's a pain but it's the only way,' he said.

Parker nodded.

'Jennings, you and Wilks take Miss Carson to the dayroom; she can interview the patients there,' Parker said.

'*All* the patients?' Jennings asked.

Parker looked puzzled.

'Even those in the Secure Ward?' the nurse continued.

'Yes,' the psychiatrist said, watching as the two men led Sheila Carson out of the room.

'And what do you want from me?' Parker enquired.

'We need to see where these occurrences have been happening so we can set up,' Hadley told him.

'Cameras, tape recorders, that kind of thing,' Beeston added.

'If you've got a problem here, we'll find it,' Hadley said, confidently.

'Can I have that in writing?' Parker said, cryptically.

'Trust us, Doctor Parker, we *do* know what we're doing,' Beeston assured him.

'Why do the witnesses need to be interviewed individually?' Parker wanted to know.

'If people are describing something in a group then they tend to elaborate,' Hadley said. 'I'm sure you can appreciate that as much as anyone. A person's frame of mind, their *state* of mind can affect their answers from one day to the next.' He paused for a moment. 'That's what makes our job a little more difficult here, I'm afraid. The state of mind of some of the witnesses.'

'You mean the patients?'

Hadley nodded.

'Mental patients don't make the most reliable witnesses,' he said.

Parker exhaled deeply.

'So, what's the procedure?' he asked.

'Well, there is a set pattern for an investigation like this,' Hadley informed him. 'First, Sheila will interview all relevant witnesses, get their descriptions on tape as well as in writing then, at a later date, she'll interview them again, to see if any of the stories have changed and to check whether any of these can be corroborated by more scientific findings, hopefully something on tape or film if we manage to get anything.'

'By interviewing repeatedly we find out if the stories are based on increased recall or just more inventiveness,' Beeston added.

'It'll be from these interviews that we decide whether or not the case is worth following up,' Hadley told the psychiatrist. 'But, in this case I can't see any need for false testimony.'

'You make it sound like a bloody trial,' Parker said. 'Why would anyone want to give false evidence?'

Hadley chuckled.

'Money to be had from a possible newspaper exposé,' he said. 'We've even had cases of council tenants claiming their houses were haunted so the council would move them to better accommodation.' He looked at his colleagues as if for confirmation. Both smiled broadly. 'Most of the stuff we find has a natural explanation, Doctor Parker. Most of the things you've experienced here probably have. Strange noises are usually down to the wind, vibrations caused by passing vehicles, water pipes and stuff like that.'

'Floorboards settling?' Parker offered.

'Exactly,' Hadley told him. 'Ghostly footsteps could be rats or mice.'

'What about objects moving?' Parker wanted to know.

'Usually it's some form of mental projection centred on one person. That's the difference between a haunting and a poltergeist phenomenon,' Hadley explained. 'A haunting centres around an area, some of them can go on for years. A poltergeist usually centres around a person.' He smiled. 'You must have seen the film, you know, where the kid disappears into the TV set.' Both men laughed.

'Yeah, we see that all the time,' Beeston said, smiling.

'If you'll excuse my French, that film was a load of bollocks as far as the psychical stuff went. Any researcher you speak to will tell you that. Hauntings aren't nearly as exciting as that in real life,' he said, grinning. 'Huge skeletal heads appearing from doorways, kids' toys flying around a room, and confrontations with exploding coffins are pretty rare in our line of work.'

'It makes for good movies though,' Beeston added. 'Like the *Amityville Horror*. Did you see that? That was supposed to be based on truth. It turned out to be a hoax. The family who were involved made a fortune though.'

Parker listened in bewildered fascination.

330

'So, you're not expecting to find anything here?' he asked, finally.

'We didn't say that, Doctor Parker,' Hadley told him. 'I'm just warning you that what we *do* find will probably have a natural explanation.'

'And if it doesn't?' Parker asked.

'Then we'll all get rich selling our stories to the *News of the World*,' Hadley chuckled.

'How long is this going to take?' Parker enquired.

'It's difficult to tell,' Hadley informed him. 'A few days, a few weeks. Months maybe. But we should be able to tell in about a week whether or not it's worth us persevering.'

The psychiatrist nodded.

'Well,' said Hadley. 'You'd better show us around. The quicker we get set up the quicker we'll know what we're up against.'

Ninety-Nine

Hadley had hardly spoken during the tour of the hospital, preferring to listen as Parker relayed information about what had been happening and where. He carried a small notebook with him and was constantly scribbling in it as the psychiatrist spoke. Only now, as he sat down in Parker's office, did he speak.

'When we spoke on the phone the other day, you said that you'd encountered something at your house, didn't you?' Hadley said.

Parker nodded.

'What kind of thing?' the investigator wanted to know.

Parker told him.

'And your wife saw these things too?' Hadley said when

Parker had finished.

'Some of them,' Parker told him, glancing out of his office window towards a van parked in the driveway. Beeston was in the back selecting the equipment needed for the investigation. Hadley and Parker were alone in the office.

'How long have the occurrences at your house been going on?' Hadley asked.

'Five or six weeks.'

'The same time as they have here?'

'What are you trying to say?'

Hadley shrugged.

'I'm not trying to say anything, Doctor Parker,' he explained. 'But it is possible that if this *is* a poltergeist phenomenon, it's centred around you.'

Parker regarded him warily.

'Have you been under undue stress lately?' the investigator enquired.

'Is that relevant?'

'Most poltergeist cases are stress related. The incidents could be projections of stress, grief, anger or frustration. Most are. Almost every poltergeist case is rooted in psychology. One particular individual will be the focus. They will cause things like you've seen.'

'Spinning pictures, exploding lights, electrical stuff switching on and off. I thought you were supposed to be a sceptic.'

'I *am*. That's why I'm more likely to believe moving objects are caused by projections of extreme emotion than by invisible ghosts who enjoy moving people's furniture and turning their lights out.'

Parker eyed the younger man for a moment then got to his feet.

'What do you know about possession?' he said, quietly, his back to the investigator.

'In what sense?' Hadley said, flatly, as if it were the kind of question he was asked every day.

'How many senses are there?' Parker snapped.

332

'Of a person, of an object, of an animal? Do you want me to go on?'

'Of a person.'

'You mean demonic possession?'

'Not necessarily demonic. Before you start telling me I've seen *The Exorcist* too many times, there are several well-documented cases of patients with multiple personalities in this field.'

'I think I'm aware of most of them. They made a film about one called *Sybil*.'

'Jesus,' said Parker, laughing. 'What would be your idea of a perfect case to investigate – a haunted cinema? Every example I give you of a supposedly supernatural occurrence, you come up with a film all about it.'

'That's because most paranormal phenomena *have* been the subjects of films,' Hadley informed him. 'That's what makes our job so bloody difficult sometimes. We interview people about, say, telekinesis and end up getting a run-down on what happened in *Carrie*!' There was a slight edge to Hadley's voice. 'Films and books sensationalise this sort of stuff and on the very few occasions we do find something which we genuinely can't explain, then the papers are all over it like flies on shit. We're trying to do serious research; the media are looking for a good story.'

Parker nodded.

'So, tell me about possession,' he said, finally. 'From your angle. I've seen people in the course of my career who claim they're possessed. Do you recognise possession as a possibility?'

Hadley raised his hands, as if in surrender.

'The cases on record, again, are based in psychology. I've never encountered it myself. Why do you ask?'

'My sister-in-law was killed about six weeks ago,' Parker said. 'Ever since she died, one of the patients here, a young woman a few years older, has been . . .' The sentence trailed off. 'She's been saying things which only my dead sister-in-law could have known. I wondered at first if it could be some kind of telepathy. I'm still not sure it isn't.'

'Why was she admitted?'

'She's suffering from puerperal psychosis.' Parker explained it briefly.

Hadley nodded.

'You think she's possessed by your dead sister-in-law?' he said, quietly.

'I don't know,' Parker told him. 'It's just that I seem to be running out of rational explanations and that one seemed to fit.' He shook his head, wearily.

'Had they ever met prior to your sister-in-law's death?'

'Not that I know of. No, I'm sure they hadn't.'

'Is there anyone who could have given this woman the information? Someone who knew you and the two women?'

'No.'

A heavy silence descended, finally broken when the office door opened.

Clive Beeston walked in.

'I'm ready,' he said. 'Let's get set up.'

One Hundred

'It looks more like a bloody bank in here,' said Frank Jennings. 'I've never seen so much security equipment.'

Cradling his bandaged hand, Damian Wilks nodded gently, his eyes fixed on proceedings unfolding before him.

At either end of the corridor leading towards the Secure Unit, two 35mm Nikon motor-drive cameras were set up on tripods. Also at each end of the corridor, one trained on the door, the other on the centre of the walkway, were a couple of Sony camcorders.

The floor of the corridor was covered by a thin film of white powdered chalk.

Five other corridors within the hospital were similarly equipped, the final piece in the investigators' armory being cassette recorders, again one placed at each end of the corridor.

'What are you hoping to catch?' asked Jennings, regarding the machinery.

'The cause of your problems here,' said Beeston, making some final adjustments to one of the video cameras.

'What do they do?' Wilks asked, almost in awe.

'All the camera equipment and the sound recording stuff is fitted with infra-red and capacitance switches,' Beeston informed him. 'If anything passes in front of them, they'll start recording.'

'What's the chalk for?' the nurse wanted to know.

'Footprints or any sign left by a presence,' Beeston told him.

Jennings snorted.

'This is bullshit,' he said, shaking his head.

'Maybe it is but this equipment is *our* way of making sure that bullshit has an explanation.' He looked challengingly at the older man.

'How the hell are we supposed to do our jobs with all this lot spread out around the hospital?' Jennings demanded.

'You don't need to enter the corridors we've set. According to Doctor Parker, there are alternative routes around the hospital and other ways into any of the wards if you need to visit them. There's no reason for you to behave any differently tonight than you do at any other time,' the investigator told them.

'And what about you?' Wilks asked. 'What do *you* do?'

'I sit and wait in one of the offices, get some sleep if I can. I'll check the cameras and tape recorders in the morning.' He stood back from the camera.

'Did you get what you wanted from the patients earlier?' Wilks continued.

'My colleague took the statements she felt were relevant,' he said.

'She disturbed some of the patients,' Jennings snapped.

'I would have thought her questions were the least of their worries at the moment,' Beeston said, defensively.

'Meaning what?' Jennings rasped.

'We're here to help,' Beeston said.

'Well, getting out as quick as you can would help.'

'You were the ones who called us in, remember?' Beeston told him. 'You either want this mess cleared up or you don't.'

'What happens if you find something here?' Wilks wanted to know. 'I mean a ghost or something like that?'

Beeston shrugged.

'We'll have to decide whether it needs further investigation,' he said.

'All this ghostbusters shit,' snorted Jennings.

Beeston ignored the remark.

'Well, gentlemen,' he said, turning towards the door. 'I'm going to find somewhere quiet to spend the night. If anything happens, if either of you sees or hears anything, I'll be in Doctor Parker's office.' He turned and walked away.

'I'm surprised Flynn allowed any of this,' Jennings said as the investigator walked away.

'Where is he, anyway?'

'Fuck knows, Parker said he called in yesterday, said he was taking a few days off.' The older man snorted. 'Perhaps he's scared.'

Wilks swallowed hard.

'I know how he feels,' he murmured.

It was stuffy inside Parker's office and Clive Beeston crossed to one of the windows and tried to open it. The sash window would only move a few inches but it was enough to allow some of the fresh night air in. He stood by the window for a moment, enjoying the breeze.

He knew that, back at her flat in town, Sheila Carson would have finished transcribing the eye-witness accounts she'd heard earlier in the day. She would question the same people the following day, asking the same questions worded differently and presented in a more random order to check for discrepencies in their accounts.

Hadley had taken the van and driven home to catch a few hours' sleep. He'd be returning later that night.

He usually stayed on the premises for the first couple of nights, like Beeston, but the equipment was all set on remote and their chances of seeing anything that first night were slim. Although, as Beeston knew only too well, every case was different.

He selected a large leather, high-backed chair in Parker's office and sat down, glancing at his watch.

It was 11.04 p.m.

Nothing to do now but wait.

Parker looked across at Beth as she slept on the sofa, the book she'd been reading lying on her chest. He smiled and walked across to her, lifting the book.

As he did she stirred and looked at him.

'Time for bed,' he whispered.

'Sorry, I was so tired,' she said. 'After what's been happening and . . .' She allowed the sentence to trail off.

'You go up,' he said, kissing her gently on the lips. 'I'll lock up. I'll be up in a minute.'

Beth nodded and wandered sleepily out of the room. He heard her gentle footfalls on the stairs.

Karen Gregson didn't stir.

Not even when Frank Jennings slipped one hand inside her nightdress and cupped one of her breasts, enjoying the smoothness of her flesh against his hand.

With his other hand he gripped the shaft of his erection

337

and moved his hand up and down swiftly, his breathing harsh.

He pulled the nightdress up, exposing her softly curled pubic hair.

He bent forward, inhaling the musky scent, then he pressed his mouth to her vaginal lips and kissed her, drinking in that heady aroma of her sex, tasting it on his lips.

She didn't move.

Not even when he began to masturbate over her face.

The body of Lucy Morton, identified by a small cardboard tag tied to her left big toe, lay in the morgue at St Angela's hospital along with two other corpses, the body of a five-year-old boy who'd died of viral meningitis that morning and a woman in her eighties who had succumbed to pneumonia.

The room was chilly, kept at its usual fifty-five degrees by a series of fans.

The autopsy on Lucy would be done the following morning.

The child was less than four inches long. Encased in an incubator it looked like some bizarre exhibit at a freak show but it clung to life and, so far, its grip on that most precious gift had not faltered.

Only time would tell.

Silence.

Deep, unbroken silence.

Then a low whirring sound.

At 3.16 a.m. the infra-red sensors on the cameras and cassette recorders in Corridor 5 of Brackley Heath psychiatric hospital were activated.

One Hundred and One

As they drew nearer to the door leading into the Secure Ward, Parker found himself quickening his step, his eyes fixed on the heavy partition ahead.

'How long has she been in this condition?' he asked, already rummaging in his coat for his penlight.

'I don't know,' Damian Wilks told him, fumbling with the key that unlocked the huge door. 'I checked the other patients this morning, as usual, but she didn't respond.' He pushed open the door and Parker hurried through, heading straight for the room in question. He pulled back the observation slot and looked inside.

Karen Gregson lay motionless on her bed, slightly on her side, her covers discarded and lying on the floor of the room.

'And you've been in to her?' Parker wanted to know, motioning for Wilks to open the door.

The nurse nodded and set about opening the door.

'Are you sure about this, Doctor?' he said. 'She hasn't been sedated yet and . . .'

'Open it,' Parker snapped, cutting him short.

Wilks did as instructed and stepped back, allowing the doctor inside.

He paused for a moment, studying Karen Gregson's position, watching the slow rise and fall of her shoulders.

He moved closer, kneeling beside her, peering closely at her face.

'Karen,' he whispered.

No response.

Wilks took a step closer.

'Karen,' Parker repeated, gripping her shoulder firmly and shaking her slightly.

Still there was no movement.

He pressed two fingers against her throat, searching for the carotid artery. He glanced at his watch, keeping the two fingers pressed firmly to her neck.

'Her pulse is normal,' he said, pushing her on to her back.

Using the penlight, Parker shone the thin beam towards her eyes, carefully peeling back the lids one at a time, allowing the penlight beam to play over the glassy orbs.

'No pupillary reaction,' he murmured.

'Is she in a coma?' Wilks wanted to know.

Parker shook his head.

'Her pulse would be much slower if she was,' he said. 'Also, her pupils are fixed but they're not dilated.'

He gently prized her mouth open and pushed the penlight to the back of her throat.

Karen Gregson gagged slightly but didn't waken.

'She's not in a coma,' Parker said again, as if to reinforce his own diagnosis. 'It's more like some kind of . . .' He paused, wondering if the words would sound as ridiculous when spoken aloud. 'Some kind of catatonic trance.' He lifted one of her hands and ran his fingertips across the palm.

Her fingers moved slightly.

'Shall I call an ambulance?' Wilks wanted to know.

'Not yet,' Parker told him. 'As far as I can tell, she's not in any danger, but it might be wise to get one of the consultants to take a look at her. Give Doctor Flynn a call too. I want him to see this.'

'I can't contact Doctor Flynn,' Wilks said.

Parker frowned.

'Why not?' he demanded.

'There's no answer from his house, just his answer machine. That's two days now he hasn't been in. Do you think he's okay?'

Parker nodded.

340

'I'll see if I can get hold of him later, you make sure someone watches Karen, if she hasn't come out of it within forty-eight hours I want her moved to a hospital.'

Wilks nodded and locked the door behind them both. Parker took one final look through the observation slot then headed off in the direction of his office.

'What is it?'

Parker turned the photo over in his hand, eyes fixed on a dark shape in the left-hand corner of the picture.

'It's not a what, it's a who,' Bill Hadley told him. 'One of your interns. Jennings. He triggered the sound and video equipment by accident while he was doing his night rounds.'

'He's in the corridor leading to the Secure Ward,' Parker mused under his breath. 'What the hell would he be doing there at that time in the morning?'

'Three sixteen to be precise,' Clive Beeston interjected.

Parker put the photo down and looked across the desk at the psychic investigators.

'Anything else?' he wanted to know.

Beeston shook his head.

'Nothing,' Hadley said. 'No disturbances, no movements. No signs either aural or visual. At least none that we picked up.'

'I'm going to re-interview the patients I spoke to yesterday,' Sheila Carson announced. 'See if we can weedle out some who might not be sure of their answers.'

Parker nodded.

'I told you, Doctor,' said Hadley. 'This isn't going to be over in a couple of days.' He smiled. 'You might be stuck with us for quite a while.'

Parker shrugged.

He touched the photo, tracing Jennings' outline with his finger, and wondered why the nurse had been leaving the Secure Ward at such a time. Perhaps he would ask him later.

'And now?' the psychiatrist asked.

Hadley got to his feet.

'We get back to work,' he said. 'See if we can find anything today but, like I said, this isn't going to be easy but if there *is* something here, we'll find it.'

One Hundred and Two

Beth hardly heard the words the priest intoned with well-rehearsed sincerity over the open grave.

Partly because of the driving rain beating against the canopy of the umbrella Parker held above them, but also because she wasn't really listening.

She could, however, hear the pattering of the raindrops against the wooden lid of Lucy's coffin, which now lay in its grave waiting to be covered by the earth piled high a few feet away.

The pall bearers had retreated to the safety of the hearse and stood mournfully in the rain, heads bowed as the priest continued with the service. Parker wondered if the cleric was aware he was rushing his words somewhat, perhaps he too was anxious to be out of this downpour.

It had been raining most of the previous night too. Another night, Parker was relieved to note, that had passed without incident and had also seen himself and Beth sleeping deep, refreshing sleep.

Dare they hope that these strange events had passed now?

He pushed the thought aside and looked at Beth who was gazing blankly at the open grave.

She and Parker were the only mourners.

It all seemed a little pathetic to Parker, Beth burying her

only sister and no one but himself and the priest for company. The priest's hair was plastered to his forehead as he spoke, the pages of his Bible soggy with rain but he continued on regardless.

Beth looked at the single floral tribute which lay alongside the grave. A simple bouquet of red carnations from herself and Parker. FROM BETH AND SIMON it read.

No love. No sympathy.

Beth could not bring herself to find any false grief or manufactured suffering at Lucy's passing. Perhaps, she told herself, she had been hardened, prepared for this day when the accident first happened.

That was what others may think. That was how her lack of grieving could be explained to outsiders.

Beth knew in her heart that she felt nothing but relief.

Lucy was dead.

Now she was buried.

Beth felt no elation, just a feeling of emptiness, an acceptance of this finality.

The priest finished and looked across at Beth who wandered forward and picked up a handful of mud. She stood in the rain for a moment, looking down into the gaping maw of the grave. She saw water all over the coffin lid, on the brass nameplate. For fleeting seconds she wanted to hurl the handful of wet earth into the hole but, instead, she tossed it gently, hearing the thud as it hit the wood. She stepped back and Parker snaked his arm around her.

She looked up at him and smiled thinly.

The priest again offered his condolences and hurried back to the shelter of one of the waiting cars.

'Let's get out of here,' Beth said, flatly.

Parker heard the edge to her voice and nodded.

They sprinted towards the funeral car and clambered in.

It had been over so quickly. A little like Lucy's life.

So short.

Beth sat in the back seat and allowed her head to loll

back as the car pulled away.

'Are you OK?' Parker asked.

'Fine,' she said, her voice devoid of emotion.

The inside of the car was warm and condensation formed quickly on the side windows. Beth drew a fingertip across the glass of the side window then wiped the rest of the diaphanous film away with the side of her hand, peering through the curtain of rain towards the grave.

Goodbye, Lucy. Good fucking riddance.

The drive home took less than twenty minutes and Beth didn't speak a word during the journey. Only when the funeral car pulled up outside their house did she open her mouth to thank the driver, then she and Parker ran for the front door.

As they got in, Parker pulled off his coat and took Beth's from her.

'I'll put these in the kitchen to dry,' he said. 'Do you want a drink?'

She was already heading for the stairs.

'When I come down,' she told him. 'I want to call the hospital.'

Parker sighed.

'What for, Beth?' he wanted to know.

'I want to see how the baby's doing.'

'Why don't you wait?' he said, reaching out and gripping her arm gently.

'I want to make sure it's all right,' she told him, looking him straight in the eye.

Parker held her gaze for a moment then let go of her arm.

'Don't *you* want to know?' she asked him, challengingly.

'Of course I do but I'm sure if there'd been any change in the baby's condition we'd have been notified.'

'They could have called while we were at the funeral.'

'There aren't any messages on the answerphone.'

'I want to check with the hospital anyway,' she insisted, and he watched as she made her way upstairs.

'Shit,' he murmured and carried the coats into the

344

kitchen where he laid them over the backs of two chairs. He could hear Beth crossing the landing, into the bedroom.

Parker wandered into the living room, to the drinks cabinet.

Above him he heard her moving about, heard the bed creak as she sat on the edge of it. She would be dialling the hospital now.

Parker poured himself a large vodka and downed it almost in one.

Outside, the rain continued to fall.

One Hundred and Three

'Why does he want her moved?'

There was a note of anxiety in Frank Jennings' question which Damian Wilks didn't detect.

'He said to give it forty-eight hours,' Wilks informed him. 'And that was yesterday, so another day and we'd better notify a hospital.'

'What's wrong with her?'

Wilks shrugged.

'Doctor Parker said he thought she was in some kind of catatonic trance; the consultant who examined her earlier today said she looked as though she'd been hypnotised but he couldn't find anything *physically* wrong. He agreed with Doctor Parker, though, that she shouldn't be left for too long.'

'Yeah, well, he *would* agree, wouldn't he? Probably one of Parker's fucking cronies. He's friendly with the consultants, isn't he?' Jennings said, dismissively.

'Do you reckon it's got anything to do with what's been

going on lately?' Wilks asked, almost excitedly. 'You know, all this psychic investigation stuff? Do you think it could have affected Karen Gregson in some way?'

'And put her in a trance? Don't be so bloody stupid,' Jennings snapped.

'They still haven't found anything, the investigators,' Wilks continued, a note of disappointment in his voice.

'What did you expect them to find? A fucking headless horseman? If you ask me, the whole thing is bollocks.'

'But you were all for them coming here. *You* contacted them in the first place.'

'Only because Parker told me to. Doctor Flynn never wanted them here.'

'I wonder where *he's* got to?' Wilks mused.

Jennings ignored the question, puffing on his cigarette then blowing out a long stream of bluish grey smoke. He watched it dissipate in the stale air of the staff room.

'What are we supposed to do about medication for Karen Gregson?' Wilks wanted to know.

'Well, if she's unconscious, she's not going to need bloody sedatives, is she?' Jennings snapped.

'I'll check with one of the other—'

'Just leave it,' Jennings said, angrily. 'I'll take care of it.' He smiled. 'Trust me.'

Beth picked up the empty bottle and tapped it with one fingernail. It made a hollow ringing sound that drew Parker's attention, and he looked round.

He noticed that she had changed out of the dark suit she'd been wearing and now wore jeans and a T-shirt. The trappings of grief had been discarded, he thought ruefully.

'Back to normal, eh?' he said, quietly.

'What do you expect me to do, Simon? Walk around in black for a week to show how much I miss her?' Beth countered. 'It'd be a bit hypocritical, wouldn't it?'

'Maybe, but the way you're acting at the moment, you

might as well throw a party and *celebrate* her burial. At least put up some pretence of mourning, Beth.'

'For whose sake? The neighbours'? Yours? Do *you* want to grieve for Lucy?' Beth glared at him. 'What was there about her for *you* to miss, Simon?'

He shook his head and finished what was left in his glass.

'Why so sad at her passing?' Beth continued, sardonically. 'Did she mean something to you?'

'She was your sister.'

'Yes, she was and I don't give a shit about her. So why do you? That night I was in London, did something really happen between you and her? Is that why you feel I should be showing a little more respect for the dead? Is it because *you* want to mourn? And mourn what, Simon, a bloody good fuck? Is that what happened that night? She seduced Mark Hennessey, why not you too?'

'Beth, this is ridiculous,' he snapped. 'All right, forget her. Forget everything that happened here, forget you ever had a sister.'

'I already have. I've told you before I never wanted her around. The only thing I want from her is her child.'

'Jesus, are you still on that shit?' He got to his feet. 'Forget it, Beth. Even if the baby survives . . .' He allowed the sentence to trail off. 'Fuck it, we've already had this conversation more times than I want to remember. We can't have children, you know that. Perhaps it's time we faced up to the fact that we're stuck with each other for the rest of our lives. Just us. You and I. Is that so bad?'

'I wanted a child, we both did, and now you're saying you don't.'

'I wanted *our* child,' he shouted. 'But we can't have our child, so I'm happy enough to live out my life with just you. I love you, Beth. That's enough for me. God knows I wanted a baby, probably as much as you did, but I didn't keep on about it. It hurt me too but now I know it's impossible. We'll be together. Isn't that enough?'

'No it isn't. Not as long as that child is alive, not as long as there's the slimmest hope that I can have it.'

'I. Me. What happened to *us*?' he said, softly.

'*I* want that baby,' she said, her voice cracking. She picked up the vodka bottle. 'Why don't *you* stick with this?' She slammed the bottle down on the table.

She turned and headed towards the sitting-room door, snatching up her car keys. He followed her out into the hall, saw her pulling on a jacket.

'Where are you going?' he demanded.

'Out!' she yelled back. 'Go back to your bottle, Simon.'

She slammed the door behind her.

He stood in the doorway, heard the revving of her engine then the squeal of rubber as she pulled away from the house.

'Fuck it,' he rasped, thumping his hand against the wall.

One Hundred and Four

Beth parked in the car park of St Angela's hospital and switched on the radio, turning the volume right down so that the music was just a gentle background accompaniment.

She leaned on the steering wheel, looking up at the great concrete and glass edifice, her eyes straying up to the fifth floor.

She knew the child was on that floor.

Fighting for its life.

If only there was something she could do to help. That was one of the worst things, she thought, the feeling of helplessness. There wasn't a single thing she could do to help the child. God and good fortune were the only things it had for aid.

An ambulance arrived at Casualty, lights flashing, sirens blaring, and Beth watched as a gurney was unloaded from the back, rushed inside and disappeared through the glass doors.

Another emergency vehicle arrived moments later and, suddenly, the air seemed to be alive with the sound of wailing sirens. She counted four ambulances screeching to a halt at the entrance of Casualty, up to three bodies were removed from one of them.

Beth wondered if there'd been a pile-up somewhere on the nearby dual carriageway.

She wound down her window slightly to let in some fresh air. It smelled fusty inside the car but the sound of the sirens seemed all the more pentrating with the window down. She wound it up again, preferring the stale air to the strident wail.

She sat back in her seat and closed her eyes.

Her eyelids snapped open when she felt something cold touch her neck.

'Don't turn around,' said the voice from the back seat and Beth shuddered as she recognised that voice.

It was Lucy.

She looked in the rear-view mirror, her heart thudding madly against her ribs.

Even with the knife pressed against her throat she couldn't contain the muted groan of terror that escaped her lips.

In the rear-view mirror she could see the face.

'You bitch,' Lucy's voice rasped, cutting through the stale air of the car.

Beth tried to swallow but felt the pressure of the knife against her Adam's apple.

The voice was Lucy's but the face she saw in the mirror wasn't.

The woman was young, early twenties, piercing blue

eyes and a slim, tapering face framed by shoulder-length blonde hair.

She knew this face from somewhere.

She knew this woman.

This woman who spoke with Lucy's voice.

'I know why you're here,' said Lucy's voice. 'You want to see the baby don't you? *My* baby.'

'Who are you?' Beth whispered, feeling the knife pressed that little bit harder against her throat.

'You know who I am,' Lucy's voice rasped.

Karen Gregson smiled.

Beth felt a sudden searing pain as the knife was drawn across her throat cutting deep into the soft flesh, slicing effortlessly through veins and arteries. Blood exploded from the wound and spattered against the windscreen.

Somewhere inside her head, Beth heard laughter.

Lucy's laughter coming from Karen Gregson's mouth.

Then the world turned red.

Parker was catapulted from the dream, his head spinning, his breath coming in desperate racking gasps.

He tried to stand but his legs buckled beneath him and he fell to the floor, gripping at the carpet as if to reassure himself he was awake.

But the vision remained in his mind.

Lucy's voice.

Karen Gregson's face.

The knife.

The blood.

'Beth,' he whispered.

It was dark. Christ alone knew how long he'd been asleep, how long Beth had been gone.

He glanced at his watch.

10.17 p.m.

The phone rang.

Parker hurried out into the hall, still feeling groggy. He snatched up the receiver.

'Hello,' he said, nervously.

350

'Doctor Parker, it's Bill Hadley at Brackley Heath, I . . .'

The line broke up, hissing with static.

'. . . something happened.' Hadley's voice was disappearing under a cacophony of hisses and crackles.

'Say that again?' Parker urged.

'Can you get here?. . .' Static. '. . . There's something you should see.'

The line went dead.

One Hundred and Five

Beth drained what was left in the tea cup and set down the empty receptacle, sitting back in her chair.

The air inside the Little Chef smelled of grease and fried food, not exactly an odour conducive to dining but one of the other occupants was busily shovelling forkfuls of baked beans and chips into his mouth while he tried to read a folded newspaper propped against the menu holder.

Beth looked across at the man who was far too preoccupied with his meal to pay her any attention.

Other than the diner and herself there were only two people in the place and they sat together over by the till. A couple in their early thirties, casually dressed, sharing a pot of tea.

Beth picked up her own tea pot and tipped it up, managing to drain half a cup from the container. She splashed in milk and sipped the luke-warm concoction, wincing as she did.

Time to go.

She wasn't sure how long she'd been there. After leaving the house she'd driven away from Oakley, twenty, perhaps thirty miles, speeding along portions of dual carriageway with almost reckless haste. Then, finally, she'd turned around and headed back, lured off course by the red sign of the Little Chef in which she now sat. People had come and gone while she'd sat there alone, and more than once a waitress had paused by her table as if expecting her to leave. Beth had hardly noticed the presence, lost in her own thoughts, gazing out into the night. She watched as the lights of other vehicles sped past, swallowed by the blackness.

She was less than five miles from home now. A ten-minute drive. Beth got to her feet and pulled on her jacket, fumbling in her pocket for some change to pay the bill. She dropped the rest of her change into a charity collection box and stepped out into the night, noticing that the air had turned chilly. She shivered as she walked towards the Astra.

Beth opened the driver's side door and slid behind the wheel.

Soon be home, now.

Perhaps he should have left a note, Parker thought as he gripped the wheel even tighter and sped through the night.

For when Beth finally got home. To tell her where he was.

Where *he* was? Where the hell was *she*?

The vision flooded into his consciousness once again.

Lucy's voice.

Karen Gregson's face.

The knife. The blood.

He shook his head as if to drive the residue of the nightmare from his mind, concentrating instead on the darkened road ahead of him.

What had Hadley found that was so important?

Parker couldn't begin to imagine.

An answer, at last?

352

He put his foot down.

Jennings looked down at Karen Gregson.

So beautiful.

He kneeled beside her, his erection already pressing uncomfortably against the inside of his trousers.

He worked quickly, pulling down the covers of her bed, unbuttoning her nightdress to reveal first her breasts then her flat stomach and softly curled pubic hair.

He licked across her cheek with his tongue, then across her lips before turning his attention to her breasts. He sucked hard on each nipple in turn then trailed his tongue down her belly to her mound, inhaling deeply.

That delicious scent.

He worked two fingers between the lips of her vagina, testing the slick, liquescence and decided that he needed more lubrication.

Jennings buried his head between her legs, salivating madly as he spread spittle over her sex and into her warm centre, tasting her, leaving her pubic hair matted with his saliva. He pushed her legs further apart and climbed up on the bed with her, freeing his throbbing penis.

He smiled and lowered himself on to her.

At last.

His penis butted against her labia then slipped inside her.

He kissed her still lips, felt the warmth of her immobile body against his own.

She did not stir. She didn't utter a sound.

Jennings continued to thrust into her.

'I don't know how it happened,' Bill Hadley said, staring down at the desk top. 'I must have fallen asleep in the chair,' he nodded towards the leather chair on the other side of Parker's office.

Clive Beeston stood close to the desk, fingertips inches from it.

353

'Don't touch it,' snapped Hadley. 'Just make sure you get plenty of pictures.'

Beeston nodded and began snapping away with a Pentax.

Scratched into the surface of the desk, deep furrows in the wood that looked as though they'd been carved with a sharp blade, were two words:

FREE ME

One Hundred and Six

The house was well lit as Beth drew up in the Astra. She parked the car and wandered across to the front door, selecting the appropriate key.

It was silent as she stepped inside.

She crossed to the door of the sitting room and pushed it open.

Empty.

'Simon,' she called but there was no answer.

The television set was on, images flickering before her. She left it on and made her way upstairs to the bedroom.

It was as deserted as the rest of the house.

She exhaled deeply, sat down on the edge of the bed

and pulled off her shoes. Then she padded into the bathroom where she crossed to the bath and spun both taps, watching as water splashed into the bath and began to fill it. Beth saw steam rising and began to undress. Naked, she walked into the bedroom and pulled the phone jack from its socket. She didn't want to be disturbed while she was in the bath; besides, if anyone called, the answerphone downstairs would pick it up.

Beth dipped her fingertips into the water, testing the temperature. Another minute or so and she'd be able to slip into its warm embrace.

She picked up a brush and began running it through her long dark hair.

Waiting.

Parker saw the lights in the distance. Dull, blue.

As he swung the car around the corner he hit his brakes.

'Oh Jesus,' he murmured, surveying the scene before him.

The cars looked as if they'd collided head on. An Audi and an Orion.

One was in the shallow ditch that ran alongside the road, the other had skidded across the road and now stood lengthways, blocking both lanes. The road was covered by shattered glass.

Parker saw two ambulances, two police cars. Uniformed men stood close to both cars.

A yellow tow-truck was also parked at the roadside, its two occupants standing against the vehicle smoking.

Cars coming from the opposite direction were also being held up by the two crashed vehicles.

Noticing that a policeman was heading towards his car, Parker wound down his window.

'How long's the road going to be blocked?' he asked, anxiously.

'Another twenty or thirty minutes,' the uniformed man told him. 'This only happened about ten minutes go. No one was badly hurt though.'

Parker realised he hadn't even thought about casualties. His route to Brackley Heath was blocked and that was all that seemed to matter.

'Where are you headed for, sir?' the policeman wanted to know.

Parker told him.

'I'd take another route if I were you,' the uniformed man advised.

Brilliant. I'd never have thought of that myself.

Parker stuck the car in reverse, knowing that he'd have to head back into Oakley itself, there was another way of reaching the hospital but it was a far more circuitous and time-consuming route.

But what choice did he have?

As he turned the car in the road he saw the uniformed man watching him. He straightened the car and accelerated back the way he'd come, watching the outline of the policeman gradually disappear from his rear-view mirror as the darkness engulfed him.

Parker glanced at the dashboard clock.

His heart was beating faster now.

He remembered suddenly.

There was another way to the hospital. A shorter way. It would still take him a good twenty minutes from where he was now and the route was badly lit but it would save him time. He indicated left and pressed his foot down on the accelerator.

The thoroughfare he sought was little more than a farm track, barely wide enough to take a car but it would do.

Another couple of minutes and he should reach it.

Despite the chill in the room, there was perspiration forming on Frank Jennings' back and forehead.

As he drove his penis hard into Karen Gregson's motionless body he gritted his teeth, supporting his weight with his fists.

The feeling of pleasure was growing.

He knew his climax was near.

She lay still beneath him, as immobile as a corpse but Jennings wasn't concerned. His only interest was his growing ecstasy.

He bent his head forward and licked his tongue across her breasts then her face, rubbing his cheek against hers, allowing some of his saliva to smear her smooth skin.

He smelled her hair, her skin.

So beautiful.

He held his lips inches from hers and snaked his tongue out, prising her soft lips apart and gliding it over the hard white edges of her teeth.

Karen Gregson's eyes snapped open.

They glinted in the half-light, boring into him.

This was no awakening from a drug-induced stupor, there was raging vitality behind those blazing orbs.

Before Jennings could react, she had seized his tongue between her teeth.

She bit through it with ease.

Jennings' tongue was severed cleanly, blood jetting from the torn appendage, some of it spurting into Karen Gregson's mouth, some spattering over her face and the pillow upon which her head rested.

She spat out the bleeding lump of tongue and grabbed Jennings' head between her two hands, gripping his skull with a power and strength he could never have imagined.

Blood was pouring down his throat, gurgling there as he screamed. A muted, liquid sound brought about by the crimson fluid coursing down his oesophagus and his agonised shock. What was left of his tongue flapped uselessly at the back of his throat, searing agony enveloping his whole body.

He felt her mouth fasten around his eye, felt incredible suction being applied.

Felt the eyeball itself being drawn from its socket by the power of her sucking.

Jennings tried to shake himself free, his rapidly shrinking penis still wedged inside her vagina, now acting like a bond which anchored him to her, preventing him from pulling away.

She gripped his skull so hard he feared she would crush it.

The suction on his eye was intolerable. It felt as if his head was filled with agonising white light.

Karen Gregson sucked hard, ignoring the blood which continued to cover her as it poured from the red chasm of his mouth.

She felt the bulbous eye come free of its socket and plop into her sucking mouth. Between her teeth there was something thin and membranous. Slippery and pulsing. She bit through the optic nerve then turned and spat the throbbing eye from her mouth, pushing Jennings back, glaring at him. At the blood which covered his face, at the empty hole where one of his eyes used to be. Blood and clear fluid were coursing down his cheek and he was lolling about on the bed like a discarded doll, trying to scream but barely able to retain a grip on consciousness.

Moving with incredible speed she snatched the ring of keys from his belt then tore off her bloodied nightdress and pulled on jeans and a sweater, pushing her feet into trainers.

The room was spattered with blood.

She wiped most of it from her face with a sheet but knew she couldn't afford to be more thorough.

Time was against her.

Already they might be coming for her. At least they wouldn't have heard him scream . . .

Jennings was sprawled across the bed, his body twitching slightly, his trousers still around his knees.

As Karen turned towards the door she felt something soft beneath one foot. Something which seemed to burst as she put pressure on it.

She realised it was his eye.

As she left the cell she looked to the right and left and saw doors at either end of the corridor.

She chose the one to the right and sprinted towards it.

One Hundred and Seven

Locals in the area called it The Cinder Path but quite why that thought popped into Parker's mind he didn't know. All he did know was that the narrow track which would lead him on to another road connecting with Brackley Heath was rutted by the passage of farm machinery and caused his car to bounce violently as he drove along it.

On both sides twigs and branches scraped against the paintwork of the Peugeot like virulent fingernails and he heard a series of loud cracks as the car hit particularly thick pieces of wood.

The track was almost pitch dark, lit only by the dull glare of the Peugeot's headlights. It was rarely used during the night because of this and also because no one in their right mind would risk their vehicle's suspension over such uneven ground. Parker had no choice.

Up ahead of him he could see the brighter lights that marked another stretch of dual carriageway. After that it was a clear run to the hospital.

The sudden loud beeping noise in the car startled him until he realised that it was his pager.

Who the hell was calling him now?

Beth?

The police?

Had Beth been involved in an accident somewhere?

He felt a sudden chill sweep through his veins as he

pulled the pager from his pocket and looked at the number illuminated there.

It was the number of Brackley Heath.

Parker frowned.

Where the hell was he going to find a phone?

Beth felt as if she were floating as the warm water lapped around her. She closed her eyes and surrendered to the feeling.

Steam filled the room, hanging like a curtain, covering the mirrors with condensation.

She lifted a leg, watching the water drip from it. Then she repeated the procedure with the other leg before soaping both limbs and reimmersing them in the water.

Beth wondered where Simon was. She hoped he was all right. Perhaps he'd gone out for a walk to clear his head. She hadn't looked in the garage to see if he'd taken his car. She hoped he hadn't. He'd drunk too much to drive. If he was stopped he'd be in trouble.

She glanced at her watch which lay on the side of the bath and wished he'd come home.

At first he thought it was an AA phone but as he drew nearer Parker saw that it was an ordinary public phone, set about two or three yards back from the roadside close to a bus shelter. He brought the Peugeot to a halt and leaped out, praying the phone wasn't broken.

Snatching up the receiver he fumbled in his pocket for change.

A few pennies, some five pence pieces. At last, a couple of tens. He pushed the coins in and jabbed the number of Brackley.

'Hello, Brackley Heath Psychiatric Hos—'

'Listen to me, it's Parker,' he interrupted. 'What's hapened?'

'Doctor Parker,' the voice said, a little startled.

The psychiatrist recognised it as that of Damian Wilks.

360

'What the hell is going on?' Parker demanded.

'It's Karen Gregson,' Wilks told him. 'She's escaped.'

Parker swallowed hard.

'How?' he said, quietly.

This wasn't possible.

'She took Jennings' keys, God knows what happened in there,' Wilks voice cracked slightly. 'She killed him. *And* one of the psychic investigators, she took his van and—'

'When did this happen?' Parker wanted to know.

'About fifteen to twenty minutes ago, we've called the police that's why I took so long contacting you. I—'

Again Parker cut him short, his whole body quivering.

'Tell the police . . .'

He heard beeps.

The money was running out.

'Call me back here, Wilks,' he shouted, searching for the number.

The centre of the dial was missing. There was no number.

'I know where Karen Gregson is going,' Parker shouted, as if raising his voice was somehow going to stop the time running out. 'Tell the police to . . .'

Dead line.

Parker slammed down the receiver in fury, his breath coming in gasps. He spun round and ran back towards the Peugeot, sliding behind the wheel, flooring the accelerator as he headed back into town.

He prayed he wasn't too late.

He had to get to Beth before *she* did.

Whoever she was.

A thought struck him.

Karen Gregson couldn't drive.

He felt those icy fingers plucking at the back of his neck.

But Lucy could.

One Hundred and Eight

She abandoned the van two streets away from her destination. After all, it was a short walk. The police would be looking for the van anyway. They'd be looking for her but it didn't matter. They would never find her in time.

The darkness was an ally too. It hid her, sheltered her from prying eyes.

And it hid the traces of blood on her fingers.

She'd wiped most of it away on the jacket of the second man she'd killed, the one she'd seen as she left Brackley Heath. It had been surprisingly easy to kill him. A blow to his face which had stunned him and then she'd slammed his head repeatedly against the hub-cap of the offside rear wheel of the van until blood had gushed from several wounds and something thick and pulsing had swelled through a rent in his temple.

Now she walked briskly through the streets, knowing what and who she sought.

She had time.

They would not know where to come looking for her.

They would not expect her to come *here*.

It was a chilly night but even though she was dressed only in a sweater, jeans and trainers she felt no hint of the cold.

One more street.

Around the next corner.

She slowed her pace as she approached the house.

There was one car parked in the driveway.

The Astra.

Her car.

There were lights on in the sitting room and the landing. She moved cautiously towards the front door, glancing around to see if anyone had seen her approach, but the street was silent.

She smiled.

It was like coming home.

She reached for the handle of the front door.

Parker glanced at his watch.

He'd been lucky so far, the road had been more or less clear. No hold-ups. The accident that had caused him to take a diversion on the way to Brackley Heath had been cleared.

He drove through the first of the estates marking the outskirts of the town doing fifty.

There were only two or three people on the streets.

One stood and watched as he sped past.

He guessed it would take another five or ten minutes to reach home. No time to stop and call the police. No time.

Please God.

He glanced down at the speedometer as he shot past a thirty-mile-per-hour speed-limit sign doing fifty-five.

As he looked he saw that the needle of his petrol gauge was nudging the red.

No. Not now.

Five, ten minutes.

Did he have that much fuel left?

He drove on.

Beth climbed out of the bath and pulled on her robe, bending to wipe the sides of the bath as the water swirled away down the plughole.

She let most of the moisture soak into the towelling robe then slipped it off, using a large bath towel to dry herself. She walked naked into the bedroom where she pulled on a pair of leggings, white socks and a baggy sweater which felt comfortingly warm.

363

The room, she noted, was chilly.

And growing colder by the second.

Jesus, it was freezing.

She hadn't noticed it in the warmth of the bath but now she felt the iciness in the air.

Beth crossed to a radiator and touched it.

It was hot.

Then why was the room so cold?

She swallowed hard.

It was then she heard the noise from downstairs.

There was no pretence of stealth now.

The front door had been unlocked.

The hallway was dark; it was the landing light that offered welcome.

The intruder passed quickly into the kitchen. She knew which drawer she wanted and with one powerful jerk, she hauled it open.

The cutlery clattered noisily as she searched through it.

It was there.

The kitchen knife was fully ten inches long and wickedly sharp.

She clutched it in one fist and headed back towards the hallway. At the bottom she paused, ears alert for any sound. She heard only the gentle creaking of floorboards. Someone moving around up there.

She smiled.

Beth felt the cold closing in upon her, crushing her.

The cold and the silence. The house was so quiet now.

First the crash from downstairs and now the silence. She knew it could not be Simon.

When the landing light went out she was certain of it.

She heard the unmistakable sound of footfalls.

Whoever was inside the house was coming up the stairs.

One Hundred and Nine

The doors leading off from the landing were closed.

The cold was intensifying. Beth was shivering but she wondered how much of that was fear.

She heard the top step creak, realised that the intruder was on the landing now. Standing. Listening.

Waiting.

Beth felt sure that whoever was out there on the landing would hear her heart thudding against her ribs. It was going like a triphammer. She gritted her teeth, tried to calm herself.

She heard footsteps moving across the landing. Stealthy, cautious.

Beth crossed to the door of the spare room in which she hid and eased open the door a fraction, enough to allow herself a view of the landing.

The intruder was a woman.

About five two, shoulder-length blonde hair, slight build.

The woman in the dream?

Only Beth knew this was no dream. It was as real as the kitchen knife the figure gripped in its hand.

The woman was heading for the main bedroom, pushing cautiously at the door.

Beth wondered what she should do?

Stay put in the spare room, pray that the woman would not come looking for her there?

Hide in the wardrobe?

Perhaps bolt for the stairs, try to make it down, beat the intruder out of the house?

The alternatives tumbled through her mind madly. And there were other questions too: who *was* this woman? What did she want here?

Beth opened the door a fraction of an inch more.

The hinge creaked protestingly.

The woman spun round and Beth stifled a scream as she just made out the dried blood on her clothes and face.

Beth ducked back into the spare room, pulled open the wardrobe door as carefully as she could and slipped inside.

The door was flimsy wood, louvered.

She would have to duck down.

If the woman entered the room she would see her through the slats of wood.

The woman.

It *was* the woman in her dream.

All she was aware of now was the slow deliberate footsteps moving across the landing towards her.

Beth hunkered down, her heart still hammering.

Her hand touched something cold and, again, she had to stifle a yell. Something metal. Something large.

Simon's tool box.

She lifted the lid as quietly as she could, fumbling around inside trying to find something, anything she could use to defend herself when the moment came.

The door of the spare room was pushed open.

Karen Gregson stood in the doorway, the kitchen knife gripped in her fist.

Parker stopped the Peugeot at the roadside and leaped out, hurtling towards the front door of his house, his lungs ready to burst.

The house was in darkness.

Please God don't let me be too late.

He flung open the front door.

'Beth!' he shouted, taking the stairs two at a time,

almost stumbling over the top one as he reached the landing and switched on the light.

Karen Gregson turned to meet him.

One Hundred and Ten

Parker couldn't avoid the razor-sharp blade.

Karen drove it forward and he shouted in pain as it sliced through the skin between his thumb and index finger.

Blood burst from the wound and it felt as if his hand had been enveloped by fire. He could feel nothing in either digit and realised the tendons had been severed.

She struck again but he managed to parry the blow with his other arm, surprised at the strength in the attack.

He dropped to his knees and kicked out at her, managing to knock her legs from under her but she rolled over and struck out at him again, narrowly missing his face.

Parker was on his feet first and Karen drove the blade forward, smiling triumphantly as it buried itself in his left calf.

Blood spurted from the wound as she tugged the steel free and Parker fell back against the wall, blood from his cut hand smearing across the paintwork.

He was only vaguely aware of movement to his right, of Beth rushing out on to the landing.

He saw the claw hammer clutched in her hand.

She swung it with fearful power and caught Karen across the left shoulder, a blow which cracked part of the scapula. The strident snap of bone was clearly audible in the silence.

367

But Karen swung round, swatting at Beth, slashing her across the right forearm, splitting the flesh and scraping the bone.

Beth backed off, blood pouring from the wound.

For interminable seconds they faced each other across the landing.

'That's no way to treat your sister, is it?' said Karen Gregson.

But the voice wasn't hers, it belonged to Lucy.

Beth almost dropped the hammer in surprise.

'Who are you?' she gasped.

'You know who I am. Sister,' Lucy's voice chuckled.

Beth shook her head.

'You won't get my baby,' that all-too-familiar voice hissed.

Parker took his chance and lunged at Karen but she was too quick for him.

She brought the knife up and buried it in his right shoulder.

The razor-sharp steel sheered through his deltoid and pectoral muscles and wedged under the collar bone. As he fell backwards the knife remained stuck there.

He tried to pull it free with his injured hand, screaming as he felt the blade grating against the bone.

Beth attacked with the hammer but Karen caught her downrushing arm and swung her round, propelling her into the wall with a sickening thud.

Beth fought against unconsciousness, noting, with horror, that Karen had picked up the hammer.

Karen. Lucy. Who the hell was she?

Parker grabbed at her leg as she passed but she struck at him with the hammer, a blow which shattered his right middle finger, splintering the bones effortlessly.

The knife still sticking out of his shoulder, blood soaking his upper body, he tried to grab her again, locking his arms through hers as Beth dived into their bedroom.

He had Karen's arms pinned, her frantic struggles

368

making it difficult for him to hold on in his injured state.

She snapped her head back, slamming the back of her skull into his face, breaking his nose.

He dropped to his knees, blood now dripping on to the carpet in front of him.

Karen turned to look at him and Beth took her chance.

Snatching up a photo of her parents from the bedside table, she ran back out on to the landing and swung it hard at Karen, smashing it into her face like a club.

The glass shattered, shards of it piercing Karen's skin, one long piece puncturing her cheek, ripping the skin easily before snapping against a back tooth.

She dropped the hammer and pulled the piece of glass free, the flesh of her cheek ripping from the corner of her mouth as far as her cheekbone. The flap of skin hung uselessly, fluttering as she sucked in breath that tasted like copper.

'You fucking bitch,' Lucy's voice screamed and she hurled herself at Beth, grabbing her by the throat, the flap of skin waving obscenely, blood from her wounds and Beth's covering them both.

She drove Beth back into the spare room, slamming her against the wardrobe door, and the entire thing collapsed inwards, wood splintering.

Beth fell back, her head cracking against the tool box.

'I'm going to kill you,' Lucy's voice said as Karen advanced upon her.

Parker crawled into the room, the knife still stuck in his shoulder, his face now a bloody mask from the shattered appendage which had once been his nose. It looked as though someone had dipped his face in crimson paint.

Beth, consciousness slipping away rapidly, shot out a hand and clawed at the tool box as Karen came at her again.

Parker heard the high-pitched scream of the whirring bit and saw that Beth had snatched up his cordless drill.

She drove it forward, the churning bit driving into Karen's thigh, burrowing through flesh, whining off bone.

Blood burst from the hideous rent, spattering Beth who pulled the drill free, pieces of flesh and bone spinning into the air.

Karen screamed in agony and fell to her knees.

The next scream was Beth's as she slammed the drill forward again.

It pierced Karen's forehead just above the bridge of her nose, boring through the frontal bone and onwards into the brain.

Beth kept her hand on the orange button, ensuring that the power was maintained. She pushed Karen back, driving the drill deeper.

It powered through the thick bone, tiny portions of which were tossed in all directions. Blood erupted from the growing hole, forcing fragments of pinkish grey tissue with it.

Beth pulled the drill free and then drove it forward again, into Karen's right eye.

The socket was riven, the eye bursting as the drill penetrated it.

Beth was sobbing now as she drove the drill into Karen's mouth, slicing through her spinal cord, the cracking of bone ringing in her ears even above the drone of the drill.

Parker looked across at them. At the blood. At Karen Gregson's body and at Beth, straddling it, the drill still gripped in one fist, blood dripping from it, more of the crimson fluid spattered all over her. On the walls, the floor. There was even some on the ceiling.

Every movement was agony for him, it felt as if his body was on fire. He knew he'd lost a lot of blood and the knife was still wedged in his shoulder.

'Beth,' he gasped, his throat dry, his nose dripping crimson as he crawled.

She looked at him impassively, her own face covered in blood. Tears were cutting through the crimson smears.

She dropped the drill, still straddling Karen Gregson's body.

The room smelled like a slaughterhouse.

Even Beth's hair was matted with the red liquid.

'It's over,' Parker managed to grunt, his head spinning.

Beth shook her head, staring down at what was left of the face of Karen Gregson.

'Is it?' she sobbed, her eyes fixed on the waxen features, on the holes bored by the drill.

Parker whispered her name then fell forward on his face.

He heard Beth sobbing.

Darkness closed in on him.

There was only silence.

He blacked out.

One Hundred and Eleven

FOUR MONTHS LATER

'It's remarkable,' said Dr Christopher Leighton, looking down at the child. 'The odds against her surviving were hundreds to one. She's a little fighter.' He smiled, watching the baby girl inside the incubator.

Beth bent over the baby and tapped on the plastic of the incubator. She felt a hand grip hers and looked round to see Simon wink at her.

'I understand you've applied for adoption,' Leighton said.

Parker nodded.

'We know it's a longshot,' he said, quietly.

(especially after what happened in the house)

'but all we can do now is hope.'

'And pray,' Beth added.

'When will you know?' Leighton asked.

'Not for another month or two,' Beth informed him. 'The Social Services department couldn't give us any clues as to how likely we were to get her. I just thought that with me being the only living relative . . .' She allowed the sentence to trail off.

'I'll keep my fingers crossed for you,' Leighton said, holding the door open for them.

They allowed themselves to be ushered from the room, Beth taking one last look back at the child.

She was so beautiful.

She was watching the mobile that hung over the incubator. Sometimes the animals on it would revolve and there would be music. The women in white who came would make that happen. The child was used to these figures in white. Their appearance meant food.

The little girl gurgled happily to herself, now left alone in the room once more. She looked up at the mobile.

It began to turn.

The child watched, fascinated.

Then something caught its eye. Something bright. Colourful.

Not the white it was used to.

This was a golden, red colour.

Long, flowing red hair.

The baby looked up at its mother, gurgling happily.

Lucy Morton smiled back.

The mobile continued to turn.

The room was empty again.

For now.

SLUGS

Prologue

The slug's eye stalks waved slowly as it moved towards the crimson lump on which several of its companions were already feeding. It slithered onto the meat and buried the long central tooth in the flesh, its rows of sharp radular teeth moving back and forth like rasps as it chewed off pieces of meat, enjoying the new coppery taste of blood.

The slugs had grown accustomed to this taste over the past few months, hidden away in the cellar beneath the old house, they had discovered this new source of food. They had tired of their hunting and concentrated, instead, on the raw meat which was tossed down into the rank, fetid darkness. A dozen or so swarmed over the rotted chop, covering it with their own slime trails, chewing until there was nothing but a tiny bone left.

At one time, the slugs had been forced to compete with the other scavengers in the cellar for the precious scraps. With the cockroaches, the wood-lice and centipedes. But now, with a regular supply of meat, they were the dominant group. By sheer weight of numbers, they had made the damp cellar their own. When there were no scraps they fed on the other creatures which shared their pitch black domain. Sometimes they fed on each other.

They had begun to breed more prolifically and many had increased in size. Even though the cellar was large, its floor was covered by them, a vast seething black mass almost invisible in the impenetrable gloom. Only a single shaft of weak light broke through the darkness, forcing its way in by way of a small hole in the cellar bulkhead. But, the slugs paid it no heed. They enjoyed the blackness and the damp and they waited eagerly for the bloodied scraps.

They had heard the footsteps above them many times, felt the vibrations. It made them restless.

In that stinking cellar they slithered over one another in their impatience like an undulating black carpet.

The footsteps seemed to grow louder each day.

One

Ron Bell got through one verse of 'Mull of Kintyre' then
threw up. He slumped heavily against the wooden gatepost,
wondering why the world was spinning round so fast. He
bent double over the fence, clutching his stomach, trying to
persuade the remaining Scotch to retreat back down his
gullet. He swallowed hard and blew out his cheeks. A thin
film of perspiration had formed on his face and he muttered
to himself as his stomach continued to somersault. He turned
and gazed up at the street lamp, its sodium glare reminding
him of a gigantic glow worm. Amused at his little analogy,
Ron started to giggle. He pushed open the gate and stumbled
down the path towards the front of the house, stumbling
once over one of the chipped granite slabs. He fell forward,
the bottle of Haig dropping from his grasp. It landed in the
thick grass on one side of the path and remained unbroken.
Ron felt something wet beneath him as he sat up and he
thought it was the whisky. He put a hand to the crutch of his
trousers and started to giggle again.

'Please let it be blood,' he said, laughing loudly. The
sound carried far in the stillness of the night and someone
walking past the gate peered at him disdainfully.

'Evening,' Ron slurred, trying to get up. He spotted the
Haig bottle lying in the waist high grass and retrieved it
gratefully, realising at the same time that he'd wet himself. A
dark stain was fanning out from his crutch, staining one leg
of his trousers too.

'Shit,' he murmured and stumbled on towards the front
door. He spotted some ants hurrying away from his clumsy
feet and wagged a reproachful finger at them.

'Isn't it about time you lot were in bed?' he chuckled.

'Dirty stop-outs.' With a gleeful whoop, he brought his foot down on the nearest group of insects, crushing them into the pavement. Laughing like an idiot, he made his way up the remainder of the path, rummaging through his pockets for the front door key. He stuffed the whisky bottle into his coat pocket and steadied himself for the difficult task of trying to find the key hole. At the third attempt he made it and tumbled into the hall, his nostrils immediately assailed by the familiar odour of damp. But it was a smell he'd come to live with, almost to welcome. He slapped on the hall light and, being careful to remove the Haig bottle first, slung his coat at the rack. It missed and landed in an untidy heap. Ron looked at it for a moment then blundered into the sitting room. He flicked the light switch. The bulb glowed brilliantly for a second then, with a loud pop, blew out.

'Shit,' grunted Ron. To hell with it, he'd manage without. At half past eleven at night, pissed out of his mind he didn't fancy clambering up step ladders to put a new bulb in. He staggered across the room towards the small portable TV set up on the sideboard. He yelped in pain as he banged his shin on the coffee table and he bent to rub the injured spot, cursing to himself. He finally groped his way to the TV and pressed the ON button, watching as a hazy monochrome picture gradually took shape. Ron fiddled with the aerial until the people on screen possessed the regulation number of heads then he fumbled in the cabinet beneath for a glass. All he could find was a pint pot. He shrugged and, clutching the tankard, stumbled back towards his chair. He bumped his shin again and, as he bent to massage the throbbing bruise, he caught sight of his own reflection in the glass top of the table. His eyes were sunken into their sockets and it looked as if someone had coloured his lower lids with charcoal. The accumulated growth of four days whiskers licked around his chin and cheeks and crackled as he ran a rough hand across them. He shook his head and reached his chair, slumping into the threadbare seat. A spring dug him hard in the backside and he jumped, almost dropping his tankard. Muttering to himself, he unscrewed the cap on the whisky bottle and half filled the pint pot, watching the bubbles rise to the top of the amber liquid. He swallowed the fiery fluid in deep gulps, gasping when he'd finished. He sat for long moments, gazing at the flickering TV screen, not seeing what was on. His mind was elsewhere. He rubbed his bruised shin once more and looked at the coffee table angrily.

Bloody monstrosity. Margaret had bought it not long after they moved into the house. She said it gave the house a touch of class. Ron scoffed at the recollection. What the hell had she known about class? He smiled, wondering what she would have thought seeing him the way he was now. It had been more than two years since she'd walked out on him. It was as if, all his life, he'd been living a false existence, trying to be something he really wasn't. He'd been manager at the local branch of Sainsbury's and it was his salary which had enabled them to buy the house in the first place. The last owner had left it in pretty good nick and there was no need for full scale renovation. A fact which pleased Ron no end, never having been one for painting and decorating. The house was old but without the feeling of antiquity usually felt in buildings erected at the turn of the century. In the beginning they had lived happily together, had built a nice home but Ron had just got bored. As simple as that. He started off by having an affair with one of the cashiers in the supermarket. He usually worked late hours so Margaret never suspected but his ruin had come with the arrival of Debbie. She had been seventeen the first time Ron went to bed with her and, at forty-two, he'd had trouble keeping up with her. By God, she knew what was what between the sheets, he remembered wistfully. He was smitten. He bought her gifts, he took her out, no longer seeming to care whether Margaret found out or not. The money dwindled. Bills didn't get paid.

Then, one weekend, Margaret had gone to stay with her sister and Ron had invited Debbie to stay. He'd never forgotten that weekend. They spent nearly all their time in bed and she was insatiable. So caught up in their wanton

11

lovemaking was he, Ron didn't even notice Margaret standing in the bedroom doorway watching them. She'd come back a day early.

He didn't even try to explain.

Margaret packed her bags that night and walked out on him.

Debbie had tired of him two weeks later and finished the affair. She'd had his money and his love but she only wanted the former. So, for the past two years he'd lived alone in the old house, watching it go to seed as he did himself. His work suffered. He received endless reprimands from his superiors until, finally, after over-ordering the wrong product three weeks running, he'd been dismissed.

After that it was onto the dole. The bills piled up, the rates were overdue and, just that morning, the eviction notice had arrived. He reached for it, picking it up from the table beside him and waving the manilla envelope before him. Inside, an official notice told him that he had twenty-four hours to come up with the money or he'd be forcibly evicted. Fuck them, thought Ron, they'll have to drag me out of here bodily. He emptied the bottle of Haig into the pint pot and tossed the empty receptacle over his shoulder where it shattered against the wall. His head felt as if someone had wrapped a blanket around it. The images on the TV blurred and Ron grunted as he downed the last of the Scotch. They were playing 'God Save the Queen' on the telly and, swaying precariously, Ron stood up and saluted until the music died away. The announcer reminded him to switch his set off and the screen dissolved into a network of lines and dots, the hiss of static making it sound like an enraged snake. Ron put a hand to his head then stepped forward to turn the set off.

Once more he banged into the coffee table but, this time, he overbalanced. Arms flailing like a human windmill, he toppled over the table and crashed heavily to the ground, catching his head on the corner of the sideboard as he fell. He felt a sharp pain as his scalp seemed to split and he went down in a heap before the hissing TV. Blood began to pump freely from the ragged cut and Ron raised one hand as if in silent reproach. Then, with a final groan, he blacked out.

It was almost three a.m. when he came round. His head was thumping from the combined effect of the fall and the whisky and, above him, the TV continued to hiss and crackle. The cut on his head must have been worse than he thought because it seemed to be throbbing mightily. His hair was matted with blood and some of it had run down over his eyes, crusting on the lids and making it difficult to see.

He felt something wet on his chin and, for a second, thought he'd vomited but then he felt something fat and slimy gliding over his lips and into his open mouth. Ron snapped his teeth together, biting down on the jellied lump, cutting it in half. A foul, obscene taste filled his mouth and, as he tried to scream, half of the sticky lump rolled back into his throat. Ron coughed, feeling the hot bile clawing its way up from his stomach. He put a hand up to his cut and, as his probing fingers found the gash in his scalp, he felt a plump, mucus-covered form burrowing into the wound itself. Ron shrieked and tugged at the pulsating shape, finally pulling it free.

For long seconds he held the slug before him, his eyes bulging wide with terror, his own blood covering the head of the foul creature. Then, with a despairing moan, he hurled the monstrosity across the room. But, it was as he did so that he became aware of the pain which was gnawing at his legs and his other arm. Scarcely able to comprehend the sight before him, he saw that his limbs were covered by a seething black mass of these creatures, all slipping and sliding over one another in their efforts to get at his warm flesh. They were on his stomach too, burrowing into the skin and muscle. With a mixture of terror and disbelief, he realised that they were eating him.

He tried to crawl, dragging the monstrous parasites with him. But his hands pressed down onto a jellied carpet of slugs which seemed to be rising from the very floor itself. He fell onto his face and one of the revolting beasts slid into his

13

mouth, fastening its razor-sharp central tooth into his tongue. He felt the bile rising once more, mingling with the taste of his own blood and the sickening mucus of the fat slug. The beast slipped down his gullet and fastened itself into the lining of his throat. Blood began to fill his mouth, spilling out onto the other slugs which were rapidly engulfing him. He felt as though his head was swelling. He couldn't breathe and even the sharp hissing of the TV seemed to have stopped. One of the slugs was burrowing into his ear, seeking out the juicy grey meat of the brain. Ron's body began to shake uncontrollably as the slugs finally swarmed over him, digging deep into his muscles, enjoying the taste of the blood which gushed so violently from his body.

One of them bored into his jugular vein and a great fountain of crimson erupted from the torn blood vessel. It splattered up the wall as if sprayed from a hose pipe.

The slugs stripped the body clean of flesh then they devoured the softer internal organs. Their eye stalks waved about as they slithered over the corpse, their mouths moving constantly, tasting the warm blood. It had formed a pool around the body, soaking into the rotted floorboards, mingling with the mucoid slime which the creatures themselves had left behind. And then, when there was nothing left worth eating, they retreated back slowly to the cellar, to the darkness.

The remains of Ron Bell lay in the centre of the room, one uneaten eyeball bulging madly in the riven socket.

Below, the slugs slithered about. There were many who had not yet eaten and they were restless, as if sensing that this was just the beginning.

Two

The alarm clock went off dead on seven, its strident ringing filling the room. Mike Brady shot out a hand to silence the clock but only succeeded in knocking it off the bedside table. Still ringing, it fell to the carpet and skidded away from his groping hand. He forced his sleep encrusted eyes open and saw that the damn thing was lying about a foot away, just out of reach.

'Oh, sod it,' he groaned, gazing at the clock as if willing it to be silent. Another few seconds ringing and he scrambled out of bed, snatched up the bloody thing and depressed the button on the top. He sat on the edge of the bed eyeing the clock malevolently. The warm shape in bed beside him didn't stir. Brady looked down at her sleeping form and smiled, then he leant over and gently bit her exposed shoulder. She awoke with a start and rolled over, looking up into Brady's smiling face. He held up the clock and tapped the perspex cover indicating the time.

'Rise and shine,' said Brady, slipping a hand under the covers. He tickled her stomach and she started to laugh, although it sounded like an effort. Kim Brady rolled onto her side and gently prodded her husband's belly.

'Fatso,' she said, tugging at a roll of fat with her thumb and forefinger.

Brady looked indignant and got to his feet, crossing to the full length mirror which covered the wardrobe door. He stood before it and drew in his stomach, holding his breath. Defiantly he turned to face her.

'Fatso my arse,' he said but then he lost control and his stomach flopped forward again. They both laughed.

'It comes with your age,' she said, smiling, watching as

15

Brady got down on all fours and began a series of jerky press-ups.

'Look, it's bad enough being forty without having you remind me all the time,' he wheezed, his face turning the colour of over-ripe tomatoes. He finally got to his feet. 'Oh to hell with it. You'll just have to like me fat.'

'I'm only kidding, Mike,' she said, smiling, motioning for him to come back to bed. He sat down beside her, his eyes momentarily straying to her firm breasts, rising and falling gently as she breathed. At thirty-five, Kim Brady still had a figure to be proud of. She blinked myopically at her husband and reached for her glasses, which were on the table beside her, propped up on two Erica Jong novels. But Brady stopped her, instead drawing her close, his mouth pressing urgently against hers, each tongue seeking the warmth of the other. He ran his hand gently across her face then kissed her softly on the forehead. She fumbled for her glasses and pushed them on.

'And stop going on about being forty,' she chided. 'It's not for another month yet and besides,' she started to giggle, 'life . . .'

He interrupted her. '. . . begins at forty. Yes I know, that's what everybody keeps telling me.'

'You know, I was thinking,' she said, the mischievous grin still on her face. 'Being married to a man five years older than me does have its advantages.'

He raised his eyebrows quizzically.

'It means we can both start drawing our pension at the same time.'

He nodded affably.

'It's after seven you know,' he told me. 'Isn't it time *you* got up?' He rose and crossed to the wardrobe, taking out a shirt and tie, hanging them on the handle while he took out his familiar two piece grey suit.

'I'm not going in today,' she told him. 'The nursery's closed for a couple of days.'

He looked round. 'Why?'

'Industrial action by the tea ladies or something,' she said.

16

Brady grunted. 'I don't blame them, the lousy bloody wages they pay them.' He sighed. 'I know one thing. I wish to Christ I didn't have to go in today.' He walked into the adjoining bathroom and Kim heard the sound of his electric razor humming.

'Why not?' she called. 'I thought you liked your job.'

'There's nothing wrong with the job,' he called back, flicking the razor off and running some hot water into the sink. 'It's just that I don't fancy what they've got lined up for me today.'

Kim sat in silence, listening as he washed his face then she heard the hiss and splutter of the shower and, a second later, a pair of pyjama trousers came flying into the bedroom. She smiled. After a moment or two, the shower was turned off and Brady re-emerged into the bedroom, a towel wrapped around his waist. He rubbed himself down and started to dress.

'They're serving an eviction notice on Ron Bell,' he told her. 'You know, the bloke who lives in that old house just outside the town centre.'

'The one near the new estate?' she asked.

He nodded. 'He's about six months behind with the rates and there's been complaints from the residents of the estate about him and the house. The garden's like a bloody jungle. I dread to think what the inside of the place looks like.'

'But I don't understand why you've got to go along,' she said, looking puzzled.

'I've got to drive the bailiff to the house,' he explained. 'They can already sling the poor sod out for non-payment of rates and because of the complaints against him but that's not enough for our council,' he said acidly. 'They want me to write a report on the state of the building, how disgusting it is and how Ron Bell isn't fit to keep it tidy. He's already hung and drawn, they've left the quartering to me'. He pulled his tie tight, smoothing it out and inspecting his image in the mirror. Brady exhaled deeply and pulled on his jacket. He gazed at his own reflection for long moments. Mike Brady, Council Health Inspector. He smiled to himself.

17

He'd held that exalted position for the last fourteen years, two years longer than he'd been married to Kim. Coincidentally, they'd first met at the offices. She'd been a secretary, he'd just arrived from London where he'd been doing the same job. Some of the jobs he'd had in Merton had been child's play after the revelations in London. He'd seen some things there which had made his hair curl. If he had a pound for every hamburger and hot dog seller he'd forced off the streets during those early days he wouldn't need to work, he told himself. Flies on the meat, sausages made out of boiled down pigs' heads, hamburgers with every known type of bacteria alive infesting them, fat two inches deep in the serving trays. Some of the restaurants hadn't been much better. He still remembered the time he'd nearly eaten a curry which was later found to contain mouse droppings, or the incident when he'd walked into one kitchen to see the chef removing maggots from a side of beef he was about to put into the oven.

But, things in Merton were quieter. Even so he'd had his fair share of incidents. Like the house where the ceiling had caved in because the kids had wet the bed so many times and the floorboards had rotted. Twelve of them in that family he remembered, most of the ten kids slept in one bed and they had about three pairs of shoes between them. Other than that there hadn't been too much to bother him, just the usual drizzle of complaints. Blocked drains, the occasional cockroach infestation, the odd shady snack bar but the thing which Brady liked most about his job was that he had no one breathing down his neck all the time. He could get on with things in his own way, as long as the reports were in on time he never even saw any members of the council. This fact suited him admirably, he had nothing to thank them for, there was no love lost between the Conservative council and their Public Health Officer who was fond of voicing his socialist views loudly and often. The only good thing, as far as Brady was concerned was that his job had enabled him to meet Kim. They'd been immediately attracted to one another and had married in less than a year of meeting. The only thing which hurt him, and it hurt more because he knew the heartbreak it caused Kim, was that they were childless and always would be.

Three years after they had married she had been involved in a car accident. Five months pregnant at the time she'd lost the baby and also, due to the severe internal damage she sustained, had been told that she would never be able to bear children. The shock had been overwhelming, hitting them both much harder than he could have imagined. Kim in particular went through a seemingly endless period of depression during which Brady began to fear for her sanity but she got through it in the end and the experience seemed to strengthen their marriage, intensifying their love beyond imagination. For the last six years she had worked in the local nursery, her own thwarted maternal instincts now lavished upon the children of others.

When Brady turned away from the mirror, Kim was getting out of bed. He watched her slip on a paint-stained blouse (the one which she'd worn when they had decorated the place after first moving in) and a pair of faded denims, having to pull just a bit too hard to get them up over her hips. She finally managed it and fastened the button, puffing slightly. He smiled as he watched her and she looked up to see him grinning at her.

'Looks like I'm not the only one who needs to lose some weight,' he said, nodding towards her.

She picked up one of her slippers and threw it at him.

'Cheeky bugger,' she said. 'I've a good mind to make you get your own breakfast.'

He slapped her across the backside and they both made their way downstairs.

Three

Brady wound down the window of the Vauxhall Victor and allowed some of the crisp morning air to blow into the car. It was less than ten minutes' drive from their house to the council offices where he was to pick up Archie Reece, the bailiff, and take him to Ron Bell's house to serve the eviction notice. Brady really wasn't relishing the trip. He'd only met Reece a couple of times but there was something about the man that he didn't like. He seemed to enjoy his job. Evicting people from their homes was more like a hobby for him. Brady remembered the last time it had happened. The house owner had decided that he didn't want to be moved and Reece had promptly whacked him over the head with a chair leg in full view of the poor sod's horrified family. The unfortunate man had spent two months in hospital after that particular brush with Reece. However, the Health Inspector somehow didn't see Ron Bell as the type to put up much of a fight.

He drove at a leisurely pace, taking in the long rows of trees which lined the roadside, already heavy with blossom they brought a sweet odour wafting into the car which Brady sucked in gratefully. Even though it was early, the sun had risen high in the sky and it promised to be a scorcher. The blossom seemed to catch the rays of the sun, holding it until it glowed pink and white like flimsy neon clusters.

A sixteen wheeler drove past in the opposite direction and Brady coughed as a choking cloud of diesel fumes swept into the car. He waved a hand in front of his face and glanced into the rear view mirror, watching the huge lorry swing up to the left, heading for the industrial part of town.

Despite its size, Merton had a prosperous industrial

21

estate, comprising a foundry, a factory which made dust-carts and, the dominant business, a huge computer complex which manufactured the machines for places all around the globe. There was also a sizeable chemical works. The town had suffered its share of closures and redundancies as had all the other towns in the area, but, on the whole, the community was thriving.

Brady swung the Vauxhall into the car park of the council offices, glancing up at the clock above the building. The metal hands had reached eight thirty and the Health Officer checked his watch. He retrieved his briefcase from the back seat, locked his door and headed towards the flight of broad stone steps which led up to the main doors of the council offices. The building itself was a large, brownstone edifice built over a hundred years ago, and a century of accumulated muck was being removed by a posse of workmen who were at this moment swarming over the lower storeys of the building like so many boiler-suited ants repairing a break in the nest wall. Brady nodded affably to the foreman as he passed. The man was sitting cross-legged on the lowest walkway of the scaffolding, drinking coffee from a thermos flask.

The Health Inspector pushed open the double doors and walked in.

Brief greetings were exchanged with the two women on the reception deck and then Brady took the stairs to the second floor where his office lay.

He found Archie Reece waiting for him outside the office door.

The bailiff tried to smile but it came out as a leer and Brady just nodded in return and walked past him into his office. The other man followed him in and stood impatiently at the door watching as Brady crossed to his desk and sat down. There were three letters lying there and Reece exhaled noisily and irritably when he saw the Health Inspector open the first of them.

The bailiff held up a brown envelope.

'The eviction order on Ron Bell,' he said.

22

'I know,' said Brady, opening the second letter.

'You're supposed to drive me there, Mr Brady.'

The Health Inspector looked at Reece with distaste. He was a big man, broad and very muscular even though the folds of his ill-fitting suit did their best to conceal that fact. Brady guessed his height to be around six two and his hair, although white, was thick and flowing, almost covering his collar. His hands looked huge, big enough to encircle Brady's head with little effort. He was tapping agitatedly against the door frame with his stubby fingers.

'Is there a bloody deadline on it?' asked Brady.

Reece nodded. 'I'm supposed to have him out by nine.' He looked at his watch. 'It's quarter to, now.' He turned his gaze back to the Health Inspector who rose to his feet, fumbling in his jacket pocket for his car keys.

'Come on, then,' he said, irritably.

'I'm only doing my job,' Reece protested, following the younger man out of the office towards the stairs. They descended hurriedly and Brady led him out to the waiting Vauxhall. Reece slumped heavily into the passenger seat and rummaged around in his pocket, finally producing a packet of Rothmans.

'Don't smoke in here please,' said Brady, looking at him disdainfully. 'If *you* want to die of lung cancer that's your business. I bank on being around a bit longer.' He twisted the key in the ignition, stuck the car into first and pulled out.

Reece took the cigarette from his mouth and pushed it carefully back into the packet. He found a packet of mints in his other pocket.

'Is it all right if I have one of these?' he asked, defiantly. 'Or are you frightened of catching diabetes too?'

Brady looked at the big man as he pushed the mint into his mouth.

'Do you know what they use as sweeteners in those?' he asked, a slight smile on his lips.

Reece shook his head, gazing out of the front window.

'Re-cycled pig swill,' Brady told him, laughing aloud as

23

the bailiff coughed and spat the mint out of the open window.

In five minutes they had reached Ron Bell's house.

Reece was out of the car with a speed implying relish and Brady could see the slight hint of a smile on the big man's lips. The Health Inspector locked the car and followed the bailiff, who, by this time, was through the gate and heading up the path to the front door of the house. Brady walked more slowly, his eyes moving slowly over the building and the garden. Jesus, he thought, talk about run-down. The grass on either side of the cracked path brushed against him as he walked and he lengthened his stride to avoid the scurrying ants which were oozing up from the crack in the granite like soil. The windows reflected the sun back at the two men, and that combined with the filth on them, made it impossible to see inside. Reece knocked three times on the front door and waited for an answer. Brady wandered across to the nearest window. It had wooden shutters on it, the wood itself rotted and yellowed in places. One was hanging off the hinges. He put his face to the pane and squinted into the gloom, trying to make out some sign of movement in what he took to be the dining room.

Reece banged the door again, harder this time.

'Perhaps he's out,' said Brady, wearily, sauntering back to the door.

Reece ignored the remark and repeated his frenzied attack on the door, as if willing it to open by itself. Brady shook his head.

'Bell,' shouted Reece, looking up at the windows of the first floor.

'For Christ's sake,' said the Health Inspector.

'I'm going to break in,' Reece told him. The bailiff strode off down the path to the window where Brady had just been. He took off his jacket, wrapped it around his elbow and, with one powerful backward stroke, broke the glass. Lumps of dirty crystal fell into the room and landed on the bare floor. Reece reached through and opened the window, hoisting himself over the sill. He landed on the broken glass which crunched beneath his heavy shoes. Brady followed him, the sound of the crushed glass reminding him of walking in heavy frost. Both men were immediately assailed by the smell of damp and Reece coughed, waving a hand in front of him. Dust particles floated lazily in the rays of sunlight which cut through the gloom.

'Bell,' Reece called again but only silence greeted his shout. He pointed to a door at the far end of the room and the two men headed towards it.

It was Brady who heard the sound first.

'Listen,' he said, lowering his voice for reasons even he didn't understand.

Reece stopped impatiently and cocked an ear in the direction of the sound. It was a high pitched, unceasing, hum which grew louder as they approached the door. The big man looked at Brady and shrugged. The handle to the door was rusty and pieces of brown metal peeled off like scabrous flesh as the bailiff turned it. It swung open with a loud creak and both men walked into the sitting room.

The stench which met them was almost palpable and even Brady recoiled at its ferocity. He just had time to register that the high pitched hum was coming from the TV which was still on, then his attention turned to the thing in the centre of the room.

Reece too saw it and Brady was vaguely aware of the big man sagging against the door frame, clutching his stomach.

'Jesus Christ,' he groaned, trying to retain his breakfast.

Brady took a step closer, the realization slowly spreading through him. The shapeless mass of torn flesh and shining bone which occupied the centre of the room was all that remained of Ron Bell. The Health Inspector moved closer, as close as the choking odour would allow him. The room was like a charnel house. Congealed blood was splattered up the walls and around the body, its rusty colour matching that of the old door handle. One sightless eye fixed Brady in a baleful stare. He pulled out his handkerchief and pressed it to his face but the foul stench even seemed to penetrate the material.

25

The corpse still retained some shreds of flesh, covering the shiny bones like wisps of gossamer, and clumps of hair still clung defiantly to what was left of the head. The mouth was open, revealing many rotted teeth, the lower jaw having been eaten through. It yawned soundlessly, the ligaments and tendons which had held it in place were gone. Part of the nose remained, the solitary nostril choked with clotted blood.

Reece seemed to have recovered his wits a little and he looked over at Brady, who was still kneeling beside the mutilated body.

'What the fucking hell happened to him?' gasped the bailiff, his breath coming in short gasps.

Brady didn't answer, he had finally managed to tear his gaze away from the body long enough to study the bare floorboards around it. They felt spongy because of the congealed blood which had soaked into the wood but it wasn't that which attracted the Health Inspector's eye. It was the shiny substance which seemed to cover the floor, sparkling like oil on water when the sun catches it. He noticed that it was all over the corpse too.

'How long's he been dead?' asked Reece, wiping a thin film of perspiration from his face.

Brady shrugged. 'It's hard to say. From the appearance of the body I'd say he'd been dead for months but . . .' He allowed the sentence to trail off. He stood up. 'You'd better phone the police.'

Reece nodded, happy to be able to escape the reeking confines of this slaughterhouse. Brady heard him exit then he leant back against the door frame, his eyes sweeping around the room.

There was more of the shiny substance on the far wall, only there it seemed to break apart into small trails each about an inch wide. He stroked his chin thoughtfully and looked down. There was more of the stuff at his feet. He knelt and felt tempted to touch it, much as a child does with something that arouses its curiosity but, at the last minute, he withdrew his hand, reaching instead to the inside pocket of his jacket. He took out a pencil and poked the end into the shiny stuff, seeing that it was fluid, but thick and sticky and, when he removed the pencil, the mucoid slime stuck to it. Brady wrinkled his forehead and laid the pencil down on the nearby sideboard.

He took one last look around the room and hurried out to see where Reece had got to.

The high pitched hum of the TV continued.

Four

Night brought with it a cloying humidity which made sleep, for many people, difficult. There was no moon and just the sodium glare of the street lamps penetrated the darkness.

Some of the houses on the new estate overlooked Ron Bell's house and some of those tenants had watched that afternoon as first the police and then an ambulance had arrived at the old place, but few had taken much notice. Perhaps the bloke had been taken ill, a heart attack perhaps. No one knew. No one cared. Some were pleased that he was gone, perhaps now the house would be sold to someone who would look after it and preferably to someone who would get that maze of a garden into some semblance of order. But, the subject of Ron Bell and his house was only of passing interest to the inhabitants of the new estate. Now, with night well and truly upon them, they tried to sleep in their little houses which had become like ovens due to the weather.

In dozens of red brick dwellings, they dozed, snored, made love, watched television or sat and talked. Crying children were attended to, pets dozed in the heat and, somewhere on the estate, a couple of tom-cats fought out their nightly duel. They hissed and spat at one another, scratching and biting in one of the gardens until a well aimed ash-tray, thrown from one of the bedroom windows, put an end to their squabble.

Silence descended once more.

In the cellar of Ron Bell's house it was silent too, except for the slurping, sucking sounds the slugs made as they slithered over one another. There seemed to be so many of them now. The cellar was filled practically to overflowing and, besides, their source of food had disappeared. Their

29

hunger became uncontrollable and they began to slither up towards the hole in the bulkhead, towards the night air. Some burrowed through the ground, others slithered through the waist high grass which parted as if moved by some invisible hand. Their jet black colour helped them blend into the night.

But most crawled to the sewer cover which lay in the garden. Rusty and covered in moss, it was surrounded by broken concrete and the slugs found many holes. They crawled down into the black depths, welcoming the wetness which enabled them to move faster. Many even slipped into the filthy water, carried along by its flow.

Through the earth, over it and swept along by the fast flowing sewers, they moved towards the new estate, an invisible unstoppable black horde.

Five

Mary Forbes watched as her two children disappeared around the bend in the road, waving to them one last time before she retreated back inside the house. She smiled happily to herself as she crossed to the windows in the front room. She unfastened them and pushed them open, allowing the slight breeze to blow in. It brought with it the heady scent of lavender and Mary looked out into the garden with pride at the blossoming purple flowers. The DJ on the radio told her it was eight fifty one and then his exaggeratedly gay banter was mercilessly replaced by the strains of a Perry Como record. Mary began to sing along with it while she bustled through the house, raising her voice as she went into the kitchen. She took the breakfast dishes from the table, shaking her head when she saw how much the kids had left on their plates. It hardly seemed worth giving them anything. Such a waste, with food as expensive as it was! She shook her head as she shovelled it into the pedal bin with a fork. Perry Como meandered on and Mary joined in mightily when he got to the chorus, her voice rising above the chink of plates as she washed them. When she'd finished that particular task she cleared the table, tripping over one of Jack's slippers as she did so. She glared down at the offending article for a second, making a mental note to tell him about it when he got back home that evening. No wonder the kids are untidy when their father sets them this sort of example, she thought to herself. She and Jack had been married for twenty-four years and, not a day had gone past during that time when she hadn't had to tell him about his untidiness. He said she should stop nagging but Mary was proud of her house and how neat and tidy it was and she

31

aimed to keep it that way. Whether the rest of the family liked it or not.

Sundays were the worst. She was always up at eight and, dead on nine, the hoover went on. The rest of the family always complained but Mary was oblivious to their protestations as she happily whizzed through the rooms with the cleaner, singing along with the radio like some demented char-lady.

Perry Como finished singing and the DJ told her it was nine o'clock. Mary dried her hands and, with the plates left on the draining rack, she scuttled upstairs to fetch the hoover.

It was the same routine every day, it never varied. Seven a.m. get up. Quarter past, get Jack and the kids up. Breakfast, get Jack off to work, make sure the kids were ready for school then, from eight fifty onwards, the house was hers. Washing up, hoovering, dusting and Mary loved every minute of it. She usually finished her housework around eleven and then she either took a trip into town (less than five minutes on the bus from the new estate) or she had coffee with one of her many friends. If there was one thing Mary enjoyed more than housework, it was a good natter.

'Did you hear about her at number 36?'

'I see so-and-so is ill.'

'Someone told me that whatsisname is having an affair with that woman, you know the one.'

But the thing which pleased her most of all was how much cleaner and tidier her house was compared to those of her friends and she felt a particular swell of pride when *they* told *her* how nice her place looked. Mary would just smile and tell them it was hard work with a family like hers but it was worth it.

Now she roared from room to room with the hoover, still singing loudly to herself despite the fact that the radio was drowned out by the din of the cleaner. She pushed it rapidly before her like some kind of jet propelled mine detector. The dusting was completed at a similarly dizzy pace and, at precisely ten fifty three, Mary tucked her duster away neatly

32

into a drawer and wiped her hands on her apron. However, with it being Friday, there was one more thing which she had to do. Retrieving a tin of polish from the cupboard, Mary armed herself with a fresh duster and headed out to the front doorstep.

As she opened the door, Mrs Banks from next door passed by and the two women exchanged brief pleasantries before Mary knelt to begin her last job.

It was as she took the lid off the polish that she noticed the first of the slime trails.

Mary looked at it, watching as it glinted in the sunlight. Then she saw another, and another. The whole step was criss-crossed with silver threads, some hardened the others still fresh and sticky. Mary followed the course of one fresh trail, noting that it ran across the step and up the inside of the concrete porch. On either side of the porch she had baskets of flowers and, as she stood up she saw a lump of what looked like phlegm hanging from the first of the suspended baskets. She leaned closer, peering inquisitively at the almost transparent lump but, as she looked closer she could see that the stuff was like frog-spawn only instead of being round, these things were cylindrical. With a dark centre they hung in clusters of about twenty or thirty. Mary noticed that there were five or six of these clusters on each of the hanging baskets and she felt an almost unnatural disgust as she looked at them. She told herself she must show Jack when he got home, then, careful not to touch the jellied lumps, she took her duster and knocked each one from the hanging pots.

She returned to the slime trails on the doorstep and set about removing them, polishing away feverishly until all traces of them were gone, then she closed the door. But, as she put the lid back on the polish, she wondered once more what those mucoid clusters on the flower baskets had been.

Brady brought the Vauxhall to a halt and switched off the engine. He hurriedly got out of the car, anxious to be free of its stifling confines, impatient to breathe the sweet summer air once more. He locked the door behind him and strode across the deserted street to the first of the houses he was to inspect. Elm Drive was the last street on the new estate to be filled, with families due to move in at the beginning of the following week. The council had asked him to give the houses a quick look over before the new tenants took up residence, just to make sure everything was all right. But Brady's mind was not really on his present job as he walked up the short front path to the first house. Burned deep into his mind was the image of Ron Bell's mutilated body. The police had arrived within five minutes of Archie Reece's call, the ambulance another five after that. The body had been removed by two young ambulancemen, one of whom had vomited at the scene of carnage in the old house. The local police inspector had been unable to offer much in the way of explanation, insisting that they would have to wait for the results of the autopsy before pursuing any investigation. Brady had mentioned the incident only briefly to Kim, telling her that Bell had been dead when they found him, but dispensing with the worst details of the ghoulish find.

Now he stood before the front door of number one Elm Drive, fumbling in his trouser pocket for the set of pass keys which he'd been given. His jacket was draped over his shoulder and Brady could feel the perspiration sticking to his back. The concrete of the path felt hot beneath him and he could feel its searing warmth even through the soles of his shoes. The sky was cloudless, the sun hanging there defiantly. The whole town was enveloped in a blanket of blistering heat. It was like walking about inside a huge oven.

Brady found the key ring and tried one of the keys, muttering to himself when it didn't fit the lock. He tried again.

Another failure.

He sucked in an impatient breath and pushed the third key in. This time it turned and the front door swung open. He stepped into the cloying humidity which was the hall way. The place smelt of fresh wood and his shoes beat out a tattoo on the concrete floor as he walked from room to room.

34

He finished downstairs, did a quick tour of the upper floor and then, satisfied, moved to the next house.

He repeated the procedure in the remaining nine buildings on that side of the road, then crossed and continued his inspection of the buildings opposite.

As he entered the penultimate house, he looked up to see a couple of kids cycling past on their way to school and the Health Inspector glanced at his watch. It was almost one fifteen. After he'd finished checking these last two houses, he told himself, he'd go and get some lunch.

It was as he closed the door behind him that he saw something glinting in the rays of sunlight which fell into the hall.

Brady paused, letting go of the front door, his attention riveted to the glistening thing before him. He stepped closer, crouching slightly to get a better look.

It was a slime trail.

The front door swung back on its hinges and slammed with an almighty crash which made the Health Inspector jump. He leapt to his feet, his heart pounding.

'Shit,' he muttered, angry with himself for being so jumpy. Then he turned his attention back to the slime trail. It was dry, crumbling away when he rubbed the toe of his shoe in it. Brady followed its shiny course into the living room (or at least what would be the living room eventually), noting that there were more of the trails in the other room, one or two of them actually stretching a couple of feet up the wall. He scanned the remainder of the room then passed into the kitchen.

There were more of the trails in there.

Brady hurried out and into the last house, twisting the key almost frenziedly, pushing his way into the hall.

The slime trails were more numerous in the last house. He counted a dozen at least. For long seconds, the Health Inspector stood in the doorway, his eyes darting furtively around the humid room then he crossed to one of the trails and peered closely at it. Like the one in the house before, it was dry. Several hours, or, for all he knew, days old. All the trails were dry but Brady suddenly remembered Ron Bell and the silvery fluid which had covered his remains and he felt uneasy, suddenly anxious to be out of the house. Not really knowing why. The air seemed to be unexpectedly fetid and he hurried out into the oppressive heat once more, locking the door behind him. He crossed to his car and sat for long moments behind the wheel before leaning forward and starting the engine. He let it idle for a moment, looking at the house which he'd just left, then, with a sigh, he stuck it into first and pulled off.

Six

Bert Crossley finished his second pint of Guinness and pushed the empty pint pot back across the bar.

'Fill that up again, Tom,' he said to the barman, fumbling in his pockets for some money. 'And whatever these two silly bastards want.' He indicated the men with him both of whom shook their heads, the first of them checking his watch.

'No thanks,' Danny said. 'I'd better be getting home, the wife will wonder where I am.' He picked up a couple of full shopping bags and left to a chorus of cheers and whistles from the few remaining occupants of the public bar. As he reached the door someone shouted, 'A woman's work is never done,' and the other men laughed loudly.

'You in a hurry too, Tony?' asked Bert Crossley, watching as the second man downed what was left in his glass.

The man nodded. 'Yeah, I'd better get back to the site. I'll see you tonight though,' he assured Bert as he left.

The big man picked up his pint and swallowed two or three enormous mouthfuls, patting his swaying belly appreciatively. He belched loudly and excused himself. Bert Crossley tipped the scales at somewhere around eighteen stone and that, combined with his height, made him a formidable sight to be propping up the bar of The Swan. Bert ran a small butcher's shop in the tiny precinct of shops situated on the new estate. The precinct also comprised a newsagent's, a small supermarket and a fish and chip shop. Bert prided himself on being the only one of the shop keepers who actually owned his own business. He stood at the bar every lunchtime between one and two p.m. nattering away

37

about football, politics and anything else anyone would care to talk about. Putting people off their ploughman's lunches by his insistence on wearing his working apron which was perpetually stained with the rusty marks of dried blood. Considering he'd been a butcher for forty-two years, Bert still didn't seem to have mastered the use of his knives and his fingers were usually swathed in blood soaked bandages, or plasters which refused to stay on and fell off to expose a jagged gash just as someone in the bar was about to tuck into their lunch. About six years back, he'd sliced off the top of his thumb while carving up a bullock carcass but, instead of calling the ambulance, Bert had calmly closed the shop and, carrying the severed end of the digit, strolled down to the doctor's surgery. That had been when he had a shop in the town centre. He'd moved into the new premises on the estate about ten months ago and had built up a good name amongst the residents. His father had always told him that there was no substitute for the family butcher's shop and Bert had been happy to find that his old man had been right. Bert had learned all he knew about the trade from his father who used to run his own shop in the days when butchers still did their own slaughtering too. Bert remembered the first time, as a child of ten, he saw his father kill a bullock. The memory was as vivid all these years later as it was at the time. In his mind's eye he could still see his father leading the animal to the centre of the yard, tethering it to an iron post there. He remembered that the animal was drooling, saliva hanging in long white streamers from its mouth. It had stood perfectly still, almost as if it realized that there was no point in running, as Bert's father had approached it with the sledgehammer. He had steadied himself, raising the heavy hammer above his head. Then, with a blow combining demonic force and years of practice, he'd brought the sledge down on the bullock's head. There was a strident snapping of bone as the skull was shattered, the beast pitching forward as its front legs buckled. It had been dead before it hit the floor. Bert had then watched as his father had hung it up, sliced open the throat to drain it and then set about

38

cutting the animal up. He had watched it all in fascination, remembering the smells too. The overpowering smell of the blood and the pungent odour of excrement which flowed out in a trail behind the twitching beast as his father had dragged it away with a meat hook.

Bert downed the rest of his pint and sighed wistfully. There'd been an art to butchering in those days. It still needed a lot of skill, granted, but the art was gone. Now the livestock were slaughtered hundreds in a day by the pneumatic gun which shot a retractable bolt into their heads. The carcasses arrived at the butcher's in storage lorries, already prepared. The only skill that remained was in cutting the damn things up.

'Another one, Bert?' asked the barman, reaching for the empty pint pot.

The butcher shook his head. 'No thanks, Tom, I'd better get back and open up.' He glanced at the clock above the bar. It was almost two o'clock. He got to his feet and lumbered out into the sunshine, wiping his face with the back of his hand. Bert perspired a lot, even in relatively cool weather, but today he thought he must have lost a couple of pounds already. He glanced up at the blazing sun and began the short walk from the pub to the shop. It took him past some old people's flats and one or two of the old dears waved gaily to Bert as he passed. He was a popular man with all the residents and many found it a surprise that he had never married but, throughout his life, Bert had always found that his business was more important than the ties of a home life. After his father died, he'd looked after his mother, nursing her through her last few painful years until she had a stroke which proved to be fatal. By that time Bert was forty-one. He had his business and, what was more, he just thought he was too old to start chasing women around.

A fly buzzed past him, attracted by the dried blood on his apron but Bert shooed it away. He reached the back door of the shop and let himself in. It was much cooler in there and he stood beneath one of the powerful fans for a moment before walking through into the shop itself. The blinds were down so the shop was in a kind of semi-darkness. Bert was about to pull them up when something made him turn to face the display cabinets.

His mouth dropped open and, for once, he was speechless.

When he had left the shop at one o'clock, less than an hour ago, the cabinets had been full. Their trays heaped with fine cuts of beef, pork, lamb, kidneys, liver. Everything. Now, Bert ran disbelieving eyes over the remnants of his stock. The meat and offal had been devoured, only tiny scraps of it remained in the stainless steel trays. Even the blood which had run from the meat was gone, every last drop removed as if by some invisible hand. There were pieces of meat on the floor too, here and there were some dark patches of blood.

Bert put a hand to his forehead, drawing in a long, slow breath.

'My God,' he murmured softly. Then, immediately, his bewilderment turned to anger. Who the hell would do such a thing? He quickly inspected the locks on the doors and windows. If some bastard had broken in Bert promised himself he'd gut the sod personally. But a swift inspection told him that the doors and windows were still secure.

He stood silently, gazing at the empty trays before him, wondering if maybe he'd had too much to drink that lunch time and he was really imagining this.

'My God,' he muttered once more.

The shop was silent but for the bluebottle which buzzed indolently around him. Bert decided to check the back door and windows and he hurried through to the rear of the building.

In his haste he failed to notice the slime trails which led from the display cabinets to the ventilator grille on the wall. Still fresh, they glittered with a vile sparkle of their own.

Seven

Brady wiped his face with a handkerchief as he walked across the car park towards the council offices. The café where he usually had his lunch was only 200 yards from the large building and could be seen from his own office window. He looked in that direction as he crossed the car park. Christ, it was hot. The tarmac beneath his feet looked as though it was on the verge of bubbling. Brady hadn't eaten much, the experience in the two new houses had quelled his appetite but he pushed the incident to the back of his mind. The Health Inspector loosened his tie as he wearily climbed the flight of stone steps to the main doors, the sun burning fiercely on his back as he turned to enter the building.

It was cool in there and he managed to ignore the frightful rattle emitted by one defective fan. The sound reminded him of a football rattle. As he crossed reception on the way to the staircase, Julie Jenkins called him across to the desk. Brady turned, running an appraising eye over the youngest staff member in the building. She was in her early twenties and had only been working there for three months but, already, most people seemed to have taken to her. The male members of the work-force in particular. She smiled sweetly at Brady who returned the gesture, managing a quick glance at her shapely figure as he did so. Because of the hot weather she wore only a light, cheese-cloth top through which he glimpsed the dark outline of her nipples straining against the flimsy material. The blouse was undone to the third button to reveal a tiny silver crucifix hanging between her ample breasts. Brady smiled to himself, administering a swift mental rebuke for taking so much interest in a girl young enough to be his daughter. Anyway, he told himself, you're

41

a married man. Nevertheless, just because you've bought the goods doesn't stop you window shopping, he mused.

Julie held up a piece of paper, smiling as Brady leant on the reception desk.

'A message for you, Mr Brady,' she told him. 'A lady rang up to complain about her drains and toilet.'

'Blockage?' asked the Health Inspector.

Julie nodded.

'Then it's a job for the sewage department, not me.'

'She says that there's a terrible smell coming from the drains. She wants it checked.' Julie looked at him, the deep blue of her eyes reminding Brady of the sky outside.

He sighed. 'OK. What's the name and address?'

She handed him the piece of paper and the Health Inspector pushed it into his pocket.

'It's on the new estate,' said Julie, as if she was telling him something he didn't know.

Brady exhaled deeply. 'Well, I can think of better ways of spending an afternoon than bending over drains and toilets, especially in this sort of weather.' He smiled. 'Give the sewage people a buzz anyway. I might need one of their blokes along, just in case it's anything below the surface.' He turned and headed towards the staircase.

Julie flicked a switch on the console before her, picking up the phone when a green light flickered on.

Brady reached his office and walked in to find the heat almost unbearable. He crossed to the window and heaved it up, allowing a blast of cool air to blow in. The perspiration beneath his arms and on his back suddenly felt very cold but he remained at the window, looking down on the people in the car park, as they scuttled around in the heat with their bags of shopping. All of them were probably complaining about the heat. Brady smiled to himself. When it was the depth of winter everyone longed for the summer but when *that* finally arrived they spent their time cursing the heat. He was the same. A knock on the office door broke his chain of thought.

'Come in,' he called, turning to face his visitor.

The door opened and a short stocky man in white overalls walked in. He smiled at Brady and introduced himself as Don Palmer. The Health Inspector caught the slightest hint of a cockney accent in the man's voice.

'You're from the sewage department?' he asked, although it came out more as a statement than a question.

Palmer nodded. 'That's right, guv. They call us "Effluent Operatives".' He smiled, broadly. A warm, infectious grin which caused Brady to smile too. 'Well,' he said, holding up a bag of tools. 'I've got my plunger. Shall we go?'

Brady followed the little man down to the car park where a white van with MERTON URBAN DISTRICT COUNCIL emblazoned on the sides was parked. Palmer hopped behind the steering wheel, Brady told him where to go and they set off.

Brady wound down the window of the van and allowed some cool air to blow in, and also to drive away the smoke from Palmer's cigarette which filled the van. The little man retrieved a packet of Marlboro from the parcel shelf and pointed it in the Health Inspector's direction.

'I don't smoke,' said Brady. 'Thanks all the same.'

'Wish *I* could give up,' said Palmer. 'It costs me about ten quid a week for fags.' He took a last drag and tossed the butt out of the open window. 'I've been smoking ever since I was eleven, doubt if I'll ever manage to kick it now. My old lady keeps on at me to stop but, well, you know how it is.'

'Which part of London are you from?' Brady asked, studying his companion's profile.

The little man laughed. 'Christ, is my accent *that* strong?'

The Health Inspector smiled. 'Well, let's say it's noticeable.'

'Islington,' Palmer told him.

'What did you do there?'

'Same as I do here. Effluent operative.' He laughed once more. 'Bloody stupid name isn't it? I don't know why they can't just call us shit-shovellers. They called us flushers when

43

I worked in the London sewers.' A wistful grin passed across his face. 'I used to do a bit of boxing before that, only amateur like. When I was a kid.'

'Why did you give up?' Brady wanted to know.

'The old lady again. She was scared I might get brain damage or something,' Palmer explained.

'Did you get very far?' the Health Inspector asked, his interest genuinely aroused by this personable little man in the white overalls.

Palmer shrugged. 'I got to the final of the ABA light weight competition one year. Albert Hall. Thousands of people there, millions watching on TV.'

'How did you get on?' Brady wanted to know.

'Well, I had the geezer worried in the third round.'

Brady was impressed. 'Yeah?'

Palmer nodded. 'Yeah.' He paused. 'He thought he'd killed me.' The little man cracked out laughing, the raucous sound filling the van and Brady chuckled too.

'What made you move to Merton?' the Health Inspector wanted to know.

'London's all right for grown-ups but I didn't want my kids living in all that smog,' Palmer explained. 'I wanted them to get up every morning and breathe fresh air instead of bloody diesel fumes.' He glanced at Brady. 'You got any kids?'

'No,' said the Health Inspector, just a little too sharply.

Palmer looked at him for a second then turned his attention back to the road ahead.

Brady changed the subject quickly. 'I used to work in London too.'

Palmer smiled. 'Yeah? Same job?'

Brady nodded.

'Why did *you* move?'

'That's something even I've never been able to work out,' he confessed. 'I think things just got on top of me. Besides, I was doing all the work in the department. I thought that if I left the other lazy bastards would have to start pulling their weight.'

44

The sewage man nodded.

'What the hell makes a bloke start in a business like yours?' Brady asked. 'I mean, crawling about in . . .' He hesitated.

'Crawling about in other people's shit. Was that what you were going to say?' asked Palmer.

Brady laughed, nodding.

Palmer shrugged. 'Well, look at it this way. It's a secure job. I mean, unless there's a mass outbreak of constipation, I've always got plenty to do.' He laughed his cackling laugh once more. 'There's a lot of difference between working these shite-pipes and working the ones in London,' he explained. 'I mean, the ones here are small, you have to crawl along the bloody things on all fours. At least in London you could walk through them.'

Brady frowned at the prospect.

Palmer suddenly slowed up. 'What was that address again?'

The Health Inspector found the piece of paper and scanned it.

'Twenty-two Acacia Avenue,' he said, looking out of the window to see that they had, in fact, arrived. Both men got out of the van, Brady leading the way to the front door. He saw one of the curtains parted slightly, a face peering out inquisitively from behind dirty net. He rang the doorbell and a two-tone Woolworth's chime tinkled. The two men waited, listening as several bolts were drawn back and Palmer suppressed a smile. The door opened a fraction and a woman squinted out at them, staying in the shadows, almost as if she were reluctant to feel the sun on her face.

'Mrs Fortune?' asked Brady, smiling.

The woman, who he guessed was well into her seventies, ran an appraising eye over the two newcomers.

'We're from the council. You rang about your drains,' the Health Inspector continued, still smiling. When he got no answer, he began to wonder if the woman was deaf so he raised his voice and repeated himself.

'All right,' she squawked. 'There's no need to shout. They're round the back.'

45

Brady nodded and was about to say something else when the front door was slammed in his face. He looked at Palmer who was laughing quietly. The two men made their way around to the rear of the house where Mrs Fortune appeared at the back door, this time emerging into the yard itself. She was a short, tubby woman, her hair done up in a bun, with horn-rimmed glasses perched precariously on the end of her nose. But the most striking thing about her was her clothes. She was wearing a huge knitted cardigan which came to well below her knees and looked as if it could have doubled as a bedspread and Brady could just detect the faint smell of mothballs.

'It's the drains,' she said, crisply.

Brady followed her pointing finger to the drain just below her kitchen window. As he stepped past her, a stench so fetid as to be obscene hit him and he recoiled. It reminded him of something between rotten vegetables and dead fish.

'Jesus Christ,' he groaned, watching as Palmer knelt beside the foul smelling drain. The sewage man pulled a pair of thick gloves from his overall pocket and slipped them on. He seemed impervious to the nauseating stench and beckoned Brady forward. The Health Inspector put a handkerchief over his nose to keep out the worst of the odour but it was so rank that it seemed to penetrate the very material itself. As he watched, Palmer took a long, hook-like implement from his canvas bag and poked it through the holes in the grate. He stirred it about, finally lifting the grille, uncovering the drain opening. There were pieces of rotten cabbage and what looked like congealed grease around the opening and Palmer scooped them away with one hand, peering closer.

'I think it's disgusting,' said Mrs Fortune, indignantly. 'Fancy letting the drains get in such a state. Why haven't the council done anything before?'

'This is the first complaint we've had from anyone on the new estate,' Brady told her, stepping back from the foul smelling opening.

She grunted indignantly.

46

'You say that your toilet is blocked too?' he asked her.

'Yes,' she snapped. 'It has been for more than a day now.'

'But how do . . .'

'It's only the outside one,' she snapped. 'The one upstairs is all right.' She pointed to a green door away to the right and Brady crossed to it, peering inside. The outside toilet was almost on the point of overflowing, the water already up to just below the seat. Brady closed the door and walked back into the yard.

Palmer had a torch out now and was shining it down the open drain. He finally switched it off and stood up.

'Well, I can't see anything,' he said. 'There's no external reason for the blockage or the smell.' He fumbled in his bag once more, closely watched by Brady and Mrs Fortune. The sewage man finally produced several lengths of steel tubing to which he attached what looked iike a small grappling hook. Carefully, he pushed the long probe down into the drain, hearing it clanking against the metal of the pipe as he pushed further.

'I think it's disgusting,' Mrs Fortune said once more and, with a disdainful shrug of her shoulders, she disappeared back into the house, slamming the door behind her.

'I bet she doesn't offer us a cup of tea,' said Palmer, still threading the metal probe into the drainpipe. He looked across at Brady and winked.

'How the hell can you stand that stink?' asked the Health Inspector.

'I must admit,' said Palmer, 'this one is a bit worse than usual but I'll be buggered if I can think what's causing it. It must be pretty deep down whatever it is.' He suddenly stiffened and the metal rod seemed to quiver in his hand. The little man gripped the rod tight, pressing one foot against the drain surround to steady himself. The tugging continued.

'What the fuck . . .' the sentence trailed off.

'What's wrong?' asked Brady, suddenly alarmed by the expression on Palmer's face.

The little man was straining to tug the rod free, using

47

every ounce of his strength to pull it from the drain.

Brady crossed to help him, fixing both hands around the probe. He felt a similar pressure being exerted from the other end.

It felt as if someone was trying to pull the rod from their hands.

'Can you feel that?' asked Palmer.

Brady nodded, anxiously. Then, finally, with a concerted burst of strength, the two men managed to heave the rod free. It came up, bringing with it a lump of brown matter. Brady looked at the lump which appeared to be a very old apple.

'Could that have been causing the blockage?' he asked.

Palmer shook his head, studying the probe closely. He sighed thoughtfully then had a quick look in the outside toilet. That done, he crossed to an iron flap which lay about ten yards down the garden. There was a disgusting smell emanating from there too. He stood on the sewer cover as if seeking inspiration.

'Whatever's causing the block is very deep,' he said. 'I can't clear it from this end.'

Brady looked apprehensive. 'Meaning?'

'Meaning, we'll have to go down.' He pointed at the rusty cover which led down into the sewer itself. 'You wait here,' he told the Health Inspector. 'I'll go and get the stuff from the van.'

Brady stood beside the flap, waving a hand before him in an effort to keep the rancid stench at bay. He heard Palmer's footsteps receding as he disappeared around the side of the house to fetch 'the stuff' – whatever the hell that might be.

He didn't have to wait long for an answer. A moment later, the little man re-appeared carrying two thick bundles of clothing and another canvas bag which he deposited on the ground.

'Put that on,' he said to Brady, pushing one of the bundles towards him. The Health Inspector picked up the bundle and opened it out, realizing that it was an overall of some kind. Made of oilskin, it looked like a shiny white boiler suit.

It fastened up the front by a zip which, in turn, was covered with a flap which both men clipped together using the large press-studs along its length. At the back, Brady found that the folds of the material could be pulled up to form a hood which was, in turn, tied at the chin with a piece of cord. As he pulled the hood up, all the sounds around him became muffled and he looked up to see a bird sitting on a nearby tree apparently whistling noiselessly. Its song could not be heard through the thick protective headgear. He pulled on the heavy gloves which Palmer handed him, watching as the little man knelt beside the other canvas bag. He finally produced a pair of large boots which Brady found he could slip over his shoes quite easily. The soles were metal and, for a moment, he found himself rooted to the spot by the weight.

The last things which Palmer took from his bag of tricks were a couple of face masks, rather like those worn by scuba divers, only curved and covering the whole of the face. Brady put his on, his breath coming in short gasps, the smell of plastic making him feel dizzy. The heat was almost unbearable. There was a small, circular, hole at the base of the mask which, Palmer informed him, was an air filter. The little man had to raise his voice to make Brady hear. The Health Inspector's breathing had slowed now, rasping loudly in the mask as he stood watching the other man.

'We've got to get this off,' shouted Palmer, his voice still sounding slightly muffled. It was as if he were talking through cotton wool. He pointed to the metal flap which covered the sewer opening and Brady looked down at the knobbed metal. Rusted with the ravages of the weather, it had two depressions in it. One at either end, both of which had a bar across them. At a signal from Palmer, both men bent, hooked their fingers under the bars and lifted.

The lid to the sewer opening came free and they deposited it on the grass nearby.

Palmer handed a torch to the Health Inspector who peered down into the darkness. It seemed to be bottomless, the iron ladder which ran down the side of the shaft disappearing into gloom so total that even the torch beams could not penetrate it for more than a couple of feet.

The sewage man looked at Brady, who was still gazing down into the darkness, and then stooped to pick up his bag of tools which he clipped to his belt.

'Last one in's a rotten egg,' he said, raising his voice once more to make himself heard. He smiled, then, watched by the Health Inspector, he clambered onto the ladder and began to make his way down into the darkness, visible, finally, only by his swaying torch beam.

Brady flicked on his own torch, took one last look around at the brightness of the day and then lowered himself onto the first rung of the ladder, his metal soled boots clanking noisily as he did so.

He steadied himself for a second, then began to descend.

Eight

Brady hadn't realized quite how narrow the shaft was until he began to climb down the ladder. Now he found that he was forced to cling tightly to the metal rungs in order to prevent his back rubbing against the other side of the tunnel. The torch wavered unsteadily in his hand and his mask had begun to cloud over, making it difficult to see. He measured his steps cautiously, careful not to miss a rung and fall. However, despite his tentative tread, he felt his left foot slide from the rung beneath him and, for a moment, his heart leapt. But he gripped the ladder tighter and continued his descent.

He heard a dull splash, signalling to him that Palmer had reached the bottom of the shaft and, a moment later, Brady himself felt his heavy boot touching something solid which he knew to be the floor of the pipe. Panting, he stood still for a moment until he felt hands tugging at his arm.

'Mind your head,' Palmer told him, shining the torch around to show him the narrowness of the pipe.

Brady guessed that it could be no more than three and a half feet from the top to bottom and both men had to get on all fours to give themselves the room to move about in it. Brady sank reluctantly to his knees, looking down to see that the trickling effluent which ran through the pipe came up as far as his forearms. He felt sick and was thankful that he had the mask on. The walls of the pipe seemed to crush in on him and the Health Inspector imagined that this was what it was like to be buried alive. Together, he and Palmer crawled through what seemed like an endless cylindrical coffin, thick with human waste and twelve instead of six feet below ground. The heat inside the suit seemed to intensify and

Brady found that he was gasping for air even though the mask was filtering it quite adequately.

'You all right?' Palmer asked him, hearing the Health Inspector's laboured, accelerated breathing. He peered over his shoulder at his companion, shining the torch at him.

Brady nodded, his breathing becoming less harsh. The perspiration was running off him and he almost slipped twice, the thought of ending up face first in a river of human excreta making him more careful.

In the darkness, neither of the men saw three or four of the slugs glide past them, carried along by the flow.

Palmer held up a hand for Brady to halt. The little man managed to scramble up onto his knees in front of a grille which was set into the tunnel roof.

'What's that?' asked Brady.

'It's the outlet from the toilet,' Palmer told him, fumbling in his bag for a screwdriver. He set to work, removing the four rusty screws which held the grille in position. As he took each one out, he handed it to Brady to hold, then, when the last one was out, he stuck the end of the screwdriver between two bars of the grille and prised it free. By torchlight he scrutinised it.

'No blockage there,' he said, puzzled.

'What now?' Brady asked, peering up the outlet.

Palmer grinned. 'We hope the old girl doesn't get taken short.'

The Health Inspector quickly withdrew his head, handing the screws, one at a time, to the sewage man who refixed the grille.

'Let's have a look at the drain outlet,' said Palmer and, pointing his torch ahead of him, crawled on. Brady followed.

'Are all the tunnels as narrow as this?' he asked.

'Most of them,' Palmer told him. 'They all work like wheels though. The pipes themselves converge in one central chamber, which is like the hub of the wheel. The tunnels are like the spokes.' He paused for a moment, steadying himself as he put his hand on something thick and soft. He grunted distastefully. He crawled on.

52

The large slug which Palmer had accidentally put his hand on slithered along the floor of the pipe, the stream of effluent and the impenetrable darkness hiding it.

'The manhole covers that you see in the road,' the sewage man continued. 'Each one of those goes down to one of the central chambers. They're dotted all over town. The chambers are pretty big.' The little man stopped once more, this time at a much smaller outlet which Brady realized must be the one from the drain. The same procedure was repeated, the grille removed. This time a lump of rotten potato fell out into Palmer's gloved hand. He shook his head and dropped it into the stream of effluent.

'I don't get it,' he said. 'Even down here there's nothing to show why the bloody pipes are blocked.' He pulled a curved implement from his bag and began scraping around in the drain outlet. Brady meanwhile shone his torch around the walls of the pipe. About half-way up the sides there was a scum mark of green mould which, in places, had extended to the roof of the pipe too. The concrete itself seemed to be cracked and the mould had crept into the rent like bacteria into a cut, turning it gangrenous. He remembered when he had found an old man living alone who had been infected with gangrene. Unable to move after falling and cutting his leg, Brady had found him after a next door neighbour complained about the smell coming from the man's house. He'd finally got in to discover that the old boy's leg was green and mottled with infection, black in places it was so bad. That image suddenly came to his mind as he ran the torch up the tunnel wall, following the course of the rent until it reached the roof of the tunnel. The torch beam shone on something silvery.

Brady felt the breath catch in his throat as he looked more closely. The marks were unmistakable.

The roof of the pipe was criss-crossed by dozens of slime trails.

Ron Bell's house. The two houses in Elm Drive and now here. With shaking hand he reached up and touched one of the trails with the index finger of his glove. The mucoid fluid stuck to the material, dropping away in thick globules when Brady removed his hand. Suddenly anxious, he shone the torch down the length of the tunnel but the beam faded into darkness less than three feet from him. Something bumped against his arm and he almost shouted aloud. Looking down he saw that it was a small piece of wood. His breathing once again became rapid but he tried to control it, clenching his teeth until his jaws ached. Get a bloody grip on yourself, he screamed inside his head. *Come on.* He clenched his fists, his eyes tightly closed for long seconds, then he felt Palmer touch him on the shoulder.

'Well,' said the sewage man. 'I can't find anything. We might as well go back up.'

The words were the most welcome Brady had heard in a long time. He crawled backwards (it was impossible to turn round in the narrow pipe) until his torch glinted on the bottom rung of the ladder. High above, he could see the blue of the sky and, with almost unnatural haste, he began to clamber up towards the surface.

Palmer waited at the bottom of the ladder, watching as Brady climbed up. When the Health Inspector was half way up, the little man followed him.

He didn't even see the large slug which had crawled onto his boot.

As he climbed, the slug crept higher, sensing the warmth beneath the overalls. It slithered onto his calf and prepared to sink its long central tooth into the material, eager to get at the warm flesh beneath. But, just then, Palmer brought his foot down particularly hard on the ladder, the slug lost its hold and fell back into the stream of waste below.

The sewage man heard the splash and thought he'd dropped something from his bag. He shone his torch down but could see nothing. Satisfied that he still had all his tools, he continued his ascent.

The slug had disappeared.

Nine

The heat hung heavily over Merton, like some oppressive cloud. As the afternoon wore on and the sun reached its zenith, the little town was bathed in a cloying, sticky heat which seemed to make the air itself hot, almost unbreathable.

Carol Wilton stood naked before the full length mirror studying the reflection which gazed back at her. Her eyelids felt heavy and she was tired, the heat seeming to sap her strength. Beads of perspiration had formed on her top lip and she licked them away, the salty taste remaining on her tongue momentarily. Another bead of clear liquid quivered at the hollow of her throat for a second before trickling slowly down her chest, between her taut breasts and across her flat stomach. She traced its path with the index finger of her right hand, allowing the digit to probe deeper, brushing through the soft curls of her pubic hair. She shuddered as the finger brushed against her clitoris and she felt a tingle run through her. She sighed, her nipples rising to erection at the same time. Carol moved her finger gently between her legs, feeling the first traces of moisture from her warm cleft. All the time she kept her eyes firmly on the mirror, watching the reflection before her. She parted her lips slightly and spoke one word.

'Tony.'

She stopped moving her finger, her expression changing from one of pleasure to one of anger.

'You bastard,' she said softly, withdrawing her finger.

Couldn't she forget him after four years? She shook herself out of her dream world and crossed to the bed, reaching for a pair of faded jeans which she pulled on, the tight material

55

clinging to her slim hips and thighs. She slid further into the denims, allowing the seam to cut into her damp cleft, then she fastened the button and picked up the white t-shirt which also lay on the bed. She let it hang outside her jeans, noting how the thin material made her hardened nipples even more prominent. She slipped on a pair of backless high heels and inspected the reflection once more. You should see me now, you bastard, she thought. The image of Tony flashed into her mind once more. No, she couldn't forget him. He'd left her a permanant reminder just to make sure. She crossed to the bedroom window and looked out.

Paul was playing on the lawn, sitting contentedly beside the rabbit's pen, watching as the small white creature hopped about, stopping every now and then to munch on the pieces of lettuce which Carol had dropped in half an hour ago. Paul was four now and he'd never even seen his father. Carol watched him and felt the anger rising once more inside her. Fate had dealt her a truly cruel blow. Not only had she been left to bring up a child on her own, the child had been born slightly retarded. She bit her bottom lip, angrily. It was almost as if she blamed Tony for her son's mental deficiency. But the real anger she felt was with herself. God, she'd been a fool in those days. A sixteen-year-old girl trying to act like a woman. Tony had been twenty-four. She'd built her world around him, ignoring the warnings from her parents and friends. What did they know? He loved her and she used to show them the gifts he bought her to prove it. He loved her and she loved him. He took her virginity but she didn't care, she had given it up willingly. She had talked about getting married, though he never seemed to take much interest when it got around to that subject but then, she had told herself, not many men do talk about marriage. They made love often and he guided her, taught her things she had never even known about, introduced her to all manner of physical pleasure. And she had accepted it all. She loved him and that was all that mattered to her.

But then she became pregnant and Tony changed. They rowed constantly and, finally, he had given her his ultimatum. Get an abortion or the relationship was over. He even offered to pay for it himself.

She refused. He left her.

'Bastard,' she muttered to herself, the memory still hurting even four years later.

Of course her parents had gone through the customary procedure of disowning her. Being Catholics in a religious area didn't help matters, she supposed. Whatever would the neighbours say? How could you do such a thing, Carol? The recriminations had flown back and forth and she'd moved out. First to a flat and finally to this house she had now, on the new estate. She'd left school at sixteen with no qualifications but she'd managed to get a cleaning job at the local hospital. The meagre wages from that, together with her supplementary benefit and child allowance just about paid the rent and kept her and the child in food and clothes. With Paul being handicapped, the Government, in its infinite wisdom, saw fit to give her an extra couple of quid on top of the usual rate. And so she managed. At times she wondered how but things never got too desperate. She'd made lots of new friends on the estate, one of whom looked after Paul while Carol went out to work at nights. Back to her old job at the hospital. She sometimes wondered what it would have been like if Tony had stayed with her. Would she have been a wife by now instead of an unmarried mother, disowned by her own family? Many a night she lay awake wanting him with her. But recently, she wouldn't have cared *who* it was who shared her bed.

She pushed the thoughts to one side and made her way downstairs. Paul didn't hear her as she walked up behind him and he giggled when she tickled his ribs. He looked up at her with wide, questioning eyes for a second, almost as if he didn't recognise her. Then he gurgled something unintelligible and returned his attention to the small rabbit. Carol knelt beside him and wiped some saliva from his mouth with the tissue which she took from her jeans pocket. He didn't move, his mind still pre-occupied with the tiny white animal hopping about before him. Carol had bought it

57

about a week ago and the man next door had helped make a pen for it. A nice bloke, Carol thought. Pity he was married. The rabbit had been an endless source of fascination for Paul and Carol could now leave him out in the garden all day, just watching the little creature.

'Paul,' she said, stroking his hair. It was blond, like her own. Soft and sleek as she touched it.

'Paul.' She gently turned his head to that he was looking at her. Once more she was faced with that vacant expression. 'Mummy's just going out for five minutes,' she told him, reaching once more for the tissue. She wiped the mucus from his nose and balled up the tissue. 'Will you be all right?'

He smiled. 'Yes,' he said, quickly. Shaking his head about. 'Yes.'

'You watch bunny, all right?' she said. 'Mummy be back in five minutes.'

'Yes,' he said again, looking back at the rabbit. He raised one chubby hand and waved in the direction of the animal. 'Bunny.'

Carol smiled. 'That's right, bunny.' She kissed him on the forehead and walked back up the garden to the house. Her purse was on the kitchen table and she opened it to reveal a pound note, some silver and an assortment of other stuff including a bus ticket, a coupon cut from a newspaper which granted her 3p off her next purchase of a certain brand of tea bag and a couple of photos. The sort taken in photo booths. The faded monochrome snaps showed her and Tony together. She snapped her purse together again and left the house. The precinct of shops was only down the road and she needed some bread and a pint of milk. Thank Christ the Giro is due in the morning, she thought.

Paul heard the clicking of his mother's heels as she walked up the path and out of the gate but he didn't turn to watch her go. He was too interested in the rabbit. He gurgled contentedly, the spittle oozing down his chin and forming a silvery pendant as it hung there.

The rabbit had stopped to eat and it crouched before him

58

devouring the remnants of the lettuce which it had been given. But suddenly, it jumped back, licking at its paw.

Paul laughed, throatily, watching the animal. He could see something red on its fur, on the paw it was licking but he didn't know what it was. Neither did he realize what the slimy black thing was that burrowed slowly up from the place where the rabbit had been crouching.

The slug pulled itself free of the ground and slid across the ground towards the rabbit, its antennae waving about in the air, the shorter forward tentacles flicking across the ground.

The rabbit watched the slug warily for a second and was about to leap aside when it squealed in pain. It managed to drag itself a few inches and this time, Paul saw one of the monstrous black things clinging to the animal's leg. The rabbit turned and bit into the second slug but the first and larger of the creatures had reached it by now and the terrified mammal was pulled down as the slug fastened itself onto one of the rabbit's ears. Blood ran freely from the wound as the slug used its sharp rows of radular teeth to shave off pieces of the animal's flesh.

Another slug, fully six inches long, broke the surface, dragging its vile form towards the stricken rabbit. It drove its sickle shaped tooth into the animal's side and the fur was suddenly stained crimson. The rabbit shook its head madly from side to side in an effort to dislodge the monstrous black thing but its efforts were useless and now half a dozen of the revolting gastropods were burrowing up from beneath it, each slithering across to join the attack. The rabbit tried to move but its tiny form was weighed down and all it could do was squeal as the slugs ate it alive.

Paul watched, mesmerised, his mouth open. Once he chuckled, not really knowing why but then he wrinkled his forehead as he saw the rabbit being reduced to a blood-spattered heap of fur. It had stopped moving and the slugs seethed over it, eager for the taste of its fresh, warm blood. One of its ears was eaten away, the other severed half way up. It hung uselessly, like a broken twig and, finally, the rabbit was pulled to the ground, its bloody fur almost invisible beneath the black mass of feeding slugs.

Paul gurgled as he watched, his head on one side.

Carol glanced down the garden as she walked round the house into the back garden. She looked down and saw Paul, still staring into the rabbit pen. Carol took her small bag of groceries into the house and put them on the kitchen table then she kicked off her shoes and padded down the garden towards her son, who, apparently hadn't heard her return.

'Paul,' she called but he didn't turn and it was then that Carol realized something was wrong.

She couldn't see the rabbit.

Hurrying down to the pen she stopped behind Paul, looking at the sight before her. The grass inside the pen was covered in blood and pieces of fur, here she noticed a lump of bone, beside it a piece of intestine. She turned away and closed her eyes, trying not to be sick. Gradually she regained control and looked more closely at the scene of carnage in the pen. The rabbit had disappeared completely.

Carol knelt beside Paul and held him tightly in her arms but he seemed unconcerned. He waved a hand towards the empty pen and shook his head.

'What happened?' she asked him, tears in her eyes. She glanced at the blood-stained grass once more and this time she caught sight of the mucoid fluid which also covered the pen. It sparkled in the sunlight, diffusing into a dozen different colours.

'Paul,' she repeated, holding him close to her.

He gurgled something and at first she thought he said 'cat', but when he spoke again she was able to make out the word.

'Black,' he said in his clumsy, clipped tones. He waved towards the pools of blood and slime.

'Black.'

60

Ten

The sun was bleeding to death in the evening sky, flooding the heavens with vivid patches of gold and crimson. Some of them eventually darkening into a cool purple as the evening drew in. Birds returning to their nests were black arrowheads against the red back-drop and the mottled sky was like a child's colouring book, layers of colour splashed brilliantly one on top of the other.

Harold Morris looked up from the begonia he was tending and marvelled at the multi-hued glory of the dusky heavens. there was nothing in the world he liked more than to be out in his greenhouse on an evening like this. Even beneath the canopy of glass and wood, the air had cooled to a pleasing temperature and Harold worked enthusiastically over his plants, tending them with a care which people usually reserve for small children.

He'd always been a keen gardener but since being made redundant from Merton's chemical works over a year ago he'd turned his hobby into something approaching an obsession. The greenhouse had been purchased with part of the sizeable pay-off he'd received. The remainder had gone into the house, new carpets and, for the first time during their thirty years marriage, a colour television. Harold's wife, Jean, was totally mesmerised by the new acquisition something which Harold himself was thankful for because it kept her out of his way while he tended to his plants. The rest of his redundancy payment had gone towards purchasing two tickets for a flight to Australia.

Their only daughter had emigrated, with her husband, six years ago and now Harold and Jean were preparing themselves to fly over for the christening of their grandson in

61

just under a month. Harold smiled happily at the thought, dropping some Baby-Bio into a pot where he was nurturing an orchid.

As well as flowering plants he also had a sizeable choice of vegetables growing in the greenhouse and, together with those in the patch at the bottom of the garden, Jean seldom had to buy any from the shops. Apart from his cucumbers and tomatoes, Harold had also been able to grow a fair crop of aubergines. They were his particular pride and joy.

He sipped slowly from the tin of lager beside him, putting the can down beside a set of shears which lay on the work top. Then, picking up his trowel, Harold set about re-potting some geraniums.

The sun had fallen far below the horizon by now and night was seeping slowly across the sky, staining the clouds like ink on blotting paper. Harold squinted in the gloom for a few more minutes then crossed to the light switch at the end of the greenhouse and snapped it on. The bank of fluorescents flickered into life bathing the place in a cold white light. He then adjusted the thermostat control, raising the temperature just four or five degrees. He picked up the can of lager and drained the last dregs, rattling the empty receptacle in his hand before tossing it into the bin beneath the work top. He looked at his watch and decided that he had time to finish tending to the fresh crop of tomatoes before he went inside to watch the football.

It was almost ten p.m. and Harold felt like another can of lager. It was warm in the greenhouse and he had worked up a powerful thirst. He pulled off his gloves and dropped them onto the work-top, then he headed up the garden towards the house.

From beneath the bottom of the work top, the first of the three slugs slithered up, its posterior tentacles waving about. Moving slowly in their mucoid trails, the black beasts, one of them as thick as a man's index finger, crawled over the trowel leaving their mark on it. They paused at the place where Harold had left his gloves and then, after a moment's hesitation, they slithered inside.

62

Harold found Jean dozing in her chair, the TV still on at full blast as yet another American cop series drew mercifully to a close. He stood in the doorway of the sitting room, rolling the icy can of lager across his forehead. Jean seemed to sense his prescence and opened her eyes. She looked round and smiled.

'I thought you were busy with your plants,' she said, yawning.

'And I thought you were *watching* that,' he said, motioning towards the TV.

Jean reached for the remote control and turned down the sound.

'I nodded off,' she confessed. 'It must be this heat.'

'It'll be a lot hotter than this in Australia,' he told her, sipping at his lager.

Jean sighed wistfully. 'You know, Harry, I still can't believe we're going to see Roger and Carol again.' She smiled. 'And the little boy too. Won't it be marvellous?'

'You'll be telling me next you were pleased I got made redundant,' he said, smiling.

She held out a hand to him and he bent and kissed her on the top of the head.

'Will you be much longer?' she asked him.

Harold shook his head. 'I'll be hurrying in to you my dear,' he said, bowing exaggeratedly.

'And the football,' she said, smiling.

He winked at her and walked out. The cool evening air seemed full of the scent of flowers and Harold inhaled deeply. In next door's garden he heard a snuffling sound and, a second later, saw a hedgehog scuttle across the lawn ahead of him, trying its best to avoid the light coming from the greenhouse.

Stars stuck to the black velvet sky like pieces of tinsel which some giant hand had hurled. Harold smiled to himself and pushed open the door to the greenhouse, the temperature immediately hitting him. He hadn't realized just how hot it was in there but, after a moment or two and a hefty pull from his lager can, he re-adjusted to the heat and looked at the waiting tomatoes.

63

He reached for his gloves.

Yes, the tomatoes were coming along beautifully this year, he thought, pulling on the first of his gloves. Last year's crop had . . .

He stopped trying to drag the second glove on, feeling something wet and slimy blocking the fingers.

'What the hell . . .'

He never finished the sentence. Suddenly, searing pain exploded through his hand as three sets of jaws fastened themselves on his exposed fingers. The slugs inside the glove eagerly devoured the flesh offered to them, quickly tearing it away until they were nearing the very bone itself. Harold was frantic, his bulging eyes watched the material of the glove undulating rhythmically as blood began to run from his wounds and dripped from his wrist. Now he began to groan in terror, the groans gradually turning to shouts.

The pain in his hand was agonizing. Already the slugs had eaten away three of his fingers and now they slithered over the back of his hand, digging deep into muscles and sinew. Harold tugged at the glove, staggering drunkenly around the greenhouse.

He couldn't get it off.

And now his shouts became screams as he wrenched at the glove, still unable to remove it. Blood was now soaking the thick material and his arm was rapidly going numb. Harold felt the bile rising in his throat and he thought he was going to faint, but, if anything, the pain in his hand kept him concious. White hot agony lanced a path up his whole arm. Again, almost blind with pain and terror, Harold tugged at the recalcitrant glove, screaming even louder when it wouldn't come off.

He groped for the shears, the realization sweeping over him. The terrifying fact of what he must do momentarily numbing even the screaming agony in his hand. He managed to push open the twin blades of the razor sharp shears and, tears rolling down his cheeks, he put his wrist between the twin steel jaws. With his free hand he brought all his weight down on the handle, shrieking with renewed intensity as the blades sliced through the flesh of his wrist. There was a sickening grating sound as they scraped the bone and Harold was splattered with a geyser of his own blood as the veins in his arm were severed. But, despite his frenzied efforts, the shears would not cut through the bone. Skin and muscle tore like fabric, exposing ligaments and twitching sinews and he pounded on the handle like a madman, sweat pouring from his face.

It was then that Jean appeared in the doorway of the greenhouse. She had heard his screams and came running and now the sight which met her caused her stomach to somersault. She saw her husband pounding madly on the handle of the shears, the twin blades of which closed around his wrist. She saw blood spurting into the warm air, saw the shining white of bone through the pulped and torn crimson mass that had once been flesh and muscle. Blood had sprayed in all directions, onto the dusty worktop, over the glass panels of the greenhouse where it trickled down like sticky crimson rain. Harold's white shirt was covered in it. He was on his knees now, a second away from unconsciousness, the shattered wrist still firmly held in the jaws of the shears and it was at that point she ran to him. Fighting back her sickness, not even able to scream, she watched the glove, moving seemingly with a life of its own as the slugs ate further into his hand.

'The trowel,' gasped Harold, his face purple, eyes bulging like a thyroid sufferer.

Her groping hands found the implement and she stood before him, mesmerised.

'My hand,' he mumbled. 'Cut it off'.

She shook her head, her own voice now beginning to rise.

'No,' she said.

'Do it,' he shrieked and his tortured voice spurred her into action. Raising the trowel above her head, she took a last look at the torn and crushed wrist then brought the blade down with terrifying force.

Both of them screamed as the heavy implement scythed through the already shattered wrist. There was a strident snapping of bone and the hand was severed, propelled some distance from the shattered stump by the jets of blood which erupted from the arteries. Harold slumped to the ground, the remnants of his lower arm spouting red geysers into the air. Jean dropped the trowel, blood from the hewn limb splashing her feet and legs.

Harold had passed out.

Jean bolted from the greenhouse, racing back to the house and the phone. Her screams had alerted several neighbours and lights flickered on in the kitchens of the houses next door.

In the greenhouse, the three slugs finished feasting on Harold Morris's severed hand then, leaving only their thick mucoid trails as evidence of their presence, they slithered away.

Eleven

'You know, we should have lived in a bloody flat. Then we wouldn't have had all this trouble,' said Brady, driving his spade into the hard ground.

He turned a few more clods then leant on the spade, the perspiration running freely down his body. He'd removed his shirt even before he started digging and now he felt the unrelenting heat of the sun on his back.

'There's two reasons why you're so worn out,' Kim told him. She was kneeling beside him, pulling weeds from the lawn which was long overdue for a cut. 'You're either out of condition, or . . .' She looked at him, a mischievous smile on her lips.

'Or what?' he demanded.

'Or you're feeling your age.' She laughed.

Brady picked up a handful of earth and threw it at her. He returned to his digging, determined to prove to her, and to himself, that he wasn't unfit. But, Christ, his body was crying out for a rest. He ached all over and he'd only been out there for an hour. Perhaps Kim was right, perhaps he was out of condition. He slowed his pace a little and looked down at her. She was wearing a pair of dirty old jeans and just her bikini top and he looked admiringly at her deep tan. His own torso was milk white, only coloured in places by the hot sun which had reddened it. Brady didn't tan, he fried. He too wore a pair of old jeans, which hung low at the backside. Together with his big wellingtons, Kim said he looked like a farmer.

Doing the garden was something which Brady had always hated and, in blistering heat such as this, he disliked the task even more. The earth was baked hard, as ungiving as

67

concrete and he had to drive the spade down with all his strength to even break it. But, he struggled on, turning the clods, stopping every now and then to mop his brow with a sodden handkerchief. In the end he gave it up, knotted the white linen square at each corner and pulled it onto his head. Kim looked up and immediately dissolved into fits of laughter.

'You look like Fred Gumby,' she said, referring to the resident idiot of past Monty Python shows. She got to her feet and padded back up the lawn towards the house. 'Fancy a drink?' she called.

He panted exaggeratedly and allowed his tongue to hang over his bottom lip.

'I'll take that as a yes,' said Kim, smiling.

Brady returned to his digging. Inside his thick gardening gloves, his hands felt as if they were on fire but the old spade had a shaft which had grown ragged over the years and he didn't fancy getting splinters, so he struggled on. As he threw himself into his job more, it began to seem less of a battle. Even so, Brady didn't think he could ever acquire a liking for gardening. He and Kim had lain in bed until ten that morning, as was their custom on a Saturday. They had woken at nine and made leisurely love, each seeming more responsive than usual. Brady smiled to himself at the recollection. They would probably just sit out and enjoy the sun when he finished digging. He wondered if he might try his hand at growing some vegetables and he surveyed his expanse of earth like some feudal baron looking out over his grounds.

It was as he looked down that he saw the first of the slugs slithering onto his spade.

Brady knocked it off, pushing the creature aside with the shovel but it was then that he noticed just how big the bloody thing was. He watched as it slithered away leaving its slime trail behind.

'Good God,' muttered Brady, watching the silvery trail glistening in the sunlight. His mind began to race. Ron Bell's house. The house in Elm Drive. The sewer pipe and

68

now here, in his own garden. He knelt, watching the vile creature closely.

Then he saw another one, as black as night and, Brady guessed, a good six inches long. He swallowed hard, feeling the urge to squash the revolting creatures beneath his spade but he could do nothing but watch in fascinated distaste as the two slugs crawled over the rough ground.

He looked back at the ground he'd already dug. There were more of them. In the six or seven yards of ground which he'd overturned, the Health Inspector counted at least a dozen of the black beasts.

'Percy Thrower, your drink's here,' called Kim, seating herself in a deckchair and sipping her own glass of bacardi and coke.

Brad ignored her, his eyes still rivetted to the slugs.

'Mike,' she called again, noticing that something had caught his attention.

'Come and look at this,' he said, without taking his eyes off the slugs nearest to him. The first one had once more slithered on to his spade and, this time, Brady watched it as it crawled up the smooth metal.

Kim joined him, the glass still in her hand. She caught sight of the slug and shuddered.

'Oh God, what the hell are they?' she said, moving behind her husband as if for protection.

'They're slugs,' said Brady, still watching the crawling monstrosity.

Kim laughed nervously. 'But slugs are small.' She felt the disgust rising within her. 'These are too big.'

The Health Inspector was adamant. 'They're slugs.'

The one on the spade had almost reached the shaft now and Kim watched it with revulsion, her eyes darting over the ground in front of her which seemed to be alive with the black creatures.

'Kill it, Mike,' she urged, watching the beast slithering up the wood but Brady merely reached out and plucked the thing up, holding it between the thumb and forefinger of his thick gloves. It writhed slowly betwen the digits and

69

reminded the Health Inspector of a fat snake. Its eye stalks swayed as if in slow motion and its mouth moved soundlessly giving the man a glimpse of its many-toothed maw.

'For God's sake, Mike,' Kim persisted. 'Kill the bloody thing.'

Suddenly the slug seemed to twist in Brady's grip, its slime making it difficult to hold, and, before the Health Inspector could react it had driven its vicious sickle shaped tooth into the tough material of his glove.

'Jesus Christ,' he yelped, the sudden attack startling him. Kim put a hand to her mouth to stifle a scream as she watched her husband pull the glove free and throw it to the floor. The slug remained anchored by the tooth, not loosing its grip even when Brady hurled it to the ground. Almost with relish he stamped on the hideous black thing, its body making a loud squish as it was crushed. The noise made Kim want to cover her ears, reminding her, as it did, of diarhoettic excretion. Brady ground the thing into shapeless pulp beneath his boot, using the end of the spade to scrape it off his glove. He pulled the glove back on, examining the hole which the tooth had made.

'The bastard tried to bite me,' he said, incredulously. Another eighth of an inch and it would have tasted flesh and that was enough to make Brady shudder.

'What kind of slug bites a man?' asked Kim, looking at the squashed remains.

'That's what I intend to find out,' said Brady, straightening up. He looked at Kim, seeing the uncertainty in her eyes and his tone softened. 'Go and get me a jar, love,' he told her. 'Anything with a screw top lid.'

She nodded and hurried back up the garden. Inside the house she picked up the money jar. They collected all their copper in it, counting it out when the huge jar was full. But, fortunately, it had only recently been emptied and there was less than thirty pence in there. Kim hurriedly emptied it, allowing it to spill out onto the kitchen table, ignoring the coins which fell to the floor. Then, she ran back to where her husband stood watching the other slugs. She put the jar down on the grass and Brady unscrewed the top. He studied the seething black shapes for long seconds then, quick as lightning, he picked one up and dropped it into the jar. He repeated the procedure with one of the larger ones, careful that the vile thing didn't take a chunk out of his finger. Kim shuddered as she saw the things slithering about on the glass, their bodies gliding on the trail of mucus they secreted. Brady snatched up a third slug and dropped it in with the others then he screwed the lid of the jar on as tightly as he could. For long seconds he watched the obnoxious animals slithering around in their efforts to escape then he crossed to the deckchair where his shirt lay discarded. As he buttoned it up, Kim looked into the jar.

'What are you going to do?' she asked.

'Find out what's happening around here,' he said. 'Come on.'

A little bewildered, Kim slipped her shoes on and followed him out to the car.

Brady fumbled in his pocket for the keys, hastily unlocking the driver and passenger doors. They both slid in, Kim yelping in pain when her exposed back came into contact with the blistering hot plastic of the seat. Brady handed her the jar of slugs which she held rather uncertainly, then he stuck the key in the ignition and started the engine. Neither of them spoke and, even as he drove, the Health Inspector couldn't resist the odd anxious look at the three slugs. Almost as if he feared they would escape their glass prison.

He put his foot down, wondering whether the perspiration on his face was entirely the product of the scorching day.

Twelve

The car park of Merton Museum was empty but for a battered old Volkswagen which lay baking in the sun.

Brady brought the Vauxhall to a halt beside it and both he and Kim got out. She handed him the jar with its monstrous black contents and wiped her hands on her jeans. Together, they approached the small flight of steps which led up to the main entrance of the museum. It was a grey stone building, three storeys high, which had been erected about ten years ago and, from the outside it looked like a block of flats but with fewer windows. The windows that were visible reflected the sun back at the two visitors as they advanced, making it difficult to see inside. A feat made all the more impossible because the venetian blinds were down. There was a small notice board outside telling of forthcoming lectures to be given there, or of special attractions to be found in the building itself but Brady was not interested in those.

Followed by Kim, he strode up the stairs, clutching the jar to him as if it were some priceless artefact he'd just dug up. The doors to the museum were open so the two of them walked straight in.

The ground floor was a natural history gallery and they found themselves faced by hundreds of stuffed birds and small animals. A thousand dead eyes followed their progress. Kim glanced into the glass cabinets. She had been here twice before with classes from the nursery and the place always gave her an odd feeling. It was almost like being in a glass fronted zoo, where all the inhabitants were in a state of permanent suspended animation. The baleful eyes of a Tawny Owl fixed her in a glassy stare and she walked on as if mesmerised by the dead orbs. The silence in the building

73

was almost oppressive but at least it was cooler in here and both of them were glad of the respite from the blistering heat outside. Despite the apparent absence of visitors (something which seemed to be a feature of the place), the museum was freshly dusted and spotlessly clean, the wooden floor in particular so heavily polished Kim could see a distorted reflection of herself in it.

They moved through the ground floor gallery, eventually arriving at a staircase. A sign at the bottom proclaimed:

ART GALLERY
LIVE EXHIBITS
ENQUIRIES

A large white arrow showed the way and the two of them followed its course eventually emerging on a landing. To the right lay a desk on which were piled various postcards and brochures depicting exhibits in the museum. There were also pencils bearing the legend Merton Museum. A black sign told them it was an enquiry desk and another pointing arrow indicated a bell and invited them to ring for attention. Brady promptly pressed the button, looking around impatiently when no one appeared. He pressed it again, keeping his finger on it this time, the high pitched ringing echoing through the silence.

A door behind the desk opened and a young man in his early twenties emerged. He held the remains of a sandwich in his hand and was chewing the rest with difficulty, as if he'd taken too large a bite. He raised a hand in greeting, still unable to speak because of the welter of bread and salad in his mouth. Kim smiled, Brady ran an appraising eye over the youth. He wore a pair of faded jeans, crisply pressed all the same, and a T-shirt with 'Iron Maiden' emblazoned across the front. He finally managed to dispose of his mouthful of sandwich and smiled happily at the waiting couple.

'Good afternoon,' he said. 'Can I help you?'

'I want to speak to whoever's in charge, please,' Brady told him.

'Fire away,' said the youth, smiling.

The Health Inspector looked surprised and the young man saw the hint of disbelief on his face. He smiled.

'I know I don't look like a museum curator,' he said. 'That is what you were going to say, isn't it?'

Brady too smiled. 'As a matter of fact it was.'

'John Foley,' he announced, offering his right hand which Brady shook, introducing himself in his official capacity and Kim who smiled at the young man.

'And you're in charge?' Brady asked, as if anxious for re-affirmation of Foley's words.

'Monarch of all I survey,' he said, smiling. 'What can I do for you?'

Brady indicated the jar. 'Ever seen anything like that?'

Foley bent lower, peering through the glass. He frowned and shook his head as he watched the slugs sliding around in their own slime. 'Where the hell did you find these?' he asked.

Brady told him. 'One of them tried to bite me,' he added, producing the holed garden glove as evidence.

'Christ,' said Foley, picking a piece of ham from his tooth. He opened a flap in the desk and walked through, leading the couple up a short flight of stairs to a room marked: 'Staff Only'.

'Come in here,' he said, holding the door open for his two visitors.

The place was like a small laboratory and Kim wrinkled her nose as the unmistakable odour of formaldehyde assaulted her nostrils. The room was small and very hot until Foley flicked on the twin rotar fans above them. Soon, a cooling breeze began to waft around the room. It contained a table with a stainless steel top, a couple of sinks and, on the work bench which took up three sides of the laboratory, there stood some empty fish tanks.

Brady set the jar down and looked around. Foley pulled up a stool and peered once more at the large slugs in the glass container.

'Do you run this place on your own?' the Health Inspector wanted to know.

75

Foley shook his head, taking a pair of plastic gloves and a set of stout tweezers from a drawer beside him. 'No. During the week I have an assistant and a woman comes in to clean up but apart from that, I do the lot. Including the exhibits.' He motioned to a newly finished badger which stood on the work top on the other side of the room. 'And no jokes about mounting and stuffing please,' he said, smiling.

Brady grinned but it faded as he saw Foley slowly unscrew the top of the jar. The young man was watching the slugs intently, still not able to believe their size. One was near the top of the jar and it was this one that he aimed his tweezers at, a little disturbed when he saw that they would not reach across its girth. He discarded them in favour of a longer and larger pair, then, cautiously, he removed the lid and inched the tweezers towards the black monstrosity.

'Be careful,' said Brady, feeling Kim take hold of his arm. They both watched as Foley made sure he had a good grip on the implement, then, with a swift movement, he gripped the slug in the tweezers. It wriggled, contracting its body, immediately exuding more slime which dripped onto the work top. Foley held it firmly in the tweezers and pulled a plastic tray towards him. He carefully deposited the slug onto it and then, noticing that the other two were slithering up to the lip of the jar, he promptly knocked them back in and screwed the lid on once more. He picked up a second pair of tweezers and pulled the slug out to its full length. For the first time, Brady saw that the tray in which he'd put it had a scale on it, like a ruler.

Foley exhaled deeply. 'Five and a half inches,' he said. 'Where did you say you found this?'

Brady repeated his story.

'Is it a slug?' Kim asked.

'Oh yes,' Foley told her. 'It's a slug all right but I'll be damned if I've ever seen one this size before.'

'What kind is it?' Brady asked. 'I mean what species?'

Foley shrugged. 'I haven't a clue.'

'I thought you were supposed to be the expert,' the Health Inspector said.

76

The young naturalist looked at him. 'Mr Brady, you probably know as much about slugs as I do. In fact no one seems to know very much specific about them and I certainly don't know anything about this kind.' He nodded in the direction of the captive slug which was writhing and contracting its body beneath the grip of the tweezers. The mucoid coating seemed to be filling the tray around it.

'What's it doing?' asked Kim, shuddering.

'Well, with ordinary slugs, the secretion of bodily mucus is used as a defence mechanism as well as a means of locomotion,' Foley explained. 'If a bird tried to eat it, for instance, the slug would secrete more slime which would cause the bird to drop it. The mucus contains an irritant.' He paused. 'That's what happens with ordinary slugs, I'm just assuming that the same rules apply to these things.' He peered closer, still keeping a firm grip on the black creature. 'You see, when a slug moves it isn't actually in contact with the surface it's on. I know that sounds illogical but what I mean is, it lays down the mucus as a kind of "carpet" if you like, between *it* and whatever it's travelling on. It's the same with snails. Someone did an experiment with one once, they let it crawl across the edge of a razor blade but it wasn't harmed because the slime acted as a cushion.'

'How do they feed?' asked Brady.

'The mouth is on the bottom,' Foley told him. 'There's three or four rows of teeth which it uses to grind up its food.'

'Which is?' the Health Inspector asked, apprehensively.

Foley shrugged. 'Green-stuff mainly. Lettuces, cabbages. Anything they can find in a garden. They're pests, any gardener will tell you that.'

There was a long pause, the silence finally broken by Brady.

'Do any of them eat meat?' he said, quietly.

Foley laughed, softly. 'Not that I know of. There are one or two species that eat earthworms and other insects but . . .' He let the sentence trail off, his tone darkening. 'Why do you ask?'

Brady swallowed hard. 'Look, I know this is going to

sound crazy but could these slugs,' he motioned to the large creatures in the jar, 'kill a man?'

Both Foley and Kim looked at him, aghast.

The young curator smiled. 'That's hardly likely, Mr Brady'.

The Health Inspector's tone hardened. 'One of them nearly took a chunk out of my bloody finger. Now that's pretty unusual wouldn't you say?'

Foley nodded.

Brady continued.

'So there might be other unusual characteristics about them too.'

'Like being able to kill a man?' There was the tiniest trace of cynicism in the curator's voice.

'Is it possible?' the Health Inspector persisted.

'Even if it were, there would have to be hundreds of them.' The young curator quickly qualified his words. 'All the same I'd say it was,' he paused, struggling to find the word, 'unthinkable.'

Kim looked at her husband as if he were a stranger. 'Why do you need to know that, Mike?' she asked.

The Health Inspector was looking at the slug in the tray, still pinned beneath Foley's tweezers.

'A man was found dead two days ago,' he said, softly. 'Ron Bell. He lived in that big house near the new estate.'

Foley nodded.

Brady continued. 'His body looked as though it had decomposed it was . . . well it looked as though it had rotted. There was no flesh left on him but there was lots of blood in the room where we found him. Now, for a corpse to be in the state he was in, it would have taken months before that amount of tissue deterioration took place and besides that, there wouldn't have been so much blood.'

Kim paled. Foley wrinkled his brow as he listened.

'But, the thing is, all over the remains and all over the room was that slime.' He pointed to the thick, transparent mucus which the slug was exuding. 'And I've seen it again since then. When I was inspecting some new houses I found slime trails on the floor and walls.' He told them about Mrs Fortune's drains. 'I saw slime trails in the sewer too.'

Foley nodded. 'That makes sense. Slugs prefer a damp environment.'

Brady nodded, distractedly and the curator looked at him, not quite sure how he should react to what he'd just heard.

'What are you trying to say, Mr Brady?' he asked.

'I don't know what I'm trying to say, I'm just telling you what I've seen.' He sucked in a worried breath. 'And now, on top of that, I find dozens of slugs, bigger than anyone has ever seen before, in my garden. When I pick one up, it tries to bite me.'

Foley stroked his chin thoughtfully and watched the slug in the tray, slithering about in its own slime.

'So you think that old man was eaten by these slugs?' he said.

'I think it's a distinct possibility. I want to know what you think,' Brady insisted.

The younger man didn't speak.

'Could these slugs kill a man?' asked the Health Inspector again.

Foley inhaled slowly. 'Like I said, there would have to be hundreds of them.'

Brady pressed him, the vision of Ron Bell's remains burning brightly in his mind's eye. 'I'm asking you for the last time.' His voice had taken on a sharp edge. 'Could they have killed Ron Bell?'

'Yes,' said Foley, flatly, his attention now rivetted to the slug. He finally turned to face the couple. 'Look, I'll take a look at these slugs, examine them, run some tests on them, do a bit of research. I'll find out all I can about them.' His tone had darkened. 'Give me a day or two.'

Brady nodded.

'Where can I reach you?' the curator wanted to know.

The Health Inspector pulled a nearby pad towards him and scribbled down their address and phone number, then beneath that he wrote down his office number. Foley scanned it once and nodded.

'I'll be in touch,' he said.

Brady extended his right hand and the young curator shook it.

'Thanks,' said Brady and they turned to leave. Foley watched them, listening as their footsteps receded away down the stairs. He sat there for long moments then turned his attention back to the slug in the tray. It was still slithering about in its own slime and had crawled as far as the lip. The curator knocked it back into the tray but, instead of withdrawing its eye stalks like any other slug or snail, it immediately began its journey to the side of the tray again. Foley glanced across at the jar beside him and saw that the other two slugs were clinging stubbornly to the top of it. It was as if the trio of black creatures were anxious to be together again. He pushed the jar closer to the plastic tray and watched, mesmerised, as the freed slug slithered over the lip and onto the glass of the jar. It crawled up the smooth side until it was level with its companions. The curator shook his head, then, taking his tweezers, he plucked the beast from the side of the jar and dropped it into a beaker. Over this he placed a piece of asbestos, normally used in conjunction with a bunsen burner. Then, he got to his feet and passed through a door on his right.

It led into a part of the museum which boasted 'live exhibits'. He flicked the light switches and the powerful banks of fluorescents burst into life. The naturalist walked swiftly towards the thing he wanted, passing half a dozen fish tanks and a Vivarium which contained a grass snake. There was also a large tank housing three or four frogs. But it was the tank at the end of the gallery to which Foley was heading. He paused before it, running a swift eye over the inhabitants.

Pond snails.

A number were feeding on the many plants in the aquarium but a large number were clinging to the glass. Foley looked at them, selecting the largest specimens, one of which was the size of a child's fist. Then carefully, he reached into the murky water and plucked the largest animal from its position on the side of the tank. The creature immediately retracted into its shell as Foley tugged it free but, ignoring the water which ran over his hand, dripping on the polished floor, he turned and made his way back to the laboratory. For some reason, as he deposited the pond snail in the tray vacated by the slug, he felt a thin film of perspiration cover his forehead and he was surprised to find that his hand was shaking when he lifted the lid from the beaker.

He seized the slug in his tweezers and held it for a moment, gripping it at the head end just in case it decided to have a go at him as it had at Brady.

The pond snail had emerged from its shell by now and was slithering slowly about in the bottom of the tray.

Foley gently lowered the slug in beside it. He pulled up a stool and seated himself beside the work top, a pencil gripped in one hand, poised over the pad before him. Quite what he expected to happen he wasn't sure but what *did* happen both shocked and revolted him.

With almost unnatural speed, the large slug slid across to the pond snail and fastened its jaws firmly into the gastropod's head. The slug held firm, its large central tooth anchoring it to its unfortunate victim. The snail tried to withdraw into its shell but was pinned down by the weight and grip of the slug which set to work on it with the numerous rows of radular teeth. Then with one powerful movement, it tore the snail in half, wrenching its soft body from the confines of the shell.

'My God,' gasped Foley, softly, hastily scribbling notes. He watched in awed revulsion as the slug proceeded to devour the remains of the pond snail.

In fact, so intent was he on watching the scene of slaughter before him, he forgot all about the other two slugs in the jar, one of which had succeeded in slithering over the lip and was in the process of heaving its form over the glass of the exterior.

Foley had forgotten to screw the lid on.

He watched the slug in the tray finish off the snail, shaking his head as he scribbled more notes.

The second black creature was half way down the jar by now, its posterior tentacles waving silently.

The slug in the tray now turned towards the curator and he reached for his tweezers once more, ready to drop it back into the beaker.

The second slug was actually on the implement when he picked it up.

With a shout of fear and surprise, Foley dropped the tweezers, the slug falling to the floor with them. He stepped away from the creature as if it were going to leap at him. A quick glance at the one in the tray told him he was going to be forced to act fast. The first slug was slithering over the lip of the tray, leaving its thick trail behind as it gained a grip on the work top. The second was moving towards him. Foley couldn't believe what was happening.

The slug was actually coming after him.

He knelt, retrieved the tweezers and seized the second slug in a powerful grip. With disgust, he hurled it back into the jar with its companion then he turned to deal with the first of the black monstrosities. This time his lunge with the tweezers was clumsy and he snipped off one of the eye stalks.

The creature immediately contracted, slime oozing from its thick body, dark blood running from the severed tentacle. It remained still for a second then, to Foley's horror, it turned towards the metal implement which hovered over its head. The second eye stalk waved around accusingly until Foley, in a fit of anger, snipped that off too. This time the slug did stop, trying to curl up into a ball to protect itself. The naturalist picked it up in the tweezers and dropped it into the beaker, replacing the asbestos mat in position on top of it. Then, he reached into a nearby drawer and took out some adhesive tape which he used to fasten the mat in place. Satisfied that it was secure he sat back on his stool.

The beaker was small, the air supply limited and Foley estimated that it would take less than an hour before the creature suffocated. He screwed the top securely onto the jar which held the two other slugs then he pulled off his rubber gloves and tossed them onto the work top. He crossed to one of the sinks and washed his hands. He was still shaking slightly and, as he dried his hands, he watched the black creatures sliding about inside their glass prisons. He would wait until the one in the beaker was dead and then run some tests on it, perhaps open it up and see exactly what he was dealing with. He decided to go and check the library, to see what he could find out about slugs in general. He folded the towel and draped it over the rail then he headed for the door but, as he reached it he paused and Brady's words came drifting back to him through a haze of uncertainty.

'Could these slugs kill a man?'

Foley closed the lab door and, after a moment's hesitation, he locked it behind him.

Brady and Kim drove from the museum in silence, Kim in particular was disturbed by what she'd heard. She studied her husband's profile for a moment longer then said, tentatively:

'Mike.'

He glanced at her.

'What you said about Ron Bell being killed by slugs. Do you really believe that's what happened?'

He shrugged. 'I don't know what to believe.'

'What did the police report say?' she wanted to know.

'There's been no police report. They're still waiting for the coroner's verdict.'

She shook her head, almost imperceptibly. 'But slugs don't attack people.'

'That one had a pretty good go at my finger,' he snapped.

He swung the car off the side-road, guiding it towards the town centre and Kim asked him what he was doing.

'There's something I've got to get,' he told her, his tone softening slightly as he felt her hand on his thigh. He looked across and managed a thin smile and she realized just how worried he really was. He guided the Vauxhall through the heavy traffic in the centre of town and was lucky to find a parking space in the main street. He switched off the engine and took out the keys.

'Fancy a walk?' he asked her and she nodded, clambering out.

The inside of Haworth's Garden Suppliers was hot and sticky and Kim found it difficult to breathe. It was a small shop but its shelves were crammed with every kind of gardening aid and the floor was littered with lawn-mowers, rakes, hoes and all manner of other equipment. Their shoes beat out a hollow tattoo on the wooden floor as they walked in and a high pitched buzzing broke the silence as Brady opened the door. Immediately a little man with greying hair and a thin moustache appeared from behind the counter. He was wearing a grey overall and had a pipe protruding from one corner of his mouth. It had long since gone out but he either hadn't noticed or just hadn't bothered to relight it. He spoke without removing it, the bowl bouncing up and down like a rampant metronome.

'Ted Haworth,' he announced, grinning broadly. 'Welcome to my little emporium, what can I do for you?'

'Slugs,' said Brady. 'I want something to kill them.'

'Well, I didn't think you wanted something to feed them with,' said Haworth, grinning at his own quip. He looked at his two customers waiting for them to smile which they did out of politeness. Kim raised an eyebrow and Brady nodded almost imperceptibly.

Haworth scuttled round to their side of the counter, crossing to the shelves which held all manner of bottles and jars.

'Having trouble with the little buggers are you?' he said, gaily.

'You could say that,' said Brady. 'What's the strongest repellent you've got?'

'Now,' said the little man, pausing momentarily. 'Do you want something to kill them or something to just shift them to some other poor devil's garden?' He laughed again.

'I want something to kill them,' Brady told him.

Haworth nodded and reached for a bottle of brown liquid. He plonked it on the counter. Brady read the label. 'Slug-it'. He nodded. 'Anything else?'

The shop owner produced a green can which had 'Slug Pellets' written on it. He crossed back to his own side of the counter.

'I'll take them both,' said Brady, fumbling in his pocket for some money.

'You really have got problems with them, haven't you?' said Haworth, smiling. He dropped the two items into a bag and handed them to Brady along with his change.

'There's full instructions on each container,' he added. 'I had trouble with the little devils one year. They ate me out of house and home. Ruined my crop of vegetables.' He smiled at Kim who tried to look interested.

Brady turned and headed for the door. 'Thanks for your help,' he said, opening it for Kim to pass through.

'They'll get rid of the little sods,' said Haworth, grinning.

Brady nodded. 'I hope so,' he said, cryptically.

It was late afternoon when they finally got home and clouds of tiny flies hovered around Brady as he scattered slug pellets and poison over the ground. Even as he did so he could see a number of the larger slugs slithering about on the dark earth, apparently oblivious to his efforts but he felt a strange kind of pleasure knowing he was sewing the seeds of death for these black monsters. The slug pellets, according to the instructions on the tin, were consumed by the animals and worked almost immediately. There was something in them which attracted the slugs to them. The poison was intended to kill on contact.

Kim watched him from the back door, the clouds of midges swirling around in the afternoon air like flies round a rotted carcass.

When his task was completed, Brady stood back.

'Right you bastards,' he said. 'Come and get it'. He turned and headed back to the house, telling Kim that he'd check on the results next morning.

As the Health Inspector trudged back up the garden a huge black slug, fully eight inches long, slithered up onto a piece of rock. Its eye stalks moved slowly back and forth, almost mockingly.

As if it were watching Brady.

Thirteen

Kath Green picked up the small watering can and poured some of the clear liquid into the pot where the spider plant was growing. The plant was increasing at a tremendous rate and its leaves draped over the side of the pot like some kind of frozen green overflow. Kath smiled to herself and passed to the next pot where she was nurturing a bizzie-lizzie. It had just started to flower, as had a number of the other plants and a heady aroma filled the air of the outhouse.

Playing contentedly on the tiled floor of the conservatory was Kath's two year old daughter, Amanda, who was having difficulty dressing one of her dolls. Finally, when she couldn't get its coat on by conventional means, she pulled the arm off in order to ensure an adequate fit. Satisfied with her efforts, she smiled happily to herself and sat the doll down beside a couple of teddy bears and a bendy model of Kermit the frog. Amanda wiped her hands on her dungarees and clambered to her feet, wandering across towards her mother who was busy watering another of her plants. She tugged on Kath's skirt and the woman looked down.

'What is it, darling?' she asked, running her free hand through the little girl's hair.

'Ice cream,' said Amanda. looking up at her with huge brown eyes.

Kath smiled. Obviously the little girl had heard the distant chimes of the van. It usually came past the house at about three every afternoon and, when she herself heard it, she guessed that it must only be in the next street.

'The man's not here yet,' said Kath and Amanda nodded, dejectedly. 'Mummy go and get you one when the man comes round.' That suggestion seemed to brighten her up

87

and she smiled broadly, her little face beaming. She returned to her waiting toys. Kermit and the others greeted her arrival with silence. Amanda picked up the torn off arm of her doll and set about fastening it back in position, chewing it angrily when it wouldn't fit back into the joint. Kath saw her and turned, wagging a reproachful finger at the child.

'Don't put things in your mouth, darling,' she said, taking the doll and its disjointed arm from her irate daughter. Kath fiddled about with the recalcitrant plastic limb for a moment and then she too gave it up as a bad job. 'We'll see if Daddy can fix it when he comes home,' she said, putting the doll on the shelf where she kept her plant food.

'When Daddy gets home,' Kath repeated her own words to herself, sighing wistfully. Ray Green had been working in Stowfield, about twenty miles away, for the past three days and he was due back that night. It couldn't be too soon for Kath. She missed him terribly, even on such short trips. She had never been very good at making friends and, despite the fact that they had lived on the new estate for the past five years, she still only knew most of its occupants on nodding terms. When Ray was on a job she only had Amanda for company and it was at times like that she was thankful they'd had a child. She'd been through a pretty bad bout of post-natal depression but Ray had helped her through it, showing a tolerance and understanding which she had never dreamed he possessed. They were happy in every respect now. Ray's business was flourishing and Kath was slowly learning to overcome her shyness. She had found interests of her own, the plants being her consuming passion. Ray had built the conservatory himself, an extension linked to the kitchen, afraid that the house was becoming like 'Bloody Kew Gardens'.

She smiled at the recollection and carried on watering. As if sensing something, Amanda got to her feet and wandered across to her once more and, just as Kath was going to ask what was wrong, she heard the familiar tones of the ice cream van outside.

88

'Mummy,' said the little girl, tugging at Kath's skirt. 'Lolly.'

'All right,' said Kath and put down her watering can. She walked through into the kitchen, retrieved her purse and headed out towards the waiting van.

The sun was still blazing away and Kath decided that she would have one herself. Why not? At twenty-six and with a figure that would make any woman envious, one ice cream wasn't going to hurt was it? She smiled to herself and got in the queue behind a couple of kids, one of whom was busily inspecting the contents of his left nostril on an index finger. Kath shook her head and smiled.

Amanda jumped up and down delightedly on the tiled floor for a moment before returning to her assembled toys. She sat cross-legged amongst them, telling them that she was going to have an ice cream. She put her hand back to steady herself and it was then that she felt something wet on her fingers. Amanda looked down and saw something glistening in the sunlight. At first she thought it was water but, as she ran her fingers through it, she noticed how thick and sticky it was. Puzzled she raised her hand, the clear liquid clinging to her fingers. Amananda brought her hand closer to her face, sniffing at the fluid, puzzled when it had no smell. She looked down and saw that it led right across the conservatory, like a trail.

Tentatively, she licked some of it from her fingers.

It was tasteless too. She swallowed quickly, wiping the rest on her dungarees. Mummy told her all the time not to put her fingers in her mouth and, if she saw her licking the sticky stuff she would be angry. Amanda ran her tongue round the inside of her mouth. The sticky stuff seemed to put her teeth on edge and she tried to wipe it away on her sleeve but, in a moment or two, she had swallowed the one or two globules and it was gone.

She heard her mother's footsteps as she returned with the ice creams and she jumped up to take hers, forgetting the sticky stuff now.

The single slug which had left the trail slithered, unseen, from the conservatory.

Kath cut Amanda's food for her and watched her as she ate. The little girl finished all her tea within about ten minutes and sat back proudly, displaying an empty plate. Kath ate her own meal, smiling as she saw Amanda rubbing her stomach the way Ray did when he had eaten. She glanced up at the wall clock and saw that the hands had crawled round to six p.m. Another three or four hours and Ray would be home. She felt a warm shudder of anticipation run through her.

She finished her own meal while Amanda scuttled off into the sitting room to watch TV. She'd brought all her toys in from the conservatory and they sat with her before the flickering picture. The multi-coloured hues reflected in their dead, glass eyes. Kath did the washing up, watching the sun slowly wane, spilling its redness into the golden heavens, tinting the clouds crimson. She left the plates to drain and padded into the sitting room. Another hour and she'd have to put Amanda to bed. The child was yawning already. Unusual for her, thought Kath. She was usually full of life and bedtimes were sometimes an impossible struggle. Getting her upstairs was bad enough but keeping her in bed was more often than not impossible. Both Kath and Ray often went through three or four story books before the little imp went off to sleep. But tonight, Amanda was dozing in front of the TV and, when seven o'clock came (traditionally a time of joyful but tiring pandemonium) she was positively insistent on going to bed. In fact, even before Kath had finished slipping on her pyjamas, the little girl had fallen asleep. Kath looked down at her as she lay on the sofa but, she reasoned, the child had been out playing all day. There was good cause for her to be tired. She lifted the sleeping form of her daughter easily and carried her up the stairs to the bedroom which had dancing rabbits on the door.

Kath laid her in bed, pulling the sheets up around her neck. She knelt beside Amanda listening to the low guttural

90

breathing for a second then she leant over and kissed her on the cheek. The child moved slightly but did not wake.

'Goodnight, darling,' whispered Kath and crossed to the door. She stood there for a moment, watching the slow rise and fall of Amanda's chest, then she quietly pulled the door shut and made her way downstairs.

Kath heard the dog barking and looked up from her book. She muttered something to herself and got up, crossing to the big bay window in the sitting room. Outside, just passing the house, Mr Steel from next door was being dragged along the road by his Alsatian. The huge dog was yanking him all over the place and Kath couldn't resist a smile. However, he smile faded as the dog stood still before the house and began barking with renewed ferocity. The blasted thing would wake Amanda, she thought and she turned back to her seat, one ear cocked expectantly, waiting for her daughter to call or to come scampering down the stairs.

But, there was no such movement and Kath settled back into her chair, reaching for the discarded paperback. She flipped it open and tried to read but she couldn't concentrate. The barking of the dog had receded into the distance but the ticking of the sitting room clock seemed to be thunderous. Kath looked across at it and saw that it was nearly eight o'clock. She checked her watch too, as if it were going to hasten Ray on his journey home. She discarded the paperback once more and got up to switch on the TV. Kath punched buttons, trying to find something to hold her attention.

A documentary about nuclear war on one channel. She hurriedly switched over. A black and white film. She sighed and pressed the last button. It was another documentary, this time about rising street crime. Kath hovered before the set where a youth with a mohican style hair-cut was being interviewed:

'Well, the fucking law ain't no bother. Me mate, he done this fucking shop and no coppers showed up so, well, I mean they're bastards ain't they? I . . .'

Kath winced and switched the set off. She exhaled deeply and returned to her chair where she sat for long moments before deciding to make a cup of tea. At least that would keep her occupied.

It was as she rose that she heard the commotion coming from upstairs. Kath stood still for long seconds, listening to the shouts and screams coming from above then, the breath catching in her throat, she raced towards the stairs, hurrying towards the landing. It was as she reached it she realized the noises were coming from Amanda's room.

Kath pushed open the door, her hand reached frantically for the light switch.

Amanda lay across the bed, her body thrashing frenziedly about, contorting like an eel on a hot skillet. Her head was rolling back and forth at a terrifying rate and, Kath noted with horror, that there was a dark, evil smelling mucus spilling over her lips. As her head shook madly, the foul sputum flew in all directions.

Kath took a step towards the bed, the sightless eyes of a teddy bear pinning her in a glassy stare. Its sewn-on smile almost mocking her.

Amanda was rasping asthmatically, her tongue lolling wolfishly from the side of her mouth, the whites of her eyes gleaming like half moons as they rolled in their sockets.

'Oh God,' gasped Kath, and reached for her daughter, struggling to hold the squirming child still in her arms. She lifted her daughter to her shoulders, the little body twisting forcefully in her arms. Tears welled up in Kath's eyes as she struggled towards the bedroom door. Her vision blurred as the salty droplets cascaded down her cheeks but she staggered on, the wriggling form of her child clasped tightly to her as the convulsions seemed to grow in intensity. Then, suddenly, with lightning speed, Amanda snaked her head forward and bit deeply into Kaths's neck, hanging on like a ferret until her mother pushed her away. Kath was screaming now. She stood motionless for a second, gazing down at the inert body of her daughter, then she staggered as she felt the warm blood jetting from the ragged wound in her neck. She clapped a hand to it and felt the torn flap of skin. The crimson liquid was running down her chest, between the valley of her breasts, staining her blouse and she felt her right arm going numb as the pain seemed to spread through her body. The landing swam before her and she gripped the bannister to stop herself falling. She felt her knees buckle but she put out a hand and steadied herself, leaving a bloodied hand-print on the white wallpaper. The mark looked black in the twilight.

'Help me,' she gurgled, the blood flowing freely from the bite. It poured down her outstretched arm and dripped onto the carpet and she felt the sickness sweeping over her. Tears coursed down her cheeks as she turned towards the top of the stairs, the phone at the bottom beckoning her.

In her haste, she missed the first step.

For a second Kath clutched at empty air, then, with a despairing moan, she fell forward. Cartwheeling as she crashed down the stairs. She hurtled to the bottom, leaving a trail of blood behind her, some of which splattered up the walls. She smashed into the phone table at the bottom and the phone itself fell to the ground. Twisted like a broken doll, Kath lay at the foot of the stairs, her tortured mind still clinging to the last shreds of consiousness. The pain which racked her body kept her awake. Even through the agony she felt the blood running from her torn neck and, somewhere in the distance, she heard a car door slam.

Ray Green made his way up the short path to the front door and paused on the step, fumbling for his key. He cursed when he couldn't find it, eventually dropping his tool bag and rummaging in the pocket of his jeans. He finally found it and inserted it in the lock smiling wearily. The job in Stowfield had been a sod. He and his partner had worked their nuts off to get it finished on time and it had been bloody hard work, but the size of the pay cheque eased the weariness somewhat and Ray knew how glad Kath would be to see him.

He pushed open the door and walked in.

Kath practically fell into his arms.

For a second, everything seemed frozen, like a stop-frame in a cine film. Ray opened his mouth to say something as he gazed into the tortured face of his wife. She was as white as milk, the blood matted thickly in her hair and stained into her blouse. He saw the vicious bite, the crimson liquid still pumping from it. The blood spattered walls, the wrecked table, the overturned phone.

And then the film was running again.

'Kath,' he gasped, looking into her reddened eyes. She tried to hold him but her fingers slipped and she slid to the floor at his feet. He dropped to one knee, his mind trying to comprehend the sight before him. She raised one bloodied hand, as if soliciting help and he tore off his jacket, laying it over her.

'Amanda,' Kath, rasped, a sudden spasm of coughing racking her body. The movement caused more of the bright red fluid to spill over her lips but she repeated the word, motioning towards the top of the stairs. He hesitated a second then bounded up to the landing taking the steps two at a time. Passing the blood flecked walls until he was looking down at the body of his daughter, now looking so tiny and helpless. Her eyes and mouth were open, a crimson smudge across her chin and lips. He knelt beside the body, shaking his head. Then, with one quivering hand, he reached out and touched her oustretched limb and the tiny hand seemed lost in his own rough one but he clasped it tightly, tears brimming in his eyes. The child's cheeks were sunken pits, her eyes ringed black. The whites seemed to glow even more brilliantly in the darkness but Ray finally tore his gaze from them and scrambled to his feet. He hurried down the stairs, groping for the phone, dialling three nines. He gripped the receiver tightly in his impatience finally managing to blurt out the word 'Ambulance', almost screaming it down the phone. He gave the address and then dropped the receiver, crawling across to Kath who still lay motionless in the hall.

Ray reached for her hand, large salt tears now spilling down his cheeks.

94

'Oh God,' he breathed, quietly.

Both mother and child were dead before the ambulance arrived.

Fourteen

Brady was up early that Sunday morning. He slid noiselessly out of bed, checking to make sure that he hadn't woken Kim. She rolled onto her back, one hand flailing across the warm area he had just vacated, but she did not wake.

The Health Inspector hurriedly pulled on a pair of jeans. He looked across at Kim once more and then at the clock which told him it was six fifteen. He pushed his feet into his slippers, pulled on his bath robe and padded out of the bedroom. Quickly but quietly he made his way down the stairs, through the house until he finally reached the back door. He unlocked it and slid the bolts back, shivering slightly as an early morning breeze whistled in through the open door.

Brady peered to his right and left, checking that no one else was around. Although at six fifteen on a Sunday morning that was unlikely. Satisfied that he was alone, he padded out into the back garden, cursing as the early morning dew soaked through his slippers and wet his feet.

'Shit,' he grunted, trying to walk on tip-toe to minimise the effect of the wet grass on his fraying foot wear. He moved across to the freshly dug area of ground, some of the slug pellets still in view, scattered on the top soil where he'd left them the day before. He swallowed hard and ran a hopeful eye over the dark earth. Many of the pellets had gone, consumed by the slugs he hoped but there were no dead animals in sight either. He stepped closer, running a hand over his bristly cheeks.

A black slug, the size of his fist, moved slowly towards him and Brady recoiled in shock and disgust. He backed off, seeing that more of the obscene creatures were slithering

97

about on the earth. Brady watched them for a second, the breath catching in his throat, then he turned and headed for the house. He opened the back door and then hurried inside, quickly locking and bolting it again.

He leant against the closed door and exhaled deeply. On the work top opposite stood the can of slug pellets and the bottle of poison.

Brady shook his head.

For all the effect they'd had, he might as well have put down sugar.

Fifteen

By noon that morning the sun had risen high in the sky and it hung in the cloudless heavens covering everything below it with a blanket of searing heat.

David Watson heard the familiar Glaswegian tones of his neighbour, Wally Mackay, and straightened up. The tall Scot had a spade over his shoulder and he sauntered over towards the wire fence which separated the two gardens.

'Hell of a bloody way to spend a Sunday morning,' said the Scot, leaning on the fence. He jumped back hastily rubbing his forearm and looking daggers at the wire which was scorching hot due to the sun. Watson suppressed a grin and tried to look enthusiastic as Mackay leant on the handle of the spade and started chattering away about the weather, his wife and any other thing which passed through his mind. David Watson loved gardening but he invariably got collared by the Scot and ended up doing nothing. It looked like today was going to be one of those days.

'My bloody old lady sent me out here to dig this lot over,' muttered Mackay, indicating the patch of miniature jungle which constituted his garden. The weeds were knee high in places and were beginning to encroach into Watson's carefully tended plot of ground.

'It is getting a bit overgrown, Wally,' he said, trying to sound tactful, but making a melodramatic effort to pull up one of the unwelcome weeds which had found its way in from the Scotsman's garden.

'Fuck it,' said the Scot, peering over his shoulder in the direction of his house. He could see no sign of his wife so he retained his position and fumbled in his trouser pocket for his tobacco tin. He swifty rolled one and then offered it to

99

Watson who, equally swiftly, declined. He returned to his own task of spreading some compost on his latest crop of potatoes. He'd begun growing vegetables as a joke to begin with and because his wife, Maureen, had bet him a fiver he couldn't do it. The joke turned out to be useful though and he had a fine crop of spuds, onions, carrots and lettuce to show for his efforts. He still didn't know the first thing about the technicalities of cultivating vegetables but he had been lucky. He'd planted the seeds and the things had grown.

Watson enjoyed the peace and solitude which the garden offered him (when he managed to avoid Mackay that was) and it came as a welcome relief from the hustle and bustle of his every day job. He worked for the computer firm in Merton as a rep and had done for the last seven years. The pay was good, he was proficient at the job and he enjoyed it. His wife was manageress of a small but profitable boutique in the centre of town and they were hoping to move from the new estate soon to buy their own place.

They were childless by choice, both of them preferring to pursue their careers rather than sink into a welter of wet nappies and midnight feeds. Maureen in particular, had never shown a desire or even a liking for children. It was something which Watson found unusual but nevertheless welcome. She, unlike others of her kind, never felt the urge to pick up a young child and hold it or to gurgle unintelligible words to new born babies. At twenty-eight, she was every inch the business woman and the emotion which most women possessed had been replaced, in Maureen, by a ruthless efficiency which Watson himself respected. They were a perfect match, for he too bore that unerringly ambitious streak which at times bordered on obsession and had, occasionally, been known to veer into vindictiveness. He was thirty-two and happy and, right now, he'd be a lot happier if Wally Mackay stopped nattering and let him get on with his jobs.

'I heard your place was making more redundant,' said the Scot, spitting out a piece of tobacco.

Watson shook his head. 'Just rumours.'

Mackay shrugged. 'I got the fucking push two weeks ago.'

'You told me,' said Watson. About fifteen bloody times, he thought to himself. 'Have you found anything else yet?'

'Nothing about. You haven't any vacancies at your place have you?' he asked hopefully.

Watson smiled thinly and shook his head. 'Afraid not.' He knelt again and pulled a lettuce from the row before him, holding it up to admire his handiwork.

'Got any of those to spare?' said the Scot, admiring the greenery.

Watson looked at him and smiled again. Good old Wally, always on the earhole. The younger man was about to turn when Mackay began talking about football. Reluctantly, Watson halted and listened politely, nodding every so often as the Scot rambled on, his harsh accent grating like fingernails on a blackboard. He chanced a look at his watch and saw that it was twelve-fifteen.

'Dave.'

The shout made them both turn.

Standing in the doorway was Maureen.

'Telephone for you,' she called.

Watson stifled a sigh of relief and made his way up the garden, clutching the lettuce.

Mackay watched the younger man disappear inside his house then he sucked hard on his fag and drove his spade into the iron hard earth. If only my bloody old lady looked like her, he thought.

Watson hurried into the kitchen and inhaled deeply, the delightful aroma of roast beef meeting his nostrils. He dumped the lettuce on the draining board and headed through to the lounge.

'Who is it on the phone?' he asked.

'No one,' said Maureen, laughing. 'I saw that old Rob Roy next door had got you cornered so I thought I'd rescue you.'

Watson laughed and came back into the kitchen. He took Maureen in his arms and kissed her gently on the forehead.

'You cunning bitch,' he grinned, flicking at her blonde hair with one dirty hand. He pulled her close to him feeling the warmth of her body against his. He cradled her head in his hands and kissed her, his tongue seeking hers eagerly. They remained locked together, her right hand reaching for the growing bulge in his trousers, her own nipples stiffening and pressing against the material of her shirt. He finally broke away, shaking his head.

'Lunch,' he said, smiling.

'To hell with lunch,' she said, prodding him hard with her long nail. She drew a line from the hollow of his throat, through the thick hair on his chest, to his navel. As her hand toyed with the button of his jeans he held it and smiled.

'Can't you wait?' he said, trying to sound stern but, when she shook her head he laughed. They finally pulled away from each other and Watson crossed to the sink to wash his hands. He looked at Maureen as he did. She was dressed only in a yellow shirt and a pair of tight-fitting canvas trousers, worn thin at the knees. Beneath them he knew she wore no briefs. She never wore underwear in the summer. The blonde colour was beginning to grow out of her thick hair and the darker roots were showing. Every time she said that she would let her hair return to its natural chestnut colour but, each time, she weakened and resorted to the dye. He watched her as she ran the lettuce briefly under the tap before returning it to the chopping board where she set about its crisp green leaves with a razor sharp knife. She cut it up hastily, dropping the pieces into the nearby salad bowl with the peppers and other vegetables.

'I had trouble finding a decent lettuce,' he said, indicating the vegetable as she tossed it in the bowl. 'Bloody slugs have been at them.'

'Slugs?' She shuddered.

He nodded. 'There's about a dozen out in the vegetable patch now. Damn things. I'll have to see about putting something down to kill them.'

Maureen set the bowl on the table and crossed to the oven, retrieving the meat. She set it on the table and handed the carving knife to Watson. Quickly and expertly he sliced the succulent joint and, within minutes, they were eating.

'No salad?' said Watson, offering Maureen the bowl after he'd taken his share.

She shook her head, reaching instead for the glass of red wine at her elbow. She raised it in salute and smiled.

'Here's to your success,' she said. 'I hope you get that contract signed tomorrow.'

'You're not the only one,' said Watson and joined her in the toast. He put down his glass once more and continued eating. She saw him wince as he pushed a lump of lettuce into his mouth. He chewed slowly for a second, grimaced and reached hurriedly for his wine.

'Something wrong?' she asked.

He motioned to the salad. 'I think I swallowed something,' he said. 'You did wash that lettuce properly didn't you?'

She raised an eyebrow, questioningly and Watson smiled. He continued eating, still aware of the strange flavour but, another glass of wine soon washed away the peculiar taste.

'Where are you taking them to eat tomorrow?' asked Maureen, running the index finger of one hand around the rim of her glass.

'The City Hotel,' he told her.

'That'll cost you.'

He winked. 'It's on the expense account.' He took a sip of his own wine, his voice turning reflective. 'Besides, this is an important contract. It'll be worth millions in the long run if I can secure it.'

'You're worried about it aren't you?' she said.

He nodded. The contract was a big one and, not only would it mean work for the firm for the next three years it would also bring Watson a sizeable slice of commission and almost certain promotion. Perhaps then, they could actually move out and buy their own house. He had two guests to entertain the following morning, one of them an American, and he didn't want anything to go wrong. Selling was his business and he would need all his powers of persuasion at the forthcoming business lunch. For the first time in his working life, he actually felt nervous. Four Mark-1

103

Computers and it would take him all his abilities to sell them and secure the contract. He sipped at his wine, pouring some more into Maureen's half empty glass with his free hand.

They ate lunch at a leisurely pace, although Watson left the rest of his salad. The strange taste seemed to have returned almost as if it were sticking to his tongue. He drank more wine in an effort to get rid of it and, even if he'd known about eating half the black slug, there was little he could have done about it.

He patted his stomach appreciatively and smiled at Maureen.

'Beautiful,' he said. 'So was the meal.'

She grinned, stood up and crossed to his chair, seating herself on his lap. She ran her carefully manicured fingers through his hair, squirming pleasurably as his left hand found its way up inside her shirt. He cupped one taut breast, rubbing his thumb across the nipple until it hardened to a firm bud. Then, with the other hand, he expertly undid the buttons until both her breasts were exposed. He bent forward and kissed each nipple in turn.

'What about the washing up?' she said, her face flushed.

He smiled. 'To hell with the washing up.'

They both laughed.

Watson checked his watch as the ten o'clock news came on. It was right to the second. He sat in the semi-darkness of the lounge with only the light from his desk lamp and the multi-coloured flickerings of the TV illuminating the room. They had only just drawn the curtains, shutting out the night but he had been sitting at his desk for more than two hours, going over blue-prints and fact-sheets. He had to be sure that he could answer any question that either of his two customers might put to him the following day. Also, he had to know every minute detail about the workings of the machines so that he could extol their worth to the best of his abilities but, as he sat, gazing at the blue-prints, his mind was not on the job at hand. His stomach felt bloated and he had already loosened his belt but, more disturbingly, he was suffering from what felt like severe flatulence. It had come on suddenly about six that evening and despite the repeated doses of Magnesia, the discomfort had not been relieved. He shifted uncomfortably in his seat, rubbing one hand across his protruding belly.

He had eaten nothing since lunch-time, but, surprisingly enough he didn't feel hungry. All he was aware of was the unrelenting pain in his stomach which sometimes felt like contractions. If he'd been a woman he might have thought he was pregnant. He smiled at his own quip but the smile dissolved into a wince as another spasm of pain hit him.

'Jesus,' he rasped, surprised at its intensity.

Maureen, crouching on the floor before the television looked round.

'What's wrong, Dave?' she asked.

He sat back in his chair. 'My bloody stomach,' he said, irritably.

She looked concerned. 'Hasn't that pain gone yet?'

He shook his head.

She got up and crossed to his desk which occupied one corner of the room. 'Do you think I should call a doctor?' she asked.

Watson grabbed hold of her and pulled her onto his knee, trying to disguise the violent stab of pain which accompanied the movement. It felt as if someone was pulling his intestines out through his navel.

'I don't need a doctor,' he said, trying to catch his breath. 'It's probably just nerves from thinking about tomorrow.'

Maureen smiled thinly, not reassured by his home-grown diagnosis. 'If you're sure.'

He nodded. 'I'm sure.' He kissed her. 'Perhaps an early night would help.'

She touched his cheek which felt hot, the perspiration beaded on it in a thin film. Maureen nodded. 'I think that's a good idea,' she said.

In fifteen minutes they were upstairs.

Watson lay in bed, the sheets pulled back. He looked down

105

at his naked body, studying each outline and contour. Lying flat, his stomach didn't seem to be so distended, indeed, when he stood up to examine it in the wardrobe mirror the bloated appearance it had shown earlier seemed to have gone.

The pain, however, persisted.

He crossed back to the bed and lay down again, glancing across at the bedroom curtains which billowed in the gentle breeze. Both bedside lamps were on but the corners of the room were in shadow. He lay still, his arms behind his head, supporting him. The pain seemed to have moved further up his body and, as he swallowed, a wave of agony seemed to sweep over his entire stomach and lower chest. He cursed silently. Perhaps it *was* just nerves. Maybe something he'd eaten? He nodded, yes, that was the answer. In the morning it would be fine, he'd . . .

He sat up as an excruciating pain tore through him from sternum to groin. He clutched the bed, the muscles in his arms standing out like cords of thick hemp but, after a few unbearable seconds, the spasm passed, even settling a little. He took a deep but tentative breath and lay back again. He heard the toilet flush and, a second later, Maureen's light footsteps padding across the landing.

She entered the bedroom and closed the door behind her, the long black, diaphanous, night-dress swirling around her like nylon fog. Through it, Watson could see the smooth outline of her body and she stood before him for long seconds gazing down at his own naked form. He shifted his position slightly, gritting his teeth against the onslaught of pain he expected. It came only briefly and he exhaled gratefully, watching as Maureen climbed into bed beside him.

Her left hand stroked soothingly across his belly.

'Does it feel any better?' she asked.

He nodded and leaned forward to kiss her, feeling that soft hand sliding further down his body until it enveloped his penis, stroking and caressing it until it reached full erection. Watson thrust his hips forward, forcing his shaft further up into Maureen's eager hand. He reached for the bow at her

106

throat and pulled it, allowing the night-dress to fall away, exposing her body. He cupped one breast in his hand, bending his head to flick the rough edge of his tongue over her swollen nipple. She held his free hand, pushing it towards her mound where his fingers brushed the soft down of her pubic hair before plunging deeper to find her slippery cleft. She writhed beneath his probing digits and he pushed deeper, smiling at the look of pleasure on her face.

Her hand gripped his organ more tightly, the speed of her movements increasing and Watson felt the unmistakable waves of early pleasure sweeping over him. He kissed Maureen gently on the lips, whispering to her to slow down but her passion knew no bounds and she pulled him onto her, guiding his hardness into her moist vagina. He thrust into her, both of them gasping at this new ecstasy.

Watson almost cried out in pain as a wave of agony tore through his stomach and chest. He gritted his teeth, sucking in a tortured breath, suddenly finding that his arms would not support him. He collapsed onto Maureen, the pain driving red hot knives into him.

He withdrew from her and rolled to one side, his penis immediately losing its stiffness.

'Dave,' gasped Maureen, breathlessly. 'What is it?'

He winced. 'Jesus.' The word sounded as if it came from miles away. Watson was clutching at his stomach, lying still on his back.

'I'm going to get a doctor,' said Maureen, hauling herself out of bed.

'No,' he said, forcefully. 'It's OK now.' He nodded, noting that the pain was, indeed, diminishing.

Maureen paused, her hand still on the knob of the door but, when she saw him stand up, she crossed back to the bed. Watson stood before the mirror once more. There was no distention, just the pain. He took three or four deep breaths, relaxing more with each one. Finally he returned to bed. Maureen lay beside him, stroking his hot cheek with one index finger. He twisted his head to one side and kissed her finger, smiling at her.

107

'Are you going to be all right?' she said, anxiously.

Watson nodded. 'The pain's almost gone now.' He smiled. 'I'll be as right as rain in the morning.'

They switched off the bedside lamps and Maureen drew herself closer to him. It wasn't long before he heard the soft, rhythmic sound of her breathing as she drifted off to sleep. Watson watched the curtains, still billowing in the gentle breeze. Beyond them the night was black, sticky with heat.

The pain gradually lessened in David Watson's stomach but, the hands of the clock had crawled round to one twenty a.m. before he finally found the welcome oblivion of sleep.

It was Maureen who heard the alarm the following morning. She reached up and turned it off, simultaneously touching Watson gently on the shoulder.

'Dave,' she murmured, her voice thick with sleep.

He didn't move.

She called his name again, rubbing her eyes and blinking myopically at the ceiling.

Still no response.

Maureen propped herself up on one elbow and leant across her husband. He was lying on his side with his back to her and, when he made no movement on her third call, she shook him gently.

Watson remained still.

Maureen swallowed hard and swung herself out of bed, crossing to her husband's side where she knelt. She pressed a hand to his cheek which was cool and suddenly she felt afraid.

'Dave,' she repeated, more urgently, this time shaking him hard.

She gave an audible sigh of relief when he opened his eyes a fraction. Crusted and heavy-lidded, they opened slowly and he looked at her almost as if she wasn't there. He seemed to be looking through her.

Maureen called his name again and, this time, he rolled onto his back. His mouth opened slightly and he made a deep rasping noise in the back of his throat.

108

'God Almighty,' he moaned, covering both eyes with his hands.

'I thought you were dead,' she said, her breath coming in short gasps.

'I think I am,' croaked Watson, massaging the bridge of his nose between his thumb and forefinger. 'It feels like there's a brass band marching around inside my head.'

'What about your stomach?' she wanted to know.

He sat up slowly, the headache intensifying to a point where he felt as though someone were hitting him repeatedly across the skull with a dozen red hot hammers. He slumped against the headboard and looked down at his stomach. No distention. No pain even. With cautious hands, he pressed the firm flesh in several places.

'No pain at all,' he said, trying to smile but the blinding white agony in his head restrained him. 'It's my bloody head now.'

'I'll go and get breakfast ready. I'll get you a couple of Paracetamols,' Maureen said and pulled on her house-coat. She padded out of the bedroom leaving Watson alone. As slowly as he could he swung himself out of bed and crossed to the bedroom door. The headache seemed to intensify as he walked across the landing to the bathroom and, when he looked at his reflection in the mirror, a haggard, white-faced ghost stared back at him. His face was the colour of rancid butter, the dark circles beneath his eyes looking all the more prominent because of that. He ran some cold water and splashed it over his face, leaning over the sink for what seemed like an eternity. When he did finally straighten up, he put both hands to his temples as if he were afraid his head was going to explode. With the red hot hammers pounding away at his brain, he began to remove his shaving equipment from the glass-fronted cabinet on the wall. He filled the sink with hot water and, carefully, lathered his face.

The prospect of a day's business and hard selling seemed to make his pain all the worse.

Sixteen

The dining room of the City Hotel was already crowded with its daily quota of businessmen as Watson and his two customers entered. He'd booked a table for one fifteen and a quick glance at his watch told him that it was over thirty minutes before they were due to eat.

'How about a drink before lunch?' he said, smiling, trying to ignore the headache which still raged, threatening to split his skull in two.

'Sounds good to me,' said Edward Canning, the first of his prospective customers. Canning's thick American drawl drifted through the air, mingling with the smell of cigarettes, liquor and the tempting aroma of freshly cooked food. Canning was in his late thirties, heavily built but without a hint of fat on his powerful body. He lit up one of his huge cigars and followed Watson and the other man, Kenneth Riggs, into the smaller of the City's three bars.

Riggs was younger by a couple of years but his grey hair gave him the appearance of someone twice his age. His face was lined and his cheeks seemed to hang down like those of a bloodhound. When he laughed, which he often did, a row of double chins wobbled fluidly, spilling over onto his shirt collar which looked so tight it threatened to strangle him. Canning had removed his tie because of the heat and, as he found a table near the window, he rolled up his sleeves. Riggs joined him while Watson stood at the crowded bar brandishing a five pound note in front of him.

He looked angrily at a man who bumped into him and the unfortunate chap apologised hurriedly when he saw the expression on Watson's face. His nerves were not so much frayed as shredded. He'd picked his two customers up at

111

nine and driven them to the factory to show them the computers in action. They had asked surprisingly few questions, only those relating to reliability, performance, output and, most importantly, cost. A fact for which Watson was grateful because he was finding it difficult to even think straight, so intense was the throbbing inside his skull. Nevertheless, he'd established a good rapport with the two men, particularly Canning. Both seemed interested and satisfied with his approach and also the computers. Watson felt almost certain that the contract would be signed but he would feel a hell of a lot happier when he could actually see their names on that dotted line. He exhaled deeply, closing his eyes momentarily. The noise in the bar seemed to swirl around him like a bank of mist yet it seemed distant, as if he were alone in a sealed compartment and everyone else was outside. He opened his eyes again, craning forward to see where the barman had got to. The little man in the red jacket was serving a couple of customers at the far end of the bar so Watson continued to stand in his place holding up the fiver as if hoping it would attract the barman. He ran one hand across his forehead, wondering if his headache was ever going to go. The two tablets he'd taken at breakfast had done nothing to help, neither had the four others he'd taken since. He just hoped that the deal could be concluded quickly. He promised himself he'd go straight home to bed afterwards.

The barman finally arrived and Watson ordered, leaning against the counter while the little man fetched the drinks. He returned with surprising speed and Watson collected both drinks and change and made his way carefully across the room to the table where his customers sat.

He almost fell into the seat, reaching for his vodka.

'Cheers,' he said, his false smile returning with effort.

The other two men echoed his toast and there was a moment's silence as they drank.

'What do you think of the place?' asked Watson, finally.

Canning scanned the bar and the dining room beyond. The walls were festooned with a mixture of rusty farming implements and old weapons. In the next, larger, bar, there

112

was a huge open fireplace stacked high with logs over which hung a full size man-trap.

'Big mice around here, huh?' said the American, smiling.

Riggs laughed loudly, spilling some of his drink.

'They used to use them for catching poachers,' Watson told his customer.

The man-trap was about the only authentic piece of apparatus in the entire hotel. It was what some people might call a 'plastic restaurant'. The wooden beams which criss-crossed the ceiling were imitation and even the massive log fire was lit by a gas flame hidden beneath the wood. The weapons and prints were antique shop acquisitions designed to give the place a feeling of age and character which was palpably second hand. Two suits of rusty armour stood guard at either side of the fireplace, as if guarding the secret of its falseness.

The dining room itself was festooned with flags bearing the emblems of dukes and lords who had probably never existed and a stag's head hung from the central wall. Canning saw it and touched Watson on the arm.

'I was just thinking,' said the American, a wry smile on his lips. 'That goddam deer must have been doing about ninety when it hit the other side of that wall.'

Watson laughed his polite laugh and Riggs once more went into a fit of giggles, spilling more of his drink.

'Is your boss expecting us to sign a contract today?' asked Canning, sipping at his drink.

Watson shrugged. 'Well, he's not banking on it, but it'd be a nice surprise for him.'

The American smiled.

'And a nice bonus for you.'

Watson nodded, the movement sending fresh jabs of pain through his head. He gritted his teeth and smiled, downing what was left in his glass.

'You are prepared to guarantee us full maintenance, free of charge for the next five years if we accept the deal?' said Riggs, studying the salesman over the rim of his glass.

'Yes,' said Watson.

113

Riggs nodded. 'So, the only thing that still is to be worked out is the price.'

'The price was agreed, Mr Riggs,' said Watson. 'There's no machine comparable to the Mark-1. You'll find nothing better for your particular needs, not at the prices we're offering anyway.' He paused, seeing that he had both men's eyes on him. 'In the long run it will be an investment. You *could* buy cheaper elsewhere, I wouldn't attempt to delude you about that. But nowhere will you find a machine with the capabilities which ours can offer.'

'How long have you been doing this job?' asked Canning, a slight grin on his face.

'Seven years,' Watson told him, slightly puzzled.

The two customers exchanged an enigmatic smile which unsettled the rep slightly.

'You're very good at it,' Riggs told him.

Watson thanked the man, wishing that he'd just put his bloody name on the contract instead of lavishing compliments on him. Riggs asked a few more questions about the computers which Watson answered with his usual thoroughness. The grey haired man nodded but didn't speak. There was an awkward silence between the trio which was finally broken when a nasal sound came over the small speaker in the bar. The garbled tones chattered on for a moment and Watson finally made out the sound.

'Mr Watson,' said the voice. 'Your table for three is now ready. Mr Watson.'

The three men got to their feet, a wave of pain so powerful it staggered him, causing the rep to support himself against the wall for a second. His head felt as if it were going to split in half and he had a mental picture of his brain swelling, trying to burst free of the confines of his skull. He stood still for a moment, his fixed smile finally fading.

Canning saw him swaying slightly and put out a hand, as if fearing that the younger man were going to fall.

'You OK?' asked the American.

Watson sucked in a laboured breath. 'Yes, just a bit of a headache.' He found the smile once more and looked at the

114

two men. 'You carry on into the dining room. I'm just going to the toilet.'

Canning hesitated but the salesman raised a hand to signal that he was all right. He watched the men walk into the dining room then he made his way to the lavatories.

The cold white light which flooded from the banks of fluorescents made him wince and his feet echoed on the white tiled floor. He found that he was alone and crossed to the nearest sink, fumbling in his jacket pocket for the jar of Paracetamol. He unscrewed the cap and scooped a handful of running water to swallow the pills with. They remained on his tongue for brief seconds, the bitter taste making him feel sick but then he swallowed them, clutching the side of the wash basin. He groaned aloud as the pain in his head pounded away. It seemed as if the red hot hammers had been replaced by hundreds of blazing chisels and someone was driving them relentlessly into his tortured brain. He bent and splashed his face with cold water, straightening up slowly to gaze at his pain racked features in the mirror.

A single drop of blood trickled from his left nostril. It ran slowly down and over his lip, falling to the sink beneath where it made a tiny crimson explosion on the white enamel.

Watson shuddered and wiped it away with the back of his hand. He washed his hands hurriedly and dried them on the nearby towel-roll then he returned to the mirror.

There was no more blood and he dabbed at the nostril with his handerchief, relieved to find that it showed no hint of red when he inspected it. He swallowed hard, steadied himself against the basin edge then walked out.

He saw Canning and Riggs seated at a table in the centre of the dining room, talking animatedly, only slowing their machinations when they saw him approaching. He smiled and sat down, draping the napkin across his knees.

'Feel any better?' the American asked.

'Yes, thank you,' Watson lied, reaching for the menu which lay before him. The waitress was approaching, order pad at the ready and Watson had only seconds to skim the menu before ordering. The waitress took the order, (steak for Watson and Canning, Spaghetti Bolognese for Riggs) and was about to walk away when the rep added a postscript.

'And a bottle of the Beaujolais please.'

The waitress nodded and disappeared.

'Well Mr Watson,' said Canning, stroking his chin thoughtfully. 'While you were elsewhere, my partner and myself made a decision.'

Watson swallowed hard, trying to forget the blinding headache for a moment.

'We'll accept the terms of your contract,' the American told him, flashing him a mouthful of capped teeth. He extended a hand which Watson shook thankfully. Riggs too repeated the gesture.

'I thought we might finalise things and sign over a drink after lunch,' said Riggs, smiling.

'Thank you,' said Watson, one hand almost unconsciously touching his nostril. He looked at the hand, relieved when he saw that it bore no crimson mark. His head was still thumping and the noise created by the many other diners made him dizzy but, the realization that he'd secured the contract was at least one worry less.

The waitress returned with the wine, uncorked it and poured some into Watson's glass. He sipped and nodded. She put it down and left them. The rep filled the other men's glasses and they raised them in salute.

'I suppose this ought to have been done with champagne really,' he said, smiling.

'What the hell,' Canning said, grinning. 'A drink's a drink. Here's to our agreement.'

They drank. The waitress returned a moment later with the food which she put down before the three men. They began eating, their conversation now veering away from business. Canning started talking about his family but the words didn't seem to register with Watson who had put down his knife and fork and was sitting motionless in his seat, his fists clenched so tightly the knuckles were white. He found it difficult to breathe and, when he tried to swallow it was almost impossible.

Canning looked up and saw him.

'Hey,' he said, a sense of urgency in his voice. 'What in the hell is wrong, David?'

Watson reached for his wine and raised it to his lips.

'I told you,' he said, his voice a dry rasp. 'It's this bloody headache.'

He managed to get a couple of mouthfuls of wine down, almost slamming the glass back onto the table. He reached for his knife and fork again and cut his steak, the pain, unbelievably, intensifying.

Riggs, peering up from his plate of spaghetti bolognese, was the first to see it.

A thin, almost watery, trickle of blood ran from Watson's nostril and dripped onto the table cloth. It left little stain but then, suddenly, it began to thicken and grow darker and within seconds, viscous clots were gushing from the nostril. They splattered onto the tablecloth and even onto Watson's plate with a force and sound which made Riggs feel sick. The rep put a hand to his face and groaned, the blood spilling through his fingers and running down the back of his hand. He remained upright in his seat, clutching at the nostril which was pouring forth blood like a tap with no washer.

'Jesus H Christ!' murmured Canning, pushing himself back and away from the table.

And now other diners had seen or heard the commotion and all eyes turned towards the horrendous scene.

Watson rocked back and forth in his seat, hands clapped to his head as the pain reached intensities beyond endurance. Blood continued to gush from his nostril and then, to the horror of all those watching, something white appeared amidst the welter of crimson. Something long and tapering which seemed to grow from the very nostril itself.

'Oh my God,' gasped Riggs.

The worm wriggled free of the nostril, its white body covered with blood. Then, as it tore its obscene form from the bursting orifice, Watson shrieked and pitched forward. He crashed into the table, plates, glasses and food cascading down after him as he grabbed at the tablecloth, which fell across him like a blood-spattered sheet. He rolled onto his back, the worm slipping down his cheek. It lay in the pool of crimson beside him.

A waitress nearby screamed and dropped an armful of plates, people began to bump into each other in their efforts to get away from the abominations before them. Only Canning remained nearby, transfixed by the sight. Watson's body was twitching madly, the muscles going into spasm so quickly he looked as if someone were tugging him about with invisible wires. Then, as the American watched, the flesh of Watson's eyelid seemed to split, as if someone had pulled it too hard. There was a small jet of clear liquid, some of which spurted onto Canning's leg and then, the eye began to bleed. The white turned crimson, the blood vessels appearing to swell and then burst.

A second white shape came writhing up from the rent in the eyeball.

The second worm was bigger and, when it finally succeeded in tearing its vile form free, Watson's eye collapsed in on itself. Blood pumped thickly from the ruined socket.

The worm slid across his face, touching the fluttering lips briefly and, with a newly awakened disgust, Canning thought that the monstrous thing was going inside his mouth but it lay there for a second then seemed to stiffen and it rolled off into the puddle of blood along with the first creature.

Watson raised one blood spattered hand as if soliciting help and his remaining eye fixed Canning in a baleful stare, then, the hand fell away and the American could see that the younger man was dead. His face a bloodied ruin, he lay amidst the spilled food and the gouts of his own blood.

Riggs had passed out.

A waiter appeared at the American's side and looked down at the body. He swiftly turned his head, fighting back the hot bile which was clawing its way up from his stomach.

'Fucking hell,' he groaned.

'Get an ambulance,' said Canning, kneeling to help Riggs up.

The dining room was filled with noise. Somewhere a woman was crying, somebody was shouting something about it being an accident. The waiter was phoning for an ambulance.

That done, he hurriedly dialled the Council Offices and asked for the local Health Inspector.

Canning took one last look at the body of David Watson, his own stomach doing somersaults but it wasn't the appearance of the body which drew his attention. It was the two white shapes which lay beside it and, finally, he lost control and retched until there was nothing left in his stomach.

Seventeen

Brady pulled up outside the City Hotel and was surprised to see up to a dozen people standing on the steps which led up to the main doorway. He locked the Vauxhall and strode across, pushing through the group into the lobby. There was no sign of any ambulance or the police and the Health Inspector wondered just what the hell was going on. He'd received the call about ten minutes ago and come straight out. Some garbled message about an accident at the Hotel, could be hygiene problems and then the caller had hung up.

The Health Inspector made his way through the group of people on the steps and walked through the lobby, his feet sinking into the deep pile of the crimson carpet. He frowned. There were more people huddled about outside the entrance to the dining room. A woman was sitting in a chair nearby and, as far as Brady could ascertain, someone was waving smelling salts under her nose.

He pushed open the door of the dining room and found several red shirted waiters standing around, all looking into the area where the tables were. There were two or three men in suits there as well and it was one of these who approached the Health Inspector. He held up his hands, as if to bar Brady's way.

'Sorry, sir,' he said. 'No one is allowed into the dining room. If you'd just like to wait . . .'

Brady cut him short. 'I'm the Health Inspector,' he said, producing a small plastic ID card which bore a very old and poorly taken photo of him.

The man looked at the card then at Brady, as if the likeness didn't fit but he handed it back, regarding the official suspiciously.

'What are you doing here?' the man wanted to know.

Brady snatched the card back, irritably.

'It's why I'm here, you should be worrying about,' he rasped. 'Now, what happened?'

'There was an accident in the dining room,' said the man. 'We're not really sure what it was.'

Brady regarded the man indifferently. 'Are you the manager?'

He shook his head. 'He's away for the .day. I'm the assistant manager, anything you . . .'

The Health Inspector cut him short again. 'Can I see your . . .' he paused, '. . . accident?'

The man in the suit snapped his fingers towards a young waiter who Brady guessed must be in his early twenties. The lad looked round.

'Show this gentleman to the . . . er . . . the body,' he said.

'Why can't you show me?' asked Brady.

The man blenched and swallowed hard. 'Robinson will show you.'

The Health Inspector smiled to himself and followed the young waiter. As he walked past tables he noticed that most of them bore plates of food; some still steaming. The aroma reminded him that he hadn't had lunch.

'There,' said Robinson, pointing to a blood-stained cloth. Beneath it lay the body of David Watson.

Brady knelt and lifted one corner of the tablecloth.

'My God,' he whispered, pulling the cloth back further to reveal the upper torso as well as the face. He looked at the corpse, the blood now thickly congealed on it, the ruptured eye socket looking as if someone had filled it with rancid crimson syrup. Watson's other eye was open. It reminded Brady of Ron Bell's head with *its* single staring eye.

'Who called the ambulance?' Brady said, swallowing hard.

'I did,' the waiter told him.

Brady looked up at the youth. 'Was it you who called my office?'

Robinson nodded.

It was then that Brady noticed the worms.

He took an involuntary step back and nearly overbalanced, the tablecloth falling from his grasp and uncovering the body. For long seconds he remained crouching, looking at the motionless forms of the worms both lying in the congealed gore, then he moved closer. He estimated that the worms must be around seven or eight inches long, but, unlike ring-worm they were not segmented. Just long white threads about as thick as two spaghetti strands.

'Was that why you called my office?' asked the Health Inspector, glancing over his shoulder. The group of waiters and the three men in suits were out of earshot but, nevertheless, the older man kept his voice low.

Robinson nodded. 'I thought those . . . worms might have come from the food.' He paled. 'I mean, the fucking things came out of his eye.'

Brady reached for a knife which lay on the floor nearby. With it, he carefully lifted one of the worms into the air, making sure he kept it at arm's length. The limp body hung there without moving.

'It seems dead enough,' he said, quietly.

'What is it?' Robinson asked, revolted by the sight of the foul thing. A jellied blob of coagulated gore dripped from one end of it and narrowly missed splashing Brady's trousers.

'Give me a glass or something,' he said. 'Anything I can put them in.'

The young waiter turned and saw an empty pint glass, he snatched it up and handed it to the Health Inspector who hurriedly dropped the first worm into the bottom. Then, he scooped the second creature up out of the puddle of congealed blood and deposited that in the glass as well. The task completed, he dropped the knife, draped a serviette over the top of the glass and hurriedly fastened it to the lip with an elastic band from his pocket.

He held the glass up, studying the blood-flecked white forms inside.

It was as he was straightening up that he caught sight of two ambulance men pushing through the dining room doors. One was carrying a furled stretcher, the second a red blanket. The latter of the two recognised Brady and nodded affably, then he looked down at the body of Watson.

'What happened to him?' said the ambulance man, holding the blanket while his companion unrolled the canvas stretcher beside the corpse.

Brady shook his head slowly, holding the glass and its vile contents down by his side. He watched as the two men lifted Watson onto the stretcher. The red blanket was draped over him and they lifted the body. The Health Inspector walked behind them, keeping the glass by his side but the people outside were more interested in the shape on the stretcher and he pushed through the crowd unnoticed. A couple of police cars, their blue lights turning silently, had just pulled up across the street and Brady saw three or four uniformed men crossing towards the ambulance. He, himself, reached his car and propped the glass up on the passenger seat. He sat still for long moments, his eyes fixed on the monstrous creatures inside and he was thankful that they were dead. Now he had to find out just what they were.

He twisted the key in the ignition and the Vauxhall engine burst into life. He drove off, for some reason, feeling the need to look at the worms every so often. The glass rocked on the seat and, once, toppled over. Brady hastily stood it up again.

He drove quickly and, this time, he knew that the perspiration which stained his forehead wasn't caused by the heat.

He brought the Vauxhall to a halt in the museum car park next to Foley's battered Volkswagen. There were a couple of other cars parked there as well and a bus with 'MERTON JUNIOR SCHOOL' emblazoned on the side.

The Health Inspector snatched up the glass, locked his door and sprinted up the short flight of steps to the main door. He entered the lower gallery and was immediately

124

surrounded by a group of kids about ten or eleven years old. They swarmed round the gallery, note-pads in hand, scrawling down the names of the exhibits while a bespectacled woman in her forties called out to them to make sure they wrote down every name. The kids babbled excitedly, one or two banging into the Health Inspector who finally fought his way through the throng and reached the stairs. He hurried up them to the enquiries desk and rang the bell, looking around impatiently when no one came. Once more he rang the ball and still no one appeared so he turned and took the three or four steps which led to the laboratory. He knocked and a familiar voice told him to wait.

A moment later, the door opened and Foley stood there. The young curator smiled broadly and ushered Brady inside.

'How's it going?' he said, wiping his wet hands on his jeans.

Brady held up the glass. 'You tell me.'

The younger man took it from him and set it down on the work top, carefully removing the makeshift cover. He reached for a specimen tray and tipped the worms into it, prodding them with the tip of a scalpel.

'Where did you get these?' he asked, his voice heavy with foreboding.

Brady caught the note of concern in the curator's voice and stepped closer.

'A man just died in the City Hotel,' he said. 'One of the waiters called me, he thought these worms might have come from the food.' Brady paused, sucking in a laboured breath. 'He said he saw one of them come out of the bloke's eye. Now what the hell do you make of that?'

Foley didn't speak, he just leant closer to the dead worms, noticing, as Brady had, that they were unsegmented.

'Well,' the Health Inspector persisted. 'That's impossible isn't it?' The question hung heavily in the air. 'I've seen ring worm, other parasites, dozens of times but never anything like this. Foley, for Christ's sake. It's not possible is it?'

The naturalist turned round to face Brady.

125

'Those slugs you brought in the other day,' he said. 'I ran some tests on them.'

Brady interrupted, irritably. 'All right, we'll talk about the slugs in a minute. I need to know about these bloody things.' He pointed at the worms.

'That's the whole point,' said Foley, raising his voice slightly. 'The slugs and these worms are linked.'

'How for God's sake?' asked the Health Inspector, sitting down on a stool nearby.

'After you left that day, I dissected one. I found out everything I could about it. I read as many books as I could find about the bloody things.'

'And?'

Foley exhaled deeply. 'Well, for one thing, they're not a new species. As far as I can tell they must be a kind of hybrid.'

'What makes you so sure?' Brady wanted to know.

'Because they're ordinary garden slugs,' said Foley, flatly.

Brady almost laughed. 'Foley, the damn things are eight inches long. That one you measured was five and a half inches and that was a small one. Now, anybody will tell you that a common black slug is about three-quarters of an inch long and what's more, they don't usually bite.'

'That's what I meant about them being hybrids,' the curator explained. 'They must have inter-bred with another species. There are three species of carnivorous slug in this country. Testacella maugei. Testacella haliotidea and Testacella scutulum. Now those three hunt and kill earthworms and other insects, sometimes other slugs.'

Brady interrupted him. 'Then they wouldn't mate with garden slugs, they'd eat them.' He paused. 'Besides, you said that these large slugs were the ordinary garden variety.'

'They certainly share all the same physical characteristics apart from the fact that they seem to eat meat,' said the curator.

The Health Inspector exhaled deeply.

'I just haven't got a clue why or how ordinary garden slugs could grow to sizes like we've seen, or why they should have become carnivorous,' said Foley, wearily. 'My theory about inter-breeding is all we've got.'

'But slugs are hermaphrodite aren't they?'

Foley nodded. 'But they rely mainly on ordinary mating to reproduce. That just compounds our problems. They can cross-fertilize and fertilize their own eggs.'

There was a long pause the silence finally broken by Foley.

'It might interest you to know that each female can lay up to one and a half million eggs a year.' He reached for his coffee and took a sip, wincing when he found that it was stone cold.

Brady didn't speak.

Foley tried to qualify his statement. 'There's a tremendously high mortality rate. These slugs seem to be cannibals too, the younger ones are eaten by the larger animals in the clutch. Out of a hundred eggs laid, only three or four slugs will actually reach full maturity. Even so, when each female can lay one and a half million eggs a year, that's still a hell of a lot of slugs. The only thing is, they *must* have damp conditions to lay them.'

The Health Inspector nodded. 'Like the sewers,' he whispered to himself.

'I also found out that the irritant in the slime trails of these particular slugs is lethal,' said the curator.

'How?'

'I gave some to a laboratory rat. The damn thing was dead in three hours. Now, working on that example I'd say that the slime would be fatal if consumed by, say a child for instance. What it would do to an adult I couldn't say.'

'How would it affect a child?' Brady wanted to know.

'Well, judging by the symptoms which the rat manifested,' he paused, momentarily. 'I'd say the victim would appear almost rabid. They'd probably undergo convulsions, mental disturbance. The rat turned savage, it killed the female that was in the cage with it.'

Brady wiped a hand across his forehead. 'I can't believe this,' he said, incredulously.

Foley nodded. 'I wish it wasn't true.'

'How do they move around?'

'Crawl. Burrow. Swim. Lots of ways.'

'So they could be using the sewers to move around in?' said Brady, although it sounded more like a statement than a question.

'Without a doubt,' said the curator. 'Anywhere there's plenty of moisture, and it would suit their egg laying habits.'

'But if they need moisture, how come there's so many of them about now? It's hotter out there than it has been for years.'

'These particular slugs have a very large mucus gland. They secrete huge amounts of slime so there's no danger of them "drying up" even in the hottest weather. That's what makes them so much more dangerous, they're not reliant on a damp environment. Although we're more likely to find them in one, they don't *need* it like ordinary slugs do.'

'My God,' groaned Brady.

'I don't know how long these slugs have been breeding,' said Foley, anxiously. 'But either way, there must be thousands of them by now. Maybe even tens of thousands.'

'You've certainly done your homework,' said Brady, trying to smile.

'It's best to know as much as possible about your enemy.'

'You make it sound like a war.'

Foley grinned cryptically. 'Perhaps it is and the way I figure it, they outnumber us about five hundred to one.'

Brady ran a shaking hand through his hair. 'I'll tell you something else. They're immune to ordinary repellents. I put some down in my garden and it didn't have the slightest effect.'

The curator frowned.

Neither man spoke for long moments then Brady suddenly turned his attention to the worms.

'And those?' he said, pointing to the tray. 'You said they were linked with the slugs. How?'

'Come here,' said Foley, getting up. He led the Health Inspector to a nearby microscope. There was already a slide set up beneath the powerful lens and Brady squinted down the eye-piece, adjusting the focus until everything merged into crystal clarity. Floating around before him were dozens of minute, hair-like organisms which, on closer inspection, he saw resembled tiny versions of the two worms which lay in the tray.

'What are they?' he asked.

'Schistosomes,' said Foley. 'Blood flukes. They're a type of parasite found in the blood stream of slugs. I took that sample from one of our slugs but they're found in every species.'

Brady stepped back from the microscope.

'I still don't see the tie-up,' he said.

'The schistosomes live inside the slugs, right? Now, if a slug is accidentally eaten, even if it's only the tiniest fraction of it, those parasites somehow transmit themselves to the human blood stream. They travel to the brain and form cysts. The worms grow inside these cysts.'

Brady swallowed hard as the curator continued.

'The disease is called Schistosomiasis. Once the worms encyst in the brain it causes nausea, headaches and, more often than not, death.' He paused. 'And there are at least three documented cases in Britain every year.'

'Then that was what happened to the bloke in the restaurant.'

Foley nodded. 'He must have, somehow, eaten part of one of the slugs. Everything about these bloody things is bigger or more lethal, it stands to reason the strain of disease carried by them is going to be more virulent.'

Brady sat down heavily. 'And the more of them there are, the more people they're likely to infect.' He sighed. 'The slime trails I kept seeing, Ron Bell's body and now this. It's been slugs all along.'

Foley nodded. 'Should we tell the police?'

'What the hell can they do? Arrest the damn things? Besides, if we went to them and said that there was a plague of killer slugs in the town they'd probably lock us up.'

'I wouldn't blame them,' said Foley, sardonically.

Brady drummed on the desk top with his fingers. 'So what the hell do we do?' He glanced across at the dead worms.

'I can try and perfect a poison of some kind,' Foley offered. 'Something we can use on them but, like I said, there must be thousands by now. And,' he paused, 'if they are using the sewers to move around in, they must be everywhere.'

The words hung ominously in the air and Brady felt cold fingers of fear plucking at the back of his neck.

Eighteen

Clive Talbot fiddled with the controls of the Ferguson hi-fi, trying to find the button which activated the record player. Perplexed by the profusion of dials and buttons which faced him he turned to face Donna Moss, who sat on the sofa.

'How does this fucking thing work?' grunted Clive, still holding the record in one hand.

Donna smiled inanely at him, put down her glass of bacardi and crossed to the set. She flicked a switch and the turntable buzzed into life.

'Smart arse,' said Clive, dropping the record into position. He watched Donna make her stumbling way back to the sofa then flop down. There was a half empty bottle of bacardi at her feet which she had drunk since eight o'clock. He noted that the solid silver carriage clock on the mantelpiece said nine fifteen p.m. Clive adjusted the volume as a thunderous bass line roared out of the twin speakers and the singer's voice rose over the strident wail of guitars.

'. . . what did I see? Could I believe, that what I saw
that night was real and not just fantasy'.

Satisfied with the volume, he got to his feet and slouched across to the sofa where he flopped down beside Donna. She looked round and moved towards him, her mouth seeking his, the taste of liquor strong on her tongue as it sought the warm moistness of his own. Clive responded fiercely, simultaneously sliding one hand up the inside of her skirt until he felt it brush the cool material of her panties. Donna pulled away, giggling.

'Stop it,' she said, her face flushed.

'What would your old man say if he could see us now?' said Clive, a triumphant grin on his face.

131

Donna shrugged and downed what was left in her glass.

'He'd probably be more annoyed to think we were using his hi-fi,' she giggled.

'Yeah, I bet he fucking would.' There was a sharp vehemence in the youth's words and his hard eyes scanned the sitting room as he spoke. He could just imagine the look on old man Moss's face if he could see his daughter now, lying across the lap of a boy he hated. Clive had never got on with either of Donna's parents. Toffee-nosed bastards they were, thought themselves a cut above the rest of the neighbourhood. Just because James Moss was on the town council and Clive's dad worked on a building site, Moss looked down on his daughter's boyfriend with ill-disguised contempt. Many times he'd tried to break up their relationship but each time they'd found a way to continue seeing each other. He'd been going out with her for over a year and she had become something of a habit. Maybe he was in love, he didn't know. Even if he was he'd certainly never let Donna know and if any of his mates should find out he wouldn't dare show his face. At eighteen, Clive Talbot was at that age when overt concern for the opposite sex was something to be frowned on. As far as his little circle of friends were concerned, girls were good for only one thing.

That was certainly true of Donna. She was a year younger than Clive but her sexual precocity bordered on nymphomania and that fact further amused the young man when he thought what her father would say if he found out his 'darling' daughter had lost her virginity at the age of thirteen. To one of Clive's mates as a matter of fact.

Clive himself was an only child and lived with his parents less than half an hour's walk from where Donna lived. It used to be a ten minute ride on his Yamaha 250 but some bastard had nicked the fucking thing about a month ago. Clive still fumed inwardly as he thought about it but he'd find out who took it and, when he did, he'd make them sorry. He wouldn't go to the police. They were bloody useless and, besides, he'd been in trouble with them a couple of times himself. Only minor offences like breaking windows

132

or fighting but, even so, he had no desire to seek *their* assistance in retrieving his stolen bike.

It had been an eighteenth birthday present from his parents. All his mates had bikes but most of them had farting little Puch Maxis or puny 150s. Nothing like Clive's. One or two of them even had jobs. Clive himself hadn't worked since he left school two years earlier. He'd looked for work sure enough, he never stopped looking, but his father's often voiced opinions about a Government *for* the rich *by* the rich were rapidly beginning to dawn on him. He'd never listened much to what either of his parents said but his father was shop steward for his branch of the Building Workers Union and, during the past two years, Clive had come to realize that his old man's hatred of the Government was well-founded. Clive now looked across at the photo of James Moss which stood on the TV and felt the anger rising within him.

'When are your parents due back?' he asked.

'Late,' Donna said, vaguely.

'Well how late is late?' he said, irritably.

'About two in the morning,' she informed him, reaching once more for the bacardi bottle. But Clive got to it first and lifted it from her clutching grasp.

'I think you've had enough,' he said, putting the bottle out of reach.

She pouted for a second then reached up and pulled him towards her. 'Perhaps I can persuade you to give it back.'

She pressed her mouth to his, her tongue forcing its way past his teeth and he responded with equal enthusiasm. He felt a tingle run through him as one of her hands fell to the rapidly growing bulge in his jeans. Donna ran her hand over his groin, squeezing his erection through the worn material of his denims. Their mouths still locked together, he reached for the buttons on her blouse and skilfully undid them, his fingers brushing against the lace of her bra. With practised movements, he reached round and undid the clasp, pulling the garment free to expose her small, taut breasts.

She tugged at his belt irritably when it wouldn't come free and Clive finally had to help her, loosening his own button.

133

Donna giggled softly and plunged her hand down inside his underpants, gripping his swollen shaft. Clive squirmed and thrust it forward into her eager, pumping, hand.

He reached across and cupped one small breast in his hand, rubbing his thumb back and forth across the nipple until he felt it stiffen. Donna sighed and, taking hold of his free hand, she thrust it beneath her skirt as if guiding him. But Clive needed no prompting and soon his eager hand was flicking against the flimsy material of her panties. He stroked the silky fabric, feeling the first hint of moisture seeping through it as he pressed harder. Donna gasped and manoeuvred herself so that he could reach her pulsing desire more easily, she felt his probing digits glide through her soft pubic hair to the hardened bud of her clitoris and she felt a comforting warmth envelop her. For her own part, she lowered her head to Clive's lap, her mouth closing over his swollen penis. He sucked in a shaking breath as he felt the hot wetness gliding up and down his shaft. He continued to move his fingers, plunging deeper until he infiltrated her sleek cleft.

Donna flicked her tongue over his bulging penis and she felt the unmistakable twitchings as he neared his climax. He stiffened and grunted and it was at that point she withdrew her head and sat up.

'What the fuck are you doing?' gasped Clive, his face flushed.

Donna smiled impishly. 'Upstairs eh?' she said.

'You are a right cow at times,' he said, panting.

'But lovely with it,' she giggled. 'Do I get my drink now?'

He gave her the bottle, doing up his trousers with difficulty. Clive looked at her once more his anger and frustration quickly disappearing. He chuckled to himself.

'What's so funny?' Donna wanted to know.

'You,' he said. 'If your fucking old man knew what you were like he'd have a stroke.'

'I think mum would like to lock me up in a convent,' Donna said, giggling.

Clive shook his head and watched her as she drank. Her

blouse was still off, revealing her breasts and her long, brown hair was unkempt and ruffled. It dangled over her shoulders as she shook her head and she ran one hand through it. The perm was starting to grow out and, only at the top and sides did it still retain curls. She wore no make-up, except a little on her eyes and, when she looked at him, those twin blue orbs held him in a hypnotic stare.

Maybe he really *was* in love, after all.

Donna sipped her drink and exhaled deeply. She glanced at the clock on the mantel and it said ten p.m. She knew her parents wouldn't be back for a good four or five hours. She and Clive had plenty of time. She watched him as he got to his feet to turn the record over then, a second later, the room was shaken once more by a series of drum and guitar blasts which threatened to reach seismic proportions. She motioned to him to turn the volume down a little which he did.

Donna, unlike Clive, had stayed on at school to study for 'A' levels. She knew that her future was already mapped out for her and there seemed little she could do to alter it. After school it would be university then, hopefully, into a job in designing. She was studying Graphic Design at school and intended gaining a degree once she reached university. But, although Donna wanted the career of her own choosing she still felt a kind of unseen manipulation. The university bit was as much for her parents' sake as her own. She could just hear them at the Rotary club luncheons:

'Oh yes, our daughter is at university.'

Both were fulfilling their own failings through her and she resented it. Of course she would never do anything to hurt their feelings or to damage her own chances of success but, sometimes, she felt the mad urge to say stuff it and walk out of school right there and then. To hell with everything.

Clive was the only thing she really cared about and that was another thing which rankled with her parents. She knew how they felt about him but she would not give him up. No matter how many times her father told her she wasn't to see the young lout (his favourite description of Clive) she always found some way of being with him. In a different kind of way, she was as trapped in her lifestyle as Clive was in his. Both knew how their futures were going to turn out, he because he was unable to get a job and she because she was fulfilling the aspirations of her parents. There seemed no way out.

'. . . Not a prisoner, I'm a free man, live my life how
I want to. Don't care, where the past was, I know where
I'm going . . .'
roared the singer on the record and the words sounded all the more pertinent to Donna. She swallowed what was left in her glass and got to her feet.

'Come on,' she said, smiling, motioning towards the stairs and, in a second, Clive was behind her.

Laughing, they made their way up to Donna's bedroom.

The first half a dozen of the slugs slithered across the glass top of the large cold frame, their posterior tentacles moving silently in the night air. On the ground nearby were many more of them, a shapeless black blot on the dark earth. They slithered over James Moss's carefully tended garden all seemingly heading for one spot.

Moving as quickly as their bloated forms would allow them, the slugs slipped into the drain, crawling up the pipe itself towards the first floor of the house where they eventually emerged in the guttering which ran alongside the windows.

They filled the pipe, overflowed like thick black rain into the guttering and then, slowly, they slid across the brickwork until they were actually on the window sill of the bedroom which faced the back garden. There were many of them and they slid over the sill, dropping to the floor of the bedroom. The darkness in there was total and it was quiet, only the slight murmur of the night breeze breaking the solitude as it set the curtains gently billowing.

The slugs continued to flood into the room.

As Donna and Clive reached the landing they paused,

136

kissing fiercely again, his eager hands searching for her breasts once more but she knocked them away and wagged a reproachful finger at him.

'Wait,' she giggled.

Clive crossed the landing towards a door which was firmly closed.

'Wrong room, idiot,' said Donna, her hand pausing on the knob of her own door.

'I know,' Clive said. 'Is this your parents' bedroom?'

Donna nodded and crossed to the door, pushing it open. She flicked on the light and walked in. Clive followed her, his heavy shoes making deep indentations on the thick white carpet. The whole room seemed to be white. The walls, the ceiling, the wardrobe unit, the dressing table. Even the bedspread was white. It was liking walking into a blizzard. It smelt of lavender and Clive wrinkled his nose.

'Fucking hell,' he said, crossing to the bed where he saw some clothes laying. He laughed and picked up a pair of large knickers.

'Who wears these?' he said, grinning. 'Your mum or your bloody old man?'

Donna laughed, too, and walked across to the wardrobe unit which dominated one side of the large room. It was covered in mirrors and she studied her reflection for long seconds. Clive noticed.

'Mirrors, eh?' he said. 'Kinky bastards aren't they? It's a wonder they haven't got them on the ceiling too.' He made a loud whooping noise and leapt onto the bed, stretching out on it with his arms folded behind his head. 'This is comfortable. Shall we do it here?' he asked, grinning.

Donna giggled. 'Come on, or they'll know someone's been in here.'

She stepped closer and Clive shot out a hand in an attempt to grab her but Donna stepped back and he missed, overbalanced and fell off the bed. Both of them began laughing and Donna hurried to the door and flicked off the light leaving him in darkness.

'You bitch,' he chuckled and chased after her.

137

He grabbed her just as she reached her own bedroom door and both of them crashed against it laughing like idiots. The door flew open and Donna stepped inside. She flicked at the light switch but nothing happened.

'The bloody bulb must have gone,' she said, snapping the switch up and down.

The room was in complete darkness, only the light which flooded in from the landing lighting their way. Clive closed the door behind him and turned the key, locking it.

'Who needs lights?' he said, and tossed the key away.

Donna giggled and held him close, relaxing as he lowered her onto the bed. In the blackness, they undressed one another until their naked forms lay side by side on the bed.

The curtains billowed in the breeze and neither noticed the gobs of slime on the window sill.

They sought the pleasurable touch of the other's hands, content in the pitch black to give way to almost invisible caresses. Donna felt Clive's hands running over her breasts before sliding down to part her legs which she moved willingly. With her own hand she guided his throbbing erection towards her slipperly cleft, gasping when he drove it into her. She locked her legs around his back, increasing the depth of penetration. He began to move rhythmically inside her and she thrust her hips up to meet his every movement, raking his back with her nails. Their grunts and cries became louder as the passion within them grew in intensity.

Neither of them heard the low sucking sounds as the sea of slugs, invisible in the darkness, flowed towards the bed moving almost soundlessly over the carpet.

The eyes of numerous pop stars watched impassively from posters on the walls as the black hordes swept nearer, the warmth and scent of human flesh attracting them.

Donna rotated her hips frenziedly as she felt her orgasm approach and she was mildly disappointed when she felt Clive withdraw from her but that disappointment rapidly disappeared when she felt him sliding further down the bed until his head was resting between her thighs. She moaned with pleasure as his tongue began to flick at her clitoris.

Clive was a tall lad and, in order to position himself correctly, he was forced to allow his feet to drop off the end of the bed. He stretched his legs out behind him, attempting to get a grip on the carpet with his toes.

He almost shouted aloud when he felt his feet touch something wet and slimy.

He raised his head, feeling a jellied movement beneath his toes, then, suddenly, he felt pain lancing through his foot as two of the slugs bit into it.

'Jesus Christ,' he shouted, pulling his feet back onto the bed.

Donna looked down. 'What is it?' she asked, dreamily.

'Something's biting me,' he shrieked.

Donna sat up, her hand reaching for the bedside lamp. She switched it on and, in that same instant she let loose a scream of terror which seemed to fill the entire house. Clive was struggling to remove the monstrous black things from his foot, blood staining the sheets as the foul creatures bored into the flesh.

Donna sat transfixed, watching the black mass of slugs seething towards the bed. A number had already begun to climb up the dangling sheets and Donna screamed again when she saw two near her hand.

With a roar of pain, Clive managed to tear one of the stubborn beasts from his foot. It came away, ripping skin and muscle as it did and he groaned, trying to remove the second. However, the effort made him overbalance and he fell off the bed onto the slippery carpet of slugs. For brief, nauseating seconds he writhed in the slime then the creatures attacked, sinking their sickle shaped teeth into his twisting body. Clive screamed in pain and tried to scramble to his feet.

'Get the fucking door open,' he yelled at Donna who was crying as she watched him struggling with the black horrors, one of which was eating its way into his back.

She sat huddled on the bed, rocking back and forth like a child, her eyes wide and filled with tears.

'The door,' he bellowed, trying to claw the slugs from his back.

But Donna couldn't move and, as more of the vile beasts reached the bed, she felt one crawl onto her hand. It bit into her and she shrieked in pain, feeling the blood running freely from the wound. Another struck at her buttocks, boring deep into the flesh and now Donna struggled to her feet but, a third slug slid up the inside of her thigh and, to her horror, Donna felt it boring into her crutch. She screamed with renewed ferocity as the thick black thing forced its way into her, like some obscene bloated penis. Blood began to flood down the inside of her legs, spraying the carpet and, in a second, the slug had disappeared inside her.

Donna collapsed. Laying across the bed, she was helpless as more of the slugs slid over her body, feeding on the warm flesh and enjoying the distinctive taste of the flowing blood.

Clive saw her body, covered by the beasts and he opened his mouth in a silent scream not sure whether to yell or be sick. His own back felt as if it was on fire as a dozen black creatures ate their way into his muscles. Others were gnawing at his feet and calves but he remained upright, throwing himself against the wall in an effort to dislodge the slugs. A mixture of his own blood and the pulped slugs left a reeking imprint on the nearest poster which regarded the scene of carnage with blank eyes. Clive staggered towards the door, one of the slugs eating into his ear lobe.

He crashed into the bedside lamp and it fell to the floor, plunging the room, once again into impenetrable blackness.

Gritting his teeth, he struggled on, over the slimy sea of blood lusting slugs. The pain in his back and legs was now almost unbearable and he wanted to scream and scream as they tore into him.

He reached the door and crashed against it, one bloodied hand grabbing for the knob.

It was then, through a pain racked brain, he realized he'd locked it. He fumbled for the key, remembering that it lay somewhere in the room.

He shrieked in agonized panic and knew that he must find the key. Must get out . . .

Must . . .

The slugs ate through the flesh of his calves and slithered up towards his thighs. He felt the sickness rising inside him and he thought he was going to faint but he punched the door hard, splitting his knuckles. White hot agony lanced up his arm, keeping him conscious. Through eyes filled with tears he saw three or four of the slugs burrowing hungrily into one of Donna's breasts. Her body was still, offering no resistance as the black monstrosities devoured her.

Clive fell to his knees, crushing a number of slugs beneath him as he groped blindly for the lost key. But the black mass covered the floor and his hands only brushed over many thick bodies. One bit into his thumb and he shouted once more in pain. Others were on his thighs now, digging deep into the muscle with their razor sharp teeth. Clive began to weaken, the loss of blood finally slowing him down but still he sought the key, struggling in the darkness.

Some of the other slugs were busily devouring the remnants of their crushed companions, seemingly oblivious to the struggle before them.

Clive groaned despairingly and hauled himself upright, swaying drunkenly for a second. He knew he would never find the key and now, as the black horrors continued to feed on his living flesh, he saw his only hope.

The bedroom window beckoned.

It was a slim hope but his only one and he blundered towards it, arms outstretched. As he reached the window he looked behind him, at the remains of Donna's body. One of the slugs was in the process of eating through her tongue, its obscene form filling her mouth as it feasted.

Clive hoisted himself up onto the sill and, still with a dozen or more of the slugs clinging to him, he jumped.

For seemingly endless seconds he hung in the air as if suspended on invisible wires then, his body plummeted earthward.

He hadn't even had time to think about the cold frame.

Directly beneath Donna's window it glinted as the watery moon shone on the thick glass panels in the top of it and

Clive's last sight was of the expanse of glass rushing up to meet him.

He smashed into the cold frame, the panels shattering with an ear-splitting crash. Lumps of jagged glass flew up as if blasted by some kind of explosion, the wood snapped like matchwood and the entire frame collapsed around him.

A shard of glass fully two feet long punctured Clive's body just below the sternum, tearing its way through his chest and erupting from his back. A fountain of blood rose with it. A smaller but no less lethal sliver sliced through his throat and a torrent of crimson gushed from the wound. His body twitched spasmodically, the blood still spurting from the wound in his back, the wind rasping in his torn lung.

Lights flashed on in houses on both sides, faces appeared at windows. Someone dashed for a telephone.

The slugs finished eating and slithered back across the bedroom floor towards the window. Then, as quickly as possible, they made their way back down the drainpipe and down into the drain itself, the familiar blackness and dampness of the sewer beckoning them.

The moon caught the point of the glass shard and it sparkled for a second then faded as Clive Talbot's blood began to congeal on it.

Nineteen

Brady had got home late that evening and Kim was surprised to find that his breath smelt of whisky when he walked in. He had come in at about seven thirty, dropped his briefcase in the hall and then slumped into a chair in the sitting room. The Health Inspector kissed Kim gently on the cheek when she bent over him.

'And where have you been?' she asked, smelling the whisky on his breath. 'There I am slaving over a hot cooker while you're out boozing.' She smiled.

Brady tried to return the gesture but it dissolved away into a sneer. Kim perched on his lap and draped one arm around his neck.

'What's the matter, Mike?' she asked, realizing that there was something wrong. He rarely drank, not unless something was really worrying him.

He shook his head and pulled her closer, loosening his tie with his free hand. 'I just stopped off at the Crown on the way home. I felt as if I needed one.'

She leant closer, sniffing his breath. 'Or two,' she said.

He smiled thinly.

'The dinner's nearly spoiled,' she told him.

'I'm sorry, love,' he said. 'But I'm not very hungry anyway.'

Kim kissed the top of his head, feeling his arm squeezing her more tightly, with an urgency he didn't usually show.

'Are you going to tell me or do I have to drag it out of you?' she said.

'What do you mean?' he asked, looking into her face.

'Come on, Mike. I'm not stupid. What's bothering you?'

Brady exhaled deeply. Should he tell her? The

143

conversation he'd had with Foley that afternoon had unsettled him. No, that wasn't really the word. To hell with it. He was scared. For the first time in his life, and he didn't mind admitting it, Mike Brady was frightened. Not just for himself, but for the rest of the town. And, most of all for Kim. He pulled her closer to him now, wondering whether he should burden her with his newly acquired knowledge. The words whirled around inside his head and he tried to dismiss them as ridiculous. Indeed, the idea of common garden slugs turning on human beings was ludicrous. As was the thought of some of them reaching lengths of six, seven and even eight inches. But, he had seen it. He had seen these creatures at first hand and, he had seen what they could do and for fleeting seconds the image of Ron Bell's remains flashed into his mind. The vision of David Watson and those monstrous worms replaced it. But, more than the problem, the solution worried him. How the hell were they going to wipe out the menace? Dare he go to the police with such information?

Brady gently moved Kim from his lap, got to his feet and crossed to the drinks' cabinet. He took out a bottle of Teachers and poured himself a large measure, dropping a couple of ice cubes in as perfunctory afterthoughts. Just to give it the appearance of respectability he thought, taking a hefty swallow. He closed his eyes, feeling the amber liquid burn its way to his stomach. He turned and looked at Kim, holding the bottle before him.

'Join me?' he asked.

She was beginning to get annoyed. 'Mike, please.'

Brady exhaled deeply. 'All right. But what I say now is just between you and me.'

She shook her head, disconsolately. 'Mike, if you can't trust me after all these years . . .'

'It's not a matter of trust,' he snapped, angrily and she was startled by the vehemence of his outburst. They regarded one another silently for long moments then Brady's tone softened. 'I spoke to Foley this afternoon.' He sighed, sipping at his drink.

144

'About the slugs?' she said.

He nodded. 'They're ordinary garden slugs.'

'But garden slugs don't attack human beings,' she said.

'That's exactly what I said,' echoed Brady going on to repeat his conversation with the curator. Kim listened intently, the hairs on the back of her neck rising slightly.

'Can you be sure about it, Mike?' she asked when he'd finally finished, her voice shaky.

'All the evidence supports my ideas. Foley's investigations just confirmed them,' he said worriedly. He downed the rest of the whisky and poured himself another.

'So you think that Ron Bell was killed by slugs?' asked Kim.

'Yes,' he told her, flatly.

'Then what's to stop them killing someone else?'

His answer sent an icy ripple of fear up her spine.

'Nothing.'

Kim sat back in her chair, the colour drained from her face. She took off her glasses and wiped both eyes and, for a second, Brady thought that she was crying but, as he looked he could see that she wasn't.

'What can you do?' she wanted to know.

He shrugged. 'Foley's working on a new poison. If only, somehow, there were a way of trapping all of the bloody things together in one place perhaps we'd have a chance of destroying them.' He took a hefty swallow from his glass.

'It's hard to believe,' said Kim, softly. She looked at him, her eyes beckoning.

Brady crossed to the chair and sat on the arm, Kim clung to him, her head resting in his lap. He stroked a hand through her hair, conscious that he was shaking slightly.

'There's something else,' he said. 'A man died today at the City Hotel. He died of a disease transmitted by slugs.' The Health Inspector decided to spare her the details.

Kim sat up. 'So the trouble is worse than you first thought?'

He nodded. 'Not only are the slugs themselves attacking human beings, the slime trails they leave contain a lethal

145

fluid and, the man who died ate part of one of them.'

Kim put a hand to her throat. 'Oh God.'

'Foley agrees that they could be using the sewers to move around in. I saw slime trails when I was down there with one of the sewage men.'

'Then they could come up anywhere?'

'Yes.'

She clutched his hand.

'There's nothing we can do at the moment,' he said. 'If I go to the police they'll laugh in my face. We can't put a warning in the papers, people will panic. We'll just have to hope that Foley can perfect a poison in time.'

'In time?' Her words echoed in the room.

'He thinks there must be thousands of them already. We've got to destroy them before they can reproduce in even greater numbers.' He swallowed the rest of his drink.

'Do you think you can?'

Brady walked back towards the drink's cabinet. 'I don't know.' Somewhere, a voice in his head was telling him that they didn't have a hope in hell. The Health Inspector closed his eyes for a moment until the voice went away then he reached for the bottle once more.

Kim got to her feet and walked slowly towards the kitchen.

'You don't want any dinner?' she said, dreamily, the knowledge she had just acquired seeming to have numbed her senses.

Brady smiled and shook his head. He walked back to the chair and flopped into it, the drink held firmly in his hand.

'Kim,' he called and she paused at the kitchen door. 'It'll be all right,' he said but the words sounded empty and reassured neither of them.

She pushed open the kitchen door.

The single scream which she unleashed seemed to shake the house. Brady leapt to his feet, the glass of whisky falling to the floor. He dashed across to her and, together they stood in the doorway, eyes riveted to the sight before them.

Slithering silently over the edge of the stainless steel sink were half a dozen of the slugs. The leading one, a huge monstrosity about six and a half inches in length, had already reached the floor and was sliding across the lino towards the two terrified onlookers. The others were close behind it and, as Brady stepped into the kitchen, he saw more crawling over the edge of the sink, the slime from their bodies making them glisten.

'Get back in there,' he shouted at Kim, pushing her into the sitting room, slamming the door behind him. The Health Inspector snatched up the broom which lay propped against the wall nearby and, using it as a club, he brought it smashing down onto the leading slug. The aim was good and the broom hit its mark. The black creature's body seemed to explode, half of it flying across the kitchen, the eye stalks still waving about silently. Brady stepped past the pulped thing and drove the bristles of the broom against two of the other slugs, watching as they dropped to the floor. He stamped on them, hearing the foul squash as they were scrambled beneath his shoes. Using the broom as a weapon he literally swept the others back over the lip and into the sink itself where, to his horror, he saw dozens more of the creatures slipping and sliding over each other.

One was on the draining board.

The Health Inspector snatched up a carving knife which lay on the drying rack nearby and sliced the foul thing in half. A gout of thick, foul smelling pus-coloured liquid spurted onto his sleeve and he tore his jacket off in disgust. He pushed the severed slug back into the sink with the blade of the knife suddenly realizing how he could destroy them.

He reached for the button which activated the waste disposal unit but his hand wavered as he looked once more into the sink, the horrific realization of how they had got there finally hitting him.

As he watched, one of the slugs eased its obscene black form from the tap.

It hung there for a second then, trailing mucus behind it, the vile beast dropped into the sink. Almost immediately, a pair of eye stalks emerged from the tap, behind it, signalling the arrival of another of the animals.

Disgusted, Brady punched the waste disposal button and the vicious blades roared into action slicing and crushing anything which came their way. Brady used the end of the broom to push the last of the slugs down into the murderous revolving blades, watching with something akin to satisfaction as their bodies were torn and pulped by the machine. He turned on both taps, flushing the last of the black creatures from its hiding place. Propelled by the powerful jet of water, the slug was hurled from the outlet and straight into the grinding jaws of the waste disposal. The water also helped to wash away the evil mixture of pus-like blood and slime which coated the bottom of the sink. Brady left the taps and the disposal unit running then bolted through the living room and up the stairs, heading for the bathroom.

As he hurtled up the stairs, visions of what he might find whirled through his brain. A bath full of the foul black animals? The whole room seething with them?

He flung open the door.

Nothing.

Breathing a sigh of relief, the Health Inspector crossed to the bath and turned both taps on full blast, the water splashing up violently when it hit the enamel. He watched for long seconds then crossed to the sink, repeating the procedure there.

Once more, there was no sign of the slugs.

Gasping for breath, Brady watched the gushing conduits finally turning them off. He reached for a towel and wrapped it around the sink taps, blocking the outlets. Then he repeated the procedure with those on the bath. Satisfied that they were secure, he hurried back downstairs. Kim looked up at him as he passed, her eyes red and puffy. Brady, breathless from his exertions and also from fear, walked back into the kitchen and switched off first the taps and then the waste disposal unit. A sudden silence descended. Only the Health Inspector's low, guttural breathing interrupting the solitude. As he fastened dishcloths around both taps, he could hear Kim in the sitting room, sobbing softly.

His task completed, he stepped back, nearly treading in the pulped mess behind him. All that remained of the slug he'd killed with the broom. He stepped back until he was leaning against the kitchen wall, his breath now slowly returning to normal.

'Mike.'

He heard Kim's subdued plea and hurried into the sitting room. She was crouching on the floor beside one of the chairs. He knelt beside her, enfolding her in his arms, rocking backward and forward as if he were comforting a child. She held him tightly, her tears staining his shirt.

'Mike,' she repeated.

'It's all right,' he said, reassuringly but couldn't resist a sly glimpse over his shoulder at the kitchen taps.

If the bastards were using the water pipes to move about in too, there was no telling where the horror would end.

Or even *if* it would.

The entire water supply of Merton could be contaminated. The thought hit Brady like a sledgehammer and he swallowed hard.

Kim looked up at him, her eyes red and bloodshot. Her glasses were steamed up and Brady removed them, wiping the big salt tears away with one finger. He held her tightly.

Brady could feel her shaking but he gripped her firmly, wondering if she could feel the powerful shudders which racked *his* body.

Twenty

Charlie Barnes struck the match, his face momentarily illuminated by the yellow light. He tossed it away, hearing it hiss on the damp grass. He sucked hard on the roll-up, leaning against the tree impatiently. The hands on the church clock had crawled on to one fifteen a.m., bathed in the cold white light of the moon, they stood out starkly against the stone face of the clock. The weather vane at the top of the spire rocked gently back and forth in the cool breeze, its squeaking carrying a long distance in the stillness of the night.

Charlie watched the metal clock hands for a few more minutes and then decided that it was now or never. He walked slowly from his hiding place behind the trees, heading towards the open grave which lay about twenty yards from him. He kept to the grassy verges, conscious of the noise his boots would make on the gravel of the path. But, he reasoned to himself, who the hell would be up and about at twenty past one in the morning? And especially in a bloody graveyard. He forgot his caution and chose the path instead, his heavy tread rattling the pieces of shale. It sounded like someone walking over a hundred bags of crisps.

His spade propped over his shoulder like some kind of mock rifle, Charlie marched up to the open grave and peered in. The moonlight glinted on the polished wooden surface of the coffin and, for a second, he could see himself reflected in it. He stood beside the grave, finishing his fag. One large lump of ash fell from the end and dropped onto the coffin lid. What the hell, Charlie thought, it wasn't going to bother the poor sod inside was it? He smiled and dropped the roll-up, grinding it out beneath his boot. Then, he rubbed his hands and drove the spade into the mound of earth at the graveside.

Charlie had been grave digger in Merton's cemetery for the last six years. Ever since he got out of the Scrubs. He'd been in and out of nick all his life, ever since he was a kid and all the people in the town knew him for what he was. But there was nothing malicious about Charlie. No GBH or mugging for him. He hadn't graduated to that, probably never would. His life of crime had consisted of things like nicking bikes or stumbling on things which had fallen from the backs of lorries. At fifty-two, Charlie was treated with something bordering on affection by the older members of Merton. 'A likeable rogue' one of the old ladies used to call him and he smiled at the recollection. The last judge had called him 'an incurable villain'. Charlie grunted indignantly to himself. Silly old sod he thought, remembering how the bastard had sat there, looking at him over the top of his hornrims like some red robed God with a plaited wig. Charlie had been caught in possession of fifty cases of Johnny Walker which had disappeared from a warehouse in Milchester, about twenty miles away. It hadn't been a case of a quick trip to the magistrate's court and a hundred quid fine (his sentence for having stolen three lawn mowers from the local garden shop). No, this time, he was hauled up to a Crown Court. The case had only taken two days and the end result had been that he'd got eighteen months in the Scrubs. A bit harsh Charlie had thought at the time but, at least, while he was in there he had had time to catch up with a couple of old friends. He smiled to himself.

When he'd come out of jail he'd returned to Merton and, much to his surprise, the local vicar had offered him the job as grave digger. Naturally he had jumped at the chance, although wondering why the old boy was so forthcoming with his offer. Charlie guessed that the vicar saw it as some kind of spiritual exercise – forgive sinners and all that. Charlie smiled to himself. Maybe it had worked because, since becoming town grave digger, he hadn't been in trouble with the law.

But, then again, dead bodies didn't make very good witnesses.

The idea had first come to Charlie after he'd seen a body laid out in the Chapel of Rest, just prior to a funeral some four years ago. The body had been of a man in his seventies and, before any mourners arrived, Charlie had wandered into the Chapel and looked into the open coffin. The body was to be buried with all its jewellery, including a gold and diamond ring which Charlie reckoned must be worth at least £500. He'd stood in awe, gazing at the glittering prize, wondering how much he could get for it if he ever managed to flog it. The point was, how could he get it? Then, that night, lying on his bed smoking, he'd had a brainwave. Along with the job of grave digger came a small wooden building which was little more than a three roomed hut. It stood just inside the main gate of the cemetery and Charlie had made it his home for the last six years. He was also entrusted with locking up the gates at night, a job which had to be done from the inside. So, from ten p.m. onwards, he was effectively sealed inside the cemetery. It became *his* domain. He was king and, as monarch he intended claiming any treasure which might lie in his mouldering kingdom.

That night, four years ago, he'd dug up the coffin, removed the lid and taken the ring from the finger of the corpse. Unfortunately, it had been a tigher fit that he'd anticipated and Charlie had winced a little when he had to sever the finger with his pocket knife. Still, what the hell, he'd collected a couple of solid gold cuff links and a diamond tie-pin too from his generous benefactor. On his next day off, Charlie had taken his little hoard up to an old friend in London. One 'Spider' Wyatt, a fence. Spider had given Charlie 900 quid for the little package, a sum which the fence knew he could recoup three times over. Unbeknownst to Charlie, the ring had been antique. But, it had been the beginning of a blossoming little business venture. Ever since that first night, Charlie had been pillaging the dead of Merton for anything he thought valuable. Just a perk of the job he thought happily as he

153

jumped down into the open grave, screwdriver in hand.

He usually had to wait until this time to do his little job and, if the body had already been buried, it sometimes took him until four a.m. to complete his task of exhuming and then re-burial. Sometimes of course he was unlucky but, on most occasions he found something worth taking and, just lately, he'd taken to inspecting the mouths of the corpses for gold teeth. The yield had been unexpectedly fruitful, although he had to confess, prizing the teeth from dead mouths was something he hadn't quite come to terms with yet. But, he put up with the smells and the clammy touch of the bodies. He collected his prizes, hiding them carefully in a locked box beneath his bed. Then, once a month, he'd take a trip up to London and see what he could get for his latest haul. Spider had asked him once where he acquired the stuff and, giggling like an idiot, Charlie had told him. The fence had paled on hearing the news but, goods were goods in his game and the source of these particular valuables made them untraceable.

Charlie grinned to himself as he inserted the screwdriver in the slit of the first screw. Things had definitely begun to look up during the last four years. Or look down as the case may be. He chuckled to himself and removed the first screw, dropping it into the pocket of his trousers. He'd removed his jacket, despite the slight chill in the air but he knew that filling the hole in would be hard work once he got around to it.

He removed the second of the six screws and wondered what prize he would find tonight. He'd seen a particularly valuable wristwatch on the corpse when it was lying in the Chapel of Rest and there was no telling what else he would find.

Smiling happily, Charlie set to work on the third screw.

Something moved behind him and the sound startled him. His hand slipped and the screwdriver scored a deep furrow across the lid of the coffin.

'Shit,' grunted Charlie and straightened up, peering over the rim of the hole to see what was happening. He strained

154

his ears for the slightest sound, the moon shining coldly down over the cemetery like an enormous flare.

He could see nothing and the only sound he heard was the low wailing of the wind as it sighed in the trees. It sounded like someone whistling tunelessly. Charlie remained upright for a second longer then bent once more and set about the third screw. That finally came free and he pulled it out of the hole and dropped it into his pocket.

The fourth one was a real bastard and seemed to have been wedged in with a power designed to thwart Charlie in his task. He put all his weight behind the screwdriver, trying to move the recalcitrant screw. Muttering to himself, Charlie strained with all his might to remove it, splitting the wood in one place where he bore down too hard. But, eventually, it began to give. He smiled, a thin film of perspiration forming across his forehead. He wiped it away with the back of his hand and set to work on the fifth screw.

That one came away much more easily and he moved towards the last one. The final obstacle between him and his goal.

Again something moved, closer to him this time, and he swallowed hard, his hand shaking for some reason. He wasn't sure whether to straighten up or not.

He remained still, the screwdriver firmly planted in the groove of the screw head.

The sound came again. It was much closer this time – less than ten feet away he guessed.

A thought swept through his mind. Had he remembered to lock the cemetery gates? Had the vicar walked in on him? Charlie strained his ears, trying to catch even the slightest sound. He slowed his breathing, the air stuck in his throat.

Very slowly he rose to his feet, the sound drawing closer. It sounded like a low snuffling, followed, a second later by a high-pitched scratching. Holding the screwdriver like a weapon, Charlie stood up.

He scanned the area around him.

Nothing moved.

Then he saw it, crouched on the marble plinth in the centre of one grave.

A mouse.

Charlie breathed an audible sigh of relief, angry with himself for being so jumpy. He watched the little mouse as it nibbled at some freshly laid flowers. Charlie was about to return to the coffin at his feet when he heard a screech which froze his blood.

Like a winged torpedo, an owl hurtled out of the night sky and, in one practised movement, snatched up the mouse in a powerful talon. Clutching its prize, it flew off towards one of the nearby trees to eat. Charlie watched it, the moon reflecting in its baleful eyes. It seemed to be watching him, looking up every so often, fixing him in that glassy stare. He turned his back on it and ducked down into the grave, removing the last screw. That done, he dug his fingers under the lid and lifted it free, pushing it up onto the side of the hole.

He looked down.

Had he been able to, Charlie would have probably screamed, as it was, he could only stand transfixed gazing down into the coffin, his mind reeling. He gagged and fell back against the grave wall.

The corpse was completely hidden beneath a slimy, seething black mass of slugs.

The stench which emanated from this vast horde was almost palpable in its intensity and Charlie tried to turn away but, with the same sort of deadly fascination with which a mongoose watches a cobra, he kept his gaze locked on the hideous sight before him. His hesitation proved to be his undoing.

A number of the slugs had already slithered over the edge of the coffin and two or three were sliding up Charlie's boots, up inside his trouser legs, heading for the warm flesh of his calves. He felt the sticky slime on his legs and, a second later, he screamed as the slugs bit into him. Blood began to course down his legs as the beasts burrowed deep into his muscles and Charlie groped at the side of the grave, trying to pull himself up but, as he turned, he stepped on one of the monstrous slugs. Its body was crushed under his boot and Charlie slipped in the pulped mess.

With horror, he realized he was falling.

He pitched forward, falling right into the middle of the slithering mass, into the coffin itself. He lay on top of the devoured corpse and, for nauseating seconds found himself staring into the skeletal face which seemed to grin up at him from its silk-lined box.

Charlie screamed again and tried to rise, dozens of the slugs clinging to his body, boring into his flesh. Eating him alive. He pulled a couple from him, horrified when they turned in his grip and drove their razor sharp central teeth into his fingers. He shook his hands in an effort to dislodge the creatures but they remained firmly anchored. Charlie felt something ripping at the muscles of his back, eating through to his kidneys. His back was covered in the vile things, the weight of their thick bodies holding him down. With a monumental effort, he rose, tears of pain and terror mingling with the blood on his cheeks as one of the slugs ate its way into his face. He grabbed a tuft of grass at the grave side and tried to haul himself up but his arms were weak. Blood gushed from his many wounds and he could feel nothing from the knees downward.

The slugs had already eaten his legs to the bone.

He managed to haul himself up, his upper torso actually leaving the hole but then the sheer weight of the creatures defeated him and, as a particularly large one began to burrow into the hollow at the base of his skull, he slipped back. He crashed heavily into the grave, falling once more onto the devoured corpse, his body twitching now as the slugs swarmed over him, one of them eating through the fluid filled cavity of his eye. Blood burst from the socket and Charlie found himself in darkness.

The last thing he saw was the gold wristwatch, dangling on the end of a half-eaten arm, just before his face. Then, with a final wail of despair he succumbed. The slugs slithered over him, seemingly galvanised by the flow of

157

warm blood which pumped from his body.

The owl looked up from its meal as it heard Charlie scream. It sat on the branch of the tree, watching as the man died. Its huge eyes blinked, then it hooted twice, the sound flowing out on the wind like some kind of death knell.

Twenty-one

Mike Brady sat gazing at the phone, a pencil stuck in his mouth like a cigarette. He finally pulled the pencil out and began drawing circles on his blotter. The air conditioner in the office had packed up and the heat was oppressive even so early in the morning. His wall clock showed ten fifteen a.m. He exhaled deeply and reached for the phone, using the end of the pencil to dial. As he did so he thought back to what had happened the previous night. The idea of slugs in the water pipes both revolted and horrified him and, once again, he wondered just how far the contamination had spread. Before he and Kim had left for work that morning he'd secured all the taps with rags. Just in case. Kim, still slightly shaken by the previous night's occurrence, had promised that she would insist all water used at the nursery would be boiled before use. He had given her some story about mould in the pipes in case any of the other staff asked why.

The line was engaged and Brady tapped the pencil irritably on his desk. He let the insistent tone continue for another moment or two then pressed the cradle down and dialled again.

It was still engaged.

'Come on,' he muttered, trying his luck a third time.

At last he heard the familiar purring and he put down his pencil, waiting for the receiver to be picked up. A moment later an officious sounding woman told him that he'd reached the local doctor's surgery.

'My name's Brady,' he told her. 'I'm the Health Inspector. I'd like to speak to Dr Warwick please.'

He was told that the doctor was in surgery.

'It's important, please put me through if you can,' Brady

insisted, picking up his pencil once more. He began turning it over and over in his hand.

The receptionist told him again that the doctor was in the middle of his surgery, adding that he had a patient with him at that minute.

'Well can you put me through when that patient leaves, I'll hand on.'

Brady was told that it would have to wait until surgery was finished.

'Listen, you put me through when that next bloody patient has left or I'll be down there myself,' he rasped, finally losing his temper. 'This is important.'

The receptionist reluctantly agreed, swayed by his angry tone and Brady heard her put the receiver down on her desk top. He held his own phone, the far off noises of the surgery drifting through to him. Finally he heard a high pitched bleep and the receptionist picked up the phone and grudgingly told him that he was being connected. There was a moment's silence, a hiss of static then Brady heard another voice.

'Dr Warwick speaking.'

Brady introduced himself. He'd known the doctor for five or six years but the men were still to reach the familiarity of first name terms.

'What can I do for you, Mr Brady? I am rather busy this morning,' Warwick told him.

'I'd like to know if there's been anything unusual this morning,' said Brady.

Warwick was puzzled. 'Like what?'

'Any patients complaining of sickness, headaches anything like that?'

The doctor was mildly irritated. 'Mr Brady, I don't discuss my patients' problems over the phone. In fact, I don't discuss them at all.'

'I realize that,' said the Health Inspector. 'All I want to know is, have there been any peculiarities? Any people suffering from the same symptoms?'

I cannot divulge personal information, Mr Brady I'm sorry,' said Warwick, condescendingly.

'I'm not asking for names and addresses for Christ's sake,' snapped the Health Inspector. 'I just want to know if you've had any patients exhibiting the same sort of symptoms, similar symptoms to each other.'

Warwick sighed. 'Mr Brady I . . .'

'Doctor, this is important. I have reason to believe that the entire water system of Merton could be contaminated. Now, all I'm asking for is a little help. If you don't want to help me, fine, but I'm warning you your bloody surgery is going to be knee-deep in people if you don't.'

There was a long silence at the other end of the line and, for a moment, Brady thought that the doctor had put the phone down but then he spoke again, his tone much more subdued this time.

'What makes you think the water supply is contaminated?' he asked.

'That's information *I* can't divulge,' said Brady.

Warwick chuckled mirthlessly. 'Touché.'

'So, doctor. About your patients, have there been any similarities in their symptoms?'

The doctor exhaled deeply. 'Well, now you come to mention it, there have. I've seen twelve patients since eight thirty and nine of those have been complaining of more or less the same problems.'

Brady reached for his pencil once more, pulling a pad towards him. 'Such as?'

'Nausea, headaches, sensitivity to light, diarrhoea. Fever in one or two cases and some vomiting. Is that enough for you?'

Brady finished writing.

'What do *you* think it is?' he asked.

'It's difficult to say without the benefit of more extended diagnoses such as blood and urine tests but at first sight I'd say it was probably a virus of some kind,' Warwick told him.

'Did you prescribe anything for it?' asked Brady.'

'Only a Kaolin solution to stop the diarrhoea and vomiting. As I said, without further tests it's difficult to say what's really causing the trouble.'

161

'If it was a virus,' said the Health Inspector, 'wouldn't you prescribe antibiotics?'

'That depends on the severity of the symptoms. But, as I've already said, I'm not absolutely sure it is a virus. However, I will admit that if it is, your theory about it being carried by water is probably correct.'

Brady felt icy fingers tugging once more at the back of his neck. 'Why do you say that?'

'Because all water transmitted viral diseases exhibit symptoms like those I've just described to you. But to be honest, Mr Brady, the likelihood of it being a virus is small. Most diseases of that kind are transmitted by animals. Yellow fever by mosquitoes, Bilharzia by snails. Those types of disease are confined to areas where sanitation is bad, you wouldn't find anything like that . . .'

Brady cut him short. 'You said something about snails.'

'Yes. There is a species of snail which spreads a disease called Bilharzia,' Warwick explained, his voice breaking up into a soft chuckle. 'But it's not that, Mr Brady. The snail which carried the disease is confined to Africa and Asia.'

The Health Inspector wrote it on his pad all the same.

'If there's nothing else, Mr Brady' said the doctor 'I do have other patients waiting.'

'Yes. I'm sorry,' said the Health Inspector. 'Thank you very much for your help.' He put the phone down and sat silently at his desk, reading the notes he'd scrawled:

1. Virus?
2. Water carried, contamination?
3. Nine cases so far.
4. Slugs in water pipes?

He underlined the last several times then got to his feet and headed out of his office towards the stairs which would take him up to the second floor and the offices of the Water Board.

Frank Phillips was trying to light a fag. He had dropped his lighter the day before and now the bloody thing wasn't working. Grunting to himself he put it back into his jacket

162

and started hunting through his pockets for some matches. He found none and plucked the cigarette from his mouth angrily. It lay on the desk before him, defiantly. Phillips was in his late fifties and had been Merton's Water Board Inspector for the last nineteen years. He was a hard, uncompromising man, disliked by nearly everyone in the building but he was good at his job and when he snapped his fingers everyone in the department jumped. He ran a hand through his grey hair and picked up the first of a pile of complaints, glancing over it. He looked at the cigarette lying beside him then continued reading the sheet of yellow paper before him, simultaneously cursing the heat. His shirt was sticking to his back, dark rings of perspiration fanning out from beneath his arm pits. He got up and crossed to the water dispenser which stood in one corner of his office. Phillips took a plastic beaker from the pile beside it and filled it, drinking the clear liquid down in two enormous gulps. He filled the cup again and returned to his desk, reaching for the second sheet of paper in the tray to his left.

There was a knock on the door and Brady walked in.

'You're supposed to wait until you're bloody asked,' snapped Phillips. 'Not just walk in.'

Brady closed the door behind him. 'Yeah, never mind that, Frank, I've got to talk to you.'

'I'm busy, Mike,' he said, indicating the pile of papers.

'It's important,' Brady insisted and Phillips sat back in his chair.

'All right, but make it snappy will you?' he said, then he suddenly remembered the cigarette. 'You haven't got a light have you?' he said, hopefully.

'I don't smoke,' Brady told him.

'I should have guessed,' grunted Phillips.

'Look, Frank, just shut up and listen will you,' Brady said, his voice taking on a hard edge. Satisfied that he had the other man's attention he continued. 'I don't quite know how to say this so I won't beat about the bush.' He inhaled. 'How long would it take to cut off Merton's water supply?'

163

Phillips raised one eyebrow. 'How long would it what?' he said, incredulously.

Brady repeated himself.

'You are joking of course?' said Phillips, sipping at the cup of water on his desk. 'What the bloody hell should I want to cut off the water supply for?'

'Because there's something in the water,' Brady told him.

'Like what?'

'A virus of some kind.'

'How do you know?'

'I phoned the local doctor's surgery this morning,' Brady told him and went on to describe his conversation with Warwick.

'So,' said Phillips. 'Nine people have got the shits, what does that prove?'

'Even the doctor thinks that there could be something in the water,' said Brady.

Phillips sat forward in his chair. 'Yes, there is.' His voice took on a mocking tone. 'There's chlorine which is added as a gas, dissolves and forms a disinfectant. There's sulphur dioxide which is also added as a gas to neutralize any excess chlorine. There's fluoride to keep everybody's teeth in such terrific shape and occasionally, in rotten water, we use aluminium sulphate. Satisfied?'

Brady was white with rage. 'All right you smart arse bastard,' he rasped. 'Nine people are suffering from a virus which they've picked up through drinking water. That's nine people, Frank. From one surgery. There's three others in the town. Christ knows how many more poor sods have got this bloody infection.'

'So, let's get this straight, you want me to turn off the town's water?'

The Health Inspector nodded.

Phillips shrugged. 'Just how did you come to this expert diagnosis in the first place?' asked the Water Board Official, his voice heavy with sarcasm. 'I mean, what made you ring the bloody doctor anyway?'

'Something strange happened at my house last night,'

Brady began, aware that the words he was about to speak would sound ludicrous. 'I saw slugs dropping from my taps.'

'Slugs,' said Phillips, nodding.

'Yes.'

Phillips exhaled deeply. 'You want me to believe that there's slugs crawling around in our water pipes is that it? And these unfortunate buggers with the runs have got that way because of these things being in *their* water pipes. Right?'

'I know it sounds incredible,' said Brady.

Phillips laughed humourlessly. 'Incredible? It sounds bloody ridiculous.'

'I saw it,' snapped Brady. 'So did my wife.'

'I couldn't give a damn if the Band of the Coldstream Guards saw it,' snarled Phillips. 'Just assuming I shut off the water. Just assuming. What the hell am I supposed to say to the council when they ask me why I did it? I can just hear it now, "Mr Brady, our wonderful Health Inspector, says we've got slugs in our pipes". You know what this bloody lot think of you already. How the hell is that going to sound?'

'Do you need Council permission to switch it off?' Brady wanted to know.

'I don't *need* it,' Phillips told him. 'But I think they're going to want a better excuse than that. And what do I tell the public when they start ringing in and complaining because they can't make a cup of tea because they've got no bloody water?'

'So you won't do it?'

'No I won't. Not until I see some proof.' He picked up the plastic cup and pushed it towards Brady. 'I can't see anything floating about in there can you?'

'What about those nine people, aren't they proof enough?' snapped the Health Inspector.

'Coincidence,' said Phillips, dismissing it.

'Bullshit,' sharled Brady. 'That's not all, haven't you noticed the amount of slugs in the gardens lately? And another thing, I've seen their trails in three or four different places but on top of that, I told you, I saw them dropping from my taps. Slugs. Big bastards too.' He had lost his temper. 'A man died yesterday from a disease transmitted by slugs.' Brady's voice had risen in volume. 'How much more fucking proof do you want?'

The two men stared at each other in silence for long moments then Phillips smiled. 'Look, I tell you what, if *I* get a case of the runs then I'll know you were right. How's that?'

Brady got to his feet, almost knocking the chair over in his anger. He turned and made for the door, pausing before he reached it.

'You know, Frank,' he said. 'You shouldn't be working for the Council. You should be on it. You're stupid enough.'

He slammed the door behind him.

'Sod off,' grunted Phillips. He sat for a moment then crossed to the water dispenser again and poured himself another cup full of the clear liquid. He looked into it for a second.

'Slugs in the water pipes,' he said, shaking his head.

He drank the water.

Brady glanced at his watch and saw that the hands had crawled round to one fifty-five p.m. He finished his half of lager and got to his feet, leaving the half-eaten remains of a ploughman's lunch on the table before him. The lounge bar of The Ruskin Arms, the only pub in Merton's town centre, was almost empty but for those last half dozen who lingered over their drinks. Brady left the pub, walking from its subdued and dimly lit interior into the blazing sunshine of the afternoon.

It was less than ten minutes' walk from the pub to the council offices and the Health Inspector took it slowly. A barmaid was outside the pub collecting empty glasses and she smiled at Brady as he passed but it was an effort for him to return the gesture. He wiped the perspiration from his face and glanced up at the cloudless sky. The heat was unrelenting and Brady stopped at a small newsagent's nearby to purchase an ice-cream. He felt mildly ridiculous standing amidst dozens of kids, waiting for his chance to be

166

served and he had to smile at the thought of what he must look like. The woman serving smiled broadly at him when he asked for a lolly. He handed over his money and eagerly tore off the wrapping. The ice-cream was pleasantly cool on his tongue.

It was as he was walking out, Brady noticed the newspaper rack which hung by the door. He scanned the dailies but his eye settled on the local paper. With one hand, Brady pulled it from the rack and ran his eyes over the headline:

POLICE BAFFLED BY MYSTERY DEATHS

He swallowed hard, folded the paper under his arm and tossed ten pence onto the counter. Then he walked out. On the way out, he dropped the ice-cream into a dustbin, as if he had suddenly decided he didn't want it. Brady paused outside the shop and scanned the article which accompanied the headline.

'Merton Police were baffled today after finding three mutilated bodies. The first two were discovered in a house on the town's new estate, the third in the cemetery. All three were badly mutilated and identification is still unsubstantiated regarding the third body. The other two have not yet been named. Policemen in the area are still looking for clues to the grisly trio of deaths . . .'

Brady folded the paper again and stood for a moment beneath the blazing sun, the thoughts whirling round and round in his mind. The cemetery. The new estate. They were nearly four miles apart. The slugs must be far more numerous than even *he'd* first thought. He shivered, despite the heat, then turned and headed back towards the council offices.

Brady walked with ill-disguised haste, almost as if he were anxious to be off the streets and back in the security of his office. He felt almost unaccountably nervous, wondering just where the slugs were going to strike next.

There was something black about two feet away from him and Brady froze. It was lying motionless on the pavement, and for long seconds the Health Inspector was unable to move. Then, he realized that it was nothing more than a

167

burnt out dog-end. He breathed an audible sigh of relief and continued walking, reaching the steps that led up to the main doors of the council offices at exactly five past two. As he walked into reception he heard the familiar clacking of the defective fan but it still offered some welcome respite from the blistering sun outside.

Brady was heading for the stairs when Julie appeared from behind the desk and called him over.

'What is it?' he asked, wearily.

'There was a phone call for you, Mr Brady,' she told him. 'A man. He said it was important. He left a phone number.'

'Did he leave his name?'

She consulted a piece of paper in front of her, finally discovering it amongst numerous other jottings and scribbles.

'Foley. John Foley.'

Brady was already gone before she could finish speaking.

Twenty-two

Brady looked down into the tray where Foley had placed the slug. The animal was slithering about in a puddle of its own slime and the Health Inspector regarded it with a mixture of disgust and foreboding. Beside the tray was a small beaker filled with a thin, orange coloured fluid and it was into this that Foley now pushed a dropper. He sucked up about half an inch of the stuff into the dropper and Brady watched as he moved it over until it was poised above the slug.

'Watch,' said Foley then, gently, he squeezed the rubber bulb at the end of the dropper.

One single droplet of moisture fell from the nozzle and onto the slug.

There was a tiny flash of brilliant white light and Brady heard a loud hiss as the fluid hit the slug. The black body seemed to explode and a small shower of pus-like blood and entrails sprayed into the air. It writhed spasmodically for a second then was still.

'Good God,' gasped the Health Inspector.

Foley looked up at him and smiled.

'Is it dead?' asked Brady, peering closer to the body.

'Too right it's dead,' Foley reassured him.

'What is that stuff?' He pointed to the beaker full of fluid.

'It hasn't got a name. I invented it,' the naturalist beamed. 'Perhaps I ought to call it Foleycide.' He laughed.

'Well, whatever you call it, it certainly works. But what made it explode like that?'

'The liquid itself is arsenic based but it's got a strong lithium content. Lithium is combustible if it touches any kind of moisture. If you emptied ten or twelve gallons of it

169

into a lake you'd have an explosion big enough to flatten this town.' He grinned triumphantly.

'Where the hell did you get the chemicals?' Brady wanted to know, his eyes still riveted to the ruptured body of the slug.

'The factory on the industrial estate,' Foley told him. 'I told them it was for use in the museum, they let me have as much as I wanted for trade price.'

'How much have you got?'

'Enough,' said the curator.

'I hope to Christ you're right,' Brady said and handed the paper to Foley. He read the article about the three deaths, his brow wrinkling as he did so.

'They got into my house last night,' said the Health Inspector. 'Dozens of them.'

'The slugs? How?'

'Through the taps. They're using the water pipes as well as the sewers to move around in.'

Foley dropped the paper. 'Then how the hell do we kill them all? We can pump this stuff into the sewers without any problem, that'll take care of the ones in there but not into the water system.'

'If what you say about this stuff being combustible when it makes contact with water is true, I'm not even sure that we can use it in the sewers.'

The curator stroked his chin thoughtfully for a second.

'The flash that you saw when the poison hit the slug,' he began. 'It looked worse than it actually was. Maybe, just maybe, we can use it in the sewers and not do too much harm.'

'By too much harm I suppose you mean demolishing the whole of Merton,' said Brady, cryptically.

'There's got to be a way,' said Foley. 'But who the hell would know?'

Brady snapped his fingers. 'Palmer.'

Foley looked vague. 'Who?'

'Don Palmer. He's one of the sewage men here. I was with him when I saw the slime trails down the sewers on the

170

new estate. He'd know whether we could use the stuff down there or not.' The Health Inspector smiled as he thought about the little cockney. 'Have you got a phone in here?'

'At the enquiries desk,' the naturalist told him.

Brady turned and headed for the door, pausing when he got there. 'You said it contained arsenic too.'

Foley nodded. 'It works two ways. Initial contact causes the reaction you and I just saw, the arsenic penetrates their skin. It works instantly. There's no way they can survive this.' He brandished the beaker full of orange liquid before him.

Brady left the room and made for the enquiries desk where he found the phone and hurriedly dialled.

The phone was picked up at the other end and he recognised Julie's voice.

'Is Don Palmer there?' he asked.

She told him she'd check.

Brady drummed on the desk top as he waited. A second later, Julie picked up the receiver again.

No. Palmer was out on a job.

'Well, as soon as he gets back, tell him to come to the museum,' said the Health Inspector. He put the phone down and hurried back up to the lab.

'No luck,' he said, plonking himself down on a stool. 'We'll have to wait for him.' He looked down at the torn body of the large slug in the tray and shuddered.

'I've been thinking,' said Foley, 'what if these slugs have some kind of social order?'

Brady looked vague. 'What do you mean?'

'Well, maybe, and it's a long shot, the larger slugs are acting as . . .' he struggled for the word, '. . . guides, leaders for the smaller ones. Maybe it's some kind of,' he paused again, 'sonar.'

'Where's your evidence?' asked Brady.

'It's supposition at the moment but it's all we've got. Now, assuming that I'm right about the larger slugs being "controllers" of the smaller ones. If we can destroy the large creatures, the others might return to their normal behaviour patterns.'

171

'You mean they'd stop eating meat?' said Brady.

Foley nodded.

'But how do we destroy them?'

'The large ones are too big to move through the water pipes, right? That means they must be using the sewers to breed and move about in.'

'What's this business about a "social order" got to do with it?' asked Brady.

'Ants and other social insects have a hierarchy within the nest,' Foley explained. 'From the queen down to the soldiers and then to the workers. The queen and the soldiers "control" the smaller workers. Kill the queen, the nest dies.'

The Health Inspector shook his head. 'But slugs aren't social insects. Christ Almighty, they're not even bloody insects.'

Foley waved a hand before him. 'I know that. But the principle is the same. There's no nest and there's no queen but I'm pretty sure that the large slugs are acting as "controllers" for the small ones and I'm willing to bet that they're using the sewers as breeding grounds. The conditions down there are perfect.'

'I can't believe this,' said the Health Inspector. 'I've seen it, I've read about what they can do but I still find it hard to believe.'

'And so will everyone else,' intoned Foley. 'Have you mentioned it to anyone?'

Brady told him about the incident with Phillips and then went on to discuss the cases of illness which the doctor had told him about.

'We can't involve the police,' he said, finally.

'They are involved,' snapped Foley, holding up the paper.

'They don't know about the slugs,' said Brady. 'And they mustn't know about the poison or our attempts to destroy these things.'

Foley nodded then laughed bitterly. 'You know, for the first time in my life I thought about dying. Stupid isn't it?' He looked up and found Brady regarding him with impassive eyes. The curator continued.

'After reading what happened to those three people . . .' The sentence trailed off momentarily. 'Whatever must it be like to die like that?' He swallowed hard.

'Let's just hope none of us have to find out,' said Brady.

The curator reached into a cupboard beside him and produced a bottle of vodka. He held it up, smiling.

'Well, the water's off isn't it?'

Brady grinned, watching as the young man poured some of the clear liquor into two beakers. He handed one to the Health Inspector who drank deeply. The fiery liquid burnt a path to his stomach and he blew out his cheeks.

'How much of that poison have you got?' he asked.

'Enough to make up five gallons,' Foley told him. 'Our only other problem is how to get it into the sewer. We can't just pour it into the first outlet we find.'

'Palmer should be able to help us there.' Brady looked at his watch. 'Where the hell is he?'

'Someone is going to have to go into the sewer tunnels,' said Foley, softly.

Brady didn't answer, he just took another swallow of vodka. That particular thought had already occurred to him.

It was nearly seven thirty p.m. when Don Palmer finally arrived. He parked the white van outside the museum between Foley's Volkswagen and Brady's Vauxhall then walked up the steps to the main entrance.

In his years of living in the town, Palmer had never visited the museum and now he walked slowly through the lower gallery, admiring the handsomely mounted exhibits and making a mental note to bring the kids along some time. They'd enjoy this, he thought. The little cockney made his way up the stairs to the enquiries desk, his footsteps echoing through the silent building.

As he reached the landing Brady appeared in the doorway of the lab and beckoned Palmer up.

'What's wrong?' he asked, grinning. 'Have they got a badger stuck down the toilet?'

Brady ushered him into the lab where he was hastily

173

introduced to Foley. The men all sat down again and Palmer gratefully accepted the beaker of vodka which the young curator offered him.

'My old lady will think I've been out boozing,' he said, smiling, taking another sip of the liquor. It was as he put the beaker down that he noticed the dead slug.

'What the fuck is that?' he said in awe, his mouth dropping open. He looked first at Foley and then at the Health Inspector.

'It's a slug,' Foley told him.

'Leave it out,' Palmer said, his smile gradually dissolving. 'Slugs are little things about that size.' He held open his thumb and index finger to indicate the length he spoke of.

'Have you seen the paper?' Brady asked him, pushing it towards him.

Palmer nodded. 'Terrible business.'

'They were killed by slugs,' said the Health Inspector flatly. 'All three of them and Ron Bell, he was killed by them too.'

'I knew old Ron,' said the cockney, softly. Then his voice took on a harder edge. 'Killed by slugs? Is that some sort of bloody joke?'

They told him. Step by step, every incident, every sighting, every death. Brady told him about the slime trails, about the creatures in his garden, of how one tried to bite him. About the taps.

Foley explained how they fed, moved and bred. Palmer listened to every word, his face set in an attitude of horrified resignation as if that was the way it was and he would just have to get used to it. He paled visibly as the catalogue of horrors continued.

They told him about the poison and about how they intended destroying the slugs. Foley even gave him a demonstration on the last remaining creature. And the little man listened to it all, waiting until there was no more to be said. Silence descended once more on the small lab and, outside, the sky began to darken for it had taken them well over seventy minutes to tell him everything. Every mind-bending, horrifying, nauseating detail.

174

'Dear God,' he said, softly. He drank what was left in his beaker and gripped it until the glass threatened to break.

'Dear God.'

'We need your help, Palmer,' said Brady, putting one hand on the sewage man's shoulder.

Palmer shrugged and turned almost robotically to look at the Health Inspector.

'It could have been my kids, my wife,' he said, quietly. Visibly shaken, the sewage man put down the beaker and shook his head.

'How can I help?' he asked.

'We need a map of the sewer system,' Brady told him. 'And we need some information.'

At last, the little cockney seemed to come out of his bewildered state. He shook his head, as if trying to dispel the horror of what he'd heard. 'I've got maps in the van,' he said, getting to his feet.

Foley, too, stood up.

'I'd better make up the rest of that poison,' he said and disappeared into a small room just off from the laboratory itself.

Brady was left alone in the lab. He looked at the body of the dead slug and felt an involuntary shudder run through him. He suddenly felt as if he needed Kim. He would have to phone her soon and try to explain what was happening. She would wonder where he was. He exhaled deeply and leant on the work top.

Moments later, Palmer returned carrying a couple of rolled up pieces of paper. He took off the elastic bands and spread them out on the work top. Brady anchored them at the corners with bottles, beakers and anything else he could lay his hands on and then the two of them began to scrutinise the maps. The plans reminded Brady of the London Underground; lines criss-crossed and intercepted each other, some drawn in red, some in black. There were large red circles on many places on the maps and each was marked with a number.

'What are those?' asked the Health Inspector, pointing to one of the numbered circles.

'Manholes,' said Palmer. 'Each number designates the street it's in.'

'How the hell do you remember which is which?' Brady wanted to know but Palmer merely smiled.

'It's all part of the job.'

A moment or two later, Foley walked back into the lab. He removed a pair of rubber gloves and dumped them on the bench nearby.

'Poison's ready,' he said.

'You reckon you're going to dump that stuff into the sewers?' said Palmer.

'It's the only way,' said Foley.

'There's already a high concentration of methane down there now. That's highly combustible too,' said the sewage man. 'If you set off an explosion down there, it'll ignite the methane as well.'

'What are you saying?' asked Brady.

Palmer exhaled. 'I'm saying that the combined effect of that poison and the methane could cause a class one explosion.'

Brady swallowed hard. 'Oh Christ.'

'Is that for certain?' Foley wanted to know.

'There'll be an explosion,' Palmer told him. 'No doubt about it, all we don't know is what the effects could be.'

'What's the worst that could happen?' asked the Health Inspector.

Palmer shrugged. 'You could blow every manhole cover in town off. If the explosion was big enough you'd blast every water appliance from its housing. You might even bring the street down.'

'Maybe?' said Foley, hopefully.

Palmer nodded. 'That's the worst that could happen. But, every house has a vent outside it. Those vents would take up a lot of the blast. They might just be able to cope with the increased pressure. It all depends on how big the explosion is.'

176

'Then we'll have to take that chance,' said Brady, flatly.

'So now we have to find them,' Foley said and, for long minutes, the room was plunged into silence.

'The first body was found near the new estate,' said Brady, finally. 'And most of the incidents have happened in that vicinity.' He scanned the map. 'Where would that be on here?'

'Ron Bell's house you mean?' Palmer said and jabbed a finger at the map. 'There. It's got a vent in the back garden and it's also got a manhole just outside in the street.'

'We could get into the sewers there,' said the Health Inspector. 'How do these damn networks connect?' he said to Palmer.

The cockney ran his index finger over three or four of the sewer pipes which were shown in black on the map. 'All the pipes converge into one central chamber. The manholes are the routes into those vaults. That's what the numbered circles are. Each one of those has got a big chamber underneath it. There's one every two or three streets.'

Brady stroked his chin thoughtfully for a second.

'Could we crawl through those pipes? Like we did under that old woman's house?' he asked.

'We could, but we'd need special breathing apparatus. Those sewers are deeper than the rest. The pressure is far greater,' Palmer explained.

'What sort of apparatus is it?' Foley wanted to know.

'Just a face mask connected to an oxygen tank,' Palmer told him. 'But there's one snag. The tanks only hold enough air for thirty minutes.'

Another heavy silence descended finally broken by Brady.

'It's the only way. We have to go into the sewers.'

'What exactly do you think you can do?' Palmer demanded. 'If there's as many of those bloody things down there as you reckon, how the hell are you going to kill them all?'

'I'll crawl along the pipes,' said Brady, quietly.

Palmer shook his head. 'You'd never make it on your

own. It's like a bloody maze down there.' He swallowed hard. 'I'll have to go down with you.'

The two men looked at each other for long moments then Brady continued.

'There's only one way of doing it,' he said. 'We'll have to crawl through the pipes and lure the slugs towards one of these central chambers. Once we've done that, you,' he looked at Foley, 'release the poison into the sewer.'

'You're acting as human bait,' said the curator, flatly.

'There's no other way,' Brady said.

'How the hell do I know where you are? Once you're down there, I won't be able to tell whereabouts in the pipes you are. If I release the poison while you're still down there, you'll be blown to pieces along with the slugs,' Foley said.

'We can keep in contact with two-way radios,' said Palmer. 'We use them all the time when we're working down there.'

Foley nodded.

'If we keep in constant contact, you can track us on the maps,' Palmer said.

'That's it then,' said Brady, flatly. 'Palmer and I will go into the sewers near Ron Bell's house. Foley, you track us on the two-way. We'll try and lead the slugs to one of the central chambers. Once we're there, give us five minutes to get out and then let the poison go.'

'And what if you're not out in time?' said the curator.

Brady hesitated a second. 'Let it go anyway.' He turned to Palmer. 'You don't have to do this you know.'

The little cockney looked at him. 'Like I said, you'd have no chance down there on your own. I can't stand by and let you kill yourself.'

'Brady. Don't you think it might be an idea to search that old house first, before you two go into the sewers?' said Foley. 'I mean, some of the slugs could still be in there.'

The Health Inspector nodded. 'You might be right. We'll do that first.' He turned to Palmer. 'You go and get the gear from the van, you and I will travel in that. Foley you take the poison in your own car.'

'What are you going to do?' asked the curator, watching as Brady made for the door.

He turned. 'I've got to make a phone call.'

Foley went to fetch the poison, Palmer scuttled off to fetch the equipment they would need and Brady wandered down to the enquiries desk. He perched on the edge of the desk and pulled the phone towards him, trying to steady his shaking hand as he dialled. Outside, the sky was like a blanket of mottled black velvet, just the pinpricks of stars glinting on it. The trees outside the museum swayed gently in the cool breeze, the wind blowing through their leaves like some disembodied voice. Brady drummed impatiently on the desk as he waited for the received to be picked up and, when it finally was, he recognised a familiar voice.

'Hello.'

'Kim,' he said.

'Mike, where the hell are you?' She sounded distraught. 'I called your office twice but there was no answer. I was getting ready to call the police, I wondered if you'd had an accident or . . .'

He cut her short. 'Listen to me, love. I'm at the museum.'

'What are you doing there?'

'Foley's found a way to kill the slugs,' he told her.

'Mike,' her voice had taken on a note of pleading.

'We've got a good idea where they are. I'm going down into the sewers with one of the men from the department.'

He heard the first unmistakable beginnings of a sob.

'Mike, please don't. You'll . . .' Her voice was cracking.

'Kim. Listen to me. They've got to be destroyed.'

There was silence at the other end of the line, only the low crackle of static breaking the solitude.

'Kim,' he repeated.

'Yes.' Her voice was strained.

'I want you to keep all the taps covered and lock the doors and windows.'

Silence.

'Kim. Did you hear me?'

'Yes.'

179

He sucked in a tortured breath, wanting so much to be close to her, to hold her. 'I love you, Kim,' he said, swallowing hard.

She was quiet for a moment then he heard her thin, worried tones once more. 'You know, I was just thinking,' she said, laughing hollowly. 'How ridiculous it is for a man of forty to be crawling about in sewer pipes.' She was crying again, sobs jerking her body as she tried to retain her composure.

Brady gritted his teeth. 'I'm still thirty-nine,' he said, trying to laugh but it wouldn't come and he could only close his eyes as he listened to her crying.

'I love you,' she said, softly.

'Keep the supper warm eh?' he said, his voice sounding empty. He slowly replaced the receiver, sitting for a moment or two on the edge of the desk. He massaged the bridge of his nose between his thumb and forefinger and exhaled deeply.

A moment later, Palmer appeared at the bottom of the stairs carrying an armful of things. He walked past Brady and up into the lab where he deposited the gear on a bench. The Health Inspector joined him.

'Put it on now, it'll save time,' said Palmer, thrusting a protective suit into the other man's hand. Both of them hurriedly pulled on the thick overalls, the little cockney completing the task first. He reached for one of the two-way radios which lay on the bench and handed it to Brady. 'Ever used one before?' he asked.

The Health Inspector shook his head and Palmer hastily demonstrated how the set worked, repeating the procedure when Foley joined them. The curator was pushing a metal drum before him and the other two men could hear fluid slapping about inside it.

'I'll need a hand to get it downstairs,' he said.

Brady helped the younger man with the bulky drum but, they eventually got it down the stairs and out into the waiting Volkswagen. The drum had a nozzle attachment to which Foley fitted a pipe. At the far end it sported what looked like the bowl of a watering can. He propped the large drum up on the passenger seat. Brady handed him the maps of the sewer and, after one final re-cap on the workings of the radio, he started the engine.

Palmer and Brady climbed into the white van and, with the breathing apparatus cradled on their laps, they drove off. Foley followed close behind.

Brady looked at his watch.

It was nearly ten fifteen p.m.

Less than fifteen minutes later, both vehicles pulled up outside Ron Bell's house.

Twenty-three

'There's the manhole cover,' said Palmer, pointing towards the large metal disc which lay in the road nearby.

Brady nodded. 'We'll look inside first.'

They clambered out of the van, leaving their masks and oxygen tanks on the seats. Foley was strolling across to join them. He'd pulled on a leather jacket just before they left but, despite the protection it offered, he was still shivering slightly.

'Cold?' said Brady.

Foley smiled, thinly. 'I'm not sure.'

'Come on,' said the Health Inspector and, led by him, they made their way up the path towards the front door of the house where Ron Bell had died. It looked even more forbidding in the darkness and Brady's mind was suddenly wrenched back to that hot morning weeks before when he and Archie Reece had discovered the mutilated remains. Weeks. It seemed like years since all this trouble began. Brady flicked on his torch and the powerful beam lanced through the darkness, lighting their way. He shone it over the front of the building and it reflected back off the dust covered windows. The waist high grass waved silently in the breeze and Foley cursed as he stepped into a patch of stinging nettles. The other two men looked round at him and he shrugged.

'We can get in along here,' said Brady, leading them towards the window which he and Reece had climbed through, what seemed like an eternity ago. Brady clambered through first, his nostrils immediately assailed by the stench of damp and decay. Next came Foley and, finally, Palmer who, as he was clambering in, accidentally brushed against a sliver of glass which opened a minute slit in his overalls at the top of the thigh.

The three men stood in what had once been the dining room and shone their torches around. The walls were peeling and the paint had come away to reveal layers of different colour, now faded and mildewed. The floorboards felt spongy as the men walked across them and Foley put a hand across his mouth, finding it difficult to breathe in the fetid atmosphere.

Something came hurtling at them from the shadows and Brady cursed.

It was a moth. It fluttered around for a second before disappearing through the broken window.

The trio moved on, into the sitting room where the corpse of Ron Bell had first been discovered. Brady showed them where the body had been lying. The room was completely empty. All the furniture had been removed, dust several inches thick showing where the sideboard had once stood. There were marks scored in the muck, tracing the path where the heavier objects had been dragged from the house. Their footsteps were strangely muffled as they moved about in the sitting room and the silence seemed to wrap itself around them like a cloak. Torch beams cut through the blackness, the tiny spots of light seeking clues, wondering if they were going to see the first slithering dark shape dragging itself along.

There were two doors leading out of the sitting room. One into the kitchen, the other into the hall.

'You two look upstairs,' said Brady. 'I'll check in there.' He moved towards the kitchen door while the other two men made their way out into the hall.

'If you find anything, shout,' Brady called after them.

'Don't worry,' Palmer said. 'If I see one of those bloody things, you'll be the first to know.'

Brady wandered into the kitchen, stopping for a second to listen to the heavy footfalls of his companions as they moved around upstairs. He could hear them going from room to room, the low murmur of their voices occasionally drifting through to him. Eventually, he turned his attention back to the kitchen, shining his torch across the filth-encrusted lino on the floor and across to the cupboards which had been ripped out long ago.

A spider had caught a crane-fly in its web and was busily devouring it. Brady held his torch on it for a second, watching the grisly tableau, then he moved the beam across towards another door to his right. As he walked towards it, Brady glanced out of the grime-encrusted windows of the kitchen and spied the sodium glare of the lamps which marked the first street on the new estate. He returned his attention to the other door, shining the torch onto the lock. There was no key and, optimistically, he turned the handle. Needless to say it didn't budge. The door was locked. He murmured something to himself and stepped back, the torch beam still directed at the peeling door. It was as he took that pace backward he noticed the small gap in the bottom of the door. He knelt to examine it, guessing it to be about two inches high. In one corner of the door something else caught his eye.

It was a slime trail.

It glistened in the torch light and Brady extended a gloved hand, touching the mucoid path with his index finger.

It was fresh.

He swallowed hard and stood up, trying the door once again, pushing his shoulder against it when it wouldn't open. But, the hinges were old and rusted and the Health Inspector heard them shriek in protest as he threw his weight against the door once again. This time the very wood itself seemed to crack. He stepped back and aimed a kick at the stubborn lock. The handle fell away, landing with a hollow thump on the lino.

'Nothing up there.'

The voice startled him and he spun round to see Foley and Palmer standing in the doorway.

'What have you found?' asked Foley.

Brady motioned to the door. 'It's a cellar or something.' He shone his torch down at the floor and both men saw the slime trail.

Palmer crossed to the door and both of them threw their weight against it, hearing the wood groan under the pressure. Finally, under their combined assault, it gave. It flew back on its hinges and slammed into the wall behind with a loud crash. The two men paused at the opening, gazing down into the blackness below. Brady swung his torch round but the beam would only penetrate the darkness a short distance. The stone steps of the cellar stretched away beneath them, the bottom invisible in the pitch black. A rancid stench rose from the cellar, an odour so rank it caused Brady to cough. He covered his nose with one hand and took a tentative step down. The torch beam wavered in his grasp and he had difficulty keeping his feet on the slippery steps. Step by step, he descended.

Palmer followed at an arm's length behind, using his own powerful torch to sweep the walls which crowded in on both sides of the staircase.

There were slime trails on them.

'Be careful,' he said, softly.

Brady could feel his heart thumping against his ribs as he neared the bottom of the steps. A thin film of perspiration had formed on his forehead. He directed the torch beam downwards, careful not to slip on the treacherous surface.

Two steps from the bottom he saw the first slug.

He stepped back, almost knocking Palmer over. The sewage man followed Brady's pointing finger and caught sight of the glistening black horror on the step, its posterior tentacles waving about soundlessly.

'What is it?' Foley called from the doorway.

'They're down here,' said Palmer, shining his torch over the floor of the cellar. The entire surface, every square inch of earth seemed to be covered by the slithering creatures. Like a glistening, undulating black carpet.

'I'll get the poison,' said Foley.

'No, wait,' Brady called and took a step down. He crushed the first slug beneath his heavy boot and walked on. He shone the torch over the slimy sea once more, noting that there were perhaps just two or three hundred of the creatures

186

down there. Those closest were moving towards him but the Health Inspector merely backed off.

'What are you waiting for?' asked Palmer.

'We can't afford to waste any of that poison,' Brady told him. 'There aren't many of them here. That means that most must be in the sewer itself.'

'So, what do we do?' the sewer man wanted to know.

Brady put out a hand and felt the damp walls. 'You've got a can of petrol in the back of your van haven't you?'

Palmer nodded.

'Go and get it.'

The little cockney hesitated for a moment then hurried back up the stairs, past a bewildered Foley who was descending the steps.

'What the hell are you playing at, Brady?' he demanded, seeing the slugs slithering towards them. 'We've got to destroy them.'

'This isn't the nest,' said Brady. 'Look.' He shone the torch over the hundreds of slugs. 'The rest of them, the big ones, they *must* be down in the sewers.'

Palmer returned a moment later, the petrol can in his hand. Brady took it from him and unscrewed the cap then, watched by the other two men, he walked into the cellar dousing the carpet of writhing slugs in the reeking liquid. They tried to crawl up his legs but there weren't enough of them and Brady crushed many beneath his heavy boots. He made sure every last drop of the golden fluid was drained from the can then he threw it into the cellar and retreated back up the stairs to join his companions.

Foley handed him a box of matches and the Health Inspector struck one, its yellow glow illuminating his face briefly before he tossed it down into the black mass.

There was a high pitched 'whump' as the petrol went up, followed, a moment later by a series of pops and dull bangs as the flames destroyed the bodies of the slugs. Yellow flames danced in the blackness, devouring the hideous creatures and filling the cellar with choking black smoke.

'What about the house?' asked Palmer, watching the fire.

187

'It's so bloody damp in there the fire will burn itself out,' said Brady with some authority.

The three men watched for a moment longer then closed the cellar door behind them. They made their way hurriedly through the house, clambering back through the broken window.

As they passed the cellar bulkhead, a thin stream of smoke rose into the night air and they could still hear the pop and crackle as the slugs were incinerated.

Palmer looked back.

'Two hundred down, 20,000 to go,' he said, cryptically.

Brady shot him an acid glance and the trio made their way out into the street. By the time they reached their parked vehicles, the smoke from the bulkhead was just a tiny plume of grey against the blackness of the night. Brady looked at it with something akin to satisfaction.

Palmer handed him his set of breathing apparatus and helped him to put it on, ensuring that he could breathe properly then the little man put on his own mask and tank. Their voices sounded muffled through the perspex and their breathing was heavy and laboured. Each of them picked up a two-way radio and Foley retrieved the third. Then, the three of them walked over to the curator's car where he quickly pulled the maps from the glove compartment.

'We're here,' Palmer told him, jabbing a gloved finger at the circle on the map marked sixteen.

Foley nodded. He got into his car and started the engine.

'We'd better synchronise watches,' said Brady.

They checked their time pieces.

'Keep in contact all the time,' said Foley and both men waved an acknowledgement.

'Remember,' said Brady. 'Five minutes after we give you the signal, let the poison go.'

The naturalist nodded and watched them as they strode over towards the manhole cover a few yards away.

It took both of them to move the huge metal disc, weighing, as it did, over a hundredweight. It fell to the road with a loud clang, spinning round and round like a dropped coin. Brady looked across at Palmer who tapped the cylinder of oxygen.

'Thirty minutes,' he said.

Brady nodded, noticing that the sewage man had a screwdriver stuck in his belt.

'What's that for?' he asked, pointing at it.

'Some of the pipes have grilles across them. I don't fancy getting caught in a dead end.'

Brady could feel his heartbeat quicken and he tried to control his breathing but it was difficult.

Led by Palmer, they began to descend.

It was eleven thirty p.m.

Twenty-four

Brady eased himself gently down from the metal ladder and stood beside Palmer, the effluent dribbling past them at about calf height. The Health Inspector swept the tunnel with his torch, noting that the beam was unable to penetrate the blackness for more than a few feet. Once again he felt that terrible claustrophobic feeling come over him as the walls of the pipe seemed to close in on him.

'We'd better check these out,' said Palmer, tapping the two-way. He switched his on and spoke into it.

Up above, the sudden crackle of static made Foley jump but the young curator picked up the set and held it to his ear.

'Foley, can you hear this?' asked Palmer, his voice buried beneath a crackling blanket of interference.

'Your voice is breaking up,' Foley told him, fiddling with the controls of the radio.

'Adjust the squelch button,' Palmer told him and, through the hissing static, Foley heard; 'Mary had a little lamb its fleece was brown not white . . .'

'Better,' said the naturalist.

Palmer continued. '. . . because the silly animal had rolled in its own shite.'

Foley laughed. 'OK, I've got it now.'

'Where the hell did you learn that?' asked Brady, smiling thinly.

Palmer shrugged and indicated that Brady should test his own equipment. A similar procedure was completed, then both men clipped the two-ways to their belts and bent low, ready to begin the tortuous crawl along the stretch of pipe which would lead to the first of the large central chambers. It was hot inside the suit and Brady felt even more

191

uncomfortable with the breathing apparatus on. Although it was light, the tank of oxygen on his back seemed to weigh him down as he crawled and he could only hear the loud, guttural sound of his breathing as he struggled along behind Palmer. Every now and then the Health Inspector would stop, almost sitting in the flowing effluent, and shine his torch behind them, just to check that there were no slugs near them. He scanned the walls and roof of the pipe for slime trails but, as yet, saw none.

The meagre shaft of light which poured down the open manhole opening began to fade into darkness as they crawled deeper into the pipes. Brady scrambled on, anxious not to lose sight of Palmer who was about two feet ahead of him.

They passed a side outlet which was less than a foot in diameter and both men concentrated their torches into the black hole.

'Drain outlet,' Palmer told him.

Satisfied that nothing was moving in there, the two men crawled on, now totally surrounded by the cloying darkness. It seemed to swathe itself around them like a shroud and the Health Inspector felt the first drops of perspiration forming on his face. His breathing was heavy and, for a second, he wondered if he might use up his oxygen supply too quickly. The vision of Kim swam into his mind and he tried to push it to one side. Her joke about a forty-year-old man crawling around sewers was beginning to take on extra significance. He closed his eyes tight, until white stars danced before him and the vision of her finally left him. He continued crawling, the progress surprisingly fast, his torch constantly sweeping the pipe in its search for the first tell-tale signs of the slugs.

Palmer stopped.

Brady shone his torch past the little cockney and saw that a grille barred their way. The sewage man pulled the screwdriver from his belt and began working on the first of the rusty rivets which held the grille in place. Brady crouched beside him and pulled the two-way from his own belt

'Foley,' he said. 'We've reached a grille. We should be through it in a couple of minutes.'

Foley acknowledged and traced their progress on the map before him.

'Another thirty feet and you'll be at the first chamber,' the younger man told him. 'Any sign of the slugs yet?'

'Nothing moving down here except us,' Brady told him.

He clipped the radio back into place and watched as Palmer prized the last rusty screw loose. He stuck the heavy screwdriver into the jaws of the grille and put all his weight on it. The grid came free and the little man tossed it away. It landed with a clang behind them. Some rotted faeces slopped onto Brady's overalls and he paled, fighting back the nausea. He shone the torch behind them once more then waited as Palmer crawled through to take the lead again.

Up above, Foley started the engine of the Volkswagen and drove slowly to the next red circle on the map, the site of the next manhole and the central chamber. He parked the car on one side of the road and guessed that it would take them about five minutes to crawl as far as the next vault. The young man exhaled deeply. He hoped that the chamber wouldn't become their crypt. A quick glance at his watch told him that they had less than twenty-five minutes.

It was eleven forty p.m.

Brady and Palmer continued on their journey, passing two more outlets as they did so. They were much larger than the first one they'd encountered and the men found that their torch beams could not penetrate the darkness in those particular pipes.

'It's a connecting pipe from one of the other main flow pipes,' said Palmer, peering into the first of the outlets.

He could see nothing in the darkness and he swallowed hard, even shining his torch into the river of effluent which occasionally washed up as high as his elbows. He, too, was beginning to perspire and he knew that it wasn't because of the suit. All he could think of was that he hadn't got the chance to kiss his kids goodnight. The little devils were

193

probably still up, waiting for him to get home. His wife would wonder what he was up to as well. He could imagine her moaning about how his dinner would be spoiled but, at that precise moment in time, Palmer would have given his right arm to have heard her nagging. To be up on the surface, at home. Instead of fifty feet below the ground acting as live bait for thousands of man-eating slugs.

The river of effluent did not flow high enough to alert him to the rip in his overalls.

He turned back from the outlet and looked at Brady who had been checking the other hole.

'Can't see a bloody thing,' he said.

'Me neither,' Brady told him.

They moved on.

It was a moment or two before the first of the slugs emerged from the larger of the outlets. Moving effortlessly in the slimy environment, it slithered over the damp wall of the pipe, the scent of man reaching it despite the assortment of smells down there.

In a matter of seconds, the entire pipe was filling with the obscene black monstrosities and, across from the first group, more were spilling from the second outlet. They slid into the water, others crawled along the roof and walls of the pipe, keeping just out of range of the probing torch beams. It was almost as if they knew.

Brady and Palmer crawled on unaware that, less than ten feet behind, the seething black mass of slugs pursued them.

The two men reached the first of the central chambers and Brady was glad to find that he could stand up for a minute. He shone his torch around, noting that the vault was about twelve feet in diameter. A rough circle with half a dozen outlets flowing into it. The effluent river was flowing swiftly here and it gushed past their feet with a low hiss. He shone his torch up and saw the iron ladder which led up to the manhole. Both of them knew that Foley was up there. Waiting.

'Which pipe do we go into next?' asked the Health Inspector, shining his torch over the numerous black holes.

194

They seemed to yawn open like huge mouths, screaming a silent warning to the men.

Palmer took the radio from his belt and raised it to his masked face.

'Foley,' he said. 'We're in the first chamber. On that map, there should be one outlet pipe marked in red, which one is it?'

Up in the car, the curator scanned the black and red lines, his finger quivering slightly as he finally found what he was looking for.

'There's about half a dozen outlets,' he said, vaguely.

'I know that,' snapped Palmer. 'Which one is marked in red?'

Foley found it. 'If you're standing with your backs to the main pipe then it's the one second from the left.'

Palmer clipped the radio back onto his belt and led Brady towards the designated outlet. They were forced to crawl once more as they entered it and the Health Inspector felt the muscles in his arms and back beginning to ache as he dragged himself along. They made their way slowly through the next pipe which seemed to narrow the deeper they got into it, but Brady told himself that his imagination was beginning to get the better of him and he struggled on behind Palmer.

He stopped suddenly as he heard a splashing from behind them.

He stuck out a hand to halt Palmer's progress.

'Listen,' said Brady and both men held their breath, torches directed down the pipe along which they had just crept. The powerful beams showed nothing.

'What was it?' asked Palmer.

Brady waved a hand to silence the sewage man and then the cockney himself heard it – the loud splashing which seemed to be growing nearer.

'It's probably just the water flowing into the chamber,' he said, reassuring no one, including himself. 'We'd better move on.'

He started to crawl again but Brady remained still, his

195

ears and eyes alert for the slightest sound or movement. He kept the torch beam directed behind him for long moments before finally crawling along behind Palmer. Perhaps the sewage man had been right. Perhaps it had just been the water gushing into the chamber.

Behind them, the vault was filled to overflowing with the black creatures, all slipping and sliding over one another in their haste to reach the two humans just three or four yards ahead.

'We should be reaching another of the chambers soon,' said Palmer, his own breath coming in gasps. His knees ached from crawling so much and he paused for a second beside a connecting pipe to get his breath.

Brady crouched beside him and rolled up the sleeve of his overall. He shone the torch onto his watch.

'Eleven forty-five,' he said. 'Fifteen minutes of air left.'

Palmer nodded. The Health Inspector patted him on the shoulder and they prepared to move on but, before they did, he swept the tunnel once more with his torch light.

There, glistening on the roof of the pipe, were a dozen slime trails.

'Palmer, look,' said Brady, pointing to the mucoid paths.

The sewage man turned his attention to the slime, watching as the Health Inspector touched it with a gloved finger. As he pulled it away, gobs of transparent fluid dripped from the material.

The trails were fresh.

The two men followed their course to a small outlet which Palmer said fed in from a drain. Brady bent close and shone his torch inside.

'My God,' he murmured and Palmer directed the beam of his own light inside.

Half a dozen of the slugs were in there, most of them larger than six inches. For long seconds they seemed to recoil from the bright lights but then, slowly, they began slithering towards the two men.

'Let's move,' said Brady and they suddenly found renewed strength, scrambling quickly down the pipe towards what they knew to be the second chamber.

Brady shone the torch behind him, puzzled when he saw no sign of the slugs.

There was a sibilant hiss which made both men gasp and it was a second or two before they realized that it was the static on the radio.

Foley was trying to contact them.

Brady snatched his two-way angrily from his belt.

'What is it?' he snapped. 'You scared the shit out of us.'

Palmer looked across at him. 'No pun intended I hope,' he grinned.

'Have you seen anything?' the curator wanted to know.

'We've seen half a dozen of them,' Brady told him. 'They're down here all right, it's just a matter of where.'

'Is it working?'

'If you mean are they following us, I don't know.'

Palmer tapped him on the shoulder.

'We'd better move on,' he said.

Brady nodded and switched off the set again, clipping it to his belt.

The two men found that the pipe curved slightly, eventually branching out into a kind of fork, presenting them with a choice of which one to enter. Palmer was about to radio through for directions when he saw the first of the slugs spilling from the left hand pipe ahead of them.

'Oh Jesus,' he said and tugged at Brady's arm.

The Health Inspector snatched for his radio.

'Foley,' he shouted into the set. 'We've found them.'

'Where are you?' the curator wanted to know.

It was Palmer who spoke next. 'They've got in front of us. They must have come from the second chamber. We'll have to go back the way we came.'

With the slugs less than a yard behind, the two men twisted awkwardly in the narrow pipe and scrambled back towards the first huge chamber. Brady now leading, held his torch before him and he was the first to see the other group of slugs. Those that had been pursuing them now blocked their way to the first chamber.

The two men were pinned between different groups of the black monstrosities, their route to the first and second chambers blocked off.

The seething mass approached slowly from both sides.

'In there,' shouted Palmer, pushing Brady towards a narrow outlet. 'It's a connecting pipe, it should take us through to another flow pipe.'

Brady squeezed through the narrow tunnel, finding it so confined that he had to crawl on his stomach to get through. His oxygen tank scraped against the stonework and the effluent splashed up against the perspex of his face mask but he crawled on, using his knees and elbows as means of propulsion. He slithered along like the monstrosities which pursued him.

Palmer threw himself into the narrow opening behind the Health Inspector, pushing the older man along in an effort to escape the hungry black hordes.

'Foley,' shouted the sewage man into his radio. 'They've got us trapped. We're in a connecting pipe mid-way between the first and second chambers. Where will we end up if we keep crawling?'

The curator's voice sounded a million miles away as he spoke.

'You should come into another flow pipe, if you crawl down that it'll bring you back out into the first chamber again,' he told them, tracing their progress on the map. His own heart was now thumping madly against his ribs.. He started the engine of the Volkswagen again and drove to the centre of the road. There, he pushed open the passenger door and struggled to lift the heavy drum of poison onto the tarmac. With perspiration running from his face, he managed to push it over towards the manhole cover. Then, he bent and took a hold of the metal bar across the top of the heavy iron disc.

It wouldn't budge an inch.

The sewer remained sealed.

Brady was crawling as fast as he could through the rancid effluent, his breath coming in gasps. Behind him, Palmer was able to see the slugs as the first of them slithered into the pipe

198

and made for his heavy boots. He crushed the first half a dozen beneath the weighty footwear but, in the beam of his torch, he could see more and more of the black things swarming into the tunnel. Fear gripped him tightly, and he found it difficult to swallow.

'Move,' he shouted to Brady.

The Health Inspector was scrambling along as fast as his aching limbs would allow but, suddenly, he let out a mournful groan.

The other end of the pipe was blocked by a grille.

'Give me the screwdriver, quick,' he bellowed, looking back to see the tunnel filling with the obscene fat slugs, all eager to reach their prey.

Palmer tore the implement from his belt and handed it to Brady who didn't even bother trying to loosen the screws, he merely jammed the blade between the slats and tried to tear the grid free. The screws were rusty, the stonework decaying, but still the recalcitrant grille kept its place, barring their escape.

'Hurry,' screamed Palmer, the leading slugs now seething over his legs, trying to bite through the thick material of his protective suit.

Brady beat at the grille with his hands in an effort to loosen it and, finally, the metal started to give. One screw came away and the Health Inspector used all his strength on the screwdriver, using the implement like a lever to tear off the grid.

'For fuck's sake,' shrieked Palmer and then he screamed in agony as the first slug found the rent in his suit and began eating its way into his thigh.

'Brady,' Palmer screamed but the Health Inspector could do nothing to help him. He just continued to wrench at the stubborn grille, hearing his companion's shrieks of pain. In that confined space they seemed to be deafening and Brady wanted to scream himself.

Blood spurted up from the gash in Palmer's leg and he tore at the first slug, managing to rip its vile form from his leg. But its head remained embedded in the flesh and it was just the bloated body which he tossed away. And now more of the creatures were swarming over him, tasting the fast-flowing blood, burrowing deep into his meaty thigh, sliding up inside the suit until they reached his genitals. The sewer man shrieked again as two of the slugs began boring their way into his scrotum. He felt waves of unbelievable pain lance through him as more of the creatures found the rip in the suit. They slithered inside to feast on his shaking body. He tried to swat at them with his hands, feeling one huge fat body burst under his fist. It squashed against his torn thigh, its own pus-like bodily fluid mingling with his spurting blood.

Brady began to shout in rage and terrified frustration when the grille wouldn't come away and, behind him, Palmer's screams became fainter as the slugs ate their way into him, a number burrowing up through his torn genitals, using his anus as a means of access in their search for the softer, more succulent parts of his body. Blood filled his mouth and gushed out into his face mask, bubbling up behind the perspex, running back down the tube to the oxygen cylinder until he was breathing the coppery fumes of his own life fluid.

With an angry yell, Brady finally tore the grid free.

He slithered through and found himself, as Foley had said, in another flow-pipe.

He shot out a hand and began to haul Palmer free of the connecting tunnel but it was too late, the little man was already dead. The only movements his body made were spasmodic contractions of the muscles and now many of the slugs were sliding over his torn body in their efforts to reach Brady.

Panting for air, the Health Inspector began to crawl back towards the first chamber.

He had just five minutes of oxygen left.

Foley tried one last time to remove the manhole cover but could make no impression on the heavy disc. Looking around in panic he saw a piece of wood lying by the roadside – the branch of a tree torn down by some kids a day before. He hurried across to it, relieved to find that it was reasonably stout. The curator stuck it into the indentation in the lid and put all his weight on it.

The lid still refused to move and Foley put more pressure on it.

There was a loud groan and the wood snapped.

He threw one half to the ground, his mind desperately searching for a means to lift the heavy lid.

The radio crackled and he snatched it up.

'Yes,' he said.

'Foley.' The curator recognised Brady's voice. 'The slugs are right behind me,' he gasped. 'I'm coming up. Get ready to let the poison in.'

Foley hesitated a second. 'I can't get the lid up,' he said, flatly.

'Oh God. Have you tried prizing it open?' gasped the Health Inspector.

Foley said that he had.

'For Christ's sake, hurry,' Brady implored him. 'I'm at the main chamber now, the bloody things are right behind me.' His voice rose to a shout. 'Hurry, Foley.'

'Rope,' the naturalist said aloud and hurried to the boot of his car. He flung it open and rummaged through the other debris in search of the thick hemp which he knew to be in there.

He found it and scurried back to the manhole cover where he slipped the rope under the metal bar in the lid. He tied a hasty knot, tugged on the rope then secured the other end to his front bumper. Then he leapt behind the wheel and reversed slowly.

Inch by agonising inch, the lid began to lift.

Foley smiled, triumphantly.

It was almost halfway up when the rope began to fray.

Brady stood in the central chamber looking up, watching as the lid was lifted. He shot a glance towards the pipes which opened into the vault and shuddered.

From every outlet, hundreds of black shapes were spilling. Like an unstoppable tide of death, they poured out of the pipes into the central chamber and Brady could only guess at how many thousand there were. Led by the huge seven and eight inch monsters, they piled on top of one another, gliding effortlessly towards their helpless prey.

He stood transfixed for long seconds, watching as the seething black mass drew towards him, then, he grabbed at the metal ladder and began to climb towards the rapidly opening gap above him.

The slugs reached the spot where he had been standing and he saw a number trying to slither up the ladder after him but they could gain no adequate hold and fell back amongst the rest of their companions.

Brady was halfway up the ladder now and his oxygen was running out rapidly. His head felt swollen, as if someone were filling it with air. The ladder swam before him and, once, he nearly lost his footing but he continued up, gripping each rung tighter than the next until he was mere feet from the opening.

It was at that point that the rope snapped.

All Foley heard was the dull clang as the manhole cover fell back into place. He looked round in alarm and saw what had happened, leaping from behind the steering wheel to re-affix the rope. He could hear Brady's weak banging on the bottom of the lid as he fastened the hemp once more. Then the Health Inspector's voice drifted wearily over the two-way.

'Running out of oxygen,' he groaned. 'I can't breathe. I . . .'

Brady found himself nearing unconsciousness, he looked down into the darkness and saw the slugs seething about below him almost as if they were waiting for him to drop into their midst. He lost his footing and thought he was going to faint but he gritted his teeth, trying to hold his breath to prevent himself inhaling his own carbon dioxide. He heard the roar of the Volkswagen's engine and then suddenly, the manhole cover was torn free. In a daze, Brady felt strong

202

arms grabbing him, pulling him from that hell hole. He felt hands struggling to remove his mask and then he was breathing fresh air again. Fresh clean air.

His head was throbbing but he scrambled to his feet when he saw Foley struggling with the large drum of poison, attempting to tip it over.

Brady joined him and both men put their weight to it, feeling the drum teeter then finally fall.

Five gallons of the deadly substance spilled from it and rained down into the sewer, onto the writhing slugs.

There was a flash of light so brilliant that both men thought they must be blinded, then a blistering geyser of white flame rose almost silently from the manhole. It rocketed up into the heavens a full fifty feet before disappearing in a billowing mushroom cloud of grey smoke. The ground shook as, beneath them, the poison set off a chain reaction which swept through the entire sewer system of Merton. As Palmer had warned them, the fire-flash set off the clouds of methane and the earth rocked. Both Foley and Brady were thrown to the floor and, below a lightning tongue of flame tore along the pipes in all directions, fanning out like some kind of fiery amoebic creature. Tentacles of screaming flame ripped through pipes and tunnels. The taps in the houses nearby were blasted from their housings and in many places, the water boiled in lavatory bowls. In the street nearby, a manhole cover was blasted a full thirty feet into the air by the explosion and, all over town, sewer vents lit up momentarily as the flames roared beneath them.

Then, as suddenly as it had come, the fire died and just a mournful plume of grey smoke wafted up from the open hole.

Brady rose slowly to his feet, the smell of burning strong in his nostrils. A moment later Foley joined him and both of them peered down into the smoke-filled maw below. They could see nothing.

'I'm sorry about Palmer,' said Foley, softly.

The Health Inspector nodded. 'The slugs killed him. The poor bastard was dead before the explosion.'

Brady was suddenly aware of a foul smell and he realized that it was his overalls. Pieces of dried excrement still stuck to them in places and he hurriedly pulled them off, dropping the stinking garments in an untidy heap on the road beside the manhole.

'What now?' asked Foley.

The Health Inspector exhaled deeply. 'The sewers will have to be checked. We can't take any chances. I'll go down again in the morning with some more men, just to be sure.'

It was as they turned to head back to Foley's car that they saw it.

Crawling in the road was a single solitary slug.

'Oh my God,' whispered Brady.

Before he could react, Foley had snatched up one of the discarded gloves and was moving towards the slug which looked to be about two or three inches long. He knelt and, watched by Brady, picked the black creature up. It tried to contract itself, anxious to be free of the grip and, when Brady stepped closer he saw that the animal had retracted its posterior tentacles.

Foley put it down on the pavement and it crawled away towards the safety of the bushes nearby.

Brady breathed an audible sigh of relief.

'Looks like my theory was right,' said Foley but there was no joy in his words, just a thankful affirmation of his beliefs.

'Let's wait and see shall we,' said Brady, patting the younger man on the back.

Lights were going on in houses all over the street, people were peering out of doors and windows and, far away, the two men heard the wail of police and ambulance sirens.

'I think you and I are going to have some questions to answer,' said Foley, pulling a packet of cigarettes from his pocket.

Brady nodded. 'Don Palmer's wife will have to be told,' he said, softly.

'The police will do it,' said Foley.

'No. It was my fault he died. It's my job to tell her.'

'He knew the risks involved,' said Foley.

'Yeah. But I'm still going to be the one to tell her.'

Foley offered him a cigarette.

'I don't smoke,' Brady said.

'Perhaps it's time you started,' said the curator and both men smiled.

Epilogue

George Thomas watched as the crates of lettuce were unloaded from the back of the lorry. He chewed the end of his pipe which, as always, remained unlit.

All around him the place was alive with the sound of crashing boxes, raised voices, laughing. The usual cacophony of noise which went to make up Covent Garden.

He'd arrived later than usual that morning due to the traffic on the roads leading into London. The drive from his farm in Merton usually took him less than an hour but he'd left at five a.m. that morning, when the mist still lay heavy on the ground, and now at seven o'clock he had finally managed to struggle through. The sun was already high in the sky above the city, pouring its unrelenting heat down over the people scurrying for buses and tubes.

George always hated coming to London. He'd lived in the country all his life and the hustle and bustle of the city unsettled him. Everybody was always in such a bloody hurry and George liked to take things easy. However, at sixty-two he was as sprightly as a teenager and ran his little farm in Merton only with the help of his two sons. It was a small piece of land but it yielded a good crop of vegetables and George had found a regular buyer for his produce. He watched now as the man picked quickly but expertly through the crates laid out before him, occasionally taking out one of the lettuces and tossing it onto a nearby pile of rotting vegetables. He went along all the crates with similar expertise, muttering to himself as he did.

'Good crop again,' said George.

'Yeah, only a few bad ones,' said the buyer, picking up another lettuce. He ran an expert eye over it, noticing something inside the inner leaves. He threw it onto the pile with the other rejects.

After about fifteen minutes he finished. The deal was concluded and George climbed thankfully back into his lorry. He waved a hurried farewell to his buyer, who was already having the crates removed, and then set off to battle his way through the traffic on his way home to Merton.

He couldn't wait to be out of the bloody city.

The pile of discarded vegetables grew higher as the day progressed, until it seemed to tower as tall as a man. Under the heat of the sun the green stuff began to wilt and smell, but no one paid it any attention. People came and went and the noise grew louder, with stall-holders shouting out their prices, bickering with their neighbours. It was a normal day really.

No one paid the slightest attention to the lettuce which lay near the bottom of the pile, one of George's crop, rejected because of the strange cylindrical objects in its inner leaves. The transparent mucoid tubes with the black centres.

Who cared about a few slugs' eggs anyway?